# THE 1

THE LIPSTICK CONFESSIONS SERIES

# THE PROMISE

**When keeping one means breaking
another**

Claire Connor

with G.P. Taylor

Authentic

First published in 2010 by Authentic Media Limited
Milton Keynes
www.authenticmedia.co.uk

**British Library Cataloguing in Publication Data**
A catalogue record for this book is available from the
British Library

ISBN: 978-1-85078-885-0

Cover Design by Phil Miles
Printed and bound in Great Britain by CPI Cox & Wyman, Reading, RG1 8EX

# Chapter 1

Sarah Abrahams hated christenings. She'd tried, but there was no getting around it. Peering into the mirror of her dressing table, Sarah smoothed imaginary creases from her mocha-coloured linen suit and reached for her cosmetics bag.

For one thing, the babies were usually disturbed by the experience and, if they didn't bawl, the parents willingly supplied the tears. Both variations were equally unpalatable. She selected a taupe eye shadow and her brown mascara. Sunlight filled the large, airy room, causing her to squint as she leaned towards the mirror.

For another, the churches were always cold, the dress code ill defined. Why couldn't the invitations be clear on this point? Though it was early May and still technically spring, the other women might well arrive in summer frocks, bedecked with hats, or worse – in suits embarrassingly similar to Sarah's own. It was tiresome.

'Are you nearly ready, darling?' Her husband's voice floated up the stairs. Sarah ignored it, flicking the mascara wand over her eyelashes with careful strokes.

It irritated her to see the way the priests held babies – gingerly, and with a kind of terrified reverence, fearing an impromptu eruption from either end. Occasionally, there was a priest who knew what he was about where babies were concerned. This simply left you wondering why he wasn't a father in the traditional sense of the word.

'Sarah?'

Sarah scattered a handful of lipsticks across the polished surface of her dressing table, the black and silver tubes standing out sharply against the soft white of the French regency furniture. She rolled her fingers over them one by one, taking her time over the decision.

'Sweetheart, we're going to be late.' His patience was wearing thin. No matter.

'Berry Kiss,' she murmured, sliding the brightly coloured gloss from its tube.

There was also the problem of gifts. How many children's Bibles, prayer books, candles or delicate silver crosses could one baby need? That said, what else were you to buy if not one of the above? Prayer vouchers?

Sarah heard heavy footsteps on the grand staircase that curved its way from the entrance hall to the first floor of her perfect home. She began to hurry a little, knowing full well she was in trouble. A quick dab of *Touche Éclat* to conceal the ever-deepening crow's feet at the corners of her eyes. One last sweep of the paddle brush through her straight blonde hair. She wore it in a long, layered bob that swung attractively when she moved her head.

'Sarah!' She stood up as her husband Lawrence entered the bedroom and stopped just inside the door. His eyes were tightly closed. 'Darling,' he announced in the long-suffering tones of someone who knows from long experience the futility of what they are about to say but feels compelled to speak anyway. 'We are late. When I open my eyes, I would like to see you dressed and ready to go.' Sarah's mouth twitched as she watched the dramatic declamation. Her husband raised an admonitory finger. 'If you aren't, I won't be held responsible for my actions,' he warned. 'But I can tell you that it will begin with me throwing you over my shoulder like a sack of potatoes.' He paused. 'And your suit will get creased.'

'You're peeking,' she accused, throwing her hairbrush at him. It scythed through the air and struck him just above the kneecap. He collapsed onto the bed with a howl. 'Don't be such a baby,' Sarah laughed, spraying a cloud of Chanel *Coco Mademoiselle* into the air and stepping through the perfume mist to ensure even application of the scent.

Lawrence picked himself up with a smile and made a show of limping across the room to offer her his arm. Sarah indulged his play-acting, a long accepted facet of their relationship.

At fifty-seven, he was still a fit, good-looking man, his black hair greying handsomely at the temples. Gentle padding around the jaw line hinted at the onset of jowls, but Lawrence's wide-set blue eyes and strong, symmetrical features were more than enough to offset this. The touch of Rome in his face made him almost commanding, imperial. Lawrence inspired respect. He knew it, but never abused the gift.

Sarah loved that about him. She brushed a stray hair from the lapel of his suit. There was no denying that men aged far better than women, she thought. Another of life's many injustices towards womankind. Not that she was bitter. Lawrence caught her hand.

'Come on, wife,' he said. 'Little Beatrice is waiting for her fairy godparents.' He glanced at his watch and grimaced. 'And if we're any later, she'll be waiting forever. Jemma will have us hung, drawn and quartered. Probably in public.'

They hurried down the stairs together, Lawrence pausing to set the burglar alarm as they left the house. Sarah eased herself into the Bentley and braced herself for the ordeal ahead. The car swung away from the kerb and set off through leafy Kensington.

The fact was, only one thing made christenings bearable for Sarah Abrahams. And . . . *un*-bearable.

The babies.

While the Bentley glided soundlessly through the London traffic, an old VW camper van was juddering to a halt on the hard shoulder of the M20, fifty miles from London. The driver sat motionless for a few seconds, feeling the van rock from side to side in the slipstream of the cars zipping past slightly too close for comfort. Then she slid across the torn leather seat and scrambled out of the passenger door. Her long, floral skirt snagged on a rusty patch of bodywork.

'Damn.'

She aimed a kick at the nearside front tyre. Never a good move in flip-flops but it felt like the traditional thing to do.

Arima Middleton was big on tradition. She narrowed her brown eyes and stared at the flat tyre, willing it to miraculously re-inflate. If her mother were here she would make an instant appeal to a higher power – was there a patron saint of motorists? Probably. Arima sighed. Since her parents had died three years ago, she might as well petition them direct.

'Mama, if you're up there . . . put in a word for me, will you?' she murmured, glancing up at the bright, cloud-dotted sky. There was no reply.

Wild black curls blew out behind her in the wind as she stood alone on the hard shoulder, wondering what on earth to do. She didn't have breakdown cover – why would she? She'd been in the country for less than five hours. Signing up with the AA was hardly the first thing you did when you drove off the ferry, tired, hungry and seasick.

In any case, Arima never bothered with that sort of thing. Benoit had always been there to sort out any technical problems with the van. Arima was the creative director of their road trips, not technical support. Not that she couldn't have learnt, she admitted ruefully. She wasn't lazy as such. Just happy to have Benoit take care of it for her, that was all.

'You're on your own now, Arima,' she reminded herself. 'You got what you wanted.' She shivered. Her white, off the shoulder peasant blouse wasn't warm enough for an English spring and her arms were peppered with goose bumps. Arima thought of the warm Italian sunshine, and of Benoit making his way there from Spain in search of work. Skilled stonemasons were always welcome at the big Italian cathedrals, and Benoit was one of the best. He was probably travelling right now, just like her. She hoped he would manage without the camper van. Arima felt a twinge of guilt. She slapped it away but it buzzed back like a troublesome fly. It would never have worked out, she reminded herself. Things had gone stale between them.

Over the winter, she had begun to have a recurring dream about choking to death, her mouth crammed with unsaid words that she could neither swallow nor spit out. She would wake in the darkness, gasping and clawing at her throat. Arima had recognized the sign and packed her bags. Time to move on. Benoit would be okay.

Partly to distract herself, she ducked back into the van and grabbed a blanket to wrap round her shoulders. It was vile – purple and holey, with a frayed ribbon trim in electric blue, one of her mother's eccentric creations. Arima treasured it. The clock on the dashboard read five minutes to twelve. Arima sighed. There was no way she was going to make the christening now, but not to worry. Nobody ever expected her to be on time anyway.

Arima stood as close to the edge of the hard shoulder as she dared and stuck out her arm, preparing for the long task of flagging down a sympathetic motorist. 'Come on, Mama,' she pleaded, casting her eyes heavenwards again. 'Have a word with the boss. What else have you got to do up there? I need help.' Preferably a man who could change tyres and was neither an axe murderer, rapist or other undesirable. But the tyre-changing was the main thing, she amended, not wanting to ask for too much. If push came to shove, she could handle the other three. Arima Middleton was no pushover.

As luck would have it, she only had to wait half an hour. Just as her shoulder started to go numb from the effort of holding her arm out, a little blue Micra flashed its lights at her and pulled onto the hard shoulder. Bingo. Arima trotted forwards, clutching the blanket tightly around her shoulders. Her smile faltered as an elderly couple emerged from the car.

They were small, the kind of small that happens to people in old age. Round-shouldered, shrunken and sort of folded in on themselves, like a badly cooked soufflé. The man wore grey slacks and a faded diamond-patterned golfing sweater. His wife wore a mid-calf pleated skirt and thick cardigan in complementing shades of brown, her stout legs ending in sensible shoes. She was wearing a headscarf, as though to protect her perm from the wind, a precaution that was hardly necessary in a Micra. Arima eyed the woman's brown cardigan enviously. It looked cosy.

'Careful, Frank,' muttered the woman as the couple approached. 'I think she might be a gypsy.' Arima stifled a laugh. They weren't going to be much help fixing the van but perhaps they'd give her a lift. She flashed them her best smile.

'I'm not a gypsy,' she said. 'My mother was Basque.' Blank stares. Arima was used to this reaction. 'Like Spanish,' she explained.

'Ah, right. I'm with you,' said the man. He extended a gnarled hand. 'Frank Paver, and this is my wife Doris. What's the trouble with your motor?'

'Arima Middleton.' She noticed Doris's face relax visibly at the English surname. 'I've got a flat tyre.'

'Not with the AA? RAC?' Frank tutted and shook his head disapprovingly. 'You ought to join, you know,' he said. 'It's not safe for a young lady to be stranded like this.'

'We could be anyone,' Doris chimed in.

'But you're not,' Arima pointed out politely. She hid another smile as an image of Frank and Doris as carjackers popped into her mind, Doris wielding a vicious set of knitting needles while Frank took care of the van.

'No,' Frank agreed, squatting down beside the van. 'And luckily for you, I'm a retired mechanic.' He rolled up his sleeves. 'Where's your spare?'

'Oh, Frank,' Doris scolded. 'You know these old VWs well enough. Sort yourself out. Can't you see the poor girl's freezing?' She took Arima by the arm. 'Come on, dear,' she said, tugging her towards the Micra. 'It'll take a while. I've got a flask of tea and a nice packet of hobnobs in the boot. Let's have a brew while you wait.'

In the murky vaulted cathedral of concrete and steel, the Bentley slid neatly into a narrow space.

'Darling.' There was an edge to Lawrence's voice as he stood beside the car, leaning on his open door. He jingled his car keys impatiently with his free hand.

'Yes, I'm coming.' Sarah was bent double in the passenger seat, ferreting around in her handbag. The multi-storey car park was dimly lit, making it difficult to distinguish one thing from another. 'I need to find my phone.'

'You need to get out of the car.'

'No, I need my phone.'

'For God's sake! We don't have time for you to make a call.'

'I don't want to make a call,' Sarah snapped. 'I need to switch it off, Lawrence. I can't have it going off during the service, can I?'

'At this rate, darling, you won't have to worry,' Lawrence observed. 'We won't even make it for the damn bun-fight.' In desperation, Sarah upended the bag and tipped the contents onto her lap. Lawrence slammed his door, strode round to the passenger side and tried to haul his wife bodily from the car.

'Look, leave it. Leave the bag, leave it all here. Let's just go.'

'You're hurting my arm!' Lawrence released her immediately.

'I'm sorry.' A look of utter weariness passed over his face. Why did it always have to be like this? He held out his hand to Sarah. 'Come on. All this dawdling only makes it worse. Let's get it over with.'

He sighed as if it were the last bout of a battle he knew he would never win and wiped his brow.

Sarah put her hand in his. 'You're right. I'm sorry too.' She stepped out of the car and left her belongings strewn over the seat, heedless of the risk. So what if the car was broken into? There were more important things than possessions. They set off at a brisk pace, past a seemingly endless line of Audis and BMWs. Even when possessions were all you had.

It was a cruel thought and she crushed it immediately. It wasn't true. They had each other, she and Lawrence. That was far more than some people had.

Lawrence squeezed her arm reassuringly as the imposing façade of Westminster Cathedral came into view. It was set back from the road, the red and cream brickwork a vivid contrast to the dull stone of the flanking buildings. Built in the Byzantine style, each mini-turret was topped with a spike-tipped dome, the stones of each one laid in identical zigzag patterns.

The design reminded Sarah of hand-knitted egg cosies, which was probably not what the architect had in mind. It was the zigzags. Did egg cosies exist in 1903 at the time of building? Possibly not. In any case, it entirely spoiled the imposing effect of the cathedral for her.

Cathedrals should inspire awe and wonder, fear of the Lord and all that jazz. Not thoughts of breakfast and toast soldiers. Perhaps this was why she struggled with religion, Sarah mused, her heels beating an erratic rhythm on the red and grey chequered flagstones carpeting the approach to the cathedral.

She was too focused on the visual, rather than the abstract. For Lawrence's sake, she tried, but her heart wasn't in it. Her stomach clenched as they approached the dark wooden entrance doors, flanked on each side by a row of stone sentinel saints. Sensitive as ever, Lawrence picked up on her heightened tension. 'It'll be fine once we get in there, you'll see,' he promised. They paused at the doors. 'Got the present?'

Sarah's face twisted with anxiety. 'Oh, Lawrence, I've left it in the car.'

'Don't worry,' soothed Lawrence, trying to stem the panic rising in Sarah's eyes. She was normally so confident and capable. Nothing rattled her. He hated seeing her like this. 'There'll be an avalanche of gifts. Jemma won't even notice.' The sound of organ music came from within the cathedral. They faced the doors together.

'Ready?' Lawrence whispered. Sarah took a deep breath. This was the fifteenth time she'd been asked to be a godmother. Every kind of ceremony, Catholic, Anglican, Baptist, Free Church . . . Sarah had done them all. If a professional godmothering body existed, she'd join. Fourteen times, each a little more poignant, a little more painful than the last. She glanced at her husband. If Lawrence's God really was merciful, the fifteenth would be the last.

'Ready.'

Far away, Arima was finishing her fourth cup of tea, served by Doris in the plastic lid of her thermos flask. 'Lakeland Plastics,' she said proudly.

It was her first taste of real tea for four years. Arima turned to Doris, who was crunching her way through her seventh hobnob without a trace of embarrassment. 'Now I know I'm home,' she said. 'That was a proper cup of tea.'

'Yorkshire Tea,' said Doris, tapping her finger against the side of her nose.

'The way tea used to be,' they chorused, and laughed.

'Do they still show that old advert?' Arima asked, a vague memory surfacing in her mind of a beaming old lady serving tea and shortbread in a comforting manner against the backdrop of the Yorkshire Dales.

'Oh, yes, now and again. I'd never buy anything else,' said Doris. 'Can't abide those daft tea adverts with the monkeys.'

'PG Tips?'

'That's the one. And there's these odd pyramid shaped bags you can buy now, too.'

'Really?'

'Incredible, isn't it?' Doris sniffed. 'Wouldn't touch them with a barge pole. Good, proper tea, that's what you want. None of this fancy Egyptian jiggery-pokery.' There was a gentle tap at the window.

Arima jumped.

'Sorry,' said Frank. 'Only me. Tyre's all done.'

Doris and Frank stood side by side on the hard shoulder to wave Arima off. Doris insisted on giving her the remainder of the hobnobs (not that there were many left but it was a sweet thought), and Frank leaned in through the open window to press a scrap of paper into her hand. 'Our address,' he explained earnestly. 'If you're ever down Rochester way, call in and see us. The kettle's always on.'

'Thank you, I will.' Arima felt tears come to her eyes as the camper van rattled into life. Travelling as much as she did had made her suspicious of people, always on her guard and alert for trouble. Most people were basically good and would help out in an emergency, yes, but the unexpected kindness of these strangers went beyond that. It touched her that such open-heartedness still existed.

In Arima's experience, help usually came at a price, either hard coin, food or exchange of skills. These people had asked for nothing in return. She glanced in her rear view mirror and saw them still standing on the hard shoulder, hand in hand, watching to be sure she was safely on her way. Arima honked the horn in farewell as they disappeared from view and put the scrap of paper into the coin box on the dashboard. Perhaps she'd see them again one day. Stranger things had happened.

She checked the time. Twelve forty-five. If she put her foot down, she might get there in time for the buffet. It was tempting to give the whole thing a miss but Arima couldn't afford to pass up the opportunity to renew the links with her English friends, most of whom had faded to casual acquaintances over the years due to time and distance. 'You need contacts,' she told herself. 'Jobs don't come out of thin air.' Jemma's invitation had come at just the right time, Arima reflected, tipping the speedo up to eighty despite the engine's noisy protests.

Almost as if it was meant to be.

# Chapter 2

'Philip? Philip! We need more seating out here. And more drinks. Can you sort it? Philip! Oh Beatrice, no!'

Lawrence moved swiftly towards Jemma, who was stranded on the manicured lawn, frazzled and dabbing frantically at the sick on her dress as her daughter roared, tiny fists waving furiously.

Instinctively, he looked round for Sarah and smiled as he saw her hurrying from the opposite direction, observant as ever. They converged on Jemma at the same time.

'It's okay,' Sarah soothed, scooping Beatrice into her arms. The baby peered up at Sarah, her cries fading to a grumble as she was expertly rocked to and fro.

Lawrence produced a clean handkerchief and put a protective arm about Jemma's shoulders to screen her from the other guests. Jemma leaned into him. Sarah watched her friend anxiously. The strain of trying to look fabulous with a six-week-old baby was beginning to show. Jemma's eyelids drooped, and beneath the make-up her skin was pale with fatigue.

'Right then,' said Lawrence calmly. 'Tell me what needs doing. More chairs, is it? The garden looks wonderful, by the way.'

The guests were milling about on the lawn beneath blossom-laden trees and bushes strung with colourful bunting.

Running down one side of the garden was a line of trestle tables set with hot and cold buffet food, and a classical quartet strummed discreetly in the white gazebo at the far end of the lawn.

'Thanks,' Jemma mumbled, bunching the handkerchief in her fist and scrubbing uselessly at the stain on her linen dress.

'More chairs?' Lawrence prompted.

'Uh, yes. Chairs. And the caterers need to serve the drinks. I don't know where Philip's got to, he's no help at all.'

'No problem. I'm on it.' Lawrence strode away, calling a couple of the guests to come and help him. Sarah held the child upright against her shoulder and began rubbing her back in small circular movements. Beatrice immediately produced a mighty belch.

'There's the problem,' Sarah laughed. Jemma stared at her through sleep-deprived eyes.

'You're so good with her,' she mumbled, half-raising a hand in a hopeless gesture. 'I've no idea what I'm doing.'

'Don't be silly, you're brilliant with her,' Sarah said briskly. 'Listen, why don't you nip inside and get changed, see if you can find Philip. We'll be fine.' Jemma hesitated, torn between guilt and the desire for a few minutes' peace. 'Go on,' she urged. 'You'll only be five minutes.'

'Thanks, Sarah. If . . . if I'm not back . . .'

'I'll come and check you haven't fallen asleep, yes,' Sarah grinned. 'I know how it is.'

That wasn't strictly true, of course, she reminded herself as Jemma scuttled towards the house. But she'd been through it so often with friends and family that it might as well be. Beatrice reared back without warning, her head flopping dangerously as she tried to get a look at this unfamiliar-smelling non-mummy person. Sarah steadied her and settled the little head securely against her shoulder. She started to hum a low, repetitive tune from her own childhood. Beatrice snuggled into her, enjoying the vibrations coming through Sarah's chest.

Jemma was right. Sarah was good with babies, a natural. Their needs were fairly transparent to her and she found a calm, confident manner usually did the trick.

Babies needed to feel safe. They liked a full tummy, warmth, predictability and noise around them. Sarah couldn't under-stand people who tiptoed around their babies, hushing anyone who breathed too loudly.

She had once visited a home where everyone was required to be silent when the baby was asleep upstairs. Sarah had been incredulous. Silence meant alone, and that was a fearful thing after nine months of constant sound and com-pany in the womb. It wasn't rocket science, but you'd think it was watching the ridiculous way some people carried on. And the number of weird gadgets and gizmos you could buy, from vibrating bouncy chairs to baby monitors so tech-nologically advanced they'd probably answer questions on current affairs if you pressed the right button. None of it was necessary. It was all just common sense.

'You're doing a sterling job there, Sarah,' called a sharp-suited man, escorting his girlfriend across the lawn to the buffet table. He threw her a mock salute as they passed. Sarah raised a hand in reply, recognizing him as one of Lawrence's business associates. The girl smiled blandly at her, struggling as her high-heeled shoes sank in the turf. Sarah was glad

she'd worn flats. She made a half-hearted attempt to circu-
late, drifting about the garden exchanging pleasantries with
the guests she knew, but avoiding being drawn into any one
group.

There was a Goldsmiths posse, which included several of
her colleagues from the Art department, a group of aggres-
sive-looking city types shamelessly exploiting the occasion
by business networking, and many unfamiliar faces besides.

'This is some party, little one,' Sarah whispered to the
sleeping baby. 'And they're all here for you. Aren't you
lucky?'

She bent her head to Beatrice's downy scalp and inhaled
her lovely baby scent, a combination of milk, talcum powder
and freshly laundered cotton Babygro. All newborns had it
but for some reason the smell vanished at about sixteen
weeks and suddenly they weren't babies any more. Someone
ought to bottle it, Sarah thought, watching Lawrence stagger
across the lawn, his face hidden behind a stack of folding
canvas chairs balanced on his outstretched arms.

His two helpers wobbled along behind him, identical
chair-towers teetering dangerously. The three of them
together looked like a bad circus act, the kind you saw at
summer variety shows in seaside towns when it was raining
and you had nowhere else to go. She waited to see which
one of them would fall first, it didn't happen.

By lowering himself to a bizarre squatting position,
Lawrence was able to offload his chairs with minimum dis-
ruption into a tidy pile on the lawn. The other men, either
weaker in the thighs or plain lazy, simply opened their arms
and allowed their cargo to clatter onto the ground in a heap.

Lawrence straightened up, frowning a little at their slapdash approach, and began snapping the chairs open one by one and laying them out in a neat, precise line. As usual, every job, large or small, got a hundred per cent from Lawrence.

Sarah made a mental note to tease him about it later, as she often did. It was another of their games. Lawrence would pretend to look hurt at the accusation of pedantry and point out that they'd had little more than the shirts on their backs when they were first married. It was entirely due to his ferocious work ethic and natural attention to detail that those first hard years were behind them, since lecturers in Fine Art, however talented, were hardly minted. Then Sarah would roll her eyes and admit with a sigh that yes, she was grateful, and that while living in a spotless home with an alphabetically ordered pantry and colour-coded sock drawer was at times a heavy burden, it was a small price to pay in the greater scheme of things.

Being the wife of a highly successful property developer was a great privilege. The game usually ended with a dramatic offer to de-organize the spice rack. Sarah traditionally refused with equal drama, declaring herself incapable of inflicting such a wound on her husband's aesthetic sensibilities. Sometimes, though, she wondered what would happen if she agreed.

'Sarah?'

'Hmm?' Lawrence was waving her over. She walked towards him, smiling sheepishly. 'Sorry, I was miles away.'

'I could tell.' Lawrence peered cautiously at Beatrice. 'Fast asleep. Let's find you a hideout before pass-the-baby begins.' He stroked Beatrice's cheek gently with his little finger.

'She'll get no rest once that kicks in, poor little kipper. Or Jemma.' He put his arm around Sarah and steered her towards a quiet spot beneath a flowering magnolia, a canvas chair ready for her in his free hand.

'So what were you thinking about?' he asked. Sarah sat down and stretched her legs out in front of her.

'You, actually.'

Lawrence's face split into a Cheshire-cat grin. 'I like the sound of that,' he said, dropping a kiss on her hair. 'Tell me more.' Sarah laughed and shook her head, pleased by the mischievous spark in his eyes. There was no need to burst his bubble. Even the best of men had fragile egos.

'Not in front of the baby,' she said primly, looking up at him through lowered eyelashes. Beatrice stirred and mewed like a kitten, breaking the moment. Lawrence's heart twisted as he watched Sarah soothe the child with a simple touch. He cleared his throat.

'Stay here, I'll get you some food. Pick and mix, bit of everything?'

'Lovely. And a drink if you can manage it, darling. I'm parched.'

Sarah glanced up at the house, feeling slightly guilty. In addition to the main body of guests in the garden, the conservatory that gave onto the patio housed a splinter group who were lounging on the wicker furniture or gossiping happily behind the leaves of the oversized tropical plants.

She caught a glimpse of Philip, looking harried and wearing an ageing female relative on each arm like grotesque, oversized cufflinks, but there was no sign of Jemma. She probably had fallen asleep, poor thing. 'I ought to go and check on her,' Sarah murmured. She glanced down at the baby and bit her lip. It was a shame to disturb her and Jemma certainly needed the rest . . . 'Five more minutes,' she decided, closing her eyes and breathing in the sweet, fresh smell of the magnolia blossom.

There was nothing in the world more calming to the spirit than holding a sleeping child. It was like a miraculous balm to cure all ills. For Sarah, though, it was never more than a temporary cure. In the end, it was just more salt in the wound. At that moment a car backfired loudly in the street. Sarah jumped and swore under her breath. Beatrice nestled deeper into her godmother's neck and slumbered on.

In the street outside, Arima jumped and swore, not at all under her breath, as the camper van backfired loudly in the middle of her shoddy parking manoeuvre. Parallel parking wasn't usually a problem but the man watching her with hawk-like intensity from the pavement was putting her off. No doubt he owned the BMW she was currently reversing towards. His hands were thrust into his jacket pockets but Arima could see them twitch with the urge to intervene each time she hauled the steering wheel round. What was it with men and parking – why did they have to watch?

She was exhausted, her shoulders ached, and she'd had nothing to eat all day except a stale croissant on the early morning ferry and Doris's hobnobs. She shoved the gear stick into first, pulled forward and prepared to try again, unable to take her eyes off the reflection of the infuriating man in her side mirror. If he offered to park it for her, she resolved to drive over his shiny leather shoes with a smile on her face.

Seconds later the man appeared at her window.

'Couldn't help noticing you're having a bit of trouble there,' he said in a jovial tone. It didn't match the expression in his eyes, which beamed the words *scratch my car and die* into Arima's hot, tired brain. 'Shall I do it for you?' Arima stared at him for a long moment, then flung the door open and jumped out, forcing him to step back into the road.

'You know what?' she slammed her keys into his hand. 'Go for your life. I'll be inside.' She jerked her thumb at Jemma's house and walked away. 'Thanks,' she added as an afterthought. No point telling him about the dodgy clutch.

Discovery was the best form of enlightenment. And at least now it'd be him reversing into his own BMW, which was a most satisfying thought. As she waited for the sound of colliding metal, Arima mounted the imposing stone steps to the porch, leaned wearily against the door jamb and rang the bell. She waited for a minute, then rang again.

Eventually, a pretty brunette with long, tousled hair answered the door and ushered Arima inside without really looking at her.

'Sorry, I'm sorry,' she mumbled, closing the heavy door with a crash. Arima flinched as an expensive-looking crystal vase wobbled on its window-ledge perch. 'Everyone's outside and I was upstairs,' the woman continued, running one hand self-consciously over some heavy creases in her linen dress. She turned to lead her guest down the hallway. 'Do come through, I'll get you a . . .' she trailed off as she recognized the girl beside her. '*Arima?* Arima!' She flung her arms around Arima.

'Hi Jem,' Arima replied, hugging Jemma back. 'Great to see you too. Sorry I'm late.'

'Oh, never mind that,' said Jemma, dismissing the apology with a flick of her wrist. She began towing Arima down the hall, talking non-stop. 'We didn't even know whether you'd received the invitation. Come on, come on, Philip will be so pleased to see you, well, lots of people will, it's been such a long time.'

'I had to come . . .'

Arima felt a little dazzled by glimpses of opulent furnishings and expensive artwork in every room they passed. She'd known from the address that her friends had gone up in the world, but this was something else. Jemma hurried her into the kitchen and on towards the conservatory.

'Some of the old Goldsmiths crowd are here, you know,' Jemma said.

*'Really?'*

Jemma laughed at Arima's surprise.

'Of course,' she said, raising an eyebrow. 'They aren't all appalling correspondents, you know.' Arima smiled back at her, easing back into the old friendship. Things had changed, but this was still Jemma.

'No offence taken,' she said.

'How could there be? It's completely true.'

'I did send a postcard once.'

'Yes, three years ago. We kept it as proof that you still existed.'

'*And* an e-mail.'

'Never got that.'

'Well, it's not my fault if you changed your account.'

Jemma stopped on the threshold of the conservatory and wheeled round, hands on hips.

'For shame, Arima Middleton. You lodged with us for three years – all the way through your degree, for heaven's sake – and you think one e-mail and one postcard in five years counts as keeping in touch?'

Arima hesitated but realized that she didn't have a leg to stand on. It wasn't that she didn't care – she counted Jemma and Philip Hever among her best friends, in fact – but she carried friendship lightly and invested little time in such attachments, confident in her ability to pick up where she left off. Emotional security wasn't something Arima had ever felt the need for.

'Okay, I'm crap. I admit it. But I love you just as much as ever,' she said with her most winning smile. 'And I'm here now.'

Jemma beamed at her. 'Yes, but where have you come from?'

Arima shrugged. 'France . . . Spain . . . Italy . . . here and there. Long story.'

Jemma wagged a finger at her. 'You'll have to do better than that, Arima Middleton. I need details.' She looked out into the garden, suddenly distracted. 'But not now. Beatrice will need a bottle any minute. Come on.'

'Right . . . yes.' Arima had forgotten all about the baby. She threaded her way through the guests in the conservatory, feeling a little dazed by the transition from solitude to the hum of a party. She squeezed past a wicker sofa where a well-built man with a shaved head was being talked at by a vapid blonde horsey type.

There was a lot of hair-flicking and simpering going on. The man looked intensely bored. He glanced up at Arima and a spark of recognition passed between them. Arima did a double take. Was it . . . ? But Jemma's hand was on her arm, tugging her onwards before either of them could draw breath to speak. Arima followed Jemma down the steps, feeling in the pocket of her skirt as she did so. The little package was there, safely wrapped in a twist of tissue paper. Jemma was scanning the garden, standing on tiptoe to see over the throng of people.

'Ah, there she is. This way.' Arima looked longingly at the enormous buffet table as they passed and tried to ignore the painful growling in her stomach. Jemma slowed as she approached a spreading magnolia tree in full bloom. Arima heard her mutter, 'I can't believe it. She's still asleep.' Then Jemma raised her voice and said, 'You won't *believe* who I found on the doorstep. Look what the wind's blown in.' Arima stepped into the shade of the tree as the woman cradling the baby raised her head. A slow smile spread across her face.

'Arima Middleton,' said Sarah, pronouncing each syllable with great solemnity. 'The prodigal returns.'

'Prodi*gy*, you mean,' said Jemma.

It was no secret Arima had been Sarah's favourite student during her time at Goldsmiths, as well as one of the more talented artists in her year. Possibly the most talented.

Arima shrugged, shedding the compliment as she always did, but Sarah laughed and extended her arm like a queen welcoming the return of a faithful subject. Arima took Sarah's hand and knelt beside the chair. It was an oddly formal moment, but then Sarah hugged her old protégé close and kissed her affectionately on the forehead.

'It's wonderful to see you again,' she said simply.

'You too, Sarah. It's good to be back.' As she said the words, Arima realized they were true. Kneeling there in the grass between her mentor and friend, she felt a sense of homecoming. Nowhere had felt like home since her parents had died.

Jemma broke the silence. 'I should give Beatrice her bottle,' she said, almost apologetically. 'We'll have to cut the cake soon, and do photos.'

'Of course,' said Sarah, raising the baby gently from her shoulder to wake her.

'Hang on,' said Arima, pulling the tiny parcel from her pocket. 'Can I just give her my present?' Jemma nodded and stretched out her hand.

'Thank you, that's so kind.'

'No, it's for Beatrice,' Arima said, her fingers closing over the gift.

'Arima, she's six weeks old.'

'So what? It's still her present.'

'She won't even be able to hold it!'

'She doesn't need to. It's for looking at.'

There was a moment's silence as Jemma wrestled with post-natal hormones. Arima waited, the package hidden in her closed fist. Sarah watched the exchange silently, only half-concealing her smile.

'Alright, okay,' Jemma said at last, unable to find a reason with which to coat her reluctance. 'But don't let her put it in her mouth.'

Sarah turned Beatrice round and settled her on her lap so she was facing Arima. Arima opened her hand and unwrapped the square of powder-blue tissue paper. A small piece of dark wood lay in her palm, no more than two inches in height and width. Its contours were smoothed into the shape of an arch and a cross had been roughly carved into the front.

'See this, Beatrice?' she said, holding her hand up to the baby's face. Arima stood the wood upright and Sarah saw there were actually two pieces, joined with tiny metal hinges. 'Like a book, you see?' Arima continued. Beatrice fastened an unblinking gaze on the object. 'Now, watch.' Arima parted the sections of wood to reveal a double-sided miniature icon painted in the Russian Orthodox style. On the left was Christ, one hand raised in blessing. On the right was Mary, head bowed demurely, her hair covered in a veil of midnight blue.

'Arima, it's beautiful,' breathed Jemma, bending down for a better look.

Sarah leaned in, her trained eye automatically examining the structure and form of the piece. The traditional forms of iconography had been adhered to, but there was something utterly original about the little miniature. There was brightness to the blend of colours that would appeal to a child without being garish. Christ was smiling, his free hand outstretched as if to draw you into the painting, and if you looked closely, you saw the Virgin's eyes weren't downcast, but peeping up at the watcher with a spark of fun. This wasn't a remote figure on a pedestal. It was a mother who would laugh and play. Sarah let her breath out slowly.

'All your own work, I take it?' she asked, knowing that it had to be.

Arima nodded, her eyes on Beatrice, who was still staring at the little wooden icon-book.

'I think she likes it, Jem,' she said.

Jemma smiled and lifted her daughter out of Sarah's arms. 'It's a treasure, Arima,' she said. 'Thank you so much. It really is milk-time now. Excuse us.' Sarah could tell by the expression on her face she'd missed the point entirely.

'Sure.' Arima closed the book up, re-wrapped it and passed it to her friend. She got to her feet, brushing grass from her skirt. Sarah stood up with her.

'Shall we get some food?' she suggested. 'I'm peckish again.'

'I'm starving,' Arima admitted. She checked her watch. No wonder. The afternoon was nearly gone.

'Are you back for long?' Sarah asked as they made their way towards the buffet table.

Arima shrugged. 'I'd like to be,' she said in a voice that suggested she wasn't sure. 'But I'm not great at staying put. I'll see how it goes.'

'Where are you staying?'

'Oh, I've got the camper van,' Arima said.

'In London?' Sarah was horrified. 'You can't sleep by the roadside, it's not safe!' Arima was amused. She'd slept in far worse places.

'I'll be fine.' She took a plate and began loading it with sandwiches and sausage rolls. There was a mountain of food, far too much for the guests. Perhaps Jemma would let her bag some up for dinner later. Sarah was not so easily put off.

'You must stay with us,' she said firmly. 'We've got loads of room. Stay as long as you like.'

'It's fine, honestly,' Arima replied. 'I'm happy in the van.'

'Well, park on our drive at least,' Sarah insisted.

'I'd forgotten how bossy you are,' Arima sighed.

'Only because I'm right,' Sarah countered.

Arima laughed. She much preferred to be independent, but she could see Sarah was genuinely concerned. As she looked at Sarah, it was as if they had never aged. There was the woman who had taught her so much looking like she always did. Arima eyed every line on her face. All was the same.

'So you will?' Sarah pressed. Arima raised her hands in surrender. 'Marvellous, that's settled then.' Sarah put her arm round Arima's shoulders. 'It'll be just like old times.'

Arima felt herself sinking into the past, layers of old, happy memories wrapping her in comfort. Somewhere deep within her, a note of warning sounded. She pushed it away.

# Chapter 3

It was getting late. Most of the guests had left, leaving the hard core that you find amid the dying embers of a good party – family, close friends and people too drunk to realize the clearing up is about to begin. Normally Arima liked this part best. It was when the real conversations happened.

Tonight, however, she stood alone on the patio, enjoying the fresh air. It was a warm night for May, but not if you were used to a Mediterranean climate. Arima was glad of the long-length cardigan she'd fetched from the camper. There was a group sitting out on the grass, smoking and drinking in the light of the garden lanterns hanging from the trees. Sarah was among them, wrapped in a man's coat and enjoying the guilty pleasure of a Marlboro Light. A second group was gathered in the conservatory, where Philip was doing the rounds with a brandy bottle in one hand and whisky in the other. A packet of cigars protruded from his top pocket. Arima wondered which group she wanted to join, and whether it would look rude to remain on her own. She was enjoying the peace. She looked up at the sky, but the stars were hardly visible through the city haze. 'Pity,' she said to herself.

'What is?'

Arima jumped and found Lawrence at her side.

'God, you startled me,' she gasped, pulling the worn cardigan more tightly round her.

Lawrence dipped his head in apology. 'Sorry,' he said. 'I thought you'd heard me coming.' He extended his hand. 'You won't remember me. I'm Lawrence, Sarah's husband. We met a few times when you were at college, I think.'

'I remember you,' Arima said, though all she remembered was his name.

'I came to ask if you'd like a drink,' he went on.

'A brandy would be great,' Arima replied. Lawrence produced a glass from behind his back.

'Thought you looked like a brandy swigger,' he grinned. 'I'm a whisky man myself.'

'No one's perfect,' Arima said, accepting the glass. Lawrence laughed.

'So, what's a pity?' he asked again.

Arima lifted her glass and sniffed, enjoying the sharp scent of her drink. She hadn't had a brandy for ages. She pointed upwards. 'The stars. As in, there aren't any.'

'Not here, no,' Lawrence agreed. 'You need to get out in the country for that, don't you.' He gave her an appraising look. 'You don't look like an astronomer, I've got to say.' Arima took a sip of brandy, coughing a little as it burned her throat.

'I dabble,' she replied.

As a child, she used to go stargazing with her father. His old telescope was buried safely in her van, almost the only thing of his that she'd kept. They would stand for hours and scan the night sky, he would always point out every celestial wonder. These were the times with her father that she had loved the most. He had smelt of whisky and pipe tobacco.

His jumpers were always snagged with patched elbows and in summer a straw hat would be pushed tightly on the back of his head.

Lawrence waited for her to say more, but Arima didn't elaborate.

'Where's Jemma?' she asked instead. Lawrence accepted the change of subject without question as he looked at the smoothness of her face and smiled.

'Upstairs with the baby. Feeding her, or catching forty winks while she can, I expect.' They both turned to look up at the house. A light shone through the curtains of an ivy-framed window on the second floor. 'Still awake by the looks of it,' Lawrence murmured. 'Poor thing.'

'Send Sarah up,' Arima suggested. 'She seems to have the magic touch.' From the expression on Lawrence's face it was clear she'd said the wrong thing. 'Wouldn't go there person-ally,' she added quickly. 'Babies look like hard work.' She dropped her gaze and picked at the frayed cuff of her right sleeve, giving him time to collect himself. It was Lawrence's turn to change the subject.

'Why don't you darn that?'

'Pardon?'

He pointed at one of the many holes in her cardigan. 'That. It's so . . .' he waved his whisky glass in the air, seek-ing the right adjective.

'Character-ful?' Arima offered.

'Raggedy,' he answered quickly as his hand brushed against her.

Arima pointedly looked him up and down, curling her lip at the silk tie and crisp shirt with all the life pressed out of it. Then she lifted the hem of the cardigan so it was level with her face.

'Don't listen to him,' she told it. 'I love you just the way you are.'

'I'm not sure that was what Stevie Wonder had in mind when he wrote those lyrics,' Lawrence said, seizing the life-line she'd thrown him.

Humour was always his safe refuge. They grinned at one another, their faces shadowy in the dim light cast by the lamps in the conservatory. On first inspection Lawrence appeared like the other sharp-suited city clones, but his confidence lacked the brash edge that tipped into arrogance in younger men, and he had a sense of humour. Arima made up her mind. Lawrence was okay. The upstairs window was suddenly thrust open, releasing cries of fury into the night air. Beatrice was making her feelings clear. Lawrence pulled a face.

'Perhaps I'll send the baby whisperer up after all,' he said, moving towards the steps. He turned and looked back at her. 'Will you be okay here?'

Arima drained her brandy and waved him away.

'Of course. I'm going to head inside. It's getting chilly.' She felt absurdly irritated by his polite concern. First Sarah, now Lawrence. Did she look as though she needed looking after or something?

She glanced at the group in the conservatory, thinking to join them after all. But it was late, and she was tired. There was only so much polite conversation she could stomach. Having accepted Sarah's offer, she couldn't leave until the Abrahams did. Arima spotted a side door set into the wall to the left of the conservatory and made her way towards it. She pushed it open and found herself in a walk-in pantry adjoining the kitchen. 'Must have been the back door before the extension was built on,' she murmured. She felt her way along the shelves of packets and tins and stepped into the kitchen. 'Blimey.' Jemma had hustled her through so quickly earlier she hadn't really noticed the décor. Now she had time to take it in.

The kitchen space was long and narrow, laid out in a galley style and illuminated by a double row of angled spotlights in the ceiling. A granite work surface stretched the length of one wall, with gleaming chrome cupboards set above and below. Arima eyed them dubiously. They'd be a nightmare for cleaning.

On the right was a funky breakfast bar with high stools in red, the colour matching the splashback tiles above the Aga, which presided over the lesser chattels from the head of the room. There was something soulless about the room, as though it had been lifted straight from a magazine picture, with no injection of warmth or personal touches added.

The only sign of use was the enormous stack of plates the caterers had left in the sink. They looked out of place, like dog mess on a spotless putting green. It was a far cry from the cramped, cosy kitchenette in Arima's camper, and very unlike Jemma. Why had she chosen it? Arima looked about for an escape route. There were two doors out of the kitchen, one straight ahead which led to the hall, the other set into the right-hand wall by the breakfast bar, opening into the conservatory.

Light filtered under the door, slicing across the dark flag-stones. Arima hesitated, wondering whether to sneak into one of the living rooms and crash out on the nearest sofa for half an hour. Then her eye fell on a brandy bottle at the breakfast bar and she decided this was as good a place as any to chill out for a while. She kicked off her sandals and pattered across the flagstones in her bare feet. The red stools were higher than they looked, but once she'd hitched herself up onto one it was surprisingly comfortable. She poured herself a generous measure of brandy and allowed herself to relax. A plan of action, she thought, swirling the liquid around in her glass. That was what she needed. Not a fixed one − they made her feel shut in, suffocated − but a working document to be going on with.

First and foremost, she needed to find work. Being on her own suddenly gave income the kind of priority it had never had when she was with Benoit. Between them they had always made ends meet, one's fallow period matching a busy time for the other. And when they were hard up, there was a kind of togetherness in being jointly poor.

She hadn't thought that through. Not that it would have made any difference to her decision, but she might have made a bit more provision before leaving. Arima sipped the brandy, reflecting on the precariousness of her immediate situation. Parking the van at the Abrahams' for a few weeks could be fortuitous in more ways than one. Sarah was bound to have contacts and would put in a word for her. She took a mental inventory of the meagre art stock in her van. There were a few bits and pieces up to gallery standard, if she could blag a bit of wall space here and there, and she could soon knock up some more of the little icons, they'd be easy enough to flog.

Arima pulled a strand of hair free of its loose clip and began chewing the end, an old childhood habit that she'd never shaken off. Really, she needed something secure . . . but temporary. She didn't want to be tied down. 'Bit of a tall order, Arima,' she sighed. 'But you never know.' A job outside London would be great – Sarah was right, the built-up city streets weren't ideal for the van – but she couldn't afford to be choosy.

At that moment the conservatory door opened and a man in dark jeans and a blue shirt backed into the kitchen, carrying more whisky tumblers than Arima would have thought possible. His fingers were splayed out, one to a glass, and there was a brandy glass wedged under his arm. '. . . sort these out, I'll be right back,' he said to someone, raising one foot to push the door shut. Arima held her breath. He hadn't seen her. The man started towards the sink, the glasses clinking and slipping in his grasp. Arima saw the brandy glass under his arm begin to slide. He wasn't going to make it. The man turned sharply as if she'd spoken aloud. His face lit up. 'It *is* you!' The brandy glass shattered on the floor. 'Shit.' He doubled over, hugging the remaining glasses to his body as they threatened to follow suit. Arima slid off her stool and ran to help, hopping through the shards of glass.

'Watch your feet!'

'It's okay. Let me take some of those.'

'I don't think I can let go of them.'

'Don't be silly.'

'I mean it. If you take one, they'll all fall.'

'Well, you can't stay like that forever. Hold still.' She bent down and slid her own fingers into the four glasses clutched in his right hand. She could feel his hands trembling with the effort of hanging on. 'Right. Let go.' She looked up at him, close enough to bump noses. 'Let go!' she ordered. He shut his eyes and pulled his hand out fast. Arima set the glasses swiftly on the work surface. 'Okay, panic over. Do you know where they keep the broom?'

'Give me a minute.' He was engrossed in getting the remaining glasses safely to the sink. Arima stuck her head into the pantry and found a dustpan and brush. She knelt down and began sweeping the smaller pieces of glass off the floor, suddenly overcome by shyness. There was no reason for it, but after all these years she didn't know what to say.

'We need some newspaper for the big bits,' she mumbled.

'I'll put them on the side for now.' His hand crossed her line of vision, picking up the largest fragments between finger and thumb. Arima saw that he wasn't wearing a wedding ring. 'I think you've got all of it there,' he said.

'Few more bits.' She kept on sweeping, knowing she was being ridiculous.

'Mima?' He said the word so easily. She flinched at the use of the childhood nickname she had thought buried with her parents. It made her feel vulnerable, and that made her angry. Most of all she felt ashamed. This wasn't a part of her past that gave her a warm glow inside.

Arima looked at the man as he smiled at her. She watched him lean back against the kitchen units, one foot crossed casually over the other. It irritated her that the laces of his brown suede boots were undone, and despite the fact that her eye-line ended at the knee of his navy jeans, she knew he was laughing at her.

'Stop messing about,' he said. 'Get up here and say a proper hello.'

Arima stood up slowly.

'What happened to your hair?' she blurted.

He burst out laughing. 'What happened to your manners?' he said as Arima flushed.

'Shut up. You had a full head of hair last time we . . . last time I saw you.' She glared at him. 'Nobody goes bald that fast.' She added silently, 'Or fat.' He was double the size he used to be, though it quite suited him. He'd been like a walking lamppost before. No wonder she'd had to look twice to recognize him.

He ran a hand over his head. 'I just shaved all the curls off one day.'

'Why?'

'Convenience.' His smile faded. 'It's been a long time, Arima,' he said seriously. 'Too long.' She swallowed hard, knowing what he would say next. Here it came. 'Where've you been?'

'Abroad. Here and there,' she said. There was silence as he digested each word. 'Who's your friend?' she asked. He raised his eyebrows questioningly. 'The blonde girl.'

'Ah.' He folded his arms and grinned at her. 'Jealous?'

'Hardly.'

'She's a friend.'

'Like me?' She hadn't meant to say that. A hint of bitterness shaded his laugh.

'No, Mima,' he said quietly. 'Not like you.' He opened his arms. 'Do I get a hug, then?' There was no polite way to refuse, and in any case, part of her didn't want to. She stood stiffly in his embrace, the familiar smell of him enveloping her. He laid his cheek against her hair. 'Five years,' he said. 'You just disappeared off the map.'

'It's good to see you, Robin,' she answered, relaxing into him despite herself.

He tightened his grip.

'Not even a goodbye, Mima,' he said. 'I deserved better than that.'

Arima felt her throat close up at the hurt in his voice. He'd been the closest thing she'd ever had to a best friend.

'You deserved better than me,' she said gruffly. She pulled away from Robin and walked to the sink. 'Might as well make a start on the washing up.'

'Mima . . .' he whined irritatingly.

'Stop calling me that!' she snapped, giving the bottle of washing up liquid a savage squeeze. She turned the taps on full and thrust her hands into a pair of flaccid washing up gloves that were an offensively bright pink colour. 'Change the subject, Robin,' she said above the sound of the water. 'I mean it.'

For a moment he said nothing. Just looked at her in that awful X-ray way he had, the one that said *I see you. Drop the act.* When they were messing around as kids and she'd pretend to be hurt, or years later when she'd concoct a lame excuse for missing a university lecture, Robin would give her *The Look*, and Arima would squirm and crumble. He was worse than her mother ever was.

Robin crossed the room, plucked a ladle from the rack above the Aga and handed it to her. 'What's that for?' Arima said crossly.

'That.' He pointed over her shoulder at the sink, where mounds of excess washing up liquid were frothing up like candyfloss, overflowing onto the draining board and dripping from the edge of the granite work surface like bubbly icicles. The water level was reaching crisis point. Arima dived for the taps and let fly with a couple of choice phrases in her mother tongue. 'Swearing in Euskara is still swearing, Arima,' Robin said piously as she cursed in the old Basque language.

Arima rapped him on the knuckles with the ladle as hard as she could. He howled and plunged his hand into the hot water.

'There was no need for that!'

'There was every need,' she sniffed. 'You deliberately provoked me.'

'I didn't.'

'You did.'

'Did not.'

'Did *too*.'

Suddenly Robin scooped up a handful of water and flung it in Arima's face, doubling over with laughter at the sight of her spitting out soapsuds.

There was a moment's shock, then she recovered and lunged at him with the ladle. He blocked her from the sink and grabbed a tea towel, snapping it back and forth like a matador to keep her at bay while he dug in the sink for a glass to fill. Arima was screaming and laughing at the same time, whacking him on the head, elbows, knees, anywhere that would hurt. The edge of the tea towel stung like a slap when it caught her.

'Robin!' she yelled. 'Pack it in!'

'I'm not falling for that,' he panted, using his fingers to flick more water in her eyes. Arima scanned the room for another weapon and spotted her brandy glass, still half-full, on the breakfast bar. She backed away, fending off tea towel blows with the ladle, then made a run for it.

She snatched up the glass and turned to find Robin waiting a couple of feet away with a jug full of soapy water. They began to circle each other like duellists, each waiting for an opening to strike. The floor was awash and without her sandals Arima was afraid of losing her footing. She needed to finish this fast. She raised the glass.

'Give in,' she commanded. Robin shook his head, brown eyes narrowing as he homed in on his target.

'No way. I've got treble the volume here.'

'Mine will hurt more. Brandy and eyeballs don't mix.'

'Your aim's not that good,' he scoffed.

At that moment the door from the hall opened and Jemma entered the room with Sarah close behind.

'What the hell is going on in here?' Jemma gasped. 'That flooring cost a fortune. Look at what you have done to it.'

Robin broke eye contact with Arima and lowered his jug. That was a fatal error. In the silence that followed, Arima struck without hesitation.

'Yesssss!' she shouted as the brandy hit him in the face.

He dropped the jug. 'Foul!' Robin yelled.

Arima gasped as the crystal jug smashed, sending yet more water cascading across the room.

'What are you doing, Arima?' Sarah asked as she strode forwards. 'Right. Cut the victory dance, Arima. Jemma doesn't need this hassle tonight.'

Arima stopped capering about and rushed over to Jemma, who was leaning wearily against the Aga.

'Jem, I'm really sorry. We were just messing around.'

'Yeah, it got out of hand,' Robin echoed, the tea towel now pressed over his face. Jemma waved their apologies away.

'Just clean it up,' she said shortly, her voice obviously strained.

Sarah wheeled round as the conservatory door creaked open. 'Stay out please,' she barked efficiently. 'I'll call you when it's safe to come through.'

Robin's blonde companion tossed her hair defiantly but stayed on the threshold.

'Are you alright, Robin?' she asked, doing her best to ignore Sarah.

'He's fine,' Sarah said, and shut the door in her face. She looked at Arima and Robin, side by side like a pair of guilty school children. 'Batgirl and Robin,' she said wryly. 'Still getting on famously, I see.'

Jemma began to circumnavigate the pools of water on the floor, her patent mules clacking on the slate tiles.

'Not that it matters,' she said, reaching round the pantry door for the mop, 'but what were you doing exactly?' Jemma asked.

Arima and Robin exchanged looks.

'Washing up?' Robin offered his beleaguered excuse.

Sarah pointed at the dishwasher with a long chastising finger.

'Never the sharpest tool in the box, were you, Robin,' she drawled. Arima giggled as Robin elbowed her in the ribs.

'Oh, give over, both of you,' Jemma sighed. 'You're worse than children.' Sarah tapped her watch with a perfectly painted fingernail.

'It's late,' she announced. 'Let's get cleared up and off home. Arima – the mop. Robin – load the dishwasher. Jemma –' her face softened a little. 'You're dead on your feet. Go to bed.'

No one was brave enough to argue with her. Sarah had spoken.

# Chapter 4

Lawrence lay in bed, listening to the sounds of the awakening city, pleasantly muted by the double-glazed windows and offset by the quiet counterpoint of Sarah's sleeping breath. He rolled onto his side and watched her for a while, hoping her peaceful aura would send him off to sleep again.

Asleep, her face was calm, childlike and ageless. Lawrence lifted a strand of hair off her face and smiled as she unconsciously twitched him away. She was a very solitary sleeper. Sarah always tucked the duvet round her body like a cocoon, bunching the edges tightly beneath her neck so no one could get her.

Lawrence found it funny that her sleep mode was the exact opposite of her personality. There was no one more openhearted than Sarah, with her impulsive warmth and knack for drawing people to her. That was exactly what had attracted him to her in the first place, all those years ago. Sarah was the laughing girl at the centre of every group. Lawrence still saw flashes of that spirit in her, and treasured them all the more for their ever-increasing scarcity. He had watched her change through the years; the girl he married had slowly been transformed.

Lawrence rolled onto his back and stared up at the ceiling, giving in to the inevitable. He had begun to shun 'downtime' of any kind. Day time was no problem. They both led busy lives and it was easy to focus the mind on something else.

This was the danger-time, late night or pre-dawn, when his troubles came squirming up through the holes in his defences like woodworm and there was nothing to push them back into the dark. Lawrence shut his eyes and let his thoughts backtrack over what he privately called '*The Battle*'. And to Lawrence it was a battle, such a battle.

He tried to think. How many cycles of IVF had Sarah endured? Five? Six? How could he have lost count, he wondered numbly, when each time was more distressing than the last? And the final times had only been possible because they were paying a private clinic. The NHS wouldn't touch them. There were others, they said, who would 'benefit more' from the opportunity. Sarah had understood, but Lawrence had loathed the careful wording of the rejection letter − as though they were being proclaimed unworthy to be parents. His heart broke for Sarah. He agonizingly remembered the day when their doctor had called her barren. It was a word that cut to the heart. It fell so easily from his lips and took life. Lawrence had watched the tears roll down Sarah's face as she repeated the word again and again. The cold wind blew down Harley Street and chilled their hearts.

Sex had changed for them years ago. It had gone from one extreme to the other. First it had been reduced to the sole purpose of making a baby. Then he suffered from the onslaught of ovulation kits, temperature charts, strange diets, even an odd Chinese birth prediction chart that claimed to give you control over whether you had a girl or a boy. Sarah had made him eat the most disgusting things and bathe in ice cold water. Lawrence had to be ready whenever she wanted him.

Then as the years passed and their failure grew more evident, their enjoyment of one another took on a hollow dimension, divorced from any possibility of creating a new life. There were months when they seldom touched or kissed and when they did, it felt empty, worthless and futile.

It was ironic, really – there were so many people who wanted sex just to be sex. No commitment, no baggage and certainly no children.

Lawrence shifted position again and the cotton under sheet rumpled uncomfortably beneath him. His mind filled with images of girls and women hunching at that moment on the edges of unmade beds across the city, trying to play it cool as their eyes hunt for discarded clothes while last night's bed-mate sleepily asks if they're okay, stumbling slightly over their name. And mostly they say sure, no worries, great night, just a bit of fun. Don't worry: I'm on the pill. The others scoop their abandoned common sense up off the floor along with their underwear, bundle themselves together and head for the nearest pharmacy to erase all potential consequences of their coupling. Or risk it and find themselves staring at an incriminating double blue line a few weeks later.

The elusive blue line. What he'd give to see one of those. He had even taken to buying the testing kits in bulk to save the timid looks of the pharmacist who gave him his usual patronizing glance.

All he wanted was a son and heir. Or a daughter. The words circled him like vultures, mocking him, waiting to move in for the kill. Call yourself a man? Too late for you now . . . your name will die with you . . . the ghostly words echoed.

Suddenly, Lawrence realized he was grinding his teeth. He threw back the covers and slid out of bed. Sarah mumbled something and half-lifted her head from the pillow. 'Go back to sleep,' said Lawrence softly. He shut the bedroom door carefully behind him and felt his way to the top of the stairs, his feet sinking into the soft carpet pile. He paused by a wall-mounted keypad, punching in the code to disable the down-stairs alarm system. Without bothering to switch on the lights, he padded silently down into the hallway and made for the kitchen. His heart leaped as the grandfather clock chimed in a low, resonant voice just as he passed. 5.30 a.m. 'Silly old sod,' he muttered, irritated at his skittish behaviour. 'How many years have you been walking past that clock?'

Unexpectedly, a muffled thump came from the darkness of the kitchen. Lawrence jumped for real. He froze, palm pressed flat against the heavy wooden door. Who could have got in without setting the alarm off? But he'd just disabled it. Someone was in the very act of breaking in. Talk about timing. The hairs rose on the back of Lawrence's neck. He sucked his breath in, deep and slow, rehearsing the next moments. Get in. Take them by surprise. Scare them off, or pin them. Call the police. Automatically, he patted the pocket of his pyjama top. He'd left his mobile on the bedside table upstairs. Typical.

There was another sound from the kitchen. Lawrence moved. He pushed the door open and stepped into the room, tensed for action. Nothing. It was empty. The gleaming units presented a blank face; the room gave no clues away. No forced entry, no signs of interference, just a lone mug and half a pint of milk marooned on the spotless granite worktop by the kettle. Sarah must have left them out by mistake. Out of the corner of his eye Lawrence caught a movement at the long rectangular window stretched across the far wall above the double sink. A cat stalked along the outer windowsill, lashing its tail. So that was the prowler.

Lawrence walked to the island unit and rested his fore-arms on it, letting his head hang down. The worktop felt cool through the fabric of his pyjama top. It had a calming effect. Lawrence shook his head from side to side. A cat? He was getting old, jumping at shadows like that.

Lawrence pushed his hands through his hair, his gaze coming to rest on the mug over on the worktop. He might as well have a cup of tea now he was up, then try and go back to bed for a bit. He straightened up, set his sights on the chrome kettle, and walked round the island.

Suddenly, Lawrence screamed.

Not a manly yell, but a high-pitched hysterical woman scream that juddered in his throat and curdled the air around him. He fell back against the refrigerator, sending Sarah's collection of fridge magnets clattering to the floor.

'What the . . . the *hell* . . . ?' he croaked, his throat constricted with shock as he looked at the body on the floor.

Arima felt around under the curtain of hair and pulled her iPod headphones out of her ears.

'I know . . . I'm scary without make-up,' she said calmly, 'but that's a bit of an over-reaction, don't you think?'

She waited but Lawrence was rendered speechless by the sight of her sitting on the floor with her back against the unit. Her long legs were extended along the heavy tiles, encased in eye-watering pink and orange floral pyjama bottoms. For some reason best known to herself, she had a frayed purple and blue blanket round her shoulders.

'What are . . .' Lawrence muttered the words.

'You scared me,' Arima said, wiggling her feet in their woolly knitted slippers. They had pompoms on, Lawrence realized. What kind of person had pompoms on their slippers? Get a grip man, he told himself. Get a grip. 'Come on, you're not even close enough to smell the death breath,' Arima joked. 'I can see there's no hope for me finding a man. If you're any kind of yardstick, it's clear he'd have a heart attack before breakfast. Never mind. The van's not really big enough for two anyway.'

She flicked her hair off her face and cocked her head on one side as she looked up at Lawrence. 'Are you going to join in this conversation at any point?' she enquired.

'I . . .'

By this point, Lawrence was squarely on the back foot, all thoughts of a lecture on sneaking around in the small hours frightening your host vanishing in the teeth of his embarrassment. Arima was staring up at him, twirling her headphones in one hand. It was disconcerting. Needing to break the silence, he said the first thing that came to mind.

'Why are you wearing a blanket?'

'I'm cold.'

'In the camper?'

She frowned.

'No, in your kitchen.'

'Why are you . . .' his brain flicked through the options – sitting on the floor / in possession of pompom slippers / out of bed at 5 a.m. / so weird – '. . . here?' he finished.

'You invited me. Sarah gave me a key.' Lawrence frowned. That wasn't what he'd meant. Arima looked a little worried. 'Hey, are you okay? You seem a bit – weird.'

'I'm fine, fine.' Lawrence slid along the refrigerator, groping behind him for the edge of the worktop. His pulse was still doing double-time. 'Cup of tea?'

Arima's face lit up. 'Ooh, yes please,' she said eagerly. 'That's what I came in for. I put the kettle on to boil, but then I got really into the plot and forgot all about it.'

'Plot?' Lawrence flicked the switch on the kettle. Was she deliberately talking in riddles to annoy him? If so, it was working. He wanted to get back to bed and away from Sarah's odd friend.

Arima held up the iPod. 'Audio book,' she explained. 'I listen to them when I can't sleep. It's *Jane Eyre*.'

'You don't look the type for classics,' Lawrence said without thinking. Busy fetching another cup and selecting teabags from the cupboard, he didn't see Arima's face change, her pleasant expression hardening into something else entirely.

'Really.' Her tone told him he'd made a gaffe. 'And what is the *type* for classics? Mousy little women in twin sets and pearls? Pale, geeky girls who spend so much time in the library their skin burns the minute they see the light of day? But not people who live in camper vans?'

'I didn't mean that as it sounded.' Lawrence dropped a teabag into each cup and doused them with milk. It was a mark of his discomfort that he didn't feel able to wait and brew a pot in the proper way.

'Just because I don't have a regular job or – or a mortgage, it doesn't mean I'm thick,' Arima said heatedly. 'I did have an education, you know.'

Lawrence rested his head against the glass cupboard door and took a deep breath.

Being dressed down in your own home before you'd even had the chance to get dressed and brush your teeth was a bit much really. He pictured his staff, the looks of incredulity on their faces at the idea of Lawrence Abrahams, *the* Mr Abrahams, being taken to task by a slip of a girl in a blanket and homemade slippers. Deborah, the super-efficient secretary whom Lawrence suspected was at least fifty percent plastic, would clutch her desk dramatically, mouth falling into a perfect lipstick-framed halo of astonishment. It wouldn't do.

Lawrence picked up the cups of steaming tea and turned to face Arima.

'I apologize,' he said. 'But frankly, I've found you sitting on my kitchen floor at five o'clock in the morning, where there are several perfectly decent chairs.'

'And?' Arima asked.

'Incidentally, wearing . . . peculiar . . . nightwear and a mangy blanket. It's hardly normal, is it?' He gestured at Arima's outfit, slopping scalding tea onto his wrist. 'Argh!'

He thrust the cup angrily at her. 'So forgive me if I seem rude, but if cultured intellectual is the image you're trying to project, the mad bag lady look isn't helping.'

Despite his harsh words, Lawrence found himself crouching down to sit beside Arima on the floor, his back protesting as he leaned back against the wall. She held his gaze for a few moments, then handed the cup back to him.

'Good point,' she said, the flash of temper gone as swiftly as it had appeared. 'Where do you keep the sugar?'

'Pardon?'

'The sugar,' she repeated, scrambling to her feet. 'For my tea.'

Lawrence pointed at a row of ceramic canisters positioned neatly below the crockery cupboard. First she makes me furious, then she refuses to argue with me, he thought. She's insufferable. Arima approached with the sugar canister in one hand and a spoon in the other. Lawrence held the cup out to her. She bent down and poured a stream of sugar straight into her drink, then shoved the spoon in for a half-hearted stir. Lawrence studied her warily.

'What?' She asked.

'Nothing . . . I've, never seen it done that way before.'

He closed his eyes. There had to be at least five spoonfuls of sugar in that cup. The girl was a complete savage. His arm twitched as he saw Arima had failed to put the canister back in its proper place. More tea slopped out, this time onto his pyjamas. Lawrence cursed under his breath and scrubbed at the spreading stain on his leg with the cuff of his sleeve. One of the fallen fridge magnets had landed face up on the tiles beside him. *Make Hospitality Your Special Care*, it reminded him in bold calligraphy strokes. His mother had given that to Sarah, it was the kind of thing she would have said.

'Always welcome strangers,' she used to urge him as a child. 'Those who welcome people into their homes have sometimes entertained angels unawares.' Lawrence's eyes would go saucer-round at this solemn pronouncement and he and his sister would spend the next week checking visitors for covert signs of flight equipment. Lawrence sighed. Arima was a guest.

Arima settled herself beside him and took her cup back.

'It's very good of you to have me to stay,' she said.

'Well, we aren't exactly,' Lawrence replied, making an effort to smile. 'You're just parked outside. Why don't you stay properly, have a room in the house?'

Arima took a slurp of her tea.

'I'm fine in the camper,' she assured him. 'It's great to be able to hook up to the electricity and use your bathroom. Your house is beautiful,' she added.

'Thank you. We've put a lot of work into it,' Lawrence answered. The smell of her perfume lingered in the air.

The room was brightening now, a strip of morning sunlight edging along the floor as the day began. Out in the hall, the clock struck six.

'I love those big old clocks,' Arima said dreamily. 'We used to have one when I was little.'

'So did we,' said Lawrence. 'And that's it. My mother left it to Sarah and I.'

'When did she pass away?'

Lawrence was momentarily startled by the question.

'Oh, she's not dead,' he grinned. 'Mum's one of those old ladies who go on forever. She says she'll die when she can fit it into her schedule. I meant she left it for us when she moved into a retirement home. You can't take that sort of thing with you.'

'Is she close by?'

'Yes, either Sarah or I see her every week,' said Lawrence. 'They're very close.'

'You're lucky.'

'So she tells us.' Lawrence put his cup down and turned to look at Arima. 'What's brought you back to England?'

Arima shrugged.

'I don't know. It was time, I suppose. I haven't been back since I left uni.' Apart for the funeral, she added silently. That wasn't up for discussion.

'Time for what?' Lawrence asked. 'To settle down?'

'God, no,' Arima laughed. 'What a thought. I like to be free to come and go.'

'It has its advantages,' Lawrence agreed. 'But don't you get lonely?'

'Not really. I've met some pretty cool people along the way,' Arima said.

'No doubt.' Lawrence stretched and felt something go pop in his back. He knew he should go back to the body alignment clinic, but it was always excruciating. 'So,' he said, more to distract himself from the dull ache in his spine than anything else, 'you've no plans to settle in one place, but you say it was time to come home. Time for what? What are you looking for?'

'Work,' Arima said.

'You can get work anywhere.'

Arima got to her feet, suddenly uncomfortable with Lawrence's line of questioning. She didn't like people who dug for information, however friendly they seemed.

'Then I'm sure I'll find work here,' she said, taking his cup without asking and dumping them both in the sink. The truth was, she didn't know why she was here. It had been somewhere to go . . . that was all. A point of reference, a familiar place and it was all she had.

'Perhaps Sarah can ask around for you at Goldsmiths,' he suggested as he got to his feet, glad her back was turned so she couldn't see him struggle. 'Or if it's gallery space you're looking for, Robin Jennings is the man.'

'Robin?'

'Yes. He's just opened a little place on the South Bank.' He pursed his lips, trying to remember the location. 'Hays Galleria, I think.'

'He didn't mention it.'

'Well, that doesn't surprise me,' Lawrence yawned, shuffling towards the door. 'He strikes me as a modest chap.'

'Yes, he is . . . thanks . . .' Arima answered softly, plans already filling her mind. She could spend a few weeks working on a couple of new pieces, offer them to Robin and see how things panned out.

'No problem. Have a good day,' Lawrence said, closing the door on his strange house guest.

As he walked, he thought there was something rather compelling about her, he mused, plodding up the stairs to wake Sarah. He could see why Sarah liked her after all. Life would not be boring with Arima about. Or tidy, he thought, cringing at the prospect.

# Chapter 5

Jemma was semi-comatose on the Circle and District line. The train carriage rocked violently, causing her head to loll forward and she jerked herself upright. Quickly, she checked the baby and tightened her grip on the handle of the fancy travel system pushchair.

Beatrice was sound asleep, her chubby face framed by a delicate white cotton bonnet. Beneath the satin-edged cellular blanket, her pink Babygro was slightly the worse for wear, but as long as she didn't kick the cover off, no one need be any the wiser. The hood of the pushchair cast a shadow over the whole ensemble, the funky lime green colour like a flare amid the faded blue upholstery of the carriage seats.

Jemma rubbed her neck with her free hand. It hurt. Actually, everything hurt. Her shoulders were tight and knotted from endless carrying of the baby, her eyes were so dry they burned and her bones ached with fatigue. This was motherhood . . . how could tiredness make your actual bones hurt? She thought back over the previous night. Was it two hours' sleep she'd got in the end, or three? *Two*, her body screamed. *Two, and I need eight. See to it, can't you?*

If only it were that simple. Jemma tried to focus on the overhead tube map, counting the stations printed above the yellow and green stripes of the District and Circle lines.

South Kensington . . . Sloane Square . . . Victoria . . . St James's
Park . . . Westminster. They had to change at Westminster for
the Jubilee line to London Bridge. Unless the baby woke up,
in which case they'd get off at Westminster, cross the river
and walk down the South Bank. The rhythm of the train was
keeping Beatrice asleep but she was bound to wake up as
soon as the motion ceased. She always did.

Jemma felt the now-familiar stab of impatience with her
ten-week old daughter. This was immediately followed by a
wave of guilt. The whole trip out was a ridiculous idea and
she knew it. Who trails a tiny baby halfway across London
just to go to the Borough market and take a stroll along the
South Bank? Beatrice couldn't distinguish night from day,
never mind appreciate the Tate Modern. Jemma wrestled
with herself, trying to decipher her determination to make
this outing happen.

They'd been in the kitchen at home that morning, Jemma
elbow-deep in an eco-nappy bucket while Beatrice yelled
for attention in her bouncy chair, brightly-coloured animals
dangling useless and ignored on the play arch. And then . . .
suddenly she'd had an overwhelming desire to do something
normal, to be spontaneous again. Just to pick up her bag and
go out.

Jemma rubbed her eyes, scratchy and still clogged at the
corners with sleep, in spite of it being early afternoon. 'Just
picking up her bag' had taken two hours, but it became a
matter of pride. She would achieve something with the day,
however small.

The carriage doors slid open and a couple of well-dressed
women got on and sat down opposite Jemma. They looked to

be in their sixties, both exuding an aura of graceful calm. Probably retired, Jemma guessed. These women moved like they had time and plenty of it, perfectly coiffed, make-up immaculate, their smiles natural, unforced. I remember that, Jemma thought, raising a hand to her own unwashed hair, tied into a scruffy knot with an old scrunchie she'd spotted underneath a chest of drawers while changing Beatrice's nappy.

The fact she couldn't remember when she'd last washed it was in itself appalling, never mind how many days ago it was. She tried to gather up her things, suddenly aware that there was a trail of baby paraphernalia across several seats and the pushchair was blocking the aisle. One of the women, crisp and sophisticated in a crimson linen suit, caught her eye and smiled.

'How old?' she asked, nodding at the pushchair.

'Ten weeks.'

'Such a precious time. Make the most of it.'

'Yes,' her companion, her blue eyes vividly offset by a carefully chosen silk scarf, chipped in. 'They're leaving home before you know it.'

'See how placid she is,' continued the first woman, craning her neck to get a better look at the baby. 'You're lucky.'

'Yes, very lucky,' Jemma parroted, her voice sounding strained. 'She's a model baby, really. Couldn't be easier. We're very happy.'

The inevitable sleep-feeding-colic conversation rolled out, Jemma's brain producing parallel answers to the ones she spoke. (Sleep – none. Feeding – sporadic, unhealthy. Colic – wouldn't be surprised. Oh, the baby? She's fine. Thank you for asking.)

'Hope you have many more,' the older of the women urged as the train rattled to a halt.

Jemma was grateful when the women got out at Victoria, saving her from further small talk. She leaned back against the carriage window as she muttered her thoughts.

'Nobody ever asks how the mother is. Nobody cares. Not even me, and I *am* the mother. I'm wearing the same top I had on yesterday, there is congealed baby sick on my left shoulder, I look like I got dressed in the dark (which is true) . . . and I don't care. This is wrong on so many levels. And Philip would be mortified to see me out in public like this.'

The occasional jolts of the train made her head bounce on the glass, but it kept her awake. She stared at the dirty white ceiling of the carriage to avoid looking at the poster warning that a sneeze could travel up to thirty feet. Hardly the ideal environment for a baby who hadn't had her twelve-week inoculations.

A bubble of anxiety swelled in Jemma's chest. She'd said all the right things, she thought, replaying the brief exchange in slow motion. The stuff all the other mums at post-natal group came out with every week. Baby was no trouble, baby slept through the night, fed like a dream, baby was the light of their life and, what's more, almost never cried, etc, etc.

Except in her case, none of it was true. Why was she the only one with a gremlin-child?

On cue, Beatrice began to stir. Jemma jiggled the handle of the pushchair desperately. Stay asleep, stay asleep, she pleaded silently. I can't feed you here. But the brakes screeched as the train stopped at St James's Park station. Beatrice's eyes snapped open like a doll from a bad horror film and, after a brief pause to fill her lungs, she began to scream. No whimpering, no gradual crescendo. It was nought to a hundred in five seconds with Beatrice.

Jemma shook the pushchair even more vigorously, feeling her anxiety crescendo into panic.

'Hold on, poppet,' she said in her brightest mummy voice. 'Mummy will feed you soon.' She glanced down and saw two matching stains spreading across her chest as the let-down reflex kicked in. Soon was evidently not good enough. Jemma gritted her teeth. I am a grown woman, rational, educated, sane, she told herself. I am a mother. I am in charge. I am not going to be dictated to by a tiny baby and a set of over-enthusiastic mammary glands. She took a few deep breaths and waited for calm to descend. Nothing.

'Shit.' Jemma started hooking bags over the pushchair as fast as she could, delving into one for a pashmina with which to camouflage her leaking breasts. It was an unseasonal Christmas green, crumpled and dirty, but she draped it round herself and hoped she looked more earth mother than fashion freak. 'You can do this,' she mumbled, getting into an upright position on willpower alone. 'Westminster and a walk.'

When the train rattled in at Westminster Jemma bumped the pushchair onto the platform and set off through the warren of underground tunnels in search of the lift. Predictably, it was miles. 'You'll *love* the Borough market, sweetheart,' she trilled in the Mummy voice, which had to be high-energy and high-pitched with exaggerated intonation in order to engage Beatrice's interest – just as the parenting books said.

As far as Jemma could tell, Beatrice didn't give a monkey's. The only noticeable effect of *The Voice* was that passers by gave her an extremely wide berth in case she broke into an impromptu song and dance routine in the manner of Mary Poppins. However, all the books agreed on this point so it must be right. Supposing she didn't use *The Voice* and Beatrice's development was adversely affected because of it? She couldn't risk it.

Jemma shoehorned the pushchair into the lift and punched the button for the upper level. Beads of sweat broke out on her upper lip. She had to feed this child soon. 'There are lots of interesting stalls and you can even buy ostrich burgers. Isn't that *funny*!' Beatrice screwed up her face and roared.

Not many miles away, Sarah was sitting in her quiet office at the university, a pile of mid-year assessment papers on her desk. The minutes of a recent departmental meeting lurked by the heavy paperweight bought for her by her mother-in-law one birthday, a delicate white butterfly imprisoned in a clear glass orb.

A scattering of random pens and erasers among some blank sheets of paper hinted at prolific activity where in reality, there was none. Sarah was ignoring all of them. On top of the assessment papers was a small booklet, currently the sole focus of her attention. She stared at it as though it was a winning lottery ticket. They never played the lottery, she thought randomly. Perhaps they should start.

The phone rang, disrupting her thoughts.

'Hello?' She picked up but immediately held the receiver away from her ear as the departmental secretary's voice boomed through the handset. Marjorie was very efficient but a little too enthusiastic at times. 'Fine, put her through.'

Sarah rolled her shoulders and tilted her head from side to side, wincing as she heard the crick-crack of tension in her neck. She needed to get back to the gym. A new voice came on the line.

'Hi, Sarah. Sorry to bother you.'

'Arima, hi. Everything okay?' Sarah listened for a moment, then reached beneath the desk for her handbag, feeling around for her address book. 'Great idea, I've got the details.' She read out an address and dropped the slim black volume back into her bag. 'Pop in and see what he says,' she advised. 'Yes, all fine here. See you tonight.' She dropped the phone onto its cradle, the conversation already forgotten, and turned her attention back to the booklet.

Lawrence needed to see this. It could be their last chance. But how best to present it? Everything hung on his reaction, and something told her he wasn't going to like the idea. How could she convince him? Sarah sat back in her chair and slowly began to formulate a plan. Dinner. A nice bottle of wine. Maybe a walk . . . if she picked her moment, Lawrence would listen. Perhaps. Sarah sighed. Compared with her, Lawrence seemed much more prepared to accept the hand life had dealt them and trust 'It would all work out for the best.' That kind of attitude drove her mad. Things didn't just work out, she thought fiercely. You had to *make* them work out.

The familiar longing seized her, so intense it was like physical pain. 'Eva,' she said suddenly. 'I need to get Eva on board.' Sarah slid the booklet into her desk drawer and reached for the phone again. Her mother-in-law would know what to do. Eva's old eyes still saw the shape of the boy in the man Lawrence had become. She was a woman who knew how to handle her child.

In the shadow of an old warehouse, tears rolled down Jemma's face as she ran along Bermondsey Street, her eyes glazed with panic.

'Oh God, there has to be a café around here,' she sobbed. '*Hold on*, Beatrice, Mummy's doing her best.'

The plan had been to get to the market, sit down at one of the little impromptu outdoor café stalls, feed Beatrice and have a proper fresh lunch. Afterwards, a leisurely browse round the stalls, like she used to do, and home. She had hoped Beatrice would hang on long enough for them to get there, and she had – just about. But it had all gone wrong at the market.

The pushchair was too unwieldy to manoeuvre between the stalls, the seating areas were much smaller than she remembered and all occupied by office people on their lunch break, none of whom had any intention of giving up their seat. An officious-looking couple holding hands over their laptops threw Jemma a disdainful glance and turned their heads away, burying their sneers in their decaff skinny lattes.

She couldn't hear over the noise Beatrice was making, but Jemma saw the man's mouth frame the words 'Stupid cow.' Then the smoke from one of the open barbecues had gone in Beatrice's eyes and sent her ballistic. Jemma had pushed her way out of the market, upsetting two baskets of fruit, and charged off, stammering an apology.

This was motherhood. The stress was unbelievable. Why hadn't she stopped at one of the places along the South

Bank? Why hadn't she brought a bottle and to hell with the mixed feed timetable in her baby care book? Feed-feed-feed, her hormones commanded. Her brain had turned to porridge and all perspective vanished.

Now she was just running, hoping to find somewhere, anywhere that she could sit down and make the screaming stop. 'Shut up!' she wailed. 'Just shut up for one minute! I can't think.' Through her tears, Jemma saw a bright red, tinsel-covered shop by a large brick archway just ahead. 'Hays Galleria,' she panted. Café Rouge. There was definitely a Café Rouge in there. 'Thank God.' She swerved into the entrance and ran on, the pushchair bouncing over the cobbles.

Inside, Robin leaned on the tiny counter tucked into a corner of his gallery. There wasn't a lack of space; he had wanted to be discreet about the exchange of money ... that was all. Both the counter and the till were as unobtrusive as possible. In contrast to this, all the work was well showcased and comfortably situated in its own place on the wall area, some pieces grouped by artist, others by style or colour.

Personally he quite liked the clash of opposing styles displayed next to one another, but it wasn't for everyone and so he'd tried to create an effect that was easy on the eye. There were contemporary canvases, gilt-framed landscapes, miniature cameos, portraits, abstracts, line drawings and charcoal sketches. No preference shown to any one style. Robin was open-minded about that. Selection would come later, depending on what sold best. The gallery was almost completely white so as not to compete with the work on show and it was a nightmare to keep clean. Robin had never spent so much time sweeping in his whole life. He felt like Mrs Mop but it was worth it. He had his own place at last.

He wandered over to the door and opened it, looking out onto the spacious courtyard of Hays Galleria, its vaulted ceiling arcing high above the worn cobbles. There were a couple of decent cafes nearby, the Horniman pub just on the corner and a beautiful view of the Thames.

Even the wacky all-year-round Christmas shop was starting to grow on him. It was a great place. Robin gave a contented sigh. He reached up and took hold of the doorframe, lifting his feet to swing gently back and forth and counting the seconds until his grip gave out. The freshly painted black and silver sign overhead implied R. Jennings was a mature artist beyond such juvenile games. Robin jumped down reluctantly. Probably best if prospective customers didn't see him hanging in the doorway like a zoo monkey. Eight seconds, though. Not bad, a two-second improvement on yesterday's score.

A breeze blew through the courtyard, carrying a layer of dust over the threshold and on to the pristine floor.

'Oh no,' Robin grumbled. 'I've already swept twice today.' He wondered how long it would be before he could afford a cleaner.

He started to close the door and was about to turn away when a figure appeared in the entrance of the Galleria, preceded by a screaming pushchair. Robin's jaw dropped. Jemma was wearing a large sky blue rugby shirt over faded jeans that were significantly too long. She had a big green scarf wrapped across her upper body and her hair was in some kind of lop-sided topknot.

Robin considered himself fairly low in the fashion stakes, but even by his standards Jemma looked pretty odd. He saw she was crying and ran to intercept her.

'Jemma, hi!' Jemma stopped short, staring blindly around her. 'Over here.' Robin jogged up to her and took hold of the pushchair. 'What's happened? Is Beatrice okay? Can I help?' Jemma buried her face in his shirt and cried even harder, overwhelmed by the sight of a familiar face.

'Please . . .' she moaned as she chewed his shirt, wiping her tears on the fabric.

'Hey, it's okay,' said Robin awkwardly, putting a hand on her arm. He was unused to this sort of emotional display from Jemma. In spite of her being an old friend he wasn't comfortable with it, but there was no one else on hand and she was obviously in difficulty.

'I need . . .' she gulped. 'I need . . .'

'Deep breaths. Take your time.'

'. . . to feed the baby,' she panted. 'Café Rouge.'

'No need for that,' said Robin. 'This way. I'll even make you a cup of tea.' He steered the pushchair towards his shop, silently marvelling at the volume Beatrice was achieving with her screams. Inwardly, he wondered how on earth the pair of them had got in such a state, but he kept his voice light and cheerful. 'Receiving you loud and clear, Beatrice,' he joked. 'Refreshments are on the way.' Jemma clung gratefully to his arm and managed a watery smile.

Half an hour later, Beatrice was fed, winded and fast asleep, a thin line of milk dribbling from the side of her mouth.

Jemma covered her with the blanket and hovered by the pushchair. 'I ought to change her,' she said fretfully. 'I didn't do it before her feed.'

'Well, she looks okay,' said Robin cautiously, wanting to reassure although he hadn't the faintest clue what he was talking about. 'If she was uncomfortable, she wouldn't go to sleep, would she?'

Jemma looked at him as though he'd cracked a previously unbreakable code. 'She wouldn't, would she? And yet, my book says you should change them before a feed or they won't settle to it.'

'Really? It didn't seem to, er, put her off.' Robin dragged his one stool from behind the counter, feeling rather embarrassed at the direction the conversation was taking. He had no desire to discuss breast-feeding in any further depth. 'Here,' he said, waving Jemma towards the stool. 'The kettle's boiled. Sit down and I'll get you that cup of tea.' Jemma wheeled the pushchair over to the stool and sat down, her eyes still fixed on her daughter. She was sitting in exactly the same position when Robin returned from the tiny kitchenette with the drinks. Watching her, he reckoned she hadn't even blinked.

'Jemma?'

'Hmm? Oh, thanks.' She took the cup from him and looked about, taking in her surroundings for the first time. 'Robin, this place is perfect for you.'

'Thanks,' he said. 'I'm pleased with it. The plan is to –'

'It's just so hard,' Jemma burst out, cutting across him. 'She never sleeps for more than an hour at a time.'

'Oh. Well, I –'

'And the feeding! It's constant, well, you've seen how she is. It's so painful. I've gone through at least three Savoy cabbages already and it makes no difference, none.'

Robin was completely nonplussed. 'That's meant to help, is it?'

Jemma nodded. 'So my book says. But it's not helping me.'

'Maybe you could try eating a few more?' he hazarded.

Jemma stared at him as though he was a simpleton. 'You don't eat them, Robin.'

'You don't?'

'No,' she said irritably.

The conversation was rapidly leaving the realms of reality. Were cabbages some kind of vegetable midwifery talisman, or was the smell appealing to babies for some weird chemical reason? Robin couldn't get a handle on this at all.

'What do you do with them then?' As soon as the words were out of his mouth, he realized he didn't want to know.

'You wear them.'

'You – you *what*?'

'In your bra.'

Robin choked on his tea.

'But it has to be a Savoy cabbage.' Jemma's face was deadly serious. 'And it isn't helping, and I don't know what to do, and Philip has no ideas and the health visitor's no good and we're doing mixed feeding with bottles which I feel *terrible* about because everybody else is one hundred percent breast feeding until at least six months and . . .' the words churned out of her, every sentence tumbling over the next in an unstoppable tidal wave of emotion.

Robin listened.

Eventually, when Jemma's untouched tea had gone cold and Robin's left leg was numb from standing so long in the same position, Jemma began to run down like an old clockwork doll, her voice gradually fading away.

'Sometimes,' she finished miserably, 'I look at her in the crib and think "Go back. I can't do this. I don't want you any more." And I really mean it.' She turned her face up to Robin, a mixture of horror and shame in her eyes. Her voice was barely audible. 'My own baby.'

Robin was silent for a moment as he tried to shape an appropriate response. He had no idea why Jemma had confided in him. Maybe it was easier to tell someone she wasn't immediately close to, or maybe she just couldn't contain it any more. Whatever the reason, one thing was very clear to Robin. He knew nothing about parenthood but the look on Jemma's face was one he remembered intimately from his own childhood. This needed careful handling.

'How long have you been feeling like this?' he asked gently.

'Weeks.'

He took a deep breath. 'I think . . .'

At that moment the door swung open and Arima stepped into the gallery. In faded brown cords and a dark blue denim jacket, windswept hair and cheeks flushed from her walk, she looked a picture of health and vitality. A tatty brown leather satchel was slung across one shoulder.

'Hi there,' she said brightly. 'What a nice surprise.' In the pause that followed, Arima read their faces, Jemma's terrified, Robin's solemn and guarded. 'Er – should my ears be burning?' she laughed, hooking her thumbs in her trouser pockets.

Robin smiled at her.

'You wish,' he replied. He could sense Jemma's eyes boring into him, *Don't tell don't tell.* 'Jemma popped in to show Beatrice my new place.'

Arima nodded at the sleeping baby.

'Bored senseless, I see.'

'I think you'll find that the tranquil atmosphere of my gallery inspires creative rest,' said Robin loftily. He winked at Jemma. 'Beatrice even went to sleep without a nappy change.'

'I should see to that now,' Jemma said, plucking Beatrice, blanket and all, from the pushchair and heading for the little kitchenette at the back of the gallery. 'She needs to wake up anyway. Through here, is it?' she asked over her shoulder.

'Yes, on the right,' said Robin. 'Sorry there isn't more room.'

Arima waited until Jemma was out of sight before moving towards Robin.

'What's wrong?' she muttered.

Robin hesitated, caught between honouring a confidence and wanting to help Jemma.

'She needs to go home,' he answered in an undertone. 'I think she's not feeling well.' Suddenly it came to him. 'Quicksand,' he said.

Arima's eyes widened and he relaxed, knowing she'd recognized their old code word. Her eyes questioned him and he nodded once to show he was sure. Nothing else was needed.

'I'll go with her,' was all she said. Arima flipped open her satchel and pulled out a handful of bubble-wrapped items.

'Well, Baby Whisperer, I came by to see if you'd think about selling a few of my pieces,' she said, raising her voice so Jemma would hear. 'They went down a storm with Beatrice.'

'Then I can't say no,' Robin smiled.

Arima set her work down on the counter and began to unwrap it. 'You'd better take a look at them.'

He caught her wrist.

'No need. I'll take them,' he assured her.

She shook him off.

'Not as a favour, Robin.'

'Absolutely not. This is business.'

Arima narrowed her eyes.

'How much?'

'Fifteen percent,' he said without missing a beat. 'Plus dinner.'

'Not if you're cooking.'

He laughed and stuck his hand out. 'Done.'

'What are you two plotting?' Jemma asked as she reappeared with a bleary-eyed and grumpy Beatrice.

'Just the usual,' said Arima with a shrug. 'Business. World domination. Robin's appalling culinary skills.'

'Old times,' said Robin softly. Arima pretended she hadn't heard.

'Ready for home?' she asked Jemma, reaching out to stroke Beatrice's downy head.

'Yes,' said Jemma, strapping Beatrice securely into the pushchair and triple-checking the harness. She looked drained but calmer, Robin thought. It had done her good to get all that off her chest. He hoped Arima would know how to approach the problem.

'Off we go then,' said Arima cheerfully. 'Can I push her for a bit?'

She took hold of the pushchair without waiting for Jemma's reply. Jemma flinched as Arima bumped Beatrice clumsily over the threshold, but she didn't intervene.

Robin followed them to the door.

'Thanks for dropping by, Jemma,' he said, as he turned and looked at Arima. His voice lowered. 'I'll call you.'

'Sure.' Arima answered with a smile that meant he'd better.

He stood in the doorway to wave them off, noting how Arima gently chivvied her friend along. Depression was a difficult thing at the best of times. There were so many aspects it was like grappling with an octopus. 'Not your problem,' he told himself, feeling half-grateful, half-guilty. He shook his head and turned away, wondering how soon he could call Arima without looking too keen.

As they walked towards London Bridge and home, Jemma turned to Arima and said, 'Nothing's changed between you two, has it? Even after all this time.'

'I don't know what you mean,' said Arima, deliberately obtuse.

'He's still crazy about you,' Jemma said. 'I'm as mad as cheese right now – no, don't argue, I know I am – and even I can see it.'

'We're just friends,' Arima replied, linking Jemma's arm through hers. 'Same as always.' And that, she added silently, was how it was going to stay. She wasn't about to make the same mistake twice.

# Chapter 6

The traffic was horrendous. Cars sat nose to tail as far as the eye could see, frustrated drivers rolling right up to the bumper of the car in front so that they resembled a giant mechanical conga line.

It was laughable, thought Lawrence. As if those extra few inches would get people home sooner. And yet everyone seemed pre-programmed to do it, himself included. When the car in front next began to crawl forwards, he deliberately waited a few seconds before teasing the clutch of the Carmen Ghia up to the biting point.

Immediately a cacophony of horns blared in the queue and a pastel-pink Nissan Figaro cut in front of him before he could close the gap. Lawrence found himself sneering. He didn't like the trend for old-style-new-twist cars, be they Mini Coopers, Beetles or the saccharine oddity sitting on his front bumper. There was something tacky about them: like new money, they tried too hard.

'Who would want to drive that?' he demanded, feeling his jaw clench with irritation. A pair of bikers zipped past on the inside, smug and stress-free in their leathers. This did nothing to improve his temper. Lawrence had campaigned for a bike for years but Sarah maintained she'd divorce him if he ever arrived home with one. He saw one of the bikers waving cockily at the static cars and hoped someone would 'accidentally' open their passenger door and send him flying. The thought cheered him up somewhat. He flicked the radio on and was soon humming along to the latest tunes on drive-time radio.

Half an hour later, Lawrence eased the car into a parking space right outside the house. Arima's van was there, parked a couple of spaces further along and looking like a rhinoceros at Crufts among the sleek, well-groomed vehicles on the street. The two-tone lilac and cream paint certainly made a visual impact and the flowers – well! Unique was the tactful description for it. Lawrence jogged up the front steps, whistling to himself.

He saw Sarah had put some new flowers in the heavy ceramic pots either side of the door. They were delicate pinks and yellows and he made a mental note to compliment her on the choice. Perhaps he'd cook up something special for her tonight as a surprise. There was some fresh sea bass in the fridge and he might just about have time to whip up a lemon syllabub for dessert.

Lawrence stepped into the hall, his thoughts on dinner, and tripped over something. He careered across the room and caught himself on the banister, skinning his knuckles in the process.

'What the . . . ?' A partially coiled extension lead lay tangled on the floor just inside the front door: Arima's hook-up for the camper. Lawrence took a deep breath, determined to cling onto his good mood. It wasn't as bad as last week, when she'd abandoned a soggy bath towel halfway up the stairs and forgotten to rinse the washbasin after brushing her teeth. He didn't begrudge her the use of their home but Arima left a trail wherever she went, like a visible stream of consciousness. You could almost map out her activities by examining the debris. Lawrence didn't do clutter or mess of any kind.

'No point getting worked up about it,' he told himself, sucking the blood from his stinging knuckles and heading for the kitchen. 'She's a guest, not a permanent . . .'

He pushed the door open and the words died in his throat.

On the south bank, Sarah didn't care about the mess.

'Madam? We're here.' The cab driver twisted round to address the attractive passenger on the back seat. She was gazing out of the window, one hand unconsciously smoothing the crease on the leg of her grey tailored trousers, the other gripping a large black handbag as if it were about to sprout legs and run off with her purse. He noticed that she was biting her lip, though whether from anxiety or excitement he couldn't tell. Either way it would ruin her lipstick but it wasn't his place to say. Instead, he cleared his throat and said again, 'Madam? St Jude's, Greenwich. That's where you wanted, isn't it?'

'Oh, excuse me. I was miles away.' Sarah pulled some notes from her handbag and passed them through the opening in the protective screen. 'Thank you.'

The cabbie glanced down at the money, then up at the woman who was already halfway out of the door.

'Hold on, you need your change,' he said.

'No, no.' Sarah shouldered her handbag and shut the door. The cabbie looked at the notes again. There was more than a hundred pounds. After a brief fight with his conscience he wound the window down and called out.

'Are you sure?'

Sarah waved a hand in acknowledgement but didn't look back. When she set off home later and found her purse empty she would realize her mistake but right now all she could think about was getting to her mother-in-law.

The cabbie shook his head in disbelief at her extravagance and his good fortune.

'She must think it grows on trees,' he laughed.

Still, his conscience twinged a little. Despite her assurances it didn't seem quite fair to take the money, which was triple the usual fare. The woman had been distracted – no, not distracted. He frowned, his fingers leafing through the bundle of crisp notes as he struggled to put a word on her mood. 'Tunnel vision,' he said finally. 'Like . . . on a mission, or, or something. Weird.' The whole thing made his head hurt. He stuffed the notes into his leather money pouch and filed the encounter under interesting stories to tell his wife during the commercial breaks of their evening television viewing. 'Never look a gift horse in the mouth, son,' he reminded himself, remembering his old dad's favourite catchphrase.

The cabbie flicked his hire light on and pulled out into the traffic, his mind already on his next fare.

Meanwhile, Sarah was nearing her destination, anticipation and fear clotting into an uncomfortable lump in her throat that made it difficult to breathe. She had stopped to sign in at reception but the cheerful girl at the desk had waved her straight through.

'I'll do it,' she offered. 'You carry on. She's waiting for you.'

Sarah recognized her as one of the staff her mother-in-law approved of. Eva sliced the retirement home staff into two categories with brutal accuracy – Amateur and Professional.

Qualifications had nothing to do with it. She used the term 'professional carer' as an insult, maintaining that they were exactly that. People for whom the habit of kindness had become so ingrained that it was a hollow, Pavlovian response, produced solely because it was expected. Their smiles were a touch too fixed and their jolly-you-along voices smacked of insincerity as they sang out their stock phrases like trained parrots.

It was the eyes that gave them away, according to Eva. Bored . . . vacant . . . cold fish. That's how she thought they looked. The Amateurs were the genuine article. 'Real,' Eva explained. 'None of the robotic pleasantries you get from the Professionals. No one can be happy all the time. It isn't normal. *They're* not normal. It's a sad state of affairs when people see kindness as something they're paid to do.' You couldn't argue with her analysis. Eva's body was failing but her mind was as sharp as ever.

Sarah waved her thanks to the receptionist and hurried onwards through the polished double doors and left down the corridor. The neutral walls were pepped up with soothing Impressionist prints.

The fresh flowers posing in every alcove and niche almost succeeded in masking the scent that pervaded every residence for the elderly, however exclusive. And St Jude's was *exclusive*: as Sarah was reminded anew each time the monthly invoice arrived.

The momentary shock on opening it never seemed to lessen, though both she and Lawrence had agreed Eva should have the best that money could buy. Eva, too, had agreed on this point, though she took issue with the name of the place on the grounds that it was unintelligent and bad for morale. On first meeting the manager she had subjected the poor man to what a lawyer would call 'robust questioning', demanding to know why any self-respecting pensioner would want to live in a place named after the patron saint of hopeless cases.

'No doubt you measure us for our coffins on the way in,' she muttered darkly as the manager floundered in his own sales pitch.

The beige carpet absorbed Sarah's footsteps. She approached a light-coloured door at the end of the corridor, bearing a small plaque. *Suite 3: Mrs Eva Abrahams* was etched in a flowing script intended to mimic handwriting.

Every suite had its own personalized plaque. Eva objected to that as well. Plaques were for dead people who wanted to be remembered with a bench. In truth, Sarah and Lawrence knew none of it really bothered her. Every little niggle and complaint was offset by her affable nature and the unquenchable laughter in her eyes. She was happy at St Jude's, well stimulated and had a tolerably good social network.

Sarah lifted her hand to knock but paused, trying to collect her thoughts for this most crucial of conversations.

'Come in, darling.'

'How do you do that?' Sarah exclaimed, entering the room with a smile.

Eva was sitting in her bedside chair, a winged leather Churchill in dark burgundy that had been a favourite of her husband's. She was as elegantly presented as ever, wearing a knee-length navy pleated skirt and tights and a green cashmere cardigan. Eva was proud of her hair and often wore it loose about her shoulders in a shock of lustrous white but today she had rolled it into a chignon, her blunt fringe emphasizing her hazel eyes and the delicate structure of her face. Physically, there was little resemblance between Eva and Lawrence. A book lay open on her lap, a pair of gold-framed reading glasses marking the page.

'Do what, dear?' Eva asked, offering her cheek for Sarah's kiss.

'Call me in before I've knocked.' Sarah perched on the edge of the bed and dumped her handbag on the floor. 'You do it every time.'

Eva smiled up at her daughter-in-law.

'Mother's intuition,' she said. Sarah didn't need to know they rang through from reception when a visitor checked in, after which Eva counted a slow twenty before speaking. It nearly always worked out right. The trick amused her. 'Would you like to move next door?' she asked, indicating the adjoining room that doubled as a lounge and private dining area for the occasions when she didn't feel like being sociable. It didn't happen that often, but she enjoyed having the option.

'No, you look cosy there.' Sarah swung her legs up onto the bed, tucking them beneath her as a little girl would.

Eva shrugged and set her book aside.

'So ... what's brought you over here in such a tearing hurry on a work day?' she enquired, getting straight to the point.

Sarah drew her breath in and opened her mouth to reply but suddenly she didn't know how to begin. Her childlessness was something she rarely spoke of, except to Lawrence, and now she wanted to, the words she needed to shape her desperation didn't seem to exist, or if they did she was unable to command them.

In a moment of insight she realized it was the return of hope that was tormenting her, not the despair. Failure had become so palatable that the taste of possibility was like acid on her tongue. Sarah turned to Eva in mute appeal, her eyes filling with tears.

Eva took her by the hand.

'News?' she asked quietly. 'Good news?'

'Perhaps,' croaked Sarah. Eva's expression didn't alter but her fingers tightened around Sarah's.

'Tell me,' she breathed.

Sarah pulled her hand free and fumbled in her handbag for the little booklet from her office. She passed it to Eva, who scooped up her half-moon reading glasses and began to read. Sarah waited, the faint sound of piano playing drifting into the room as the weekly tea dance started up in the community room.

The music surged and faded as the minutes crawled by, unmarked by the tick of a clock. Eva read on. Someone knocked on the door to offer tea and biscuits. A car door slammed. The sounds of everyday living that were normally such a comforting backdrop jarred on Sarah. Her nerves were in tatters.

Finally, Eva closed the booklet. She continued to stare at it for a minute before handing it back to Sarah. With careful deliberation she removed her glasses and tucked them into her cardigan pocket. Then she looked out of the window and slowly shook her head.

'This is not the way,' she said quietly. 'Not for you. Better adoption than this.'

Sarah seized her hand again, as if to prevent this last fragile chance from slipping away.

'Why?'

Eva faced her daughter-in-law, tears in her own eyes at the sight of Sarah's distress. She chose her next words with care, not wanting to inflict more hurt.

'It's too risky, Sarah. I know how difficult the situation is, but think objectively about what you're proposing for a minute.'

Objective wasn't a concept Sarah was capable of applying to the subject of being barren.

'I can't,' she gulped. 'You – you *don't* know.'

Eva dipped her head.

'No,' she admitted. 'I don't. But I know you, Sarah, and I know my son. Please.' Her eyes strayed to the plain wooden cross above her bed, small and unobtrusive but an unmistakeable presence in the room. 'Don't give up hope of carrying a child of your own. I know it seems hopeless to you but I've always believed it would happen.' She leaned out of her chair, folding Sarah into her arms. 'I still do. I think, deep down, Lawrence does too. Won't you take strength from our faith in it?' Sarah sat stiffly in the circle of Eva's arms, taking no comfort from the embrace. 'Not a stranger, Sarah,' Eva murmured, kissing Sarah's hair. 'It should come from you. Think of the risk involved, the legal loopholes . . .'

A sensation of cold descended on Sarah as Eva tried to rock her rigid body to and fro, the unconscious maternal gesture cementing the realization in her mind that she would do anything to have a child, whatever the cost. Anything at all. It frightened her.

Sarah took her leave of Eva as soon as possible and physically ran from St Jude's, shaking off Eva's words of warning as she went.

'Greenwich pier please,' she said, hurling herself into the first available cab and already running through the quickest route home in her mind. Cab to the ferry, ferry to Westminster, cab home.

Usually she'd take the tube but today there was no time to lose. With shaking hands, she pulled her mobile from her bag and punched in the number from the booklet. Her heart thumped in time with the dialling tone as she waited for a reply. Answerphone.

Sarah left a garbled message, giving every contact number she had. No matter. She flipped the phone closed and bit her lip, reworking the plan in her mind. She'd been counting on Eva's support. Now, she would simply have to convince Lawrence by herself. All her earlier thoughts of caution fled, swamped by an overriding sense of urgency. They would discuss it tonight. Sarah crossed her fingers and hoped Lawrence had had a productive, stress-free day. That would certainly help her cause.

Lawrence was up a stepladder scrubbing the kitchen ceiling when the doorbell rang, so he chose to ignore it. He ignored it the second time as well. Finally the visitor leaned on the bell and held it there.

'For God's sake!' yelled Lawrence, climbing down and stamping to the front door. He was wearing Sarah's Cath Kidston rosebud apron over his business suit and a pair of primrose-yellow marigolds. There were shards of bullet-hard eggshell scattered like dandruff in his hair. If this was Arima without her key, guest or no guest, he was going to tear a strip off her, he vowed. What kind of a moron went out and left an egg boiling in the pan? She'd gone too far.

'Yes?' He yanked the door open, already convinced it was her.

A group of neighbours stood clustered on the doorstep. At the sight of Lawrence they fell back, partly aghast at the thought this odd attire was *de rigueur* for the respectable Mr Abrahams behind closed doors, but mainly because he smelled strongly of rotten egg. After a moment, Mr Bertram-Wirral from number 20, a fat, bald man with the head of a toad, stepped forwards. He looked nervous but resolute. The man checked the position of his wispy comb-over, adjusted his tie and cleared his throat several times before he spoke.

'I'm sorry to disturb you at a time like this, Lawrence.'

Lawrence leaned against the door, suddenly very aware that his J-cloth was dripping water onto the carpet.

'What's the problem?' he said tersely. 'Because, if you don't mind me saying, it's damn rude of you to stand on the bell like that.'

Mr Bertram-Wirral coughed as he tried not to laugh at the sight of Lawrence in rubber gloves and an apron.

'Yes, well. I'm sorry about that but it really couldn't wait. I – that is to say, we – we've come about *that*.' He jerked his head to the left. Lawrence stared blankly at him.

'About what?'

'That . . . vehicle.'

'I can see about twenty-five from here.' Lawrence knew perfectly well what his neighbour meant but had no intention of making it easy for him.

Mr Bertram-Wirral drew himself up to his full height of five feet and five inches.

'I think you know,' he said pompously, 'the vehicle to which I am referring. We would like it removed from the area immediately.' He paused but Lawrence said nothing so he pressed on, his voice becoming more officious with every word he spoke. 'It is an eyesore, a damned nuisance and, what's more, the – lady – residing in it keeps uncivilized hours.'

Lawrence snorted. 'Uncivilized hours?'

There was a murmur of assent from the three cronies hiding behind their spokesman. One of them, a Russian woman in her eighties who Lawrence thought lived at number 24, spoke up.

'Is she a *lady of the night*?' she asked in scandalized tones, her wrinkled mouth puckering with distaste.

'No,' said Lawrence, hardly believing he was rushing to Arima's defence given the current state of his kitchen. 'She most certainly is not.' He rounded on Mr Bertram-Wirral, whose confidence was rapidly deflating. 'And how do you know she keeps uncivilized hours? If they're uncivilized, I assume you're asleep.' He realized he was gesturing with the soggy J-cloth and quickly put his hand behind his back.

'Well, I, I, I . . .' stammered Bertram-Wirral as his only strand of hair slipped from across his bald head to form a long braid across his face.

Lawrence sighed.

'Look,' he said. 'I'll offer you a compromise. The camper van remains where it is, but our guest will stay in our home from now on.' The deputation went into a huddle.

Lawrence could take no more. 'Tell you what,' he said. 'You can get back to me. Enjoy your evening.' He stepped back into the hall and kicked the door shut. Then he kicked it again for good measure. 'Great,' he said through gritted teeth. 'You might as well call yourself Stig of the Dump from now on. Sarah will have to have words.'

He plodded back to the kitchen in search of a beer. What he really needed, he thought, was a bit of peace and an early night.

Arima rounded the corner of the street, tired and drained from dealing with Jemma. Something needed to be done there, but she wasn't sure. Sarah might know what to do. Sarah was good with children. She stopped short, seeing the huddle of neighbours on the doorstep and guessing instantly why they were there. She saw one of the old ladies was the one who had been peering through the windows of her camper van late at night. Slowly, she backed up until she was out of sight again. At that moment, her mobile rang.

'Robin, hi.' She turned and began walking back towards the bus stop. 'Yes, she got home fine. I'm sure we can sort it out.' She paused and glanced back at the house. It might be politic to keep a low profile this evening, keep out of the way of the neighbourhood watch. 'Listen, how about that dinner you mentioned? Tonight would be great for me. Brilliant, see you there.' Arima pocketed her phone and picked up her pace, anxious to get well out of the way until the fuss had died down. It wouldn't be so bad having a catch-up evening with Robin after all.

# Chapter 7

It had been a busy evening in the Thai restaurant in Bermondsey. Waiters sped to and fro, weaving between the tables. They tried to maintain a service that was both discreet and attentive.

Robin had booked a table on the balcony, where the deep red walls were softened with angled spotlights and a large window gave them an unrestricted view of the river. The low-level hum of conversation from the other tables just reached them. The crisp linen tableware, slim, high-backed leather chairs and multi-level floor plan created a relaxed feel. It was the perfect venue.

Robin could hardly believe his luck when Arima had agreed to dinner so readily and had done everything in his power to maximize the chances of a perfect evening for this, their first proper meeting for five years. And it had been perfect. Though neither of them referred to it, their shared history drew them to one another, an invisible web settling over them, its trailing threads ready and waiting to be picked up again.

'A toast,' said Robin, raising his glass of red wine in a salute.

'To what?'

'Er . . .' Flushed with wine and pleasure, Robin was momentarily stumped. 'I dunno. Absent friends?'

'But that's everyone we know,' Arima pointed out, scraping the last of the curry sauce from her plate. 'We're the only ones here.'

'True.' Robin took a swig of wine while he tried to think of an alternative. Arima reached over and topped up his glass. 'You should have finished that,' he protested. 'It was the last bit.'

'So we'll get another.'

Robin frowned, his wine-soaked brain trying to process the wisdom of this suggestion. Another bottle sounded good to him but he shouldn't have too much. He liked to have the shop open by ten o'clock and that generally meant an early start with the commute. 'How many bottles have we had now?' he asked.

'Two.'

'Right. Probably enough?'

'Probably?' Arima picked up the empty bottle and gave it a little shake, eyeing the tannin-darkened dregs. 'Seems a shame, though,' she said sadly. 'It's a nice bottle.'

'Do you still use them as candle-stands?' Robin asked, picking up on her thought.

'All the time,' Arima assured him, making her eyes large and solemn. 'Actually, they're my main source of light. The electrics are dodgy in the van.'

'So . . . if we don't get another bottle, you won't be able to see at night?'

'So right.' Arima started an enthusiastic nod but stopped abruptly as the room began to spin. On the other hand, if they did have another bottle, it was likely she wouldn't be able to see at all. She leaned back, glad of the high padded back on her brown leather chair.

Robin beckoned to a waiter and held up the bottle. The waiter bowed, smiled and glided away, privately marvelling at the volume of alcohol these Westerners could drink. Not that he minded. Generally they left a larger tip, plus he could amuse himself by telling them the fresh orchid garnish served with every dish was edible. It added an element of fun to a busy shift. He located the correct bottle of wine, mounted the steps to the mezzanine and politely asked if Arima would like to sample it first.

'No, that's okay,' she said, beaming at him. 'We're going to drink it anyway.'

'Of course, Madam,' the waiter said smoothly, filling Arima's glass. 'Would you like to see a dessert menu?'

Robin looked at Arima, who nodded. When the waiter had taken their order, Robin raised his glass once more.

'Right. Where were we? A toast to . . .'

'Spontaneity,' Arima suggested randomly.

'Eh?'

'You know, seizing the moment. Going with the flow.'

'I know what it *means*,' he laughed. 'But why that?'

'Because that's me. My code,' she replied.

'Okay. Spontaneity.'

They chinked glasses and shared a smile. Robin was quiet for a moment, watching as Arima swirled the wine around in her glass. She was absolutely right, he thought. Spontaneity summed her up precisely. Living how and where she wanted, no method to her decision-making and certainly no thought for the consequences. No guarantee from one day to the next. She was like a cat. Beautiful and capable of wonderful companionship, but ultimately without reference to anyone but herself.

There was no malice in her and Robin knew that. Arima was simply content to live in the moment and was utterly self-sufficient, happy to wait around until the next opportunity presented itself. It was emasculating for a man to feel so obviously dispensable. Robin felt his mood plunging into melancholy. The descent was speeded by alcohol.

'What are you thinking about?'

Arima was watching him over the rim of her glass, her eyes warm and teasing. A trio of gold bangles on her arm clinked and jingled when she took a sip of wine.

Robin opened his mouth and discovered the word 'you' on the tip of his tongue. For a second he panicked. Don't spoil it! You've had a beautiful evening. He swallowed the word and said instead, 'Just wondering whether to have coffee and then a liqueur, or a coffee liqueur.'

'It's a tough call.' She removed one of the gold bangles from her arm and spun it on the table as you would a coin. The delicate twisted rope design appeared to writhe as it revolved in the candlelight. 'Hey, do you think they'll bring any more of those little flowers with dessert?'

'Hope so. They were delicious.'

She was so beautiful, just as he remembered her. He warned himself not to fall in love with her again. Arima tilted her head to rest on her cupped palm and smiled at him in that particular way she had, and a small voice within him declared it was already too late.

Sarah arrived home at eight o'clock. It was a full two hours later than normal. She would have been home by seven had it not been for her mistake in overpaying the cab driver on the way to St Jude's. On arrival at Greenwich she had made the embarrassing discovery that the coffers were bare and had to beg to be driven to the nearest cashpoint in order to pay her fare.

The knock-on effect of this was missing the ferry, and so on until the entire journey plan had toppled like a stack of dominoes and she was horribly late, something that always put Lawrence on edge, especially if he was cooking dinner.

Last summer, Sarah had accepted the offer of an after work drink with her colleagues, thinking Lawrence was working into the evening to close a big deal. Inevitably, one drink had turned into two drinks, then three, then dinner. When she got in at eleven o'clock she'd found Lawrence asleep at the kitchen table, her favourite scented candles burnt down to a multi-coloured waxy puddle and a congealed romantic dinner slowly charring in the oven. There were twenty-three missed calls on her mobile. Despite copious apologies and painful grovelling, he still brought it up a year later.

She stood on the doorstep now, house keys dangling as she tried to compose herself. How was she going to do this? Dinner first, then talk, or get it off her chest straightaway? Sarah took a deep breath and stepped into the house.

'I'm home,' she called, shedding her jacket and hanging it neatly in the coat cupboard under the stairs. There was no reply. Sarah poked her head into the kitchen. No Lawrence and no sign of dinner. She frowned. His coat was on its usual hanger in the cupboard so he was definitely here. 'Lawrence?'

'In here.' At the sound of his voice, all thoughts of having '*The Talk*' fled. Sarah entered the lounge and saw Lawrence lying on the enormous Churchill sofa, still in his suit. One arm was flung across his eyes and a bottle of Black Sheep ale stood daringly on the carpet without so much as a coaster. A bad sign. The remote control lay limply in his hand. He hadn't even switched the television on. Lawrence was beyond weary.

'Hi, darling. You okay?' Sarah kicked off her shoes and joined her husband on the sofa, curling herself up by his feet. The crushing sense of urgency in her chest eased a little as she looked at Lawrence's face, the lines and furrows of stress and worry softened by his smile. Tomorrow, she promised herself. A nice breakfast before work, then float the idea and leave him to mull it over during the day. 'Sorry I'm late,' she added hastily, patting his leg. 'I popped in on your mum.'

'I know,' he mumbled. 'She called.'

'She did?' Sarah felt her entire body tense like a drawn bow.

'Yeah.' Lawrence pulled himself up and gave her a tired smile. 'God, what a day. What kept you?'

'There was a mix-up with the taxi. Long story.' No need to tell him it was a one hundred pound mix-up. Sarah relaxed, realizing that Eva hadn't said anything. 'Tough day?'

'Long and stressful. But productive.' He leaned over and kissed her. 'Better for seeing you.'

Sarah recoiled. 'Ugh! You stink of eggs.'

'Arima,' Lawrence grimaced. He gave a brief synopsis of the evening's events. Sarah hugged him.

'Thanks for sticking up for her,' she said softly.

'Well, she hadn't done anything wrong.'

'I know, but I also know she's not your favourite guest,' Sarah replied, snuggling in under his arm. 'Are you sure you're okay with asking her to stay in the actual house?' She felt him shrug.

'It won't be forever,' he pointed out. 'We're just a pit stop for Arima while she gets herself sorted.'

'True. And I think I've got work for her at the university next term if she wants it,' Sarah said.

'Sarah, that's two months away,' Lawrence moaned. 'The house will be trashed by then.'

'I'll make it up to you,' Sarah promised. 'Anyway, it's your idea to have her in the house, not mine.'

'I know, but I thought we were talking weeks, not months,' he sighed, running a hand over the fast-growing stubble on his jaw. 'Oh well. There's nothing else for it.' He grinned at Sarah. 'Listen to us. We're talking about her as though she were some kind of feral pet we keep in the shed. Poor girl.' He sat up suddenly. 'She wouldn't hook up with Robin Jennings, would she?' he said hopefully. 'He's a nice bloke.' That would be a neat solution.

'No-o,' Sarah said. 'Hell would freeze over.'

'I thought they went back a long way?'

'They do. That's the problem. Too much history.'

Lawrence frowned. 'You've lost me.'

Sarah giggled and slid off the sofa. 'Forget it. I don't know the whole story myself. Let's open a bottle of wine and order a takeaway,' she suggested. 'It's too late to start cooking now. Come on.' She reached down and pulled him to his feet. There was a resounding crack. 'Lawrence, was that your back?' she gasped.

'Yes,' he groaned. 'I'm getting old.'

'Distinguished,' she corrected, kissing him on the nose. 'You need to see the body alignment man again.'

'But he hurts me.'

'Don't be a wimp,' Sarah laughed, disappearing into the kitchen. 'I'll make you an appointment for next week. White or red?'

'White,' he called, shuffling towards the phone. 'Chinese? Korean? Thai?'

'Thai, please.'

'Okay.' Lawrence rummaged in one of the drawers of the merchant chest coffee table, searching for takeaway menus. The pleasing sound of a cork popping carried through into the lounge. Lawrence sighed contentedly. Things were looking up. He picked up the receiver and jumped as it rang in his hand. 'Hello?'

Sarah padded back into the room and waved a large glass in front of him. 'Sorry, I think you've got the wrong number,' said Lawrence, dropping the bundle of menus and taking a large swig of wine. Sarah collapsed back onto the sofa, cradling her own glass in her lap. 'Yes, she does live here, but . . .' Lawrence turned towards her, a frown suddenly darkening his face. Sarah smiled up at him, her fingernails tapping idly on the stem of her glass. Probably a telesales call. He loathed them but was always polite on the grounds they were only doing their job, however irritating. On the other hand, she was starving and Lawrence was still patiently listening to the double glazing salesperson or whoever it was today.

Sarah pointed at her stomach and mouthed, 'Hurry up.' Lawrence stared at her, his cheeks slowly flushing an angry red. Uh-oh. The caller must be attempting a hard sell. Sarah held her breath and wondered if he was going to let rip. Lawrence didn't often get angry – his natural authority was such that he rarely needed to – but he was pretty magnificent once he got going, provided you weren't the subject of his rage.

'I'm going to stop you there,' Lawrence said, his voice clipped and perfectly even. 'Thank you for calling. Please don't contact me again. No, I won't change my mind. Goodnight.' He switched the phone off and tossed it onto the sofa, then tipped his head back and drained his wine glass.

'Steady on,' said Sarah. 'These glasses hold almost half a bottle each.' Lawrence ignored her, taking one final swallow before placing the glass on the coffee table with deliberate care.

'Darling, who was it?' A thread of anxiety crept into her voice. Something had really got under his skin, that much was plain.

'That,' Lawrence announced with visible self-control, 'was someone calling to arrange a meeting.'

'At this time of night?'

'Indeed.'

'That's ridiculous,' Sarah sniffed. 'It's almost nine o'clock.'

'I'll tell you what's ridiculous, Sarah,' Lawrence said, his voice now dangerously low. He really was furious. 'The idea of me fathering a child with a complete stranger. *That's* ridiculous.'

Sarah's stomach turned. 'Lawrence –'

'Especially,' he interrupted, 'especially when you appear to have made all the arrangements without any reference to me.'

'That – that's not true,' she stammered. 'It was just an enquiry, just a . . . I was meaning to . . .' she wilted under the force of his stare.

'Just a what, Sarah? A joke? A bit of idle research?' Sarah eyed him fearfully. Lawrence was so angry he was barely containing himself. He'd gone white around the lips, his hands bunching into fists at his sides. 'How dare you,' he said, his voice scarily calm.

Sarah rose, her hands outstretched in supplication. 'So you won't . . . you won't consider it?' she whispered. Tears were rolling down her cheeks now but Lawrence made no move to comfort her.

'You're damn right I won't.' He turned his back on her and strode to the door.

'Lawrence!'

He wheeled round in the doorway, fury in his eyes. 'No, Sarah. No. I love *you*. I want a child with *you*, not some rent-a-womb woman I've never even met. How could you even think it? I know you think little of my faith, but I believe God has promised us a child, a child of our own.'

'Darling, please.' Sarah started towards him but he threw up a hand, warning her to stay where she was. 'It's not – she's a counsellor, it's just to discuss the, the possibilities. That was all, I swear it,' Sarah wept. She hung her head, unable to bear the look in his eyes, a collision of love, anger and – was it disgust, or despair? 'It would still be your child,' she whispered. 'And mine, through you. Might not this be the way your God answers our prayers?'

Lawrence was silent. When at last she dragged her gaze upwards, he was gone. Sarah's legs gave way beneath her. She crawled on shaking limbs to the sofa, lay face down and wept as she'd never wept before. Lawrence had never been so angry with her, not in all their years together. She wondered if he would ever forgive her. A vivid image appeared in Sarah's mind as she sobbed – a giant sand timer, with her trapped in the bottom half. Sand was raining down on her, filling her mouth and nose, blinding her eyes and suffocating her as she searched desperately for a way out. Soon it would be too late. Even as her despair plunged to new depths, her determination rose up to meet it. While her heart cried out that there was no way forward, her will hardened in response.

*I will find a way.*

# Chapter 8

It was nearly midnight when Arima arrived home. She zigzagged up the street, stumbling against parked cars and privet hedges like a human ping-pong ball. It had been a long time since she had had so much to drink. Despite being distinctly out of it, she clearly saw the bedroom curtains of number 24 twitching as she passed by.

Arima paused, leaned heavily on the gate, and waved up at the window with one of the empty wine bottles from the restaurant.

'Lovely evening!' she yelled. 'Thanks for waiting up!'

The curtains trembled furiously in response. Arima giggled and staggered on. It was rude, but no ruder than Mrs 24 poking around the van at 6 a.m. No doubt she'd be there again in the morning. Arima briefly considered sleeping naked and leaving the curtains open to give her a fright but decided against it. The old bat was irritating but she didn't want a heart attack on her conscience. Anyway, it was too cold. July or not, she was still using a hot water bottle most nights, unable to adapt to the cool climate of west London.

Arima stopped by the van and bent over, placing her two wine bottles on the kerb by the front wheel with the exaggerated care of the seriously drunk. She straightened up, fishing around in the pocket of her dress for her keys, and struck her head on the wing mirror. 'Ow!' Where were her keys? 'Think, Arima, think,' she mumbled. Not in her pocket, and she had no handbag. Had she given them to Robin to look after? She rested the heels of her hands against her eyes, trying to summon a bit of focus. They were . . . they were . . . 'Got it.' Arima swung round and tottered towards the house. She'd put them on the kitchen counter beside the hob when she'd been boiling her eggs in the . . . oh, nuts. She'd gone out and left the eggs on, hadn't she. Arima giggled. 'Shut up,' she reprimanded herself, pushing clumsily against the front door and finding it still open. 'It's not funny.' It was a bit, though. Lawrence must have been beside himself.

She tiptoed through the darkened hall, hoping to get in and out without being spotted and told off. It was like being a teenager again. A floorboard creaked underfoot as she passed the lounge door.

'Lawrence?'

Busted.

'No, it's me. Arima.'

She opened the door and peeped in. It was almost pitch black inside. One small table lamp perched on the piano, achieving little more than an interesting shadow-shape on the far wall.

'Hello?'

'Over here.' Arima could just make out the shape of Sarah curled up at the end of the sofa. She felt her way around the coffee table and flopped down beside her.

'Sorry, I forgot my van keys,' she slurred. 'Just came in to find them.'

Sarah ignored this remark and held up a bottle of wine. 'Drink?'

'Why not?' One more wouldn't hurt. Sarah produced a full glass out of the darkness with a flourish, as if by magic.

'Good night?' she asked in a hollow voice.

'Uh, yes. Lovely. Dinner with Robin.'

Arima didn't stop to wonder what Sarah was doing, lying alone on the sofa in the dark at this time, and failed to notice her pale face and red-rimmed eyes.

'How nice.'

'Mm.' Arima stifled a yawn and stretched her legs out onto the coffee table, pointing and flexing her toes to release the tension in her calves. The little kiss at the end of the night was probably ill advised, she thought fuzzily, but no matter. Robin was an old, old friend, and he was so sweet. Plus she hadn't seen him for a very long time and he'd paid for dinner, so she was practically obliged really. He wouldn't even remember in the morning. Suddenly she remembered her misdemeanour in the kitchen. 'Sorry about the eggs,' she said, trying to look penitent in case Sarah was bothered. After the evening she'd had, Sarah couldn't have been less bothered.

'Forget it,' she said, making a huge effort to halt the downward spiral of her thoughts. 'But I'm glad you came in. I need a word about the van.'

'Oh?' Arima feigned ignorance and crossed her big toes, another of her mother's superstitious habits. Arima had carried out extensive trials on the theory in her childhood and discovered that crossed toes yielded a far better success rate than fingers. When ten-year-old Robin had scoffed at her, she had stuck her nose in the air and explained in lofty tones there were thousands of things that modern man was unable to account for, such as the big bang and why a watched pot never boils. Toe-crossing was simply another one of those things.

Briefly, Sarah explained the situation.

'So we think it'd be best if you moved into the house,' she finished. 'As our guest, of course. No rent.'

Arima sat up. 'Really?' She couldn't hide the relief in her voice, sure that she'd been about to receive her marching orders, literally. Being moved on wasn't something she'd ever got used to. Apart from the embarrassment of it, authority didn't sit well with Arima. She liked to be the one who decided where she went, and when. The prospect of leaving made her realize how much she wanted to stick around.

Sarah smiled at her.

'Did you think we were about to throw you out on your ear?' she asked. 'Far from it. In fact, I might have a bit of work for you after the summer. Practical tutorials, seminars. We're losing a PhD student. Just temporary, but . . .' she couldn't bring herself to say that it was for maternity leave.

'That would be fantastic. Sarah, thank you so much.'

Arima was elated. What a coup. A job and digs all in one night. They drank in silence for a while, Arima congratulating herself on her good fortune, Sarah sinking back into her private grief.

Arima was nodding over her wine glass when a fragment of dinner conversation surfaced in her mind.

'I saw Jemma today.'

'Oh?' Sarah was staring off into the dark, absorbed in her own thoughts.

'Yes. She's . . . not well, I think.' Depressed was such an awful word, perhaps because of its descriptiveness. It was exactly as it sounded, Arima realized. Depressed. Held down against one's will by an invisible force. 'Would you have time to pop in and see her, maybe look after the baby for a couple of hours?' she asked. 'Jemma I can handle, but I know nothing about kids. They're more your thing, aren't they?'

Sarah made a peculiar choking sound and Arima shot up on the sofa, almost spilling her wine. After a few seconds, she realized Sarah was laughing. It was the most horrible sound she'd ever heard.

'My God, Sarah, what is it?' Arima pitched forwards and grasped her by the shoulders as the great, gurgling rasps gave way to tears. 'Shall I get Lawrence, should I . . . tell me what to do!' It was deeply unsettling to see someone she'd previously looked up to crumbling before her eyes like this. The Sarah she'd known was always composed and capable, a problem-fixer, not this shaking bundle of nerves clutching a wine glass as if her life depended on it.

'Everything,' Sarah wept. 'It's everything. I can't go on.'

'What? Sarah, no,' Arima replied, desperately trying to stem Sarah's tears with the sleeve of her cardigan. She felt groggy and disorientated, her brain unable to process this sudden shift in mood. What could be so wrong? 'Listen, you've had a bad day, maybe, bit too much wine. It'll all look better in the morning, honestly it will. Trust me.'

Sarah's head lifted at the sound of those words. She stared at Arima, her face haggard in the gloom. 'Alright,' she whispered, putting the crumpled surrogacy pamphlet in Arima's lap. 'I will.'

'What is it?'

'Read it.'

Arima squinted at the lines of close-set print. 'Wait, I can't see.' She crossed the room to sit on the piano stool, in the tiny circle of light cast by the lamp. She began to read, swaying a little on the stool as she tried to absorb the information. The beginnings of a hangover started to pulse behind her eyes and she felt a sudden yearning for her bed. After some time, she looked up at Sarah and frowned. 'So this, um –' she checked the leaflet again, 'this surrogacy thing. That's what you're doing, you and Lawrence?'

'No.' Sarah's voice was flat. 'He refuses to consider it.'

'Oh.' Arima stumbled back to the sofa. 'I didn't realize you wanted children.'

'Very few people do,' answered Sarah, her mouth twisting in a bitter imitation of a smile. 'Everyone thinks I'm a career woman.'

'Aren't there . . . other *options*?'

'Believe me, we've tried.' Sarah reached out and took the pamphlet from Arima's hand. 'This is the only option left.'

'Adoption?'

'We want our own child.'

'I can . . .' Arima floundered, unable to say she understood. 'That's fair enough,' she finished.

Sarah proffered the wine bottle and she nodded gratefully. More alcohol was definitely needed. This was way out of her comfort zone. Babies were – well, they were delightful, but they'd never figured in Arima's life. Not even theoretically. Arima had always thought of kids as something that . . . happened . . . in due course, or not. The concept of wanting a child at all, let alone wanting one this badly, was completely alien to her.

'I suppose if it's meant to be . . .' It was like flicking an invisible switch in Sarah's brain. She slammed her glass down in fury.

'Don't. Don't say it. That's what Lawrence says. Time and time again, he's like a damn parrot.' She raked her hands through her hair, becoming more agitated by the second. 'Every failed IVF cycle, every period, year in, year out. Don't give up, it'll happen. It's meant to be. Well, I'll tell you something, Arima,' she spat, jabbing a neatly painted nail in the air for emphasis, 'I'm not like Lawrence and his mother. This irrational faith, this . . . this *belief* that we'll have a child of our own one day, it's ridiculous. I'm forty-five, Lawrence is fifty-seven.' She folded in on herself, rocking to and fro with her arms wrapped round her body. 'The writing's on the wall. I have to do something, *anything* to make it happen. It has to happen, do you understand?' She turned a tear-streaked face towards her friend and pupil. Arima didn't understand but the anguish in Sarah's eyes was more than she could bear.

'Let me help you,' she said, trying in vain to take Sarah's hands and make her still. 'How can I help?' Sarah shook her off, wrapping her arms more tightly about herself.

'You can't,' she moaned. 'No one can.'

Arima cast around for something to say, something useful, productive. Anything to get Sarah out of this dreadful state. 'Why won't Lawrence consider the surrogacy idea?' she asked tentatively.

Sarah tossed her head. 'Because it would mean involving a third person. Putting our trust in a stranger.'

'Surely that makes it easier?' Arima said, rubbing her temples as the headache began in earnest. She really wanted to go to bed now. 'More businesslike?'

'There are risks,' Sarah mumbled, glaring at Arima as though she'd dragged the admission from her by force. She was reluctant to give credence to Lawrence's objections. 'Legalities.'

'So ask someone you trust.'

'It's not that *simple!*' Sarah wailed, starting to rock again. It was disturbing. She was almost out of her mind with pain. The force of it radiated from her like a perpetual mental scream and Arima reacted instinctively, driven by a simple need to make it stop.

'I'll do it,' she said in a rush. 'I'll have your baby.'

Sarah froze, open-mouthed, her dishevelled hair hanging over her face. 'What did you say?'

'I'll have your baby,' Arima repeated, with words inspired by chardonnay.

Sarah pushed her hair back and leaned forwards, staring at Arima as though she were a ghost. 'Why would you do that for me? For us?' she whispered.

Arima shrugged.

'Why not? I'm here, for a while anyway. Call it payback if you like.' She laughed. 'It's only nine months. I don't want kids myself, so it'll be an experience.'

'You don't?' Surely every woman wanted children.

'Sarah, I can barely look after myself, let alone another person,' Arima said with disarming frankness.

'True.'

'You didn't have to agree with me so quickly,' Arima grinned, not at all offended. She closed her eyes as the room began to spin. There was a very real chance she was going to vomit, and that would not be a good idea. 'Listen, I really have to go to bed. Let's talk about it in the morning.'

Sarah watched Arima weave across the room, mumbling to herself about keys. This was . . . unbelievable. It couldn't be happening. She seemed sincere but was there a catch? 'Arima, wait!'

'Yeah?' Arima swayed in the doorway, feeling dead on her feet.

'Promise me you're serious about this. Promise.'

'I promise.'

Arima waved groggily and left the room. She had a job, a place to stay, and she was going to be a baby greenhouse. It was without a doubt the weirdest conversation she'd ever had, but that's what happened at the end of a good night out, she reflected. It had been so long since she'd had one that she'd forgotten, that was all.

Sarah remained motionless on the couch as Arima banged about in the kitchen, located her keys and stumbled out of the house into the night. She switched off the lamp and climbed the stairs to her own bedroom in a daze. She lay on her side beside Lawrence all through the night, her mind working furiously, churning out possibilities as she watched him sleep. The fact he was against the idea of surrogacy now seemed a minor obstacle compared with the mountain it had been earlier.

Arima had promised. A friend, not a stranger. Here was her chance.

Sunlight filtered through the thin curtains of Arima's van, announcing the day. Tendrils of light laid themselves gently across her face, hinting at a perfect English summer's day ahead. The delicacy of this gesture was wasted on Arima. She flinched and groaned, tugging her mother's purple and blue blanket up over her head. It was no good. Once woken, she could never get back to sleep, however tired she was. She propped herself up on her elbows. Surely it couldn't be morning yet. Arima opened one eye experimentally. The effect was not dissimilar to being stabbed with a hot needle.

'Bright. Too bright,' she moaned, scrunching her eyes shut and using her arm as a flimsy shield against the day. Why was it so bright? Keeping her eyes closed, she put out a hand and felt around on the narrow shelf beside her bed, dislodging several objects, including, by the sounds knifing through her head as items struck the floor, a cup, several books and a shower of loose change.

After further blind shelf patting, her fingers found their target – an oversized pair of Jackie O sunglasses. Arima put them on and somehow managed to attain a more or less upright position without throwing up. This felt like an achievement worthy of a national bravery award, or a public standing ovation at the very least. Anything resembling full physical motion was definitely out of the question. Arima breathed in slowly and deeply. 'Okay. I'm okay,' she repeated, as though a banal mantra was capable of curing a killer hangover.

Without warning, her mobile phone launched into a tinny rendition of 'No Woman, No Cry,' at full volume. 'Oh God, oh no. Make it stop. Somebody make it stop.' Arima rolled to one side, hung over the edge of the bed and vomited colourfully onto one of her mother's lovingly crafted rag rugs. From her upside down position she spotted the phone flashing beneath her bed, the display light penetrating the smoky lenses of her sunglasses. Arima pulled it out and lifted it to her ear.

'*Mor*-ning!' Jemma chirped in her best Mary Poppins voice. 'Are you ready?'

'Urgh.'

'Breakfast, remember? Beatrice and I have been up for hours. It already feels like lunchtime to me.'

'Where are you?'

'Outside. Thought we'd pick you up since we were already out and about.' There was a tap on the door of the van. 'Can we come in?'

'No! No!'

'Why not?'

'I'm, uh, not dressed.'

Arima fought past the nausea and struggled to her feet. She had no recollection of making the arrangement but cancelling wasn't an option. Any social engagement was a big deal for Jemma at the moment. She clutched at the trailing bedclothes as her stomach heaved. What had she *eaten* last night? *Where* had she eaten, come to that? How had she got home? Arima yelped as Jemma's voice lanced through her ear again.

'Hello? Are you still there?'

'Ugh, yes. Yes.' The pain in her head was blinding. She hadn't had a headache like this since she'd strayed into a Morris dance at a village fair and taken a blow to the head from a beribboned staff. Her mother had been immensely proud when the hospital staff commented on her remarkably thick skull and boasted about it to all her friends as though Arima were a seven-year old medical prodigy. Arima had been taunted with shouts of blockhead at school for weeks. This hangover was far, far worse. 'Five minutes,' she said thickly. 'Wait for me in the car, okay?'

'Okay. Come a-*long*, Beatrice!'

Arima took a deep breath. Right. New mantra.

'I can do this. I can do this.' First, clothes. She leaned over very carefully and opened the cupboard she used as a wardrobe, trying not to make any sudden movements that might set off further vomiting. 'No, wait.' She caught sight of her arm, still swathed in a flowery sleeve. 'I'm still dressed. Okay.' Arima lifted her sunglasses just enough to allow a quick scan of her dress. Crumpled, but no vomit. It would do.

Tooth brushing was out of the question but she managed to locate a flannel, dampened it with cool water and held it to her forehead to soothe the throbbing. Finally, she scrabbled under the sink for her deodorant. It was a brand that claimed to leave no white marks on your clothes. 'One way to find out,' she muttered, spraying a cloud of it over herself. She winced as Jemma's horn sounded and gathered her strength for the sliding door on the van. 'Coming!'

'You're hung over,' Jemma said, more than a touch of jealousy in her voice as Arima crawled into the passenger seat of Philip's Audi.

'What gave it away?' Arima groaned, trying vainly to fasten her seatbelt. The clippy bit kept moving.

Jemma laughed.

'Let me see,' she said, setting the car in gear. 'Was it the sunglasses, the fact you can hardly walk, never mind in a straight line, or the low-level whimpering?'

'I hoped you might think that was Beatrice.'

'There's nothing low-level about Beatrice's whimpering,' Jemma said, sending the car swooping round the bend and onto the main road. Arima moaned again and gripped the door handle. 'And by the way, you stink.'

'Shut up,' Arima said through gritted teeth, 'or I'll puke on Philip's walnut dash.'

'Don't even think about it, lady.' Jemma glanced at Arima and slowed down a little. Her friend looked genuinely ill, her skin waxy-white against the black of her hair. 'Seriously, are you okay?' she asked. As Arima opened her mouth to say yes, her memory bank uploaded the previous night's events into her consciousness, where they replayed on her closed eyelids in sharp, painful detail. Her phone bleeped in her lap and two messages appeared. Arima raised the phone to eye level, opened her eyes to slits and read the names with difficulty. Robin. Sarah.

'Arima?' Jemma prodded her on the arm.

'I think I've made a big mistake,' she gulped. 'Wind the window down, quick.'

# Chapter 9

Tucked into a little side street off Kensington High Street, *La Cucina di Mama* lived up to its name, exuding a homely feel that was the stuff of dreams. Children's felt-tip pictures proudly adorned the walls and the smell of freshly baking bread and cakes wafted over the sprawl of tables and mismatched chairs, seemingly shoved into the space any old how but carrying it off with insouciant style. It managed to be kitsch, chic and welcoming, with an unusually broad spectrum of customers right through from pensioners and teenagers, both with a surfeit of time and a deficit of money, to harassed businessmen with the reverse and strung-out parents striving for the elusive balance between the two. In other words, one big family.

Jemma was a recent convert, having heard the couple who ran the place were child-friendly and willing to mop up projectile vomit. Under the circumstances, it had seemed the best choice. She jiggled Beatrice on her knee and shook a few drops of milk onto her wrist to check the bottle's temperature. Somewhere in the changing bag there was a stretchy bib but she lacked the third hand necessary to reach it. Jemma glanced at her daughter's outfit. It was a designer label but it had been in the sale, she reminded herself, trying to stay calm. A couple of stains wouldn't hurt. She sighed.

'Sit up, darling, or you'll spill.'

Arima groaned and did her best to comply. She was slumped over the table, head resting on the cool wood, a mug of coffee held weakly in one hand. The hot liquid sloshed to and fro in her trembling fingers, threatening to slop over the rim onto her matted hair. She felt like a puppet with its strings cut. Death would be preferable to this. 'Put me out of my misery,' she pleaded.

'Put me out of mine and I'll think about it,' Jemma retorted. 'What's this terrible mistake? What happened last night?' Arima raised her head a few inches from the table, just enough to enable her to hover over the mug. She inhaled the caffeine fumes, trying to build up to taking a sip.

The café owner glided up to the table and set her tray down, her chic polka-dot apron straining across an ample bosom as she bent over to serve the food. She was frighteningly well-groomed in the manner of Roman women, dyed blonde hair pulled up into a bun, every nail perfectly manicured and buffed to a pearly sheen. She wore designer glasses and had impeccably made-up eyes. Jemma could never decide how old she was but reckoned mid-fifties. If you looked closely there were definite crow's feet under that make-up, and faint laughter lines that spoke of a happy life. There was also a reassuring maternal air about her, but not in a frumpy, bedtime-stories-and-good-home-baking way. It was more that she carried herself with the conviction of a woman who had seen and done much in her life and would somehow always be able to make things if not right, then substantially better. A curer of ills both large and small, from scraped knees to first love. This was a level of parental greatness Jemma could only aspire to, or so she told herself.

'Granola, yoghurt and fruit platter?'

'Here, please.' Jemma said, pushing the cafetière aside to make room.

The woman looked Arima up and down, assessing the matted hair, pasty complexion and floaty black dress hanging loosely on her frame. The girl was wasting away. Feeding her was an act of Christian charity. She nodded, satisfied that she'd made the right choice in altering the girl's order. 'Breakfast roll,' she announced, sliding a hot plate under Arima's nose. 'Eat.'

Arima looked at the bulging dome of bread. 'It's just fried egg, isn't it?' she asked, detecting an unfamiliar smell. 'I only wanted egg.'

'Italian breakfast roll,' the woman repeated. Arima lifted the lid and eyed the contents. A fat round of steaming black pudding squatted on top of two rashers of bacon, topped with onion and – were they *raisins*?

'What . . .?'

'Sanguinaccio,' said the woman. 'Black pudding. Iron for your blood.' She pushed the plate closer to Arima. 'Trust me. You will feel better. Eat.' Her voice carried the authority of generations of Italian mothers.

'I'm a vegetarian,' Arima protested, sitting as far back in her chair as she could to escape the smell.

The woman smiled and tapped the side of her nose. 'Call it a special occasion. I won't tell anyone,' she said, and swept off to serve a fresh batch of customers. Arima knew with terrible certainty she would be back to check.

'So?' Jemma prompted. Arima took her knife and shaved off a sliver of black pudding, squeezing her eyes tight shut as she inched it into her mouth. It was hot and gritty on her tongue, but not unpleasantly so.

'It's . . . quite nice.'

'Not that.' Jemma lifted Beatrice up to her shoulder and started to wind her. 'I mean what's the problem?' She rolled her eyes as Arima gave her a blank look. 'This so-called big mistake of yours last night?'

'Oh. Yes.' Arima took another bite of black pudding, deciding to go for the dissection method rather than whole-scale demolition of the roll. For a few blissful seconds she'd forgotten the mess she'd landed herself in.

'Arima, if you don't spit it out, I swear I'm going to shake it out of you!' Jemma realized she was patting Beatrice's back harder than she ought to be and lowered the baby to her knee.

'Sorry.' Arima swallowed hard and braced herself. 'I went for dinner with Robin.'

'And?'

Arima kept her eyes on the bacon rashers. 'And I, sort of, accidentally . . . you know.'

'You *slept* with him?' Jemma screeched.

'Keep your voice down!' Arima hissed as heads swivelled in their direction from every corner of the café. 'No, I did not,' she said. 'I didn't!' she protested as Jemma narrowed her eyes suspiciously. Had they been in a more appropriate setting than a side road in Bermondsey she couldn't hand on heart say that she wouldn't have, she admitted privately, but that was by the by.

'Well, thank goodness,' said Jemma, tipping Beatrice back for the second half of her feed. 'We don't want a repeat of last time.'

'Oh, come on. It wasn't that bad.'

'You weren't here, remember?'

'Alright, okay. There's no need to go on.'

'So in that case, what did you do?' Arima concentrated very hard on crumbling a piece of bread into little grains on the tablecloth. 'Arima.' An edge crept into Jemma's voice.

Arima cradled her thumping head in her hands. 'I might have . . . kissed him a bit,' she mumbled.

'A bit?'

'Alright, a lot. But we were drunk as lords. And he did pay for dinner.'

'Oh, *well*. That's fine then,' said Jemma sarcastically. 'That makes it all okay.'

'Stop,' Arima moaned. On one level she felt this conversation was all wrong. She was a grown woman and it was no business of Jemma's what she chose to do, or with whom. There was no need for this fierce interrogation, it was just a bit of kissing, for God's sake. It was like being a teenager again, honour-bound to donate every encounter with the opposite sex to the shared pool of experience in the eternal quest to shed light on the mystery of boys. On another level, Arima knew she was in the wrong and lacked the mental reserves to construct an argument in her defence.

'I will not stop,' Jemma snapped at her, hoisting Beatrice onto her shoulder for more winding. 'I warned you he was interested and you told me that you were just friends! You know how he felt about you, how he still feels about you.'

'That was five years ago!'

'So what? You didn't stick around to see the state he was in. We were the ones picking up the pieces for months on end after you left. Now you've started it all up again and nothing's changed. It's thoughtless and selfish and . . . and cruel.' Beatrice received a firm pat on the back and obediently delivered a body-shaking belch.

'Are you done ranting?' Arima queried.

'For now.'

'Right.' Arima held up three fingers and ticked them off one by one. 'I'm sorry, I'll sort it out and I'll make sure he knows it's still just friends, capital J, capital F. Happy?'

'Happy's pushing it, but okay,' Jemma grunted. 'Change the subject.'

'Beatrice has puked on your trousers.'

'Change the subject again.'

'Okay.' Arima began to tuck into the meat in earnest, now certain she wasn't going to throw up. 'This stuff's really working, I feel better. I should never have gone veggie.'

Jemma reached for a baby wipe to mop her jeans with, then checked herself. Better to wait. Beatrice usually threw up at least twice after a feed and it was highly distressing when it happened just after she'd finished cleaning herself up. 'What else is new?' she sighed, spooning yoghurt into her mouth and trying to mentally disassociate herself from the woman who was happy to chat with sick on her leg.

'Lots,' Arima replied, as the latter part of the evening came back into focus. 'Sarah's got a bit of work for me at Goldsmiths after the summer and they've invited me to stay in the house. The locals are complaining about me being in the van.'

'I thought you preferred to be in the van,' Jemma said.

'Generally speaking, I do,' Arima agreed. 'But I haven't been back to England in years, and I'm freezing to death out there.'

'You can't be,' Jemma laughed. 'It's July.'

'I know,' Arima said with a shrug. 'My blood must be too thick, or too thin.' She stabbed a chunk of bacon with her fork and chewed it with gusto. 'Maybe this meat will help. Anyway, I'll be better off in the house with Sarah and Lawrence for now.' Suddenly she remembered her conversation with Sarah. 'Oh yeah, and something really cool.'

'Mm?' Jemma was only half-listening now, intent on shovelling as much breakfast into herself as she could before Beatrice kicked off.

'I'm having a baby for them.'

'Very funny.'

'I'm serious.'

'You are?' Jemma stared at her friend, the colour slowly draining from her face. Arima's gaze didn't waver. 'You are,' Jemma said faintly. It couldn't be true. The room swam before her eyes, Arima's smile splitting into two smiles, two Arimas. Without warning she thrust Beatrice over the table, almost impaling her on the plunger of the cafetière. 'Quick, take her. I think I'm going to be . . .'

'Sick.'

Robin lifted his head from his arms and tried to open his eyes. He was lying face-down on the floor of his gallery. Why had he come here instead of going home last night? 'Got to be sick,' he mumbled, crawling on hands and knees to the

bathroom. Long minutes later, he gripped the sides of the
basin to steady himself, opened his eyes one at a time and
blearily took stock of the damage. The badly glued mirror
tiles on the wall reflected a gruesome image. At some point
in the night he'd thought to roll his sweater up as a make-
shift pillow. It must have seemed like a good idea at the time
but now one side of his face appeared to be covered with a
strawberry birthmark, complete with indented cable knit
pattern. On the plus side, he hadn't been sick on his clothes.

'Excellent,' said Robin. His tongue felt like a foreign
object in his mouth, obstructing rather than aiding his
speech. He glanced at his watch. Half past nine. Well, the
gallery was always quiet in the mornings, he reasoned. Plenty
of time to get back to his one-bedroom flat in Vauxhall,
shower, change – there was a knock at the front door. 'Would
you believe it?' Robin asked the mirror. 'First time in weeks
someone's come before lunchtime.' He wiped his clammy
hands on his trouser legs, pushed off from the basin and
made it to the door with the rolling gait of a newly landed
sailor. There was a girl waiting outside. She looked familiar,
Robin thought, as he struggled with the bolts on the door.
Mousy brown hair framed a pale face that was utterly unre-
markable except for a pair of huge, deep-set eyes. They were
unnaturally green, like a cat's. She was small and dumpy, and
held herself with the slightly inward-curving posture adop-
ted by people who prefer not to be noticed if at all possible.
Robin opened the door slowly.

'Hello Robin,' said the girl. Oh no. She knew him. Robin
gave her a panicky smile, aware that if he got too close his
breath would knock her out. His brain started flicking

through a catalogue of casual acquaintances. There were no matches. Who was she? The girl looked up at him expectantly, her eyes fixed on his left ear. Whoever she was, she was cripplingly shy.

'Er. Hello, um –'

'Hannah,' she supplied. 'From the Christmas shop?'

That was it. A vague memory came to mind of seeing her in the shop doorway on his way through the arch into the Galleria. More than once, now he thought about it. Sometimes she waved. 'Of course. Sorry, I didn't recognize you,' Robin said feebly. 'Without your flashing Santa hat.'

Hannah flushed, red blotches appearing unevenly on her face and neck.

'They make us wear them for work,' she stammered. 'I don't wear it all the time.'

'No. Right.'

Hannah dropped her head and plucked anxiously at the cheesecloth fabric of her gingham summer dress as if to emphasize the point. The conversation hadn't gone like this when she'd rehearsed it in her head. He was saying the wrong things and her carefully prepared answers no longer fitted. Robin automatically followed her movement, his gaze passing down the line of her stout calves to the seashell-encrusted flip-flops cutting the skin on her pudgy feet. This was excruciating. All he wanted to do was get home, re-humanize himself and call Arima.

'You came to the shop to introduce yourself when you first opened up,' Hannah blurted out. 'And you've been here a while now and, and I thought how rude that none of us had returned the gesture, not from the Christmas Shop anyhow, so I . . . I came.' It was a Herculean effort.

'That's very thoughtful of you,' Robin replied. Hannah seemed genuinely nice and it wouldn't do to offend the neighbours but he really needed to get home so he could call Arima. And get the shop open at a reasonable time, of course. Hannah delved into her bag and pulled out a small tin printed with squirrels ice-skating on a frozen pond. She thrust it into Robin's hands.

'I brought cookies,' she said desperately. The smell of freshly-baked food had an instant effect.

'Oh God.' Robin bent over and threw up on Hannah's feet.

'I'm sorry, I'm so sorry!' Hannah squealed.

Robin hauled himself up on the door frame, wiping his mouth on his sleeve. 'No, I'm – wait, your cookies!' But Hannah was already squelching away, her dress flapping around her as she ran. Robin looked down at the squirrel tin. He'd have to return it to her another day, with some flowers or something by way of apology. He couldn't believe he'd actually thrown up on the poor girl. 'What a loser,' he muttered, heading inside for a mop and bucket. At least it hadn't been Arima. Robin felt this was fast turning into the kind of day where you were grateful for small mercies.

Back in *La Cucina di Mama*, Jemma and Arima had reached a stand-off.

'Tell them you've changed your mind,' Jemma ordered.

'But I haven't.'

'Then change it.' Jemma made a chopping gesture with the flat of her hand, almost knocking her abandoned granola off the table. 'Arima, you can't do this.'

Arima cuddled Beatrice close. 'Why not? Look, she's adorable.'

'That,' said Jemma, 'is exactly my point.'

'I'm not following you.'

'Don't you see?' Jemma hissed. She lowered her voice and leaned in, sensing rather than seeing Mama, and every customer in the café, mirroring her while trying to look nonchalant and engaged in their own conversations. 'You can't just grow a baby and hand it over like a prize marrow. It doesn't work like that. They've got feelings, you know.'

'I know, Jemma,' Arima said patiently. 'Look, I've researched it and everything, it's all covered.' It was sort of true. The booklet was at least ten pages and it had been small print. 'Surrogacy isn't that uncommon, you'd be surprised. Oh, what now?' Jemma's hand had flown to her mouth as a new horror occurred to her.

'You're not going to *do it* with Lawrence, are you? He's pushing sixty!' A gust of air rippled through the café as the listeners sucked in their breath as one. This was better than reality TV.

Arima shrugged. 'I don't think so,' she said wickedly.

'You don't *think* so? You don't think so?' Beatrice observed her mother with detached fascination. If Jemma's eyebrows climbed any higher they would launch off her forehead and go into orbit.

'Chill out, I'm joking,' Arima snorted. 'I can't. It makes the whole process illegal. Pity, though. He's cute in a Dad sort of way.' She laughed. Jemma started to hyperventilate. 'Oh, Jemma, lighten up. This really isn't a big deal to me. I don't even want kids. No offence, Beatrice,' Arima added, kissing the baby's head. 'It means a lot to Sarah and I'm happy to do it for them. I promise you it's all above board. Lawrence hasn't even agreed yet.' On cue, her phone bleeped.

'Oh, speak of the devil.'

'He's texting you now? I can't believe this.' Jemma pulled her lips back and began to pant, a tried and tested labour technique.

'No, silly. It's Sarah.' Arima scanned the message and shoved the phone into the pocket of her dress.

'What does she want?'

'She wants me to speak to Lawrence, tell him I'm cool with it all.'

'And you're going to?'

Arima sighed, stood up and began fastening Beatrice into her pushchair. The conversation was going nowhere. 'Yes, Jemma, I'm going to.' She put a hand out to help her friend up. 'Look, I appreciate your concern and everything but it's totally fine. Can we go home now?'

'Yes,' said Jemma. 'Beatrice needs a lie down. So do I.'

The old lady at the table nearest the door dug her husband in the ribs as the trio passed. 'Close your mouth, Arthur,' she said. 'You're not catching flies.'

'No flies on her anyhow,' chuckled her husband, watching Arima stride down the road with her arm round Jemma.

'I don't know about that,' answered the woman. 'Playing with fire, that one. I suspect she's in for a couple of nasty burns before too long.'

# Chapter 10

Lawrence let himself into the house quietly and stood in the hallway listening for signs of life. After a couple of seconds he picked up the faint strains of Sarah singing along to the radio in the kitchen, probably preparing him another gourmet supper which he would refuse to eat. There was a momentary twinge of guilt but Lawrence shook it off, reminding himself this was no petty row to be smoothed over with dinner and an expensive bottle of wine. Sooner or later they would have to slug it out and resolve the issue, but it would happen at a time and place of *his* choosing, not hers. Lawrence had no intention of being manipulated. He removed his shoes, slid his jacket off and prepared to sneak upstairs. His tactic for the past week had been simple – work late, arrive home 'tired' and make sure he was either in the bath or in bed before Sarah detected his presence in the house. Any conversations they did have were kept brief and trivial, and he cut her off if she so much as looked like broaching the surrogacy idea. Like many of her ideas before, he prayed it would soon go away, starved of attention and conversation.

This silent battle of wills was both childish and exhausting but once locked into it, Lawrence refused to buckle. They had been engaged in a kind of psychological tennis game for several days now.

Sarah had left the surrogacy booklet on his bedside table. He had returned it to her handbag. The next day it appeared in his briefcase. He replaced it in the drawer of her dressing table. Two days later it showed up in the inside pocket of his jacket. This time, Lawrence had scanned the infernal thing, dismissed it, then screwed it up and put it in the top of the compost bin.

She hadn't found it yet but Lawrence had no doubt she would. Every time he turned back the duvet he expected to find it on his side of the bed, stinking and covered with rotten vegetable peelings. He ought to have put it in the recycling bin, he thought, moving silently up the stairs in an intricate step pattern to avoid the creaky patches. That would have given him game, set and match.

Lawrence paused at the turn of the stairs, checked his watch and debated the options. Nine o'clock. There was no chance of getting to sleep at this time, despite his early morning start. 'Bath it is,' he muttered, swinging round the upper banister and aiming for the bathroom.

He'd never been so clean in his life. Lawrence had always treated the bathroom as a functional room, but he had to admit it was a surprisingly pleasant place to hole up in. He had even taken to lighting candles. The heated floor and sunken spa-style corner bath they'd put in last year helped. That, and the wonder of watching the scented bath balls explode in the water. Was it possible to spend so long in the bath your entire skin soaked off? It was a worry.

If this stand-off went on much longer he'd have to get himself a garden shed. He had a colleague at work who was adamant his marriage had been saved by the purchase of a shed. He had even had cable TV installed. Lawrence strode into the bathroom, pulled off his tie and began unbuttoning his shirt, gnawing at the problem like a dog with a bone. He wasn't one to judge others but the whole concept of surrogacy appalled him. He desperately wanted a child, of course he did. Sarah knew that, but implicit in the wanting was the desire for the child to be truly their own. It was what prevented him from seriously considering adoption. While full of admiration for men willing to take on other people's children and raise them as their own, it wasn't something Lawrence felt capable of attempting. Sarah had always agreed with him, or so he thought. But *this* – a surrogate child would be completely separate from Sarah in every possible way, genetically, physically – she wouldn't carry the baby or give birth. It wouldn't belong to her. For her it would be an adoption and for him . . . well, in his mind it was tantamount to having an affair. How could Sarah have got so low that she was ready to consider this? There had been no warning, none.

The heat seeped up through his socks, warming his feet. Lawrence sighed, trying to will the tension in his muscles away. The décor was very relaxing in here, no question about it. Sarah had gone for a Mediterranean feel, soft terracotta tiling, white Roman blinds, adjustable spotlights and fresh ivy plants trailing from the windowsill. Bit like being in a greenhouse in some ways, Lawrence thought, but he liked the smell the plants gave off when the room heated up. There was enough floor space for you to turn cartwheels if the mood took you, with two large wicker chairs either side of the sink and the bath tucked away almost as an afterthought in the back corner of the room. These long baths were dull, but the prolonged soaking did seem to be doing his back good. He popped the final button on his shirt and turned round to switch on the bath taps.

'Hi.'

Lawrence yelled in fright and stumbled back against the slatted doors of the towel cupboard.

'Honestly, Lawrence. I wish you'd stop doing that,' said Arima petulantly, her face just visible above clouds of scented bubble bath, hair tied up in a rough ponytail to keep it dry. 'You're giving me quite a complex.'

'You wish *I'd* stop doing it?' Lawrence spluttered, adrenalin pumping through his system. 'You're the one who keeps jumping out on me in, in . . . unexpected places. What are you playing at?'

A hand appeared from the bubbles as Arima tapped the side of her face, pretending to think about this. 'Er, let's see,' she said, frowning as she looked about her. 'I'm in the bathroom . . . up to my neck in hot water . . . covered in bubble bath . . . naked . . .' Lawrence felt his face heat up, his eyes fixed on the frothy water. Arima snapped her fingers, her face lighting up. 'Got it – I'm having a bath.' She cocked an eyebrow at him and made a show of moving over. 'You carry on, though,' she said, her grin as wide and predatory as a crocodile's. 'There's plenty of room.' She was thoroughly enjoying his discomfort.

'Arima, stop messing around! I've had a long day.' Lawrence tore his gaze away from the bath and backed towards the door, pulling the edges of his shirt across his bare chest. 'And lock the door next time.'

'Stop right there.' Arima's hands shot out of the bath and gripped the mosaic-tiled rim. 'Stay where you are or I'm getting out.'

'Don't be ridiculous.' Lawrence was beginning to panic. What had got into her? Was she drunk?

'I mean it,' she said warningly, making as if to sit up.

'Arima, stop! Stop it!' He released the door handle and averted his eyes.

'Sit down,' she said, waving him towards the wicker chairs.

'For God's sake, Arima,' Lawrence said, moving stiffly to the chair furthest away from the bath. He refused to look at her, fixing his gaze on one of the ceiling spotlights. 'What's this about? I'm tired.'

'Me too,' she replied. 'I've been trying to speak to you for days. Since this seems to be the place you go to hang out lately . . .' she shrugged eloquently, droplets of water glistening on her tanned shoulders. 'I figured I'd hang out here too and sooner or later we'd bump into each other.'

Lawrence took a deep breath. The girl was barking mad. 'Make it quick.'

'Well . . .'

'Two minutes, Arima. I'm low on patience today.' Lawrence could feel her stare, frank and unperturbed. He wished he could say the same for himself.

'Chill out, Lawrence,' she said calmly. 'Let's take it from the top. You want a child. Sarah wants to try surrogacy. You won't consider it with a stranger. You're making her miserable.'

'This is none of your business, Arima,' Lawrence said tightly. Who did this kid think she was, trapping him in his own bathroom and talking to him like this?

'But it is,' she replied. 'I'm not a stranger.'

Maybe not, but she was pretty damned strange, thought Lawrence, still avoiding looking at her. What kind of woman ambushed you in the bath? Aloud, he said, 'Get to the point.'

'I'll do it,' she said simply. 'Sarah trusts me and you can too.'

Lawrence was dumbfounded. Quite aside from the insane scenario of talking to a naked girl in the bath who wasn't his wife, the idea of Arima – hippy, happy-go-lucky, mad as a hatter Arima – having his child was completely off the map. He was struck by the sudden crazy thought she might expect him to leap into the bath there and then to do the necessary and began to size up the distance between his chair and the door. One burst of speed and he could make it.

'I'm not kidding, Lawrence,' Arima said quietly. 'I'll do it.'

'Absolutely not,' he said, his voice harsher than he intended. 'It's out of the question. Forget it.'

'Okay. But not until you've discussed it with Sarah. Go downstairs, she's got dinner ready.' Arima hooked one leg over the side of the bath. 'I'm getting out now. Go on.' She grinned rakishly. 'Unless you're getting in after all?'

'Enough, Arima,' Lawrence growled, fairly sprinting for the door. Arima chuckled.

Lawrence bolted from the room and nearly collided with Sarah, who was waiting at the top of the stairs, her hands outstretched. 'Please, darling?' she said, the faintest of tremors in her voice.

Lawrence had the sense to know when he'd been out-manoeuvred but he wasn't happy about it. 'Let's eat,' he said gruffly and walked past her down the stairs, refusing her hand.

Arima stuck her head out of the bathroom door and gave Sarah a thumbs up. 'Told you it would work,' she whispered, shivering a little in her strapless bikini as she towelled her hair dry. Sarah smiled and hurried downstairs after Lawrence. Arima's methods of persuasion might be unortho-dox but they were certainly effective. Now it was up to her.

The kitchen was pleasantly cool after the humid warmth of the bathroom. Instead of using the table, Sarah had set two places at the end of the worktop, something she tended to do when they were eating a casual, light supper. A couple of tealights in glass holders camouflaged the unclaimed space between their place mats. No-man's-land. That's where they were at the moment, Lawrence thought, taking his usual seat facing the long, low window and the garden beyond. A bottle of red wine stood ready beside two empty glasses. He poured himself a glass and stared into it as though an answer might appear from the opaque depths. He didn't raise his head when Sarah entered the room, nor when she placed a beautifully cooked steak and green salad in front of him. They ate in silence. Not the companionable quiet of two people so familiar with one another communication is unspoken, but the kind of awkward hush that grows until the absence of noise is so loud it makes you want to cover your ears.

Finally, when they were staring at their empty plates, it couldn't be avoided any longer. Lawrence put down his cut-lery and laid his hands flat on the table, palms down. Sarah inched her own hand across the table, her fingers stopping just short of his. She had skinned one of her knuckles, Lawrence noticed, and her nail polish was badly chipped.

She never let it get tatty, never. Funny how such a tiny detail could reveal so much about a person's state of mind. For Lawrence it had the same shock value as arriving at St Jude's to find his mother hadn't bothered to get dressed and do her hair. This was so improbable he couldn't even conjure up a theoretical image of it. As he stared at Sarah's hands, his throat constricted with love and pity. She had won the first round without even saying a word.

'How would it work?' he asked.

'Wh-what?' Sarah was taken aback.

Lawrence moved his hand to cover hers, eliminating the gap between them. 'Explain to me,' he said quietly, 'how this would work.'

It was so unexpected that Sarah took a few seconds to react, staring slack-mouthed at her husband as she wondered how the storm of objections she was braced for had been replaced with the calm resignation in his voice. Slowly, she uncurled her legs from their clenched position beneath her chair, stretching the cramped muscles in her toes. The pressure on her hand increased.

'Sarah?'

'Yes,' she said, clearing her throat and trying to reorganize her thoughts. 'It's like this.' Quickly, she sketched out the broad shape of a surrogacy arrangement, being careful to stress the elements of trust and goodwill between the surrogate and the intended parents and answering his questions as best she could from what she remembered of the surrogacy booklet.

'How does the surrogate manage financially during the pregnancy?'

'We can't pay her but we can cover pregnancy costs and loss of earnings.'

'Could we be there at the birth?'

'Provided she agreed, yes.'

'What about rights? To whom does the child belong?'

'To the birth mother, and to the biological father if named on the birth certificate.'

'But not to you.'

'No.'

Lawrence saw the tiniest flinch, the hint of a shadow on her face. 'So the child would be mine, but you would have to . . . what? Adopt?' Another flinch.

'No. A parental order through the courts is sufficient. It's very straightforward, much more so than adoption. No hoops to jump through.'

'What if she changed her mind and wanted to keep the baby?'

'That never happens,' Sarah said quickly. Too quickly.

'Never?'

'Hardly ever,' she amended, ducking her head to avoid his eyes.

'But if it did?' he pressed.

Sarah gave a half-shrug. 'There would be nothing we could do.' She looked up and gripped Lawrence's hand more tightly. 'That's why Arima's offer is so generous, so perfect. A friend would never do that to us,' she said, her words tumbling over themselves in her haste to get her point across. 'Arima doesn't want children, she's a wanderer, a free spirit. She can never settle in one place for long. It's in her nature.'

'So she'd have the baby, hand it over and move on? Is that what you mean?'

'Exactly.'

Lawrence slid his hand free of Sarah's and sat back. Doubts filled his mind, and his every instinct told him this was a bad idea, a dangerous idea. There was no security in it, no assurances. His instincts warned him the deal couldn't be watertight. They would be vulnerable. With years of success under his belt, Lawrence had grown used to operating from a position of strength, being the man to hold most of the bargaining chips when striking a deal. You didn't willingly expose your neck to an opponent, however honourable they seemed. One thought kept presenting itself.

'What's in it for her?'

'Nothing. She just wants to help,' Sarah said, her eyes wide and earnest.

Lawrence shook his head. 'I don't believe it. Why would she do this for us? What does she want?'

'She doesn't want anything,' Sarah insisted. 'Lawrence, remember that this is Arima we're discussing. She doesn't think like other people, doesn't live by the same rules. She's . . . different.'

'That's certainly true, but even so.' Lawrence ran a hand through his hair, trying to put his finger on the source of his unease. Arima was different. Unconventional, easy-come, easy-go. And she seemed genuinely good-hearted. She certainly wouldn't care about what people might say. Sarah gave him no time to think.

'Darling,' she said, taking both his hands and looking him squarely in the eye. 'You've always said yourself you believed we'd have a child, even when the doctors told us there was no hope. If I'm honest, I stopped believing it a long time ago. But look – you were right all along. Just when we'd given up, Arima comes back into our lives after all this time. She can make it happen for us. God works in mysterious ways, isn't that what your mother says?'

'She does, but –'

'So why shouldn't this be God providing for our needs in a way that we could never have guessed?'

'But Sarah, it wouldn't be your child,' Lawrence said gently.

'It would,' she said, refusing to acknowledge the flaw in her argument. 'Your family name, your bloodline. They became mine when I married you, and the child would become mine too, in every way that counts.'

Lawrence sighed. 'It's not that simple, Sarah.'

She smiled at him and stretched over the table to cup his face in her hand, an old gesture of tenderness from their younger days. 'It is if we make it so,' she said. 'And we will.'

Lawrence shut his eyes. He was tired, too tired for this kind of conversation. His instincts were sounding the alarm but he lacked the agility to translate the warning into logical, coherent thought. What Sarah said almost made sense, but . . . all he had was the but, and it wasn't going to be enough to dissuade her.

'Lawrence?'

He turned his head into her palm and kissed it. 'Okay,' he said. 'Let's try. No, listen.' He raised his hand, forestalling Sarah's cry of joy. 'Three attempts, that's all. Then we call it quits. Agreed?'

Sarah clasped his hand between both of hers. 'Agreed,' she said, beaming. Her smile faltered as a look of panic came into Lawrence's eyes. 'Darling, what's wrong?' Surely he wasn't going to change his mind now? Please God, no. She was so close. 'Tell me,' she urged.

Lawrence shifted uncomfortably on his chair. His earlier fear seemed improbable but he had to ask the question to be sure. 'I don't have to . . . you know . . . do I?' he mumbled.

'No,' said Arima from directly behind him. 'I was only winding you up. You're not my type.'

'Arima!' Lawrence shot off his chair, catching his plate with his elbow and sending it crashing to the floor. 'Will you stop *doing* that?'

# Chapter 11

The trio of women huddled together at the mouth of Westminster tube station, just beside the steep steps leading onto the bridge. They looked like Macbeth's witches, except their focal point was a pram instead of a cauldron. Arima resisted the urge to cackle, judging rightly it wouldn't ease the tension. It was a hot day, and scores of tourists were emerging from the underground into the sunlight, where they shambled around like lost sheep, clutching their A to Z books and gawping at everything in sight. Why was it that people lost all road sense when they went on holiday? Arima wondered, watching a portly middle-aged man attempt to step off the kerb into the fast-moving traffic while reading his map. A dozen horns blared and his wife pulled him back by his shirt collar, snatched the map from him and used it to beat his chest while she yelled at him. Two skinny teenage boys cowered in the background, gangly limbs poking out scarecrow-like from baggy shorts and T-shirts, looking grateful it wasn't them on the receiving end for once. Arima smiled at them and turned away, trying to tune back into her own mini-drama.

'Are you sure you've got everything?' Jemma asked for the hundredth time.

'Yes,' Sarah said, doing an impressive job of keeping her voice level. Standing a little way behind Jemma, Arima

managed to catch Sarah's eye. Sarah took the hint, albeit reluctantly. 'Shall we have another check just to be sure?' she said,
trying not to sound as though this would be a complete chore.
They had checked four times already and Sarah was eager to
be off and have the baby to herself. A whole three hours on her
own with Beatrice. As good as she was with children, most of
her godchildren lived some distance away so it wasn't often she
had them to herself. With any luck this might become a regular event, she thought, stooping to flip open the changing bag.

'Nappies?' asked Jemma.

'Check.'

'Wipes and nappy sacks?'

'Check.'

'Spare clothes, there should be two full changes and a
third vest just in case?'

Sarah poked around in the bag. 'Check, check, check.'

'Six-ounce bottle, three-ounce bottle – remember they're
sterile – and flask?'

'Yes.'

'Factor 50 sun cream?'

'Got it.'

'Spare sunhat? Bibs?'

'Under the pram.'

Jemma faltered. 'I . . . think that's everything,' she said anxiously. 'Was there anything else?'

'No,' said Arima swiftly. 'And Sarah has both of our mobile
numbers.'

'What if reception's bad?'

'Different providers. You're Orange, I'm O2.' Arima
squeezed Jemma's arm. 'We're covered.'

'Right then,' Sarah interrupted, seizing her chance before Jemma could think of something else to fret about. 'See you back here at two o'clock. Come on, Beatrice, let's go and catch the riverboat.'

'You're taking her on the riverboat?' Jemma's voice went up about three octaves. 'She's never been on a boat. I thought you were getting the train to Greenwich!'

'This is quicker. Cheerio!' said Sarah firmly, and hustled Beatrice away before Jemma could say another word.

'Do you know how to use the brake?' Jemma called after her. Sarah didn't look back. 'Oh my God, she could roll right in.'

Arima grabbed her by the arm and dragged her towards Westminster bridge before she could set off in pursuit. 'They'll be fine,' she panted as Jemma struggled in her grip. 'Listen, you made her godmother, didn't you? Sarah's a whiz with babies, you know she is.'

'Yes, but –'

'No buts.' Arima forcibly linked Jemma's arm through hers and kept hold of her hand for good measure. 'We're going for a nice walk, maybe pop into the Tate Modern if you fancy, and then you're going to have lunch with Robin while I mind the shop. Just as we discussed, okay?' There was no response. She tapped Jemma's hand. 'Okay?'

'Okay. She will be on time, won't she?' Jemma fretted as Arima propelled her up the steps and onto the bridge.

Arima snorted. 'This is Sarah we're talking about. Her entire life is run with military precision. Now turn your head round or I'll walk you into a lamp post. You're not an owl.' Jemma did as she was told. 'Good. Now smile, and look like you're enjoying yourself.'

'But I'm not.'

'Pretend then.'

The first quarter of an hour was hell. Try as she might, Jemma couldn't help stealing backward glances every thirty seconds, even when Sarah and Beatrice were well out of sight. As ridiculous as it sounded, she felt as if the umbilical cord was still in place and could only stretch so far before the distance between herself and Beatrice became too painful to bear. She had only ever left the baby with Philip, and then only at home once or twice for an hour or so. Despite feeling completely incompetent as a mother, she realized that neither did she trust her daughter with anyone else, not even Sarah. It was a no-win situation. Arima kept tight hold of her, knowing if she let go for a second Jemma was likely to launch herself into the Thames and swim after the nearest ferry. She kept up a bright monologue of inane chatter and strode along at a brisk pace, cutting efficiently through the August holiday crowds. The anxiety rolled off Jemma in waves, but Arima absorbed it all and ploughed on. It felt almost cruel, but she and Robin had both agreed Jemma needed the break, and Philip had backed them up wholeheartedly.

'She's gone a bit . . . I don't know, queer,' he'd whispered down the phone when Arima had telephoned him with the proposal. 'Taking everything to heart, worrying about germs and getting everything right and I don't know what else. Nuclear war, probably. She doesn't eat, hardly sleeps. The other day she actually sprayed me with Dettol when I got in from work before she let me go near the baby. I don't know what to do for her.'

'She probably just needs a break to get her perspective back,' Arima had said. 'Too much time on her own, I should think.'

'Definitely. She's much better when she's with people,' Philip had agreed. 'Does she, er –'

'Yes?'

'Er, does she do the spray thing on you?'

'No. She behaves pretty normally.'

'Thank God for that. It's just me then.'

'Don't take it personally, Philip.'

'I'm trying not to,' he sighed. 'But it's doubled my dry cleaning bill.'

Arima watched her friend as they walked along the South Bank, waiting for the tension in her face to ease. Sunlight sparkled on the waters of the Thames and a cooling breeze offset the heat of the midday sun. The place was buzzing with life. This was one of Jemma's favourite places, Arima reminded herself. Sooner or later it would work its magic on her. She was counting on it. After about twenty minutes, Jemma turned to her with a shaky smile.

'It's a gorgeous day, isn't it?'

'Yes,' Arima replied, hiding her relief. 'You're doing brilliantly, by the way.'

'Does that mean you'll let go of my hand?' Jemma enquired. 'You're crushing the life out of my fingers.'

'Oh, sorry.' Arima took her phone from her pocket and checked for messages. 'Look.' She held it out to Jemma, shading the screen from the sun. *All well. Walking to Greenwich Park. B sleeping.* 'No need to worry, you see?'

Jemma nodded bravely. 'Do you know something?' she said. 'I'm rather looking forward to having a completely uninterrupted meal and being able to eat it with both hands. Is that terrible of me?'

'Nope. It's normal. Speaking of which . . .' Arima checked the time on the screen display. 'We should give the Tate a miss. Robin's expecting us about now.'

'Maybe we'll have time on the way back?' Jemma suggested, her stomach knotting at the thought but determined to show willing.

'That's the spirit. Come on.'

Sarah was strolling along one of the well-tended paths in Greenwich Park, enjoying the sensation of the sun warming her back through the fabric of her summer dress. This was one of her favourite places in the whole world. She glanced down at the pram and felt a thrill of pleasure at the thought she could be leading her own child through the park in years to come. She imagined herself walking along this very path, hand in hand with a little girl of seven or eight years, smiling down at her upturned face, bright eyes hungry for knowledge. 'And it was in this park that your father asked me to marry him,' she would say, laughing as the eyes widened in astonishment.

'Right here?'

'Well, not right here. A little way over there, near the Observatory,' she would reply, pointing over at the building with its distinctive ball-topped turret.

There would be a pause as the little head tilted mischievously to one side, blonde pigtails trailing over skinny shoulders. 'Was it a long time ago?'

'Yes, many years.'

'When King Charles the second lived here?'

'Certainly not. Cheeky thing!' There would be a squeal of laughter as her daughter twisted free of Sarah's hand and ran off, looking back to be sure she would be chased, caught and tickled into submission.

Tears misted Sarah's eyes as the image faded. The thought it might one day happen was exquisitely painful but the possibility was becoming more tangible with every passing day. Sarah felt she could almost touch it with her fingertips. Not quite reality, not yet, but much more than a dream. Gurgling sounds came from the pram as Beatrice awoke.

'Oh, hello,' Sarah said, bending over to address the baby. 'You've decided to join me, have you? Are you ready for some milk?' Beatrice yawned and tried to pull her sun hat off. 'It is getting a bit hot out here, isn't it,' Sarah smiled. 'I'll take you to the Pavilion Tea House. They've got baby-changing facilities and everything. Mummy would be very impressed with Aunty Sarah, wouldn't she? Come on. Look at these lovely sweet chestnut trees. When you're older I'll tell you all about how these gardens were designed. It was all done by a clever Frenchman . . .' She wandered on, keeping up a soothing running commentary to distract the baby. Beatrice didn't understand a word but Sarah saw no reason to dumb down and start talking strangely, as seemed to be the current vogue. It was the reassurance of her voice the child wanted, so the content may as well be interesting. Sarah toyed with the idea of popping in to see Eva after lunch but decided against it. She hadn't asked Jemma's permission and she didn't want to overstep the boundaries on their first trip out. 'I hope Mummy's having a nice time, Beatrice,' she said. 'Aunty Arima will take good care of her, don't you worry.' Sarah stopped the pram for a moment and sent another text message. Better to be safe than sorry.

Arima rolled her eyes as the words flashed up on her phone. *No alcohol with lunch, don't forget! XX*

'Is that another message from Sarah?' Jemma asked, immediately fearing the worst. They were sitting outside the Horniman pub waiting for Robin. He was dealing with a customer when they arrived at the shop so they'd gone for a quick drink to give him time to finish up.

'Yes,' Arima replied. 'But the baby's fine. She's just being irritating.'

'Beatrice is?' Jemma looked affronted.

'No, Sarah,' Arima laughed, passing her friend the phone.

'It doesn't make any sense,' Jemma frowned.

Arima took the phone back and dropped it into her bag, leaving it switched on only for Jemma's sake. 'I'm supposed to be keeping myself in tip-top condition,' she explained. 'My body is a temple and all that.' She prodded herself in the stomach. 'Sarah's pumping me so full of vitamins and folic acid supplements I'm surprised you can't hear me rattle.'

Jemma clutched Arima's arm. 'You're not . . . ?'

'No, no. The first attempt is next week,' Arima said breezily. 'I can't say I'm looking forward to it, if I'm honest.'

Jemma shuddered. 'I'm not surprised.'

'Well, apparently it doesn't hurt, and needs must.'

'I know, but . . . it's so . . . eugh.'

Arima raised her eyebrows mockingly. 'This from the woman who tries to discuss baby poo at the meal table?'

'I do not.'

'You certainly do.'

'Well, it's important to monitor the colour, you know, because if their digestive system isn't working properly it –'

'Stop!' Arima covered her ears. 'I'm still scarred from the last time you told me about it.'

Jemma's eyes filled with tears. 'Hey, I'm teasing,' Arima said hurriedly, putting her arm round her friend. 'I don't mind what you tell me.'

'I'm sorry, Arima, really,' Jemma snuffled. 'I suppose I just don't have anything else to talk about these days. It's weeks since I read a paper or even watched television.'

'Well, that's no great loss,' Arima said. 'There's never anything decent on in the summer anyway. Think how I feel – at least you're not five years behind in all the soaps. You've only missed a couple of months, but I'll never catch up.'

Jemma blew her nose and managed a smile. 'You always look on the bright side,' she sighed, twisting her lemonade glass round and round on the table. 'I wish I was like that.'

'You are,' Arima said stoutly. 'Oh look, here's Robin now.' Her hand shot out as Robin sauntered round the corner and sent his shop keys flying through the air towards her.

'Good catch,' he said admiringly as Arima caught them one-handed.

'Oh, please,' she sniffed, getting to her feet and gathering her things together. 'That was the lamest underarm lob I've seen for a long time. Beatrice could have fielded that.'

'No,' said Jemma warningly as Robin produced his house keys from his pocket and started to back up for a second throw. 'Robin, don't.'

Robin pulled his arm back but thought better of it when he saw Jemma's face. She was genuinely agitated. 'Sorry,' he said, stuffing them back into his pocket. 'Are you all set?'

'Yes, but we haven't got long. I'm collecting Beatrice at two.'

'Plenty of time,' he said easily, offering her his arm with a little bow. 'Shall we?'

'See you in a bit,' Arima said, giving Jemma an encouraging smile.

'Try not to wreck the place, Arima,' Robin said over his shoulder as they walked away.

'No one would notice if I did,' she smirked.


'Why do you do that?' Jemma asked, looking up at Robin as they made their way past the grey bulk of HMS Belfast and along the riverside path in the direction of Tower Bridge.

'What?' he asked, the picture of innocence.

'Wind each other up all the time.'

Robin shrugged. 'I dunno. We always have. Sign of affection?'

Never a truer word, thought Jemma, biting her tongue to prevent herself from enquiring about their current relationship status. Arima had completely clammed up over it and Jemma was too absorbed in Beatrice to actively pursue her for details. Added to which the surrogacy bombshell had eclipsed all other matters in their friendship. Jemma wondered how Robin felt about it. She suspected he had strong opinions on it, not that Arima would take any notice. Having said that, he didn't seem unduly bothered, she thought, leaning comfortably on his arm. He was wearing jeans and a blue and white checked shirt that reminded Jemma of her father. Or perhaps it was the fact that Robin had such a solid and reassuring presence that made her think of times spent with her dad.

'Good old Robin,' she murmured.

'Pardon?'

Jemma jumped and found him looking quizzically at her. 'Oh,' she said, flustered. 'I didn't mean to say that out loud. I just meant . . . you're lovely.'

'Thanks,' he grinned.

'Reliable.'

'Can we stick with lovely?' he asked, looking slightly pained. 'Reliable makes me sound like a golden retriever.'

Jemma swallowed her giggles as Robin ushered her through the door of a sassy-looking riverside French bistro and decided not to mention how sweet he looked with his three days worth of head stubble. Like an oversized cute hedgehog. Mr Tiggy-Winkle was probably not the image Robin was trying to create. But that had always been his problem, Jemma thought as Robin held her chair for her and handed her the menu before taking his own seat. He was unfailingly reliable, endearing and a hundred percent trustworthy. A safe person to be with. Robin was the human equivalent of a golden retriever. Every girl wanted a man like him . . . but only as a friend. It was tragic someone so nice could be damned by the very things everyone loved about them. Arima would probably want him in the delivery room when she had the baby. She'd have the cheek to ask, at any rate.

After waiting five minutes for Jemma to express any kind of food choice and sending the politely hovering waiter away twice, Robin rolled his starched white napkin into a cone shape. 'Earth to Jemma. Are you receiving me?' he said in a fake American accent.

'Hmm? Oh, sorry. I was thinking.'

'About whether to have pork, beef or the goat's cheese tart?'

'Um . . . yes,' Jemma lied. 'The goat's cheese, please. No, wait. It's unpasteurized. Is that okay to have when you're breast-feeding?'

'You're asking me?' Robin said, spreading his hands wide and looking to the waiter for assistance.

'I believe goat's cheese is acceptable for breast-feeding mothers,' the waiter said with quiet assurance. 'At least, it is in France.' He saw the fear in Jemma's eyes and knew nothing short of a signed medical declaration would convince her. 'The pork medallions, however, are delicious,' he added smoothly.

'That sounds perfect,' said Jemma. She picked at a chunk of crusty baguette and tried not to keep looking at her watch while they waited for the food to arrive. Robin did an excellent job of keeping the conversation going, asking lots about Beatrice with the occasional gentle question about how Jemma herself was feeling. He was so easy to talk to and Jemma found she was able to be honest with him, even to the point of confessing about disinfecting Philip. 'The thing is,' she said, her voice trembling with shame, 'part of me knows that I'm being ridiculous but another part of me knows that if I don't do it, the worry will drive me mad. And so I do all these stupid things but it doesn't make any difference because there's always something else to worry about.' She hung her head, unable to go on.

Robin covered her hand with his. 'It's going to be okay, Jemma,' he said softly. 'The fact you can talk about all this is a huge thing.'

'Is it?' she mumbled.

'Yes. Trust me, I know about this stuff. Look, here comes our lunch.'

Jemma sat up, grateful for the change of subject. Robin sensed that she'd done enough soul-baring for one day and began hacking at his roast potatoes with such enthusiasm that his portion of peas scattered across the tablecloth. 'Sorry, my table manners are dreadful,' he said cheerfully. 'Now, onto the gossip. I hope you've got some. Any punch-ups at baby yoga class this week?'

'No,' Jemma giggled, tucking into her own food. 'But Arima's got her first attempt next week. I won't talk about it over lunch, though.'

'No, carry on. Don't mind me,' Robin said through a mouthful of pork.

'Well, it's a bit gross, isn't it,' Jemma said, warming to the subject. 'I mean, having babies is a messy business, fair enough, but artificial insemination? It makes me go all shud-dery. Really, I just can't see how it's going to work out, can you?' She looked up from her plate. 'Robin?'

He was sitting with his mouth open, a forkful of carrots suspended halfway to his mouth as though someone had pressed freeze-frame on a television remote. Jemma dropped her cutlery and covered her eyes with her hands. 'She hasn't told you.' She heard the fork clatter onto the table.

'It appears,' said Robin bitterly, 'she's left that dubious pleasure to you.'

# Chapter 12

Out of the blue, Arima dreamt about flying for the first time in years. The flying dreams stemmed from star watching when she was a little girl. Her father would wake her unexpectedly on clear nights, wrap her up in her dressing gown and a blanket and lead her out into the garden where his telescope would be set up on the patio. 'Hush,' he would whisper. 'Don't wake your mother.' These words always sent a thrill of disobedience through Arima, though in later years she worked out her mother not only knew but gave permission. Her father was a dour man with a silent, forbidding manner, prone to what her mother called 'black fits'. These nights were precious to Arima because when he stood outside beneath the stars, he came to life. Arima would clamber onto the white metal step stool borrowed from the kitchen, put her eye to the telescope and listen as her father taught her about the constellations and quizzed her on the phases of the moon.

'What's the first quarter of the moon?'

'Waxing crescent.'

'How about the third?'

'Waning gibbous?'

'Well done. And tonight?'

'Waning crescent.'

'Top of the class again, Miss Middleton. Now then, who can we see tonight? There's Ursa Major, the Great Bear, see him up there? And his friend the Herdsman close by. Who else can you see?' Watching his face, so animated and passionate, Arima felt the stars must know how much he loved them and made him shine at night in return. Afterwards, the two of them would creep into the kitchen for hot chocolate and biscuits before Arima was carried back to bed. They never spoke about it in the morning.

Often, she would have the flying dream for several nights afterwards, soaring through the night sky in her nightdress like Wendy in *Peter Pan*, weaving fearlessly in and out of the stars. Arima never looked down at the earth in these dreams, only up and out into the universe. Endless sky, endless stars.

When at last she grew cold, Arima would swoop downwards, arms pointing the way like a diver, zooming through the open bedroom window and back into her bed. She would wake gripped by a tremendous sense of possibility. Much later, she came to wonder why the stars her father loved couldn't make him feel that way. Their magic always faded in the light.

Arima awoke with a start, floundering in the king-size bed in the main guest room. Her room, for now. After the eclectic clutter of the camper van it felt enormous and completely alien to her, being decorated entirely in cream. Aside from the bed, the room contained only a wardrobe and a dressing table. While this created a feeling of space, the minimalist approach seemed deeply impersonal to Arima and not at all cosy. Everything felt bleached and clinical, every wall and surface completely bare of photos, pictures or prints. The only colour in the room came from the distressed pine furniture. Arima didn't know which she found more distressing – the pine or the cream. She sat up, her eyes automatically straying to the window. It was closed, the curtain drapes exactly as she'd left them last night with the hems puddling fashionably on the carpet.

'That old dream,' she murmured, wiping tears from her face. The euphoria of flying stayed with her as she pushed back the covers and got out of bed. She felt powerful, like there was a bubble of energy pulsing around her body. Perhaps it was a sign. Arima pulled open her underwear drawer and took out a foil packet. Maybe it was a little early to be certain but it wouldn't hurt to try. 'First time lucky, who knows?' she wondered, heading for the door. Out on the landing she bumped into Sarah, fresh-faced and already dressed and pressed for the first day of the new academic year.

'Good morning. Sleep well?' asked Sarah. 'You've seemed tired these past few days.' She made it sound as though this was a good thing.

'No, I'm fine,' Arima yawned, trying to slide the packet up her pyjama sleeve. Hope was all very well but false hope was the last thing Sarah needed. She wasn't fast enough.

Sarah spotted the movement and was on her like a flash. 'Arima! Do you think you're . . . ?'

'I don't know,' Arima said a little testily, showing Sarah the unopened packet.

'But you're about to do the test?' she squealed.

'Um, yes,' Arima replied, trying to inch towards the bathroom door. 'But don't get excited. It's just to check.'

'I can't believe it!' Sarah went to throw her arms round Arima, then changed her mind and ran to the top of the stairs. 'Lawrence? Lawrence!' she shouted.

He appeared at the foot of the stairs with his tie half done and his hair askew. 'Everything alright?'

'Oh, good grief,' Arima muttered and made a dive for the bathroom. 'Invite the neighbours in while you're at it.' With the door safely locked, she ripped the packet open with her teeth and read the instructions. 'Right. Pretty straightforward.' She lifted the lid of the toilet and sat down.

'Arima?' Sarah was knocking at the door. 'Can I come in?'

'What? No!'

The door handle rattled. 'Just me, not Lawrence.'

'No!' This was unbelievable.

'Sarah, come away. Leave her in peace,' she heard Lawrence say. As a man he was more comfortable with the concept of group urination but was well aware it wasn't the female way, however confident Arima was.

'In a minute,' Sarah hissed. Arima shut her eyes and tried to concentrate on the task in hand. Sarah crouched by the door and tried not to breathe too loudly. Lawrence leaned against the wall, flicked his leather slippers off and rubbed one foot against the other, poking at the hole in the toe of one sock. As they waited, he pondered the thought that once you'd embarked on a project like this, the normal social boundaries disintegrated. There was going to be very little privacy or dignity at any point on this bizarre journey. The trip to the fertility clinic had proved that. Lawrence shuddered at the memory of the no-nonsense nurse who had shown him to the appropriate room.

'Here you are, Mr Abrahams,' she said briskly. 'I know this part of the process may seem a little distasteful, but try to keep in mind the end result.' Lawrence hadn't been able to keep anything in mind, nor was he able to meet the eye of any of the couples in the waiting area as he waited for Arima and Sarah afterwards. It was the thought that everyone knew what he'd been doing. And he would never, ever be able to look at a specimen vial again. God willing, he wouldn't need to.

After ten minutes of loaded silence, the bathroom door opened and Arima stomped out.

'I can't do it with you listening at the keyhole,' she said irritably. 'It's a physical impossibility.'

'I'll go, I'll go,' Sarah gabbled.

'There's no time now, we'll be late for uni,' Arima said. 'That's not good on my first day, is it?' Lawrence gave his wife a look that clearly said *I tried to tell you*, and silently ordered her downstairs with a jerk of his head.

'Sorry, Arima,' he sighed, rubbing at a stray patch of stubble that had escaped his morning shave.

'No worries.' Arima retreated to her bedroom, more than a little alarmed at the thought of weeing for an audience every month until she fell pregnant. And then what? This was only the start. A few ground rules might be needed if this carried on. When the coast was clear, she showered quickly and ran downstairs, shoving the test into her bag. Best to try again later when Sarah wasn't around.

Sarah was waiting in the hallway, the contrite look on her face at odds with the sharply-tailored charcoal suit she'd chosen. Lawrence had obviously had a stern word. 'Ready?'

she asked, itching to ask for more details. How many days late was the period? Did she feel sick? Tired? What made her think she should do the test? Lawrence had forbidden any further questioning but Sarah was practically writhing with the need to know. Arima wondered if he had threatened to tape Sarah's mouth shut. If he hadn't, she might drop it into the conversation herself.

'All set,' she smiled. 'Let's go.'


Robin entered the building and headed straight for the studios, his body automatically programmed to follow the old familiar route. He had popped into Goldsmiths now and again over the years, usually to visit Jemma in the textiles store and persuade her and Philip out for a drink, but he'd never been back into the studio space. It ought to feel good, but any pleasure was swamped by the urgency of his errand. He had to make Arima see sense before it was too late. She might have been successful in dodging him over the last three weeks but he knew she'd definitely be here on the first day of term. Robin turned a corner and there she was, a flash of distinctive curly hair and bright, trailing skirt disappearing through a doorway.

'Arima?' Robin called. 'Hang on, I want to talk to you.' He broke into a run when Arima didn't reappear, hand outstretched ready to power through the door and pursue her. He was halfway through before he registered the symbol on it.

'Shit.' It was the ladies. He reversed at speed and knocked instead. 'Arima?' His voice floated through the door and reached the cubicle where Arima was sitting, pregnancy test at the ready. She raised her eyes to the ceiling in disbelief. Was nothing sacred? 'Mama, come on. What are you doing up there?' she moaned. Who was the patron saint of pregnancy anyway? Probably a man, knowing the Catholic church.

'Arima? I know you're in there. It's Robin.'

'Oh, for the love of God,' she muttered. 'I *know* it's you,' she said, raising her voice. 'Nobody else would stalk me in the toilet,' she added under her breath. She stared at the white test stick for a moment to see if anything was happening. 'Now I wait,' she sighed, exiting the cubicle and moving to the row of basins.

After five minutes Robin hammered on the door again. 'Are you going to stay in there all day? I'm not leaving until you talk to me.'

'Will you give it a rest? I'm washing my hands,' Arima snapped. She glanced into the mirror. If she stayed in here long enough, might he start beating his head against the wall and knock himself out? 'No chance,' said her reflection. 'His skull's way too thick.' Arima dropped the test stick into her bag, rinsed her hands and yanked a couple of green paper towels from the dispenser. She dried her hands roughly and then kicked the door open. 'What exactly is your problem?' she demanded, striding into the corridor and squaring up to Robin.

'I'll tell you over lunch.'

'I don't want to go for lunch.'

'I don't care.' He took hold of her arm and began marching her towards the exit.

'Let go,' she ordered, using her free hand to try and prise his fingers off her arm.

'No.'

'You're bang out of order, Robin.'

'So sue me.'

'You're actually hurting me.'

'I seriously doubt it. That would mean you had feelings.'

Arima gasped. 'Right, that's it,' she spluttered, digging her heels in and dragging Robin to a standstill. 'No lunch. Say your piece and then get lost. I'm not taking that crap from you.'

Robin shrugged. 'Whatever. Coffee, then.' He towed her onwards, gritting his teeth with the effort. 'But you *will* listen to me, Arima. That's not negotiable.' Arima said nothing. Listening and hearing were different things.

Robin dragged Arima into the first coffee shop they came to, an odd place that looked as though its owners had fallen out repeatedly over the image they wanted to project. Either they were terrible negotiators or just plain indecisive because they had thrown in a bit of everything, in the manner of a television chef rustling up a creative meal from a random selection of ingredients.

The effect was unpleasant, even to Arima's forgiving bohemian eye. Retro walls, modern leather furniture, cheap-looking prints outclassed by their shabby chic frames. The final jarring touch was a collection of decorative plates and saucers lined up along the high Delft rack that skirted the room. Needless to say, the place was quiet, so much so that the young waitress looked first nonplussed when Robin burst in, then a little irritated at having to interrupt her daily nail-filing session.

He marched Arima up to the counter and bought two lattes without letting go of her for a second. Then he propelled her to a window table with a couple of leather tub chairs squashed in on either side, their backs grazing the flocked wallpaper – which was covered in clashing flowers of orange, pink and green. The waitress carried the drinks across and ran to take cover behind the counter, sensing an imminent explosion. Robin and Arima sat and glared at each other over the steaming cups.

'You can't do this,' he said bluntly.

Arima skimmed some froth from the top of her latte and sucked it off her finger. 'That's not for you to say.'

'Yes, it is.' He rubbed his hand over his shaved head, an unconscious gesture of nervousness. 'Look Arima. We've known each other, what, fifteen years? Sixteen?' He paused but Arima just shrugged indifferently. 'Well, a long time,' Robin continued. 'I think I know you better than anyone except your parents. What on earth are they going to make of this weird arrangement?' Arima stiffened, the blood rushing to her face as the dull ache she so carefully contained flared up, beating its own ugly rhythm in her heart. *Mama.*

Robin mistook her expression for anger. 'Don't start shouting at me,' he said. 'I know fine well you haven't told them, for the same reason you didn't tell me.'

'And why's that?'

'Because we're the only people you might actually listen to.'

'Don't flatter yourself,' she said, turning her head away from him so he wouldn't see the tears in her eyes. She concentrated on the flow of traffic out on the street while she tried to get herself under control. It had got to the point where it was easier not to tell any of her friends here, but especially not Robin. He had loved her mother so much, and she knew he would never forgive her for not inviting him to the funeral. There was never a good time to bring it up. 'Hey, by the way, I forgot to tell you my parents died in a house fire three years ago. Sorry, it completely slipped my mind.' Why drag up the past and show off her grief like dirty laundry? It was nobody's business but her own. Oh, no. Robin was trying to take her hand. It was going to be impossible to stay cross with him. Arima snatched her hand back and sat on it, picking up her cup with the other hand before he could make a grab for that one.

'I don't understand you,' Robin said, the confusion plain in his voice. 'I'm the one who ought to be cross here.'

'How do you figure that out?'

Robin said nothing. He just looked at Arima until she began to squirm. 'Alright. I just − I didn't mean to cause offence, okay? I just . . . didn't get around to mentioning it. I was going to.' *Plus you were still sore over the Just Friends thing and I thought it would tip you over the edge.* She was wise enough not to say it.

'No you weren't,' he replied evenly. 'You thought I'd try and talk you out of it and you didn't want a fight.'

'Okay, that too.' Arima took a sip of her latte. It was luke-warm and too sweet. She wished Robin had bought espressos instead. Still, the sooner she drank it the sooner she'd be out of here. She drank another mouthful and made herself meet Robin's eye. He was trying to look stern and reproving, but even with a sober grey V-neck pullover to help him along, he couldn't carry it off. His face was too kind. Good old Robin. 'Listen,' Arima sighed, 'I don't see what the big deal is. I'm happy to do this for Lawrence and Sarah, and I'll stick around to see it through.' She threw him a questioning look. 'Is that what you're worried about? That it'll take months to get pregnant and I might get itchy feet and take off before it happens? Leave them high and dry?'

Robin frowned. 'No, Arima. What I'm worried about is you getting hurt.'

Arima laughed out loud. She couldn't help it. 'By carrying their baby?'

'Your baby,' Robin corrected. 'Your own flesh and blood, Arima.'

'It won't be my baby,' Arima said. 'I'll just be the incubator.'

Robin's fist clenched beneath the table. Did she really not see it or was she choosing to be obtuse? 'It would be your baby,' he repeated. 'And whatever you think you'd do, I know you, and I'm telling you – begging you – to reconsider. If you do this, it will hurt you in ways you've never imagined.'

'And you know that because . . . ?'

'Because it's true, Mima,' he replied. Arima shook her head and took several large gulps from her coffee cup. Robin groped for the right words, the best argument to persuade her. It had to be there, he told himself in desperation. He just needed to find the right angle. 'Suppose you have the baby and they change their minds?' he said suddenly. 'You've always said you don't want children.'

Arima dismissed the notion with a wave of her hand. 'That's not going to happen,' she said scornfully. 'They're desperate to have a child.' She drained her cup, gagging on the globules of sugar welded to the bottom. 'Thanks for your concern, etcetera, etcetera, but this is between Sarah and I. And Lawrence,' she added. 'And yes, it'll be my baby, but that's just a technicality until the legal papers are signed.' She stood up and squeezed through the tiny gap between her chair and the table. 'I have to go.'

Robin caught her shoulder as she bent down and kissed him on the cheek. 'Arima, please listen to me. You know I'm talking sense.' Arima shook her head and pulled away. 'Catch you later,' she said. Robin tried to follow her but found himself wedged against the wall, the edge of the table cutting painfully into his thighs.

'I'll phone you,' he called after her. 'It's not too late to change your mind!'

Arima raised a hand as she left the café but didn't look back. It was obvious what was going on here, she thought as she hurried back to Goldsmiths. Robin was being eaten up by jealousy, as though carrying this baby would give Lawrence some kind of romantic claim on her. 'How prehistoric can you get?' she sighed, wondering idly if Robin would ever get over her. He ought to go on a few dates. She was utterly blind to the fact that by renewing their friendship, she herself was preventing him from moving on, her presence a constant reminder of everything he wanted but couldn't have. It never crossed her mind that she was being both selfish and cruel. But that was Arima. A hundred percent action and no thought for the consequences. She put her hand in her bag and withdrew the slim white test stick as she bowled through the entrance and headed for the art department.

'Good job I didn't show him after all,' she murmured. It was a shame, though – after all his complaining about being left out of the loop in her life, Robin could have been the first to know.

# Chapter 13

Three nights later, Sarah, Lawrence and Arima sat in the kitchen, wordlessly examining the evidence on the tabletop between them. It was irrefutable. Four tests. Eight blue lines. Sarah had wanted to be absolutely sure. Lawrence cleared his throat.

'I think that's fairly conclusive,' he said, eyeing the white sticks with the same caution he would give a grenade with a dodgy pin.

'Yes,' said Sarah in awed tones, touching one of the tests with her fingertip. 'And on the first attempt. It's a miracle.'

'Great,' said Arima, sweeping them off the table and strolling over to the bin before Sarah could move to stop her. 'Now I can stop peeing onto a stick every morning.' She rolled her eyes at Sarah's stricken expression. 'You weren't seriously thinking of keeping them? That's gross. I've peed on them, every one.'

Sarah blushed. 'No,' she protested, embarrassed that her thoughts were so transparent. Surely it wouldn't have hurt to keep just one of them? Hygienically, of course. She slid off her stool and ran to the fridge, where a pre-emptive bottle of bubbly had been chilling since the first test. 'Champagne,' she said. 'Lawrence, fetch some glasses – oh.' She stopped in the act of uncorking the bottle over the sink. 'How stupid of me. You can't drink it, Arima.'

Arima looked at the champagne flute Lawrence had just put into her hand. 'I'm sure one glass won't . . .' she began.

'Coffee,' Sarah declared, abandoning the bottle and making a beeline for the kettle, her heels slipping on the slate floor. 'I'll make a nice, fresh pot of . . .' she trailed off, looking crestfallen. 'No, you can't have that either. Caffeine . . .' she glared at Lawrence in a *help me out here* sort of way.

'What?' he asked. 'You want me to put the flutes away?'

Arima handed her glass to Lawrence and made for the door. 'I think I'll have a quick bath and get an early night,' she said, giving an exaggerated yawn.

Sarah rushed towards her, a manic look in her eye. 'Can I get you anything? Fresh towels? Bubble bath? Soothing music?' she babbled, trying to dodge Lawrence as he moved to intercept her.

'No, I'm good, thanks,' Arima said, hastily ducking out of the room. She pelted up the stairs, dashed in and out of her bedroom, then locked herself into the bathroom with her pyjamas, a book and the packet of emergency ginger nuts she kept under the bed. She hated to be crowded or fussed over, and with Sarah behaving like Mrs Mental downstairs, she might need to stay in there for a long time. She set the bath running and stripped off, returning to the door twice to check she'd locked it properly. Satisfied Sarah wasn't going to burst in unannounced, she examined her stomach, running her palm over the taut muscles and smooth, unmarked skin. It was weird to think there was an actual person in there, or the beginnings of one. 'No sign of you yet,' she murmured. 'I hope there's going to be room in there.' Arima decided not to dwell on that particular thought. That side of things would come later. Much later. She sank into the bath and buried herself in her book.

Downstairs, Lawrence was attempting to talk some sense into his wife. 'You've got to calm down, darling,' he implored, pressing a cup of tea into her shaking hands and guiding her into the lounge. 'It's a start but we've got a long way to go.'

'Are you saying something might go wrong?' Sarah asked, clutching at his arm.

'No,' he said patiently. 'But if you rush around in this hysterical state for nine months, we're all going to go insane. Just back off a bit. Give Arima some time to adjust.'

'But she seems fine,' Sarah objected. Lawrence collapsed onto the sofa and closed his eyes. He couldn't argue with her. Arima did seem fine, even nonchalant about the pregnancy. It was Sarah who needed to adjust to the situation. *And me*, Lawrence admitted to himself. Now that they were in business, so to speak, he felt besieged by doubts again. There were so many pitfalls, so much they hadn't yet discussed. He had thought they would have more time to arrange things – their previous experience of attempts to fall pregnant had involved a lot of time and waiting – but this had all happened very quickly. Lawrence liked Arima but he abhorred any form of dependency, and they were now wholly dependent on her. On her integrity; her discretion; her word. On her body, for goodness' sake. It couldn't get much more personal than that.

Lawrence felt deeply uneasy without being able to say why. He had a strong desire to withdraw from the entire situation, like a tortoise retracting into its shell. But how could he? This was his child. The realization hit him like a blow to the head, swiftly followed by a second, more deadly strike — where was the happy feeling he'd always envisaged?

Sarah stood up and began pacing round the coffee table, glancing upwards every few seconds as if to see through the ceiling. Lawrence watched her despairingly.

'Do you think I should pop up and check if she needs anything?' she asked.

'No.'

'But she —'

'No.'

'Well, I might just —'

'No!' Lawrence roared. Sarah sat down with a bump and gulped her tea. Lawrence stood up. 'I'm going for a walk,' he said tersely. 'I can't handle you like this.' A few seconds later the front door slammed hard enough to make the pictures rattle on the walls. Sarah winced.

'Really,' she muttered, setting her tea down on a frosted glass coaster. 'He's overreacting a bit. I was only trying to help.' She felt let down by Lawrence's apparent lack of enthusiasm at the news. While he was bogged down in the fine details of the process, only one detail mattered to her, and that was the baby. Sarah fetched her address book from her handbag, curled up on the sofa and picked up the phone, intent on sharing the good news with someone who would understand.

Jemma was creeping down the stairs, her senses alert to the slightest change in the steady breathing coming through the baby monitor clipped to the waistband of her jeans. It was so sensitive it occasionally picked up transmissions from the local taxi rank. This was extremely painful if you happened to have the monitor held to your ear at the time, but apart from the risk of a perforated parental eardrum it was reliable. Jemma made it to the bottom of the stairs and let her breath out in a rush. If she managed to get all the way downstairs it usually meant Beatrice would sleep through the night. Not always, but mostly. The signs were good.

She poked her head into the dining room to see whether Philip had set the table as she'd asked. After months of living off slow-cooker casseroles, Philip had put his foot down and insisted they attempt a proper dinner together once a week in an effort to wrestle an element of normality back into their lives. Granted, it was nearly always takeaway dinner for two from the local Italian restaurant but the food was fresh and the deal included a bottle of wine, so it didn't feel like a takeaway. Jemma preferred to think of it as 'dinner cooked elsewhere'.

'Philip?' He was sitting in the carver at the head of the table, the French polish giving the mahogany a deep, glossy sheen that reminded Jemma of black treacle. He had slung his tie over the back of the chair and unbuttoned the collar of his salmon-pink shirt, signalling freedom from the stranglehold of the stock market for another day. One hand hung limply over the arm of his chair, while the other held a tumbler of whisky. In the centre of the table, the crystal decanter gleamed like an enormous amber jewel, the phone lying beside it looking out of place amid the cutlery and glassware. Its red battery light blinked a repeated S.O.S message as its power faded.

'Wakey-wakey,' Jemma said, grabbing the phone. 'Dinner will be here any minute. Have you got your wallet?' She left the room to return the phone to its base on the telephone table in the hall. Philip was still staring at the table when she came back. 'I said, have you got your wallet?' Jemma repeated. Philip raised his head, a bemused expression on his face. Jemma sighed, reached over him and fished in the inside pocket of his suit. 'Here we are.' She dropped a kiss on his blonde hair, which was rapidly thinning at the crown. When had that happened? 'Why are you sitting there looking dopey?' she asked, taking the tumbler from his hand and eyeing the contents dubiously. 'How many of these have you had? We've got a bottle of wine coming, don't forget. Are you going to finish this?'

'That was Sarah on the phone for you,' Philip said, ignoring Jemma's barrage of questions.

'Oh? Do I need to call her back?'

Philip shook his head. 'I wouldn't. She's high as a kite and making no sense. Arima's pregna – arrgh!' Jemma had sat down on his knee with a bump.

'Straightaway?' she gasped. 'First time?'

'Yes,' Philip winced. 'Something you'll never be again if you do that to me too often.' He picked up his tumbler and swirled the dregs once or twice before draining it. 'I don't know, Jemma. It's a funny old business. I don't know what to make of it.' He buried his face in her hair, enjoying the smell of her perfume. 'We're lucky, aren't we,' he sighed. 'To have Beatrice, I mean.'

Jemma curled her arms round Philip's neck and hugged him, resting her cheek on his head. 'Yes,' she agreed. 'Even though I'm a sandwich short of a picnic as a result.'

'Stop it.'

'Well, I am.'

'We're dealing with that,' he reminded her. 'The tablets are making a big difference, aren't they?' He meant it as a statement of fact but didn't quite manage to keep the question from his voice.

'Yes,' Jemma replied. 'They are.' In some ways, she added silently. She no longer found herself staring at Beatrice and hating her for taking over her life and ruling her every waking moment, for example. This was a huge improvement. However, there were still days when she was crippled by the anxious thought that everything must be done correctly or she would have failed as a mother. Jemma was on the brink of awareness at the moment, becoming vaguely conscious that the second instinct might be an over-compensation for the first, and that the whole thing was tied up with hormones. If the tablets weren't quite balancing the hormones yet, they were at least ring-fencing a mental space from which Jemma could see with perspective once more. It felt like putting her head above the clouds to remind herself that the sun was still there, even if she couldn't see it all the time. 'It's a relief,' she said aloud. 'I thought I was going mad.'

'Well, I didn't,' Philip lied, sweetly loyal. 'But it's been a bit of a rollercoaster at times.' He splayed one hand in Jemma's lap and studied it. 'My skin's still peeling off every which way, though,' he observed. 'All that scrubbing with the hand sanitizer gel. One of the guys at work asked me if I have eczema the other day.'

Jemma swatted him on the arm. 'They did not.'

'They did!' he protested. 'I said yes to protect your honour.'

'My hero.'

'Better that than saying the wife's developed OCD.'

'I *have* apologized about the hand-scrubbing,' Jemma sniffed. 'More than once.'

'I'm teasing.' Philip pulled her head down for a lingering kiss. Just as things were beginning to look promising the doorbell rang and Jemma pulled away, grabbed Philip's wallet and slid off his knee.

'That'll be dinner.'

*And all hope of dessert gone with it*, Philip thought sadly, watching her leave the room. By the time they got to bed they'd both be dead on their feet, and Beatrice was waking around five o'clock at the moment. There was never any time.

He heard voices and footsteps in the hall and got to his feet, thinking there wasn't enough cash in his wallet and Jemma had brought the delivery man in to settle up. He almost collided with her at the door. 'Lawrence is here,' she whispered, giving him a significant look, the kind women effortlessly decode and men puzzle over for hours before drawing the wrong conclusion. Philip hated them.

'So?' he whispered back.

'So go and sit with him.'

'But what about dinner?' he said plaintively.

'You like cold pasta. Go on.' Jemma put her hand between his shoulder blades and shoved him towards the lounge. 'I'll bring the whisky. I think he wants a chat.' She gave him the look again. Philip shrugged helplessly. This was worse than the annual family game of charades at Christmas. 'The baby,' mouthed Jemma.

'Ohhhh. Oh, right.' Philip felt irrationally annoyed at her spelling it out. *A couple more seconds and I'd have got it*, he thought, pushing open the lounge door to find Lawrence staring out of the bay window, hands clasped behind his back. 'Hi, Lawrence,' he said jovially. 'Good to see you.'

'Philip.' They shook hands, the friendship still quite formal despite their long acquaintance.

'Sit down, make yourself at home,' Philip said, indicating the long white sofa, a lunatic impulse buy just before the birth of Beatrice.

'Thanks.'

Philip took the matching armchair, which gave him a clear view of the front door through the window. It was going to be torture seeing dinner arrive and knowing Jemma was tucking into all the best bits in the kitchen while he played agony uncle. If she left the kitchen door ajar he might be able to smell it. Torture. The men faced each other, neither one sure how to approach the conversation. It was delicate.

'Sorry to call in unannounced,' Lawrence began.

'You know you're welcome any time.'

'I was out for an evening walk and realized I was close by.'

'Right.' Philip intuited Lawrence was psyching himself up to reveal the big news. 'So congratulations are in order, I hear?' he said, trying to make it easier for his friend to open up. It didn't have the desired effect. Lawrence's face registered shock and dismay, not what Philip expected from a man who'd been trying to have a child for years.

'How do you know about that?' Lawrence demanded. 'Who told you?' At that moment, Jemma ploughed in, balancing the whisky decanter and two fresh glasses on an art deco tray.

'Here you are, boys,' she said, clattering it all down on the table. 'I'll be in the kitchen if you need me.' They all jumped as the doorbell rang again. 'Goodness, who could that be?' Jemma trilled. 'I'll go. It's probably the neighbour wanting to borrow some Darjeeling again.' Philip saw the delivery man on the doorstep, a bag in each hand. The neck of a bottle of red wine extended over the rim of the bag closest to him. Philip's face brightened. Jemma would only have one glass, so there would be something left for him to drink, if nothing else.

'Who told you?' Lawrence repeated.

'Hmm? Sorry. Sarah rang earlier this evening.'

'Ah.' Lawrence relaxed a bit and sat back, having noticed he'd been holding himself bolt upright on the edge of the sofa.

Philip watched him, unable to gauge Lawrence's odd mood. 'We, er, assumed it was good news?' he said cautiously.

'It is,' said Lawrence emphatically. 'Definitely. Yes. The best.'

Philip hesitated for a fraction of a second, then decided it was best to tackle this head-on. 'Look,' he said, getting up to pour two whiskies and handing one to Lawrence. 'We can go through the pleasantries and skate round the issue if that's what you want, or we can cut to the chase.' And my dinner, he added, realizing that his estimation of his wife's cruelty had been correct. She'd definitely left the kitchen door ajar. 'Because to be frank, you don't look like a man who's had good news.'

Lawrence fidgeted with his glass, looking out of the window. 'To be honest, Philip,' he said eventually, his voice so low Philip had to lean forwards to hear him properly. 'I don't feel like one.'

Now they were getting to it. 'Well, it's natural to feel a bit daunted,' Philip said reassuringly. 'I mean, it's a big deal. Especially when you've waited so long for it.'

'No,' Lawrence replied, his foot tapping nervously on the floor. 'That's not it. It doesn't feel right.' He put his glass down and stood up, too wired to be still. 'I ought to be happy about this but I'm not. There's no connection.' He crossed to the window and stared out at the darkening sky, the sun dipping behind the London skyline. 'So much could go wrong,' he said.

Philip rose and joined his friend at the window. 'Well, that's always the case,' he offered. 'It's better after the first trimester.'

'Not the pregnancy!' Lawrence burst out, frustration overriding his good manners. 'Arima, Sarah — this arrangement. The whole thing's a house of cards.'

To his credit, Philip didn't ask the obvious question first (how on earth Lawrence had been talked into it?) though he was dying to know. Instead he said, 'Have you formalized the agreement?'

'No.'

'Mind if I ask why not?'

'Because whoever gives birth to a child is legally its mother.' Lawrence turned to his friend. 'Don't you see, Philip? I could have an agreement drawn up by a solicitor tomorrow. Arima could sign twenty of the wretched things and jump through whatever hoops we asked, but in the end it makes no difference. None of them can be enforced.'

Philip's eyes widened at this, and Lawrence saw that he had grasped the implications. 'So it's all on a promise,' Philip said. 'That's not good business sense.'

'Exactly.' Lawrence was immensely relieved to find some- one other than his mother who understood the rationale. 'But everyone seems determined to gloss over this detail, as though it's a minor point. It's a massive deal-breaker.'

Philip puffed out his cheeks, thinking it through. 'Why did you agree to it?'

Lawrence's head dropped in an uncharacteristic gesture of defeat. 'I don't know,' he murmured. 'I don't know. For Sarah. For us, I suppose.' He closed his eyes. 'She was so sad, Philip. Always so sad on the inside, for years and years. I couldn't bear to see her like that, so I gave in.' His fists clenched in his pockets. 'My God, Philip, this goes against the grain. It's all too quick. We haven't even thought about what to tell people, what everyone will think. I must be mad.'

Philip was silent for a while. 'No,' he said finally. 'Arima's a good person. You can trust her.'

'I know,' Lawrence mumbled. 'She's an absolute fruitcake but I believe she's genuine. I just . . .' he struggled to ident- ify the fear sitting like a cold stone in his stomach. 'Is there such a thing as father's instinct?' he asked.

Philip smiled ruefully. 'No,' he said solemnly, putting an arm around his friend. 'That's why we have wives. And baby monitors.' Lawrence laughed. 'That's better,' said Philip, clap- ping him on the back. 'Look, it'll be okay, you'll see. Let's have another drink before you go.'

'Thanks, Philip.' They sat down and began to talk about other things – work, business, cars. Safe topics. Lawrence found himself relaxing for the first time in days as they drank and bantered back and forth. Maybe Philip was right, he thought, nodding as his friend enthused about a killer deal he'd closed last week. This was all needless worry. Of course things were going to change, but feeling it was not going to be for the better was melodramatic speculation on his part.

Everything was going to be fine.

# Chapter 14

Everything was not fine. Rarely had they been less fine, in fact.

Arima knew this the minute she opened her eyes, or tried to. Her brain was sending awake signals but her eyelids weren't co-operating. This wasn't normal. Dozing wasn't something she had ever really got the hang of. Either she was asleep, or she was awake and got up, however tired she was. An awake brain inside a resistant sleeping body was a whole new experience. It felt as though her body had divorced her brain and acquired a mind of its own. Every mental instruction was being smoothly repelled.

*Open your eyes.*

*Don't want to.*

*Open!*

*Nope.*

*Sit up, then.*

*Sorry, no can do.*

She couldn't even reach out to turn off the alarm clock that had been beeping persistently for the last quarter of an hour, though the repetitive sound set her teeth on edge. Arima tried to force her body into a sitting position. Nothing. Had the earth's gravitational pull been cranked up overnight by some joker? Her limbs felt like lead. This was taking fatigue to a whole new level.

The door burst open and Sarah whizzed in with a tray. 'Breakfast!' she beamed.

'Gnnnrrr.' Arima watched her through slitted eyes. There was nothing wrong with gravity in Sarah's personal orbit. It was just her. How could a minuscule bundle of cells wreak this much havoc on a grown woman? It was David and Goliath all over again. This baby was small but deadly.

'Decaff tea and toast,' announced Sarah, putting the tray down on the bed. Arima managed to raise her head a couple of inches off the pillow, just in time to inhale the smell of hot buttered toast. The nausea struck her like a slap and she fell back, gagging. Sarah watched the blood drain from her face. 'Oh dear. Hold on, I'll fetch the ginger nuts,' she said. 'I hoped you might feel better today. Don't move.' She clicked the alarm clock off and hurried from the room. Arima would have laughed if her stomach wasn't churning like a washing machine.

It had been this way every morning for weeks. Sometimes she was able to get out of bed after an hour and several ginger nuts and get on with the day. Other days she felt too weak to do anything but potter about the house, any activity she attempted interrupted by frequent bouts of sickness. While Sarah fussed over her, leaving small, nourishing meals in the fridge and urging her to rest, Lawrence kept his distance, as though pregnancy was contagious. As far as resting went, Arima needed no urging. She had no choice in the matter. By five o'clock in the afternoon her eyes were closing of their own accord and the heavy-limb syndrome kicked back in with a vengeance. Nobody warned her it would be like this, she thought angrily, managing to roll onto her side to check the time. In fairness, Sarah couldn't have warned her but Jemma could have. Arima was unreasonably piqued about this.

'I didn't really get any morning sickness,' Jemma protested when Arima had confronted her about it.

'But you knew about it, didn't you?' Arima snapped back. 'You knew it existed.'

Jemma gave a bewildered shrug. 'Well, yes,' she said. 'But so did you.'

'But I've never been pregnant,' Arima countered. 'So I didn't really know. You did.'

Jemma had looked to Philip for support. His wry smile and accurate quip of, 'I see the hormones have kicked in already,' did nothing to help the situation. Arima had stormed off, in fact, although this was partly in order to throw up. Again.

'Apparently it wears off after the first trimester,' Sarah had said one morning as Arima emerged, whey-faced, from the bathroom.

'*Apparently*? So you don't know for sure?'

'Well, I . . . no, but – so everyone says.'

'Brilliant,' said Arima as she slouched past. 'Everyone. Let's hope they're right.'

Even if Sarah was right and the morning sickness wore off after the first three months, it wasn't much comfort since Arima was only eight weeks pregnant. Another four weeks and she'd have wasted away altogether, she thought. Somehow, she managed to prop herself up on the pillows, knocking the breakfast tray with her leg and sending lukewarm tea cascading over the plate of toast. It swamped the meagre crust defences and set about destroying the hardened structure from within, crumb by crumb. Arima managed to right the cup before the entire contents were lost. She looked at the drops of spilt tea on her hand and considered for a moment before wiping it on her pyjamas. Better to keep the sheets clean.

Sarah reappeared, breathless from her run up the stairs. 'Never mind the tray,' she panted, handing Arima a steaming mug of lemon and ginger tea and a plate of ginger nuts. 'Dig in.'

'That's a bit optimistic,' Arima groaned, wafting the mug under her nose. Ginger really did the trick but the thought of digging into anything food-related was stretching the boundaries of possibility way too far. She picked up a biscuit and screwed her face up in disgust. 'I hate it when they're crunchy.'

'Dip it in your drink,' Sarah suggested.

'You can't be serious!' Arima was aghast. 'It has to be proper tea. You can't dip them in just anything, Sarah.'

'Well,' replied Sarah in the sort of measured tone normally reserved for awkward children, 'why don't you dip your biscuit in *this* cup . . .' she pushed the half-spilled cup of tea along the tray, 'and drink from *that* one.' She pointed at the mug in Arima's hand with a triumphant flourish. 'Problem solved.'

Arima scowled at her. 'S'pose,' she acknowledged grudgingly. Rather perversely, she hadn't wanted the problem solving. She wanted to feel cross and thwarted by the world at large. Now she had the feelings but with no good reason for them. 'Can you move back a bit? Your perfume's going to set me off.'

'I've made you a doctor's appointment,' Sarah replied, backing towards the door. 'Ten-thirty. You can come to work afterwards if you're up to it, but don't push yourself. Please,' she said as Arima scowled her refusal. 'You have to register in any case, and they might be able to give you something for the sickness.'

'I doubt it,' said Arima, sucking miserably on a soggy ginger nut. 'But I'll go.'

'Wonderful. I've written the address out and left it on the kitchen table for you. Have a good day.'

'Not likely.'

Sarah smiled. 'See you later.'

Arima opened her mouth to say, 'If I'm spared,' but managed to stop herself by lodging another ginger nut between her teeth. Fortunately, Sarah had already left the room. 'If I'm spared?' she muttered. 'Get a grip!' What was *wrong* with her? The last person she'd heard say that was her paternal grandmother, who used to intone the words dramatically every night before mounting the rickety stairs to the bedroom of her tiny cottage. Arima used to wonder if she sat up in bed each night, wrapped in her shawl and armed with a Bible and a small sherry, waiting to see if God was coming for her. At any rate, that was how they'd found her when she died. 'I'm going insane,' Arima decided. She pushed the bed-clothes aside and prepared to mount her attack on the day.

The doctor's surgery was crowded and noisy. The low-level piped music designed to promote an atmosphere of calm and quiet could barely be heard above squalling toddlers, a scattering of the elderly and a hefty dose of foot-tappers, looking highly aggrieved that precious minutes of their day were being stolen by illness. Arima sat down on a burgundy faux-leather seat beside a red-haired lady, whose freckled offspring had just tipped a carton of organic smoothie down his cardigan. 'Henry, no!' wailed the woman. 'It's *Boden*, darling.' The child gave her a puzzled look before emptying the rest onto the carpet. Arima grinned at him. Clearly, he found the flecked brown-beige as offensive as she did. 'You have to log in,' the woman said to her, dabbing hopelessly at the creamy mess on the treasured cardigan.

'Pardon?'

'Over there.' She pointed at a flat-screen monitor mounted on the wall beside the reception desk.

'Oh. Thanks.' Arima crossed the room and checked out the screen. She tapped in her details and waited for them to go through. A red sign flashed up on the screen. 'Patient not recognized. Please consult staff for assistance.' Arima turned to the counter and found a platinum-haired woman with red lipstick like a slash across her face and gold half-moon spectacles ostentatiously perched on the bridge of her nose. It was obvious Arima was waiting to speak to her, but the woman kept her gaze on her own computer screen for several seconds before flicking a glance at Arima, as though she was beneath proper notice.

'Sign in on the touch-screen system, please,' she sniffed, assessing Arima's dishevelled hair and scruffy clothes with disapproving eyes.

'I have. It told me to consult you,' Arima replied, needled by the woman's manner.

The woman clicked her tongue and made a show of shutting down whatever she was doing on the computer. 'Name?'

'Arima Middleton.'

'Are you registered with us?'

'No. It's an emergency appointment. But I'd like to register as well.'

The woman tapped a couple of buttons on her keyboard. 'Ten-thirty, Dr Colman?' she barked.

'Yes.' Arima leaned on the counter, feeling bile rise in her throat.

The receptionist thrust several forms through the glass hatch with a pen. 'Fill these in. I'll need to see your passport, and a recent utility bill as proof you're in catchment for the surgery,' she said.

'I didn't know I needed to bring those,' Arima apologized. 'And I don't pay any utility bills at the moment.' The woman threw her a sneering look. *I thought as much.* The thought was projected with such clarity that Arima almost heard the words aloud. 'The people I'm staying with are with this surgery,' she said defensively. 'They made the appointment.' Why was she defending herself? She hadn't done anything wrong.

'NHS card?'

'Um. No, not on me.'

'Then I can't register you,' she said triumphantly. 'You'll have to come back another day, when the surgery's quiet.'

'I don't expect it's ever quiet,' Arima objected.

'No,' agreed the woman, smiling thinly.

Arima glared at her.

'Are you trying to tell me to get lost?' she demanded.

The woman pursed her lips, the skin around her mouth tightening into the puckered grooves of a hardened smoker.

'I'm telling you that I can't register you without the proper identification,' she said. 'And you should know that without proof of domicile, you will have great difficulty in registering anywhere.'

Arima felt her hackles rise. She opened her mouth, preparing to give the woman a piece of her mind, but at that moment a buzzer sounded and a calm voice spoke over the intercom system.

'Arima Middleton to Room 3, please. Arima Middleton, Room 3.' Arima drew herself up and glared at the receptionist before turning on her heel and striding into the corridor.

She found Room 3, gave a perfunctory knock and marched in without waiting for a reply.

Dr Colman looked up from his desk, not at all perturbed by the wild-haired girl barging in and throwing herself down in the chair by his desk. He was middle-aged and slightly built, with a dark beard and moustache cropped close to his face, giving him a groomed, sprightly look. Put together with his impossibly neat suit and tie, he looked too perfect to be real, as though he'd stepped out of a comic book or magazine. He reminded Arima of a leprechaun. The thought made her smile.

'Ah, that's better,' beamed the doctor. He thrust his hand across the desk. 'Dr Colman. How can I help?'

Arima found she didn't know where to begin, and the sharp, musky smell of aftershave was making her stomach roll.

'I'm sorry,' she blurted, charging across the room to throw up in the wastepaper bin.

'Quite alright,' replied Dr Colman cheerfully when she staggered back to her seat. 'Would you like a glass of water?'

'No thank you,' Arima mumbled, her cheeks flaming with embarrassment. 'I'm sorry,' she repeated, moving her chair back to put herself out of smelling range. 'It's your after-shave.'

Dr Colman raised his eyebrows in surprise, then laughed. 'Ah. You're pregnant.'

'Yes,' Arima replied miserably. 'And I'm really sick. And the baby isn't mine.'

'Pardon?'

'Well, it *is* mine, obviously.' Arima scrunched her eyes up, trying to think of a way to explain without making herself sound like a nutcase. 'But the father is my friend's husband . . .'

Dr Colman's eyebrows were sternly forced back into place but he couldn't do anything about his eyes, which were wide with shock. Patients didn't usually admit these transgressions so candidly.

'No, it's not like that,' Arima said hastily, realizing she'd dug herself into a hole. 'I'm living with them, and . . .' she panicked as the shock began to turn to disgust behind the professional demeanour, 'We went to a clinic. The baby is for them,' she said desperately.

Dr Colman's face cleared as understanding dawned.

'You're a surrogate?'

'Yes,' Arima gulped, wondering why she hadn't just said so in the first place. Her brain was like a sieve lately.

'And is this a straight surrogacy or host surrogacy?' he asked, the interest evident on his face.

'I –'

'Is the fertilized egg your own, or was it harvested from the other lady and implanted?'

'It's mine.'

'Fine, fine.' He was jotting notes down on a pad as he spoke. 'And how have you come to this arrangement?' he enquired. 'Are you working via an intermediary organization that deals with surrogacy?' Arima shook her head. 'May I ask why not?' he asked mildly. 'I understand that they offer counselling and support throughout the process.'

'It's a private arrangement,' Arima replied. 'I don't want children right now, and I'm happy to be able to help.'

'Fine,' he muttered as he gave her a shrewd look. The girl seemed intelligent, but unnaturally blasé about her situation. 'I would advise some form of counselling or discussion at the very least,' he said. 'Pregnancy is a shock to the system, body and mind. This is a major decision, quite apart from the surrogacy aspect.'

'You're telling me,' Arima said fervently. 'But I don't need counselling. I just want to stop being sick.'

Dr Colman smiled.

'That's perfectly understandable,' he said, 'but there's a lot more to it than morning sickness.'

'I'm aware of that.' Arima was beginning to feel uncomfortable. She just wanted to get some medicine and get out of there, and this man was looking at her as if she was an incredibly rare specimen. The doctor picked up on her discomfort instantly.

'I apologize for all the questions,' he said. 'I'll be completely honest with you. I haven't dealt with a surrogate before, and I want to be sure I understand the situation before we go any further.'

'That's fair enough,' Arima sighed. 'But I'm getting the third degree from everyone at the moment.'

'I'm afraid that's something you're going to have to get used to,' the doctor said frankly. 'Surrogacy isn't common in this country, and many people regard it with suspicion.' He tapped his pen on the pad and considered for a moment, choosing his words with care. 'If the sickness is severe, I can help with that,' he said. 'And we need to make you a booking-in appointment with a midwife. What concerns me more is that you are fully aware of the implications of a surrogacy arrangement.'

'I am,' Arima replied. She couldn't understand why the doctor was making such a meal out of it. He was as bad as Robin. 'After the birth we get a parental order through the courts, and Lawrence and Sarah – that's my friends – become the legal parents of the baby. Lawrence is the father in any case, so it's more for Sarah.'

'Fine,' replied the doctor. He put his pen down and sighed. 'I'm at the very edge of my knowledge when it comes to surrogacy, but I do undoubtedly know you must be very careful to remain within the letter of the law throughout the pregnancy. No money can change hands, for example, but expenses incurred by your pregnancy can be covered by the couple. Are you aware of all this?'

'Yes,' Arima said. 'I read up on it all beforehand.'

'And you're absolutely sure you want to proceed with the pregnancy?' he pressed. 'It isn't too late to change your mind if you're having second thoughts or doubts of any kind.'

Arima stared at him. Was he suggesting an abortion? 'I'm sure,' she said, meeting his eye squarely.

The doctor sat back, making an odd movement, halfway between a shrug and a shake of the head. 'Well, it's an admirable thing you're doing,' he said. 'But I still strongly advise you to consider counselling, and make sure you have a strong support network around you.'

'I'll keep it in mind,' Arima said blandly.

Dr Colman knew when he was beaten. 'Have you filled in the registration forms?' he asked, moving the conversation along.

Arima explained she didn't have the right documents with her. 'The receptionist didn't seem to think she'd be able to register me at all, actually.'

'Was it the blonde-haired lady?'

'Yes.'

Dr Colman smiled broadly. 'Don't worry. Your passport and any piece of formal post with your address on will suffice. Now, tell me about the morning sickness.'

Ten minutes later, Arima left the surgery clutching a prescription for anti-sickness tablets and an appointment with the practice midwife. She felt like brandishing them in the receptionist's face on her way out. She studied the prescription as she sat at the bus stop, kicking idly at a pile of russet-gold leaves lying in a high drift against the side of the shelter.

Dr Colman had told her to rest and stressed if the sickness got any worse she would need to be hospitalized for monitoring.

'I'd rather eat my own foot,' Arima said, pinching the neck of her coat closed against the October wind. 'These had better work.' She glanced up at the scudding clouds. 'See to it, Mama.'

# Chapter 15

Lawrence was running late. He paced around the kitchen in his suit, cupping a cereal bowl in one hand and cramming porridge into his mouth as fast as he could. Every time he completed a circuit of the room, he took a swig from his coffee mug before setting off again. He wouldn't be finished any quicker than if he sat down to eat, but being on the move made him feel more efficient. He glanced up at the clock and grimaced. It was all very well having a contemporary creation with odd metal hands shaped like bolts of lightning, random blotches of clashing colours and no numbers on the face, but it made telling the time virtually impossible. Sarah refused to replace it on the grounds that it had been a gift from a departing student. Lawrence could see why the student hadn't wanted it in their own home. It appeared to be half past six, or thereabouts.

Outside it was still dark and the wind was flinging rain against the kitchen window in petulant, intermittent blasts. Lawrence hunched his shoulders, anticipating the unpleasant dash from the front door to his car. He hated these dark mornings, especially having to rely on artificial light. It muddled his thoughts, made him feel he should still be in bed and generally set him off on the wrong foot for the day.

Sarah swept into the kitchen; her grey wool coat looped over one arm and a pair of leather gloves in the other. A tangled red pashmina trailed from one coat-sleeve, threatening to trip her up. 'I'm just off,' she said, pecking Lawrence on the cheek as he strode past. 'See you at two-fifteen, okay?'

'Will I?' he said, with his mouth full.

'It's Tuesday,' Sarah said. It was clear from her tone that this was significant, but to Lawrence's sleep-fuddled brain it made no sense.

'So . . . ?'

'Oh, Lawrence. You can't have forgotten.' Sarah shrugged her coat on and began buttoning and belting herself in, her sharp movements conveying her displeasure more eloquently than words.

'Um . . .' Since he clearly *had* forgotten, there was no point denying it.

'The scan,' Sarah replied. 'Please, Lawrence. Make an effort to be there.' She wound the pashmina several times round her neck and yanked it into a knot. 'You will be there, won't you.'

'Yes, yes, I'll be there,' Lawrence replied grumpily. 'If I can get out of my meeting in time.'

Sarah pulled on her gloves and turned to leave. 'You'll have to,' she said tartly. 'I've told Arima to call you if she's too unwell to take the tube.'

'I don't want her throwing up in the Bentley,' Lawrence spluttered, spraying porridge onto his suit. 'Oh, damn. I've just had this back from the dry-cleaners. Listen, Sarah, about this scan. I'm not really comfortable with the idea of being there. Hospitals aren't my thing.'

'Tough,' Sarah said. 'It's about time you took an interest. Arima's been ill for weeks and you haven't lifted a finger to help her.'

'That simply isn't true.'

'Then you have a funny definition of truth, darling,' Sarah replied coolly. Lawrence was silent. 'Two-fifteen,' she repeated, and left the room, leaving Lawrence thoroughly out of sorts.

He slammed his bowl into the sink and stamped off in search of the shoes he'd forgotten to polish. The last thing on earth he wanted to do was sit huddled round a monitor in a poky hospital room with Sarah and Arima, peering at a grainy shot of Arima's innards and a partially formed foetus. Even imagining it made him feel decidedly twitchy. This . . . was the realm of women . . .

Lawrence stood at the front door, eyeing up the distance to his car through the curtain of rain and putting off the moment when he had to step into the deluge. He probed his thoughts gingerly, as you would a sore tooth. It was becoming difficult to avoid the fact that he was in denial about the surrogacy.

Apart from Philip and his mother, he hadn't told a soul. So far neither of them had been much help. Philip was tactfully neutral and his mother remained tight-lipped, saying only she hadn't lost faith he and Sarah would have a child of their own.

'You've always believed it, Lawrence,' she chided on his last visit. 'You told me once you felt God had given you that assurance.'

'It was just a dream,' Lawrence mumbled, always uncomfortable when she raised the subject. 'Dreams don't mean anything.'

'Sometimes they do,' replied Eva. 'God speaks in all sorts of ways, including dreams. Read your Bible.'

'I don't need to read my Bible,' Lawrence snapped, swatting her words away like a troublesome fly.

'There's no need to take that tone with me, dear. I understand your frustration, but -'

'I am not frustrated, mother. It was a long time ago, and it was just a dream.'

'Well.' Eva had folded her hands in her lap and fixed him with the kind of stare she'd used when he was a child, clearly in the wrong about something but stubbornly refusing to back down. 'We won't argue about it.' Lawrence had left the room grinding his teeth so loudly Eva could hear it.

'That child will come, Lawrence,' she said to his retreating back. 'I'm still praying for it, and you.'

'I know, Mother. Tell that to Sarah – she can't wait any longer – perhaps this is the way God will answer your prayers?'

Childishly, he had slammed the door on his mother and her pie-in-the-sky notions, thinking he might very well stop paying for her Sky television contract. She watched too much of the God Channel and this was the result.

Lawrence was still grappling with his feelings about the whole thing, constantly seesawing between the positives and negatives, unable to find any kind of equilibrium. On the one hand, to be getting what he and Sarah had always wanted was unbelievable after all this time . . . but in such a way.

Arima was doing a wonderfully generous thing for them . . . but Lawrence couldn't rid himself of an instinctive dread that resonated with his mother's warning. Somewhere in all this there was a loose thread; not the possibility that Arima could renege on the deal, he'd thought about that. It was something else, something he hadn't considered.

All he knew was that if the thread was found and pulled their lives would unravel. The words beat at his brain like the raindrops bouncing on the concrete. He felt as though he was spinning blindly in the dark, anticipating a surprise attack from an unknown quarter but knowing neither the form nor the assailant, only that danger was near. Lawrence shook himself free of these faceless fears.

'You're being ridiculous, man,' he said for the hundredth time. 'And you're late.' He turned up the collar of his rain-coat and made his move, pelting down the steps to dive into his car. The door slammed behind him, almost catching his coat. Lawrence punched every heater button in sight and sat shivering while the engine warmed up. 'I'm not in denial,' he muttered, wiping droplets of water from his face. Which meant he was in denial about being in denial. Worse and worse. A psychiatrist would have a field day with him. Lawrence set his jaw and drove away, vowing to do every-thing he could to make his meeting overrun.

By eight-thirty the rain showed no signs of abating. The wind whipped the waters of the Thames into foamy peaks, the slate-grey sky mirrored in the choppy waves. Few people wanted to brave the riverboats on such a morning, a choice reflected in the suffocating press of commuters on the underground.

Robin got off at Westminster instead of his usual London Bridge stop, unable to bear the crush. He crossed the bridge and walked briskly along the South Bank, his upper body hidden beneath an enormous striped golfing umbrella. The view from the London Eye must be comical on a day like this, the pavements and walkways of the city appearing to be dotted with brightly striped spinning tops twirling in the downpour.

The rain soaked through his loafers and began to seep up his trouser legs, staining the stonewashed denim a dark blue. Jeans were a bad choice for wet weather, thought Robin, as the line of damp crept up towards his knees. They held the water and took hours to dry, so you were wet and chilled for most of the day. With the onset of winter, his little gallery was getting draughty and the electric heater he'd bought to ward off the damp, though heroic in its efforts, was largely ineffective and dealt a crippling blow to his wallet. It was only November. God alone knew what the electricity bill for the entire winter would be.

On top of fretting about his overheads, the daily battle of mud versus white floor was becoming a personal vendetta. There were days when Robin had to remind himself people coming in to browse was a good thing, even if their shoes were filthy. The previous week a couple had arrived wearing wellingtons, and Robin had found himself with his hand on the mop, about to follow them round to erase their offensive trail of muck from his pristine floor as soon as could be. It was possible, he mused, passing under the archway of Hays Galleria, he was spending too much time on his own. Or too much time brooding over Arima. Robin retrieved his phone from the pocket of his raincoat and checked the messages. Sure enough, there was one from her already.

*Sick as a dog again. Run out of ginger nuts. Disaster! A x*

Robin wrestled with himself for several seconds, coming to a standstill at the far side of the arch. 'Don't answer,' he muttered, but his fingers were already moving over the keys.

*Poor you. Better stock up.*

*Too sick to go out in this. Will drown.*

The plea was unspoken but most definitely there. Robin squeezed his eyes shut and counted to ten, fighting the pull. It wasn't his problem. Running out of biscuits shouldn't even qualify as a problem. He was on the opposite side of the Thames to Arima, for goodness' sake. What could he do about it from here? Besides, she had freely chosen to enter into this, he reminded himself. She'd made her bed and so forth. His sympathy was, therefore, a limited commodity. Very limited. Another message flashed up.

*Batgirl needs Robin. Come in, Robin.*

It was no use. No matter how much he tried to resist, Arima Middleton was like Robin's magnetic north, and he the compass needle drawn inexorably to where she was. He pressed quick dial and put the phone to his ear. 'Hey, Batgirl. You okay?'

'I've been better.'

The last of his resistance dissolved at the sound of her voice. Robin had never heard her so forlorn. He wanted to sweep her into his arms and protect her, tell her that he'd take care of her and make everything right. She'd probably kick him in the goolies if he tried.

'Can I do anything for you?'

'Ginger nuts?'

'I'm at work, Mima.'

'Oh.' A heavy sigh gusted down the phone. 'Never mind. They'd be soggy by the time you got here anyway.'

Robin smiled. 'But that's the way you like them.'

'Yeah.' There was a pause. 'Twelve-week scan today.'

'I wish you weren't doing this.'

'I'm too sick to go over it all again. Just be there for me, Robin.'

'I'm here for you, Mima. Good luck today.'

'Thanks. See you soon?' There was an unfamiliar note of vulnerability in her voice.

'Promise.' Robin closed the phone and stared at it for a long moment, heedless of the rain dripping on his collar from a rogue spoke of his umbrella. He knew the pregnancy was affecting Arima more than she understood, or cared to admit. She was changing. 'I'm always here for you,' he said softly. 'Whether you need me or not. That's the trouble.'

Robin crossed the large courtyard to the gallery on the far side, his shoes slipping a little on the cobbles. As he patted his pockets in search of his keys, his eye fell on a pair of smudged muddy footprints flaunting themselves on the front step. Robin bent down to examine them.

'The postman again,' he tutted. 'I need to have a word with . . .' he froze, acutely aware of how stupid that sounded. What exactly did he intend to say to the postman? Excuse me, mate, but would you mind stretching up to deliver my post because I don't want you messing up my step? 'Oh God, I'm going mad,' he groaned. 'I am actually becoming Mrs Mop.' Shaking his head, Robin fumbled the key into the lock and stepped into the gallery, vowing not to mop the

floor for the entire day, come what may. Instantly, his stomach clenched. 'Okay,' he amended. 'Just for the morning.' A
full day of dirt was something he needed to work up to.
Robin was unnerved by his burgeoning neurosis. He wasn't
a neat freak by nature, quite the opposite. Where had it come
from?

As he scanned the post and made his ritual pre-opening
cup of tea, a random conversation with an old lady at a bus
stop in New Cross during his student days surfaced in his
mind. The bus had been over twenty minutes late and the
waiting crowd was getting shuffly and impatient, anger rip-
pling through the queue like the breeze through a wheat
field. Robin hadn't cared. It gave him a valid excuse for missing his lecture, which was an unexpected bonus on a Friday.
The lady next to him was also unaffected by the mood,
humming and smiling to herself as the minutes dragged on.
Robin had found the contrast between themselves and the
other waiting passengers so intriguing that in the end he
asked her why she was so cheerful when the bus was late.

'Us old fogeys,' she'd said confidentially, the smell of her
Yardley perfume almost rendering him unconscious as she
leaned in close. 'We fall into two camps. Some of us don't
worry about anything, because we've seen a lot, done a lot
and know there's no point fretting. I'm one of them. The
others, like him –' she paused to point at another pensioner
in the queue, a fastidiously dressed little man fidgeting with
his watch and loudly complaining that the bus service
wasn't a patch on what it used to be and moreover, he was
going to miss the one o'clock news. He was turning a bat-
tered trilby round and round in his hands as he spoke, his

fingers gripping the brim so hard that it was all bent out of shape. 'They worry about all the little things because they don't have any big things to deal with any more, and because they've got too much time to think.' The old lady had loose, leathery skin on her face and her neck was crinkling up like crepe paper as she spoke. 'So the little things become the big things, see?'

At the time, Robin hadn't seen at all. Now, years later, he thought he did. What with renting his own flat and being cooped up in the gallery six days a week, he was definitely spending too much time on his own, and introspection didn't suit him. This was the problem. He saw lots of people, of course. London was crawling with life, but the appearance of community created by the sheer volume of bodies was a sham. Catching someone's eye in the street and exchanging the odd pleasantry with customers wasn't proper social interaction. There was no mental stimulation, no real engagement with anybody. For each person who might acknowledge your existence, there were twenty more who would probably step over you if you lay bleeding in the street. Part of it was a survival mechanism.

At times, travelling by tube was such an invasion of personal space that ignoring everyone was the only way to cope. It was the same at the gym where he occasionally worked out. A nod and a smile here and there, no more. It wasn't enough. Robin swilled his cup out in the sink and stared vacantly into the stainless steel basin, gnawing absently at a hangnail as he processed this mini-epiphany. He hadn't thought the combined impact of a bachelor pad and a one-man business could shrink his sense of perspective to such an extent.

Outside of work, there was barely any time for seeing friends, and what time Robin had he gave to Arima. Worrying about her filled his mind, mushrooming until all other thoughts were excluded. If he wasn't with her, he was thinking about her; and neither scenario was particularly peaceful. No wonder he was on edge.

'You need to make some changes, mate,' he told his reflection. 'Before you become a total basket case.'

So when Hannah from the Christmas shop appeared on the doorstep half an hour later, flushed and sweaty in her mauve pac-a-mac, Robin didn't make an excuse and turn her away, as he had when she'd come to thank him for the 'sorry for being sick on you' bunch of flowers, and the time after that as well. When she held up two cups of takeaway coffee and a bag of blueberry muffins like a shield, cringing slightly as she stammered a greeting, Robin smiled and held the door wide. 'I'm not busy this morning,' he said, stepping back to usher her in and trying not to focus on the drop of rain hanging from the end of her nose, or the way her wet fringe was pasted across her forehead in clumped, unattractive stripes. 'Come on in. The coffee smells great.' He didn't know which of them was more shocked by the invitation.

'Thanks,' gulped Hannah, stumbling slightly over the threshold. 'I'm on an early break today.'

'How long have you got?' Robin asked, holding out his hand for the pac-a-mac. 'Let me hang that up for you.'

'Okay.' Hannah peeled it off, revealing a pair of black jeans and a baggy, bright red sweater. 'I have half an hour.'

'Brilliant. It'll warm up in here soon,' Robin promised, ducking into the kitchenette to add her waterproof to the single hook on the back of the door, with his own sodden coat. 'Well, this bit will,' he amended, crossing the room to draw a tiny square with his arms in the airspace around the electric heater. Hannah giggled, the sudden sparkle in her green eyes transforming her plain features. She put the coffee cups on the counter and offered the bag of muffins to Robin.

'My favourites,' Robin smiled. 'So, tell me your secret.'

'Pardon?' Hannah blushed and buried her nose in her coffee cup.

Robin pointed at her trousers.

'Your jeans,' he explained. 'How come they're dry? Did you teleport to work this morning? Mine are soaked.'

Hannah raised her head cautiously. 'I brought a dry pair in my rucksack,' she said, trying not to stare at Robin's two-tone jeans and failing.

'It's not a good look, is it?' he laughed, lifting one leg up to examine the cut-off point of the water stain, just above his knee.

'Not really.' She turned her head aside to examine some of the paintings but not in time to hide the flash of humour in her eyes. Hannah seemed okay, he thought as the conversation slowly began to flow. If he made the effort she could be a mate. Right now, she was doing a good job of taking his mind off Arima's scan and that was a start.

He wasn't alone. In their respective morning habitats, Arima and Lawrence were also striving to bury their heads in the sand. Arima because she couldn't contemplate the thought of being upright and out of the house without a ginger nut safety net, and Lawrence because his lunchtime meeting had been cancelled and there was to be no escape from the scan appointment and the gritty reality of impending parenthood.

Sarah, however, could think of nothing else. She didn't *want* to think of anything else. Cocooned in her office at the university, she pressed her hands against her stomach, feeling the butterflies flutter and jump and imagining her child doing the same inside Arima. She couldn't concentrate on her work. Every few minutes, her eyes strayed to the clock, willing the hands on. In a few hours she would have her first picture of the baby. Her baby.

'I can't wait to see you,' she murmured. This would be her first chance to forge a bond with the baby. The unbreakable bond of mother and child. She wouldn't miss it for the world.

# Chapter 16

At one o'clock Sarah gave up all pretence of doing any constructive work. If you counted the list of children's names she'd drawn up while feigning interest in her students' comments during a mixed year group tutorial on aspects of constructed textiles in contemporary art, you could argue she'd achieved something productive with her time. Other than that, she'd done nothing but alternate between staring at her laptop screen and the clock.

Everyone had days like it, she told herself, trying to justify her total lack of focus. The trouble was, she was having them all the time lately. If she carried on, the gaps in her work were going to show. However, she had recently had a performance management review so nobody was going to be breathing down her neck for the next few months.

'By which time I'll be gone,' she murmured, switching off her laptop and snatching her coat from its peg behind the door. She was halfway into it when the door opened to admit Marjorie, the much-loved departmental secretary. She was a woman with a glorious disregard for both colour and style, with the result that she generally looked as though she'd wandered blindfolded through a jumble sale and put on whatever came to hand.

Today's ensemble was a brightly striped skirt and blouse in orange and blue and a red knee-length chunky cardigan, which added unfortunate bulk to her middle-aged figure. Combined with her unique dress sense, Marjorie's broad Birmingham accent ensured that every encounter with her induced a sensory overload, which Sarah had never got used to, despite working with her for several years. Sarah could imagine Arima looking like this in thirty years, her eclectic style bleeding into eccentricity as time went by. She hoped it wasn't a genetic trait.

'I'm just off, Marjorie,' she said, pointing rather unnecessarily at her coat and scarf. 'Long lunch. I'll be back later.' She was bursting to tell someone about the baby but had reluctantly agreed to wait until the pregnancy was further on, at Lawrence's insistence.

'Right. Well, just a quick word before you go,' replied Marjorie, planting herself squarely between Sarah and the door. Sarah stifled a groan. Marjorie had a habit of doing this. She was prodigiously efficient but her ability to hold lists and queries in her head meant that 'quick words' were rarely that.

'I really don't have long to talk, Marjorie,' she said apologetically, attempting to move towards the door.

'Oh, not a problem,' said Marjorie cheerfully, shifting ever so slightly to block Sarah's way. 'This won't take a minute. Just a couple of things to run past you. Firstly, the Christmas Carol Service. We need a reader from the Art Department . . .'

While Sarah tried desperately to escape from the office, Lawrence was trying equally hard to find reasons not to leave. He had successfully mired himself in contracts for the entire morning, giving his secretary, Deborah, strict instructions that no calls were to be put through. When he had run out of contracts, Lawrence began hounding Deborah to update his schedule.

'Let's not waste time,' he said when she teetered into his office mid-morning with a cafetière and biscuits. 'Now that the midday meeting has been cancelled there's a two-hour window in my diary. Make some calls, see if you can re-jig the schedule. Surely something can be slotted in.'

'Well, I – it's a bit short notice, Mr Abrahams,' Deborah replied, every muscle in her over-botoxed face straining as she attempted a disapproving expression. In the end she settled for frowning on the inside.

'This is a business, Deborah, not a charity,' Lawrence said testily. 'I don't expect my staff to sit around all day and I've no intention of doing it myself. Please do your best to arrange something.'

Deborah had flounced from the room, muttering ill-disguised profanities under her breath, her stilettos striking the wooden floor so hard that Lawrence actually got up to look for gouge marks when the door clicked shut. As bosses went, he was one of the best and rarely raised his voice to his staff, considering it bad people management. He found it tended to make them uncooperative.

Deborah was no exception. It was now one o'clock, and nothing had appeared in the blank segment of his electronic diary. Lawrence considered his options. Deborah was either sulking or hadn't come up with the goods. Most likely both. How was he going to get out of this wretched scan appointment? He eyed the door. Could he barricade himself in? The bookcase to the left of the doorway might just fit, if he slid it along and . . .

The phone on his desk rang. Lawrence ignored it for a count of fifty, at which point Deborah kicked the door open with one pointy leather-clad foot and announced in glacial terms that she was putting a call through.

'I said no calls, Deborah,' Lawrence reminded her calmly.

'It's urgent,' she hissed, her eyes communicating what her facial muscles no longer could.

Lawrence gave up and reached for the phone, motioning for Deborah to close the door. He winced as the reverberation felled a picture from the wall. Further words with Deborah were needed. 'Hello?'

'Lawrence?'

'Yes?'

'It's Jemma. Where on earth have you been?'

'Uh – at work. Is there a problem?'

'Only that Arima's been trying to get hold of you all morning.'

Lawrence thought she sounded slightly on edge.

'I've been in meetings,' he lied. 'Is everything okay? Beatrice all right?'

Jemma gave a harsh bark of laughter.

'Beatrice is fine. Arima is throwing up in my kitchen and needs a lift to the hospital for her scan.' Her voice sharpened. 'Apparently, you were supposed to be available to take her, but she hasn't been able to get through to you.'

'Right, yes. The thing is, I'm completely snowed under here,' Lawrence gabbled, hoping that Deborah hadn't said otherwise. 'I, don't suppose . . . '

'No. Beatrice and I are due at Shake, Rattle and Roll in an hour and we can't miss it. I've paid for the term and baby music classes have a huge waiting list. Arima walked all the way over here, you know. She really isn't well enough, Lawrence.'

'Right, right. Poor thing.' Lawrence looked around the room, seeking inspiration. 'Shake, rattle and roll, eh? Sounds like fun.'

'Give it a few months and you can enrol for yourself.'

'Right. Excellent.' There was a painful silence on the line as Lawrence prayed for a solution.

'Just get over here, will you?' Jemma said, and hung up.

Lawrence stared glumly at the receiver before following suit. There was to be no escape. He threw on his raincoat and strode out of the office. 'I'm just popping out, Deborah,' he said briskly. 'Lunch meeting.'

'I'm so pleased. Silly to waste valuable time over a meal when you could be working.'

Deborah gave him a cat-like smile and turned back to the letter she was typing. Women, thought Lawrence, punching the lift button for the ground floor. They were all in it together.


'Men,' said Jemma scathingly. 'I love them but they're useless.'

Arima lifted her head from the sink, catching her ear on the mixer tap. 'He can't come?'

'Oh, he's coming,' answered Jemma, swinging Beatrice off her hip, into her high chair and snapping the buckle into place in one fluid movement before Beatrice could wriggle free. 'I didn't give him the option. Here.' She took a tumbler from the cupboard and passed it to Arima. 'Try and have some water, see if you can keep it down. You mustn't get dehydrated.'

'Okay,' croaked Arima, staggering to the breakfast bar and laying her head down on the cool granite surface. A few months ago she'd sat in the same place and kicked off her shoes, sipping brandy and having water fights with Robin. It seemed a lifetime ago and a world away from this. 'To be honest, I think dehydration is the least of my worries,' she mumbled.

Never a truer word, thought Jemma, biting her lip at the unhealthy pallor and lethargy of her normally vivacious friend. Pregnancy was not agreeing with Arima so far.

'You'll pick up in the middle trimester,' she said brightly, spooning pureed carrot into Beatrice's mouth and doing her best to shield Arima from the sight and smell of the stuff. 'Your energy levels will be through the roof and your hair and skin will look amazing. You'll see.' Arima lifted a hank of greasy hair and stared miserably at it. 'When will that kick in exactly?' she sniffled. 'I can't wait for this part to be over.'

Jemma tactfully turned away so as not to see her friend's tears. This was just the beginning, she thought grimly. Arima had bitten off more than she could chew and there was no going back.

Stranded in her office, Sarah felt a scream beginning to build in her chest.

'Marjorie, I really have to leave. Now. I'm going to be late.'

'Fine. I just need a quick word about the maternity cover post for the textiles department. That doesn't seem to be working out, does it?'

'What do you mean?' She was going to miss the appointment. She couldn't miss it.

'Well, I think we need to be realistic about the limitations of the current set-up,' Marjorie said, her tone even and oh-so-reasonable. Sarah put a hand to her head as the blood started to pound in her temples. Marjorie trundled on, unaware of the impending explosion. 'I mean, Ms Middleton has had more days off sick than at work so far,' she pointed out. 'At the moment, we're having to find cover for the maternity cover, if you follow me.'

'What of it?' said Sarah faintly, afraid if she opened her mouth fully the scream would blow the door off its hinges, and Marjorie's efficient head with it. Perhaps that wouldn't be a bad thing.

For the first time, Marjorie hesitated.

'I know she's a good friend of yours, Sarah,' she said carefully. 'And I'm not asking for any personal information. But I was wondering if you knew whether this . . . ill health . . . is likely to be an ongoing thing, because, really, if it is, I don't think the cover job is viable, do you?'

That did it.

'If you'd let me get to this blasted appointment, I might be able to answer that question!' Sarah screeched. She barged past the secretary and opened the door. Marjorie gave a squawk of surprise, arms windmilling as she tried to regain her balance. 'Marjorie, I can't do this now. I'm sorry.' Sarah closed the door on Marjorie's stunned expression and ran. By the time Marjorie got out into the corridor Sarah was long gone, racing for New Cross Station and the next train into London.

'*Well.*' Marjorie smoothed her chunky cardigan over her wounded dignity and returned to the departmental office to await Sarah's apology, whenever that might be. 'And,' she said vehemently, thumping stacks of paper from place to place on her desk, 'it had better not be long in coming.' Suddenly, she remembered there were works on the line that afternoon, making it highly likely that Sarah would be late for her precious appointment. It was a pleasurable thought. Marjorie began to hum a little tune as she returned to her work.

The waiting room of the antenatal unit at St Thomas's hospital was situated on the eighth floor of the North Wing. Lawrence gazed out of the window, trying to distract himself by picking out familiar places among the sprawl of buildings visible from this height. It wasn't a patch on the London Eye but for a static view it wasn't bad, he thought, shifting to a more comfortable position on the hard seat. He awarded himself a point for every place he recognized, excluding the Thames and the London Eye. Too easy.

After a while, Lawrence became aware the couple sitting directly opposite were staring at him, or rather, trying not to stare. The woman, her bump protruding through a jade green jersey dress, was doing a poor job of hiding her smirk. Her companion, still wearing his full-length charcoal winter coat despite the warmth of the waiting area, was openly staring. Lawrence wondered if he had been inadvertently mouthing words as he silently named places in his game. Their stares were fair enough if so. He himself was suspicious of anyone who talked to themselves in public. When Lawrence gave a smile and a nod, hoping to reassure the couple of his sanity, he was unable to catch their eye. With a sense of dread, Lawrence turned his head to the right. Arima was sitting with her eyes closed, apparently picking her nose.

'Arima,' he said through clenched teeth. 'Stop it.'

Arima opened one eye.

'Stop what?' The overcoat man tried to turn his snort of laughter into a cough. Lawrence blushed. She was worse than a child.

'You know very well what.'

Arima ignored him. Mortified, Lawrence reached up and tried to prise her fingers away from her nose. Arima twisted away from him, keeping her thumb firmly pressed over her left nostril, her fingers fanned out vertically beside her nose as though she were a child poking fun at him.

'Alternate nostril breathing,' she informed him, her blocked nasal passage creating a comedy cartoon voice, 'helps with the nausea.'

The woman spluttered into her husband's shoulder. Lawrence couldn't stand the humiliation any longer.

'Find another coping mechanism,' he said bluntly. 'You're embarrassing me.'

Arima turned to face him, releasing her left nostril and blocking the right with her middle finger. 'Have you got a bag?' she enquired.

'No.'

'Ginger nuts?'

'No.'

'Anti-nausea acupressure wristbands?'

'No!'

'Then put up with it. Look the other way or something.'

'You don't do this at home,' he protested.

'Course I do. You're just not there to see it.'

The overcoat man leaned forwards in his chair.

'You might as well get used to it, mate,' he said, still chuckling at Arima. 'Few months' time and you'll be on the labour ward. There's a lot worse than alternate nostril breathing waiting for you, believe me.'

Lawrence gave a tight smile and went back to staring out of the window. Labour ward with Arima? Sarah would have to deal with that side of things. Personally, he'd rather walk over hot coals.

Sarah stood on the crowded platform at New Cross Station, grinding her teeth in frustration as the minutes dragged on and still the train didn't come. There was no way of knowing how long the delay would be. Taxi was an option but it would cost a fortune to get to St Thomas's from here. She shifted from foot to foot, jostling for a good spot on the platform. At five minutes to two, her nerve broke and she elbowed her way to the exit, ignoring all complaints as she trod on toes and dislodged bags from shoulders in her haste to get out. She was on the verge of hysteria at the thought of missing the scan.

'St Thomas's hospital,' she panted, throwing herself into the back of a taxi. 'Hurry.'

'Nothing serious, I hope?' asked the driver politely.

'Life and death.'

In the hospital waiting room, a door opened and the sonographer stepped out and looked around.

'Arima Middleton?'

'Oh, that's us,' Arima said, nudging Lawrence. 'Let's go.'

Lawrence trailed after Arima into the consulting room.

'Come on in, Dad,' smiled the sonographer, blue eyes dancing as she ushered him through the door.

Lawrence did a double take and almost turned around to see whom she meant before realizing it was him. *Dad*. It was the first time anyone had called him that. Such a small, everyday word but it certainly packed a punch when you weren't expecting to hear it. Lawrence felt winded. He wasn't ready for Dad. He took the chair beside the bed and tried not to look as Arima pulled up her top to expose her stomach. There wasn't anything much to see anyhow. No more than a subtle rounding of the abdomen that most women seemed to have as a matter of course.

'I feel enormous already,' Arima complained.

The sonographer laughed.

'Everyone says that,' she informed them. 'It's amazing how much stretch you've got in you, and you'll need it. Especially if it's twins.' She winked at Lawrence, who nearly sprang off his chair at the mere mention of it. How could she joke about something like that, he thought angrily. First Dad, and now this. People ought to be more sensitive. The sonographer scanned Arima's notes, her blonde ponytail bobbing up and down as she moved her head from side to side. 'Ah,' she said. 'You're a private patient.'

'Yes,' said Lawrence, looking pained. Sarah had given him no choice in the matter.

The sonographer bit her lip. 'I'm terribly sorry,' she began, 'but the private scans are usually from 5 till 8 p.m. on Tuesdays and Fridays. There must be some mistake.' Arima leaned over to peer at her notes.

'We are going private, but I think my GP referred me here because of all the morning sickness,' she explained. 'I think it might just be the birth bit that's private, I don't know. Sarah's in charge of that, isn't she?' she finished, directing the question at Lawrence, who nodded blankly. The sonographer glanced from one to the other.

'Well, since you're here and booked in, we may as well go ahead,' she said, putting the notes aside.

'Er – we're actually waiting for a third person,' Lawrence interrupted. 'Is there any chance we could hang on for a few minutes till she gets here?'

'I'm afraid not,' the sonographer replied. 'But you can buy a photo for four pounds if you like. Now, this will be a bit cold, I'm afraid.' Arima yelped as the woman smeared a clear jelly over her stomach and pressed the ultrasound device against her lower abdomen. Lawrence looked away, focusing on the vivid turquoise wall. Even that offended him.

'So,' said the sonographer, addressing Arima since Lawrence was clearly pretending to be elsewhere, 'here's baby. Just the one foetus, nice strong heartbeat.' She put a finger on the monitor to mark the spot. 'See it?'

'Yes,' breathed Arima. 'That's incredible.' Her heart swelled at the sight of the tiny dot pumping furiously on the screen. 'It looks very determined.'

'Yes, they're tenacious little things,' agreed the sonographer. 'Surprisingly hardy.' Arima started as something swished across the front of the screen.

'What was that?'

'A hand.'

'You're kidding.'

'No. There it goes again, look. And here's the head.' Arima stared at the monitor in disbelief. 'Lawrence,' she gasped. 'You have to see this.'

'I – I'd rather not,' said Lawrence, still looking away. 'I'm a bit squeamish.'

'It's okay,' said the sonographer kindly. 'There's nothing gory, I promise you. Take a look. You don't want to miss this.'

Unwillingly, Lawrence swivelled round and glanced at the screen. He froze.

'My God,' he whispered. 'That's . . . that's unbelievable. It's like a miniature person.'

'I know,' Arima smiled, tears rolling down her cheeks. 'I didn't expect it to be so clear.'

Lawrence was gaping openly at the monitor as he examined the tiny, perfect profile. The forehead, the eye socket, the slope of the jaw, the tiny spine. He had seen scan pictures before but you just looked impressed and said something enthusiastic to the cooing parents. This was a completely different experience. The foetus was moving about freely. It was . . . alive.

'I think it has my nose,' he said in astonishment.

'You can't possibly tell that!'

'I can. My nose is very distinctive.'

'That's one way of putting it.'

Lawrence moved closer for a better view. 'And look, look! It's waving at us.'

'It does look that way, doesn't it,' the sonographer agreed as the little arms whooshed to and fro across the front of the monitor.

She never tired of seeing people's reactions on seeing their child for the first time. Watching this couple, she couldn't decide which of them was more overcome. Possibly the man. That made sense, she thought, too professional to mention the surrogacy information on the woman's medical notes. And yet, the woman seemed equally smitten.

Lawrence's head was reeling. It was the most mind-blowing thing he had ever seen. There was a person in there, an actual person. He was overcome by an urge to make contact with this little creature, to put his mouth to Arima's stomach and shout, 'Are you alright in there? Hold on, we'll get you out!'

He forgot all about Sarah, stuck in a traffic jam on Westminster Bridge Road. The world shrank to the size of the consulting room, the sonographer's presence fading into the turquoise walls. Nothing was left but Lawrence, Arima and the baby. 'Thank you so much,' he said, his voice cracking with emotion. It was a powerful, intimate moment.

Arima felt it too. Suddenly, she saw why she had left Benoit and her nomadic life. Deep down she had become tired of rootlessness and wandering. The unnamed malaise that had driven her home was the oldest and most basic of desires – a yearning to settle down. Not to be always leaving, forever saying goodbye, but to have and to be and to stay. To belong.

Lawrence felt a surge of protectiveness rise up in him at the sight of his child. His hand found Arima's, their fingers intertwining as tightly as their lives. He looked at Arima as if he saw her for the first time.

Arima spoke into the silence.

'I wonder who it is.'

'It's our baby.'

'Yes.'

They gazed at one another, their eyes mirroring shared tears and each of them glimpsing in the other something they had not seen before. Or, perhaps, it had been there all along, shrouded on the edge of their conscious thoughts, and they had failed to recognize it, or had pushed it away.

Alone in the taxi, rain pounding the metal roof and lashing the pavements, Sarah wept tears of rage and frustration, pierced by a fear she could not name.

# Chapter 17

On Christmas Eve Robin stood in the doorway of his shop, chafing his hands together as he looked out across the court-yard. At half past four it was already dark and the traditional decorations of the Galleria made him feel as though he'd stepped back in time, the garlanded pillars and bristling holly wreaths in every door and window conjuring images of a Dickensian Christmas.

The Horniman was selling warm mulled wine by the gal-lon and the air was laced with the smell of chestnuts roast-ing somewhere close by. All very tasteful, if a little stylized for Robin's liking. On the fringe of the Galleria, the Christmas Shop was a lone outpost of festive tat, with an abundance of multi-coloured lights, flashing Santas and dancing snowmen decorations. They were the annoying kind activated by movement sensors so they sprang to life when you got too close. Robin had once had a bad experience with a singing reindeer at two o'clock in the morning when tiptoeing to bed at a friend's house after one too many sherries. He shud-dered at the memory.

The shop could not be seen from where Robin stood but he imagined he could perceive a faint glow coming through the archway, cast by a million tiny LED lights. The combined energy output was probably enough to power a small country.

Robin chuckled at the thought of Hannah trapped in the midst of it all, valiantly trying to draw attention to the many sleek and sophisticated decorations on offer, eclipsed by their brash, overstated cousins. She'd said as much on her last tea-break visit, which was becoming a regular thing.

'It is the Christmas Shop,' Robin pointed out, trying to hide a smile at her indignation. 'People will expect them to go to town on it at this time of year.'

'I know,' Hannah mumbled through a mouthful of mince pie. 'But there's such lovely stuff in there all year round and it's like . . . like we morph into the Blackpool illuminations on December the first. There's no need.' Robin had appreciated the analogy.

In his opinion it wasn't just shops but people who were supposed to morph into the human equivalent of the Blackpool illuminations on the first of December, brimming with festive cheer, bonhomie and love for all fellow men. For Robin Christmas meant an extended visit home, which entailed none of those things. He glanced at the rucksack leaning behind the counter and closed his eyes. Even with catching the latest possible train to Gravesend tonight, he'd still be with his parents a whole five days. It was hard to muster any sense of enthusiasm for the trip but he had promised and his dad had been embarrassingly grateful.

Arima was with the Abrahams for Christmas. Robin was unreasonably hurt that she hadn't offered to visit his parents. Not that he would expect her to stay, of course, but just for a day.

'Should old acquaintance be forgot' and all that. Okay, she wasn't his girlfriend, but they were close. There was history between them. Long history. He had hinted heavily and in the end came right out with the idea over lunch the previous week but Arima had deflected the invitation.

'Sarah wants me to stay at home in case of any problem with the baby,' she explained, standing on tiptoe to plant a kiss on Robin's cheek. 'Give them my love, though, won't you? Especially your dad.'

It was a decent excuse, though they both knew she wouldn't have come even if she could. If Arima ever bumped into his parents in the street she'd be genuinely delighted to see them but she shied away from formally arranged meetings. They weren't her style. For the first time since Arima had burst back into his life, Robin wondered how *her* parents were getting on. How could he have failed to ask after them? He didn't even know where they lived these days. Robin felt a pang of something like homesickness at the thought of seeing Arima's mother again. She had been like a parent to him.

'There's my first new year's resolution,' he decided, trying to stamp some warmth into his feet. His grey fingerless gloves were doing a poor job of keeping the circulation going in his hands. The blood had leached from his fingertips, leaving them numb and yellow-white like the hands of a corpse. Robin blew on them and flapped his hands in the direction of the electric heater. Another hour and he could close up.

'That won't do any good,' Hannah called, appearing from the tunnelled archway. Robin's gloom lifted at the sight of her trotting towards him, cheeks ruddy with cold and her regulation Santa hat askew on her head. Her hands were encased in thick woollen mittens and a bright blue scarf muffled her throat, one end trailing right down to her knees. She looked like something between a Muppet and a Christmas elf.

Robin felt his face break into a smile. 'Why won't it?' he called back. Hannah was so innocently comic it felt mean to laugh at her, and yet, he thought, seeing her eager face lit by those luminous green eyes as she drew nearer, she was such a nice person she wouldn't mind him laughing if she thought it would cheer him up. Knowing Hannah, she'd probably encourage it and take no offence, or at least not show it.

'Because,' she puffed, stopping in the doorway to catch her breath, 'your heater is useless.'

'That's a bit harsh,' Robin objected, feeling obliged to defend his property, however shoddy its performance. Hannah stepped inside and produced a paper bag from inside her coat.

'Truth hurts,' she said with a shrug, passing him a steaming cardboard cup.

'Yes, but there was no need to be so brutal. Ohhh!' Robin closed his eyes as the smell from the cup reached his nose. 'Is that . . . ?'

'Yep.' Hannah grinned triumphantly. 'Mulled wine. And I brought stollen too. Home-made.' She delved back into the bag and produced a couple of hefty-looking slices of cake wrapped in green paper napkins.

'You're an angel,' declared Robin, wincing a little as the heat from the cup set the blood pumping back into his numb fingers.

Hannah blushed prettily and raised her own cup in a toast. 'Merry Christmas.'

'Merry Christmas,' echoed Robin. 'And thanks, Han. This was just what I needed.' Hannah's stomach did a happy flip. Robin had never shortened her name before. That meant they were really friends. They huddled round the pathetic heater, talking and laughing about the minutiae of their day. 'What are you doing for Christmas?' Robin asked.

'I volunteered for a homeless charity this year.' Hannah wiped the last crumbs of stollen from her lips and scrunched her napkin into her pocket. 'My parents are on a Caribbean cruise.'

'Wow. Didn't you want to go too?'

Hannah wrinkled her nose.

'Nah. It's a bit decadent for me, lazing about on sun loungers and drinking cocktails all day. I'd get bored.'

'You'd really rather be serving Christmas dinner to the homeless?'

Hannah shrugged.

'Yes, I suppose I would. Signed up at church.' She looked up at Robin, anxious she'd said the wrong thing. 'Is that a bit weird?'

'Nope. Remarkable, I'd say.' Robin put his cup down and stooped to hug her. 'Saint Hannah of Bermondsey,' he pronounced, pecking her on the cheek.

'Oh, give over,' Hannah replied, swatting at his arm. 'I have to go.'

'You're a good sort, Hannah Templeton,' Robin called out as he waved her off at the door. Hannah raised a hand as she disappeared into the tunnel, feeling as though she'd hit the jackpot. Devastatingly beautiful and a passionate clinch would have been better, but a good sort and a kiss on the cheek wasn't a bad start. Usually nobody noticed her at all – unless she was physically in their way.

As Robin locked up and reluctantly shouldered his rucksack for the walk to London Bridge station, he realized he was going to miss Hannah's visits. She had a quiet, solid decency so lacking in people nowadays. When things got bad at his parents, Robin knew he would think of her decked out in an apron and that awful Santa hat, serving up Christmas lunch. Then he'd smile, take a deep breath, and make the best of it.

Arima didn't like to make a big deal of Christmas. This was a shocking betrayal of her roots, since Christmas was a huge celebration in the Basque country. On the other hand, Basque traditions were very much community-based so it was nigh on impossible to recreate them alone. Once or twice, Arima's mother had tried to fuse the Basque and British Christmases but the food and customs were too radically different. In the main, childhood Christmases had been spent with Arima's relatives in San Sebastián as far back as she could remember. The last few years had been just her and Benoit in the camper, doing their thing.

Christmas was business as usual. Midnight Mass, then a couple of drinks, followed by a quiet day. They didn't really bother with presents either. Like most men she knew, Benoit always left buying a present until the last moment on Christmas Eve. She had gathered a collection of strange gifts usually bought from the late-night petrol station. He would smile, say he loved her and then give her something to use in the camper. Somewhere, she still had the miniature vacuum cleaner from last year. It had never worked very well and attempted to suck up dust like an asthmatic dachshund.

For some reason, Arima had imagined Christmas with the Abrahams would be much the same. Just the three of them, with Lawrence's mother if she felt up to it.

Had she known what lay in store she would have made swift arrangements to be elsewhere, even to the point of accepting Robin's invitation to Gravesend. As it was, when Christmas Day came Arima had no choice but to go with the flow.

'Arima?' the voice whispered close by.

'Urgh?' It was still dark. Was there somebody sitting on her bed?

'Merry Christmas,' said Lawrence.

'Same,' Arima mumbled without waking up. Lawrence remained perched on a corner of the mattress, waited five minutes, then tried again.

'Arima?'

'Yes?' she answered, wondering why Lawrence was in her room.

'It's morning. Merry Christmas.'

'You too.' She rolled over and began to snore. Lawrence couldn't help smiling at her, limbs flung out like a starfish and long curls of hair tangled every which way on the pillow. She was so different to Sarah. For several moments he couldn't take his eyes off her. Lawrence wanted to touch her face, to feel her skin. Then, he reigned in the thoughts, took control. He rattled the gargantuan breakfast tray balanced on his knee and coughed loudly. Arima grunted.

'Arima?'

'What?' Oh God. It was a recurring nightmare. Lawrence again.

'It's Christmas day. I've brought breakfast.'

'What?' Arima woke too quickly and experienced the sleeper's equivalent of the bends, like a deep sea diver surfacing before his body makes the necessary adjustments. She thrashed about in the bedclothes, temporarily unsure of where she was. 'Merry Christmas, hi. Um, breakfast, I can't ... I don't . . . can't find my arm, sorry.' Lawrence reached out and snapped the bedside lamp on. Arima realized her arm was pinned beneath her pillow and pulled it out. 'Oh. Thanks.'

'It's a pleasure. Are you going to sit up?'

'Er . . . yes?'

'Great.' Lawrence plonked the enormous tray onto Arima's lap and flourished a teapot at her. 'Lemon and ginger?' Arima was too busy examining the daunting array of breakfast choices to reply. Smoked salmon and cream cheese, Parma ham, cinnamon spiced buns, croissants, pain au chocolat, champagne and some kind of non-alcoholic pretend champagne. Her eye fell on the packet tucked incongruously between the teapot and cafetière.

'Just a ginger nut to be going on with,' she mumbled. 'Then I'll see after that.'

'Your wish is my command,' said Lawrence, splitting the wrapper open and shaking three biscuits onto a delicate china plate.

She noticed his smile. He was still good looking – for an older man. After a couple of biscuits, Arima's brain settled back into her body.

'I could get used to this,' she mused, stretching out and wriggling her cramped toes.

'Merry Christmas!' cried Sarah, bursting into the room. She wore a classic navy shift dress and had immaculate hair and make-up. Or, maybe not, thought Arima, as Sarah also took up a position on the end of the bed.

'Merry Christmas, darling.' Lawrence calmly handed Sarah a mug of coffee and proffered the tray in her direction. Sarah helped herself to a little of everything and settled down to eat. It was too weird.

'Do you always congregate on someone's bed for a picnic on Christmas day?' Arima asked, reaching for a croissant. If it made her sick, Lawrence and Sarah might leave her in peace.

'No,' chuckled Lawrence. 'We usually have a posh breakfast downstairs but since you've not been too well we thought we'd come to you.'

'Mohammed and the mountain sort of thing,' Sarah chimed in. 'And it's such a manic day we thought you'd appreciate an extra half hour in bed.'

Arima shrank back against the padded headboard. That didn't sound good.

'Manic? Manic how?'

'Don't panic,' Sarah said. 'It's not that bad. Just Christmas lunch for ourselves, Eva and a few friends, then some of the godchildren over for the afternoon . . .'

'And their families . . .' Lawrence added.

'Open house for the neighbours . . .'

'. . . and the annual Trivial Pursuits match in the evening,' Lawrence finished, pouring himself a glass of champagne.

'Who with?' Arima tried to keep the horror from her voice. If there was a hell, general knowledge trivia games were surely in it.

'Oh, whoever's still here,' Sarah explained. 'Usually two or three teams. Then we do all the clearing up about midnight and have a large mulled wine or two before bed.'

'But you don't have to do that part,' Lawrence put in.

'I . . . I thought it would be a quiet day,' Arima stammered. 'Just us?'

'Oh, no!' laughed Sarah. 'Imagine how miserable that would be, the three of us sat staring at each other all day long. We'd barely be able to play charades.'

'You know, I'm not feeling so good today,' Arima began, squirming beneath the covers.

Lawrence patted her gently on the arm.

'We anticipated that,' he said earnestly. 'So we've toned things down this year. You must go for a rest whenever you need to.'

'What time is it?' Arima enquired.

'Half past eight,' Sarah replied. Arima wondered whether nine o'clock would be too soon for a nap.


The schedule of events was every bit as bad as it sounded. In fact, it was worse because Lawrence had omitted to mention the singsong round the piano, obligatory Christmas quiz and the treasure hunt for the children. It was bedlam.

Usually, Arima threw herself into parties but now all she wanted to do was curl up by a warm fire with a drink and a good book. Socializing was fine as long as you could retreat from it. Her stomach protesting from the small amount of roast dinner she had managed to keep down, Arima took refuge on the sofa as wave after wave of people arrived throughout the afternoon. The normally pristine house was transformed into a chaotic thoroughfare, with bits of food and wrapping paper crushed underfoot and a drink spilled roughly every two minutes.

The Christmas tree loomed over the proceedings, shedding its needles like spiky tears as an ever-changing menagerie of children whooped and danced about, tugging rudely at its decorations and diving beneath the laden branches in search of presents, as if they hadn't already received more than most people did in a year.

'Obscene, isn't it?' said a voice in her ear. Arima turned and found Eva settling herself down beside her on the sofa. 'All this, I mean,' she explained, waving a hand at the throng of guests. 'Bit over the top.'

Arima was at a loss. Was the expression on her face so obvious?

'Well, it's . . . very busy,' she said, in what she hoped was a neutral voice.

'That's putting it mildly.' Eva tucked a fringed plaid blanket over her knees and checked that her pearl-drop earrings were still in place. 'Sarah and Lawrence like a busy house at Christmas. The empty spaces in one's life need more camouflaging at this time of year, I always think.' Arima was still grappling for a diplomatic reply when Eva abruptly changed the subject. 'How do you feel, my dear?'

Arima panicked. 'Uh, fine. Thank you.' Did Eva know? Was she allowed to tell?

'Lawrence keeps me up to speed,' Eva said quietly. She was smiling but something in her eyes kept Arima on her guard. This lady didn't trust her, or suspected she had reason not to. Why?

'The baby seems healthy, so it's all looking good,' she replied.

'Excellent news, of course,' said Eva, swaying gracefully to one side as a toy aeroplane zoomed past her ear and crash-landed onto the piano. 'But that wasn't what I meant. How do you feel about . . . losing a child?' She looked Arima directly in the face, her eyes diamond-hard, ready to ferret out the things Arima might leave unsaid. 'Because that *is* what you've agreed to.'

'It's really not like that,' Arima said, one hand creeping across her stomach. The gesture wasn't lost on Eva, whose mouth tightened as she saw that her words had hit their mark.

'Is it not?' she murmured. 'How would you describe it then?'

'I'm just the incubator.' Arima scanned the room, looking for Lawrence to come and call his mother off. What was her problem? Eva didn't miss that either.

'I think my son is in the kitchen, serving drinks,' she said lightly. 'No doubt he'll be back in a minute, if you need him.'

The old lady was scaring her now. 'Excuse me,' she mumbled, almost falling off the sofa in her haste to get out of the conversation. 'I'm going upstairs for a rest. I'll be in my room if anyone needs me.'

'Of course, my dear,' said Eva, baring her teeth in a smile. 'Off you go. If – anyone – needs you, I'll send them up. And please forgive my bluntness. It's my age, you know.' Fear coiled round her heart as she watched Arima stumble from the room, stepping over two small girls engaged in a tug-of-war over a toy pony. 'So,' she whispered. 'I was right.' Hell would freeze over before that girl gave up the child. Strangely, the girl herself didn't yet seem aware of it. Eva shook her head. There was nothing she could do but wait, watch and pray, knowing much but able to do precious little. The curse of old age.

Once out of the room, Arima ran for the stairs, desperate to put some distance between herself and Lawrence's mind-reading mother. She was deeply disturbed by Eva's frank questioning and the manner in which she'd framed the questions. 'How do you feel about losing a child?' No one had put it to her as baldly as that before. Everything had been couched in careful terms, the surrogacy spoken of as a gift from one woman to another; making a childless couple's dream come true. 'How do you feel about losing a child?' put an entirely different spin on things. Arima bit her lip. Maybe, after all, it would have been wise to speak to one of those surrogacy counsellors Sarah had flagged up in the early stages. But it had all seemed so straightforward until she saw the little baby inside her.

To complicate matters, Lawrence had switched from ignoring her to being sweet and attentive and instead of feeling suffocated, she loved it and found herself seeking him out at every turn. Everything felt right and wrong at the same time. Arima had gone from being cool and controlled to feeling like a child on a rollercoaster, with no idea which way was up and screaming to get off.

She crashed into her room and threw herself on the bed, breathing in angry gasps. Hormones, she told herself, just more of the dreaded hormones. She lay on her side, forcing her breath into a regular rhythm and willing sleep to come.

Just as Arima was starting to relax, a scuffling sound beneath the bed sent her heart rate rocketing. Surely not a rat . . . not in here. Arima held her breath and listened. There it was again.

'Who's there?' she called stupidly, as though any lurking rodents would pop up with a cheery greeting and an apology for disturbing her. There was further scuffling, then a forehead and two eyes rose up at the edge of the quilted throw like a little hippo emerging from the water. Arima couldn't tell whether it was a girl or a boy.

'Don't tell,' it whispered hoarsely.

'Okay. Are you hiding?' The head nodded.

'For a game?' A shake for no ruffled the blunt-cut fringe.

Arima felt rather nonplussed by the hippo child. Then it came to her.

'Ah. You're running away.'

Hippo child nodded.

'On Christmas day? That's a shame. Have you been told off or something?'

Another vigorous shake of the head. They regarded each other in silence for a few moments, Arima wondering how to resolve this odd predicament, the child's eyes at once pleading and defiant. She thought she recognized the face, what she could see of it anyhow, from dinner. In any case, she could hardly go to sleep with a runaway child crouched under the bed.

'Tell you what,' she said, sitting up and swinging her legs over the side of the bed. 'I know a much cooler hide-out than this.' The eyes widened as the hippo child mulled this over. It was wrong to go places with strangers but . . . this lady seemed strange in a good way. She hadn't shouted, for example, or said that running away was naughty. Also, she had left at least half her vegetables at the meal table earlier on *and then* had pudding. Arima's credentials were good. The child, a boy of about six, stood up cautiously as Arima held out her hand. 'Come on,' she said. 'I'll show you some pictures of a *real* Christmas. Then we can decide where you're running away to.' Hand in hand, they tiptoed down the stairs.

'I'm Arima, by the way.'

'Funny name.'

'So's Arthur.'

'How did you know my name?'

'It's what everyone was calling you at dinner.'

'Oh.' The boy looked crestfallen. 'For a minute I thought you might be magic.'

Arima laughed.

'No, but I've got a stash of ginger nuts and a house on wheels. Will that do?'

'*Cool.*'

In his parents' cramped, chilly house in Gravesend, Robin, like Arthur, was also hiding out from his mother, though for different reasons, and on the pretext of being useful. After eating their Marks and Spencer's turkey dinner on trays in the lounge, Robin had parked his mum in front of the

Queen's speech with a small sherry and bolted to the kitchen to do a bit of clearing up.

To begin with, the kitchen work surfaces were tacky to the touch and the units were in dire need of a scrub. While down on his hands and knees Robin couldn't help noticing the state of the floor. The blue and cream checked lino was bubbling up in places where water had got in underneath. There was nothing he could do about that but he could certainly attack the stains, many of which looked to have been there a long time. It was something to do and it made him feel more productive than sitting in the lounge with his mother's unflinching apathy all too obvious. Still, she had got dressed today in honour of Christmas. That was something to be grateful for. Robin cocked his head towards the lounge.

'Okay, mum?'

'Fine, son. Fine.'

Robin leaned on the long-handled mop and surveyed the magnitude of the task ahead of him. Generally, his dad would keep on top of the housework as best he could in between his shifts as a bus driver at the local depot and his church choir commitments. Like his son, Tom Jennings was a conscientious, caring man. Seeing the kitchen in this state conveyed more to Robin about the current lie of the land than anything his dad might have said. Robin dunked the mop into the old-fashioned metal bucket and swished the disinfectant solution across the filthy floor, glad that he had persuaded his dad to go out for the afternoon. The church was hosting a Christmas dinner for the elderly and disabled of the parish, and the choir were providing the entertainment.

'Go on, Dad,' Robin had urged, practically pushing him out the door. 'I'm here nearly a week. What's one afternoon? You'll enjoy it.'

'But it's Christmas Day, son,' his father protested weakly. 'Family time.'

'We'll still be here when you get back,' Robin said firmly and closed the door.

Quicksand. The old code word between Robin and Arima. Their childhoods were mirror images, except that the depression hit Arima's father, whereas in Robin's family it had taken his mum, attacking the heart of the home. In their childish way, their secret code had captured the essence of the illness in a single word – quicksand, slowly, inexorably sucking people into the ground until even breathing became a struggle. They had watched, beleaguered onlookers to the mortification of a parent consumed by gloom.

As children, Robin and Arima had understood each other's lives so completely that nothing ever needed to be said beyond that one little word. For both of them, the relief of having no need to explain or dissemble was immeasurable, but this was true for Robin most of all.

His home life was blighted by his mother's illness. Though his dad did his best to cover all the bases, no friends could ever be invited for tea because there might not be food in the house. His mum lived in her dressing gown for days on end, her eyes dull and her hair unwashed.

Robin was always the scruffy kid, late to school with odd packed lunches he had foraged from the meagre fridge pickings. It was different for Arima. Her father, though equally affected, tended to sleep a lot in the daytime and this enabled Arima's mother to shield her from the worst.

Alaia Middleton was a slight, birdlike woman of formidable character who created a warm, loving home where all visitors were welcome at her table. Whatever time Robin arrived at the house next-door-but-one, his needs were met. If he came during the day, a meal was set before him. If he appeared at night, Alaia tucked him into bed in the spare room with a mug of hot milk and the same strict lights-out curfew she gave Arima. Once he was asleep she would quietly let Tom Jennings know where his son was, deflecting his every attempt at gratitude. In the morning, Robin would find his clothes folded at the end of his bed, washed, pressed and even darned when necessary.

Those years, taking him from aged nine to twelve, were the happiest of Robin's young life. Even now, tears came to his eyes at the memory of the Middletons' departure from Gravesend. Itchy feet, Alaia said, trying to press all her love for him into one last hug, but Robin knew better. When the depression was at its worst, the Middletons moved on. New place, new face, new start. It was Peter's way of coping. It was as if the house was so full of the gloom it became a living creature to be left behind. Robin had thought he would never see them again.

'Just shows how wrong you can be,' he sighed, wiping the sweat from his brow and examining his handiwork. 'About all sorts of things.' Arima, so like Alaia in looks, had inherited her wanderlust from her father. Alaia's rare gift for home-making and hospitality remained her own. Robin was convinced her horror at Arima's surrogacy would know no bounds, but that wasn't his battle to fight. He already had his hands full.

Holed up in the camper van, Arima was discovering that ginger nuts and tales of a traditional Basque Christmas were a winning formula with Arthur. She had dug out the last surviving photo album of her mother's to illustrate her stories as they squashed up together on the padded bench-style seat that doubled as her bed. Arima had draped one of her mother's blankets over their knees to ward off the chill. Arthur gazed up at her, his brow furrowed in concentration.

'So, where you come from, Father Christmas doesn't come?'

'That's right,' said Arima. 'It's always Olentzero, the coal man.'

Arthur was appalled. 'We only get coal if we're naughty. Didn't you ever get presents, not even if you were really good?' At six, he lacked the vocabulary to express his outrage at this towering injustice, but he squeezed Arima's hand in wordless sympathy.

Arima smiled at him. 'No, no. Olentzero brings the presents instead of Father Christmas.'

'So . . . it's like a swap then? Olent – Olent –' he screwed up his face, stumbling over the unfamiliar syllables.

'Olentzero.'

'Yes, him. He does the job to help out because Father Christmas is so busy?'

'That's it,' agreed Arima, impressed by Arthur's rationale.

'And Father Christmas takes the coal to Basque children who are naughty?'

'Oh, I don't know about that,' Arima said, keeping her face poker-straight. 'I was always very, very good.'

'Hmm. That's lucky.' Arthur continued to browse through the album on Arima's knee, stopping to ask questions whenever a photo caught his interest.

Arima hadn't seen the photos for years and had to think hard to remember all the names. Satisfying Arthur's lively curiosity stretched the limits of her memory but as she explained the old customs of the Basque people to the eager boy, Arima recalled her mother doing the same for her – patiently fielding each question so the knowledge would be handed on to another generation. That was how it should be, Arima abruptly understood. From mother to daughter, father to son. If the chain was broken the old traditions would die out.

On the last page of the album they came across two black and white photos pasted side by side. Arthur prodded the first one.

'So this one is you,' he said, indicating a ten-year-old Arima in cut-off jeans and a ragged sweatshirt, her hair scraped into bunches. 'But who's this you're cuddling?'

Arima glanced at the photo. 'That's Robin,' she said. 'A very old and dear friend.'

'He's not old,' Arthur scoffed, flicking a disdainful finger at the tubby boy with a pudding basin haircut.

'I mean I've known him for a long time,' Arima explained patiently. 'Many years.'

'Oh.' Arthur turned his attention to the last photo. 'And this one?' The photo had captured a woman with long, black hair in the act of tossing Arima into the air. Her head was thrown back, beaming up at the child screaming with laughter.

'My mummy,' said Arima softly. 'Alaia.'

'What's that mean?'

'It means joy.'

'She looks like a nice mummy,' Arthur said authoritatively.

'She was.'

'Is she dead then?' he asked, as if he was blessed with the wisdom of the ages.

Arima hesitated before nodding.

'Oh. Sorry about that.'

'That's okay.' Arima closed the album and laid the memories aside. She couldn't cry in front of Arthur. After a few hard swallows she mustered a smile and said, 'So. Are you still running away from home or shall we go back indoors?'

Arthur considered his options.

'In,' he said finally. 'I haven't got my bedtime bear with me so I can't sleep out. Anyway, I reckon they'll be good and worried by now.' He gave Arima a hopeful look as she slid the door back. 'But can I run away here another time?'

'Be my guest.' Arima helped him jump down to the pavement. 'If you let me know you're coming, I'll have the ginger nuts ready.'

When they reached the front door, Arthur slipped his hand into hers. 'I wish you were my mum,' he said. 'You'd be ace.'

# Chapter 18

At six o'clock on a bitter January morning, Sarah woke Lawrence with a sharp jab to the ribs.

'Team talk,' she announced, pulling the covers back and exposing her husband to a blast of cold air.

'Why now? Why today?' Lawrence moaned, curling into the foetal position in a futile attempt to retain body heat.

'Because I've been awake half the night,' Sarah retorted. 'Thinking.'

'Is it the boy names again?' Lawrence asked wearily, pressing his face into the pillow. At least his nose was warm. 'I thought we'd agreed to let that lie for a while.'

The last thing he wanted right now was another stand-up row over the suitability of Maximilian, Horatio and Jared, Sarah's current top three choices. Max he could live with but to call a child Horatio was setting them up for a lifetime of bad Hamlet jokes. You might as well stick a sign saying 'pick on me' on the poor kid's back. As for Jared, the less said about that, the better. Lawrence was well aware that his role in name choosing was on a strict consultation level only but he felt honour-bound to fight the poor child's corner as far as possible.

'It's not about that.' Sarah grabbed his dressing gown and strode to the door. 'Bathroom, five minutes.'

Lawrence rolled out of bed and landed heavily on the floor. Why did the women in this house have a thing about bathrooms and heavy conversations? He was still traumatized from the last one. The discovery Sarah had taken his slippers did nothing to improve his temper. However, it would be impolitic to keep his wife waiting. It had taken her a long time to get over her disappointment at missing the twelve-week scan and since then Lawrence had found himself on thin ice on several occasions.

At times, Sarah seemed almost jealous, as though she had been deliberately left out of the equation that day. She had mounted the photo of the scan in a frame and put it on her bedside table, where it could be seen and enjoyed solely by her.

Lawrence made no comment, nor did he mention he had bought two photo scans. The second could be found poking out from beneath Arima's pillow if you looked carefully when delivering her morning tea and ginger nuts, and Lawrence did look carefully at Arima now. He often found himself staring at her, examining her every contour, wanting to be near her.

The connection he had felt with the little life inside her was getting stronger with every passing day and he fussed over Arima, attending to her slightest need so swiftly that Sarah was left standing every time.

Lawrence padded barefoot onto the landing, his toes bunched up against the cold. As he passed Arima's bedroom he saw that the door had been left ajar. Before he was consciously aware of what he was doing, he had pushed it open and stepped inside, moving quietly to the bedside.

In the dark he could just make out the silhouette of the sleeping girl, the cover turned back to reveal her arms folded loosely across her swelling stomach. She looked so vulnerable. Lawrence had to fight back the urge to climb into the bed and wrap himself around Arima and the baby like a human shield, to know beyond doubt that they were safe. He forced himself to back away, shocked at the fierce response Arima evoked in him. How long had he been standing there? What if she had woken and found him by her bed in the dark? How would that make him look?

'Keep it together, man,' Lawrence muttered, moving swiftly to the bathroom.

'Finally,' called Sarah from behind the shower screen.

'Sorry,' Lawrence replied, fumbling in the cupboard beneath the sink for his shaving equipment. 'Dropped off again.' He filled the basin, massaged shaving foam onto his face and focused on long, smooth strokes with the razor, leaving snowy tracks across his cheek. Sarah shut the water off and stepped out of the shower, briskly towelling herself dry.

'I think Arima should give up work altogether,' she said bluntly, crossing the room to stand beside Lawrence at the sink. 'Let's face it, she's hardly been at work for weeks as it is. Her health hasn't been good and we need to be absolutely sure she's looking after herself properly.' Lawrence swished his razor in the sink and started on the other cheek. Sarah's eyes followed him in the mirror, trying to read his reaction. 'We've already had the referral to the hospital because of all the sickness and weight loss,' she went on, taking his silence for dissent. 'And there have been moments when she's been borderline for hospital admission. I've read up on it. If the sickness causes prolonged dehydration your kidneys can fail.'

'I agree,' said Lawrence, reaching for a flannel.

'You *must* take the risk seriously, Lawrence,' Sarah snapped, pulling a second towel from the rail to wrap her hair in a turban. 'We have to take every precaution with the baby's safety. And Arima's, of course,' she added as an afterthought.

'I said I agree,' Lawrence repeated.

'Oh.' Sarah was momentarily silenced, all the arguments she'd carefully constructed while lying awake last night made redundant by Lawrence's lack of resistance. She waited as he patted his face dry with a towel.

Lawrence looked up, feeling her eyes on him. 'What?'

'Nothing. It's just – that's it? You agree? No conditions?'

Lawrence shrugged.

'No. It's Arima you need to convince, not me.'

'Right. Well, I'll talk to Arima today and let work know,' Sarah said, perplexed but delighted by his support. 'There'll be no problem once I explain.' She waited for his customary objection to going public about the surrogacy.

'Fine.' Lawrence ditched his pyjamas and went towards the shower, extremely glad of the under-floor heating Sarah had insisted on. Emboldened by this unprecedented level of compliance, Sarah pressed on.

'Oh, Lawrence?'

There was more coming and Sarah's tone said he wasn't going to like it. Lawrence turned, one foot already in the shower tray. 'Yes?'

Sarah took a deep breath.

'I think you should take Arima to visit your mother. Eva seemed a bit cool towards her at Christmas, did you notice?'

'I'm a man, remember?'

'Good point. Just take my word for it, then.' Sarah adjusted her towel as the turban began to slip. 'I know Arima will be moving on in due course anyway but we don't want any hostility in the meantime. I could take them for a girlie lunch if you like?'

'No need. I'm on it.' Lawrence slid the door shut and hit the power. 'In fact,' he called over the spray, 'I might take a long lunch and go today if Arima's up to it.'

'Okay.' Sarah marched over to the shower and stuck her face against the screen, peering in suspiciously. 'Who are you and what have you done with the real Lawrence?'

'Don't knock it,' Lawrence laughed, kissing the inside of the screen where Sarah's face was squashed against it.

'I won't.' But I'll keep my eye on you, she added silently, shivering as she left the warm bathroom in search of clothes.

Lawrence was exhibiting very non-Lawrence behaviour and it was more than a little strange. It was such a relief to know that he was finally on board with the surrogacy but after months of wrangling and heavy persuasion it was, well, odd, that he should suddenly be so keen. 'You're never satisfied, Sarah,' she chided, pulling a warm woollen dress from the wardrobe. 'You want something but when you get it, you're still not happy.'

She could tell herself whatever she liked; the incongruity remained. Lawrence had never wanted to spend any time with Arima at all, quite the opposite. Sarah wrestled on a pair of opaque tights and tried to thrust aside the insidious whisper that had begun weaving through her thoughts of late, tightening like a noose around her mind and attempting to throttle her careful rationale. *It's only natural, Sarah. It's their child, after all. Theirs.*

'No,' she said stubbornly, reaching for the reassurance of the framed picture by her bed. '*My* child. Mine and Lawrence's. Our gift.'

The day was cold. Lawrence still thought of the morning conversation with Sarah as he drove through the streets with Arima next to him.

'Could we go for a walk in the park before we call in at the home?' Arima asked, casting a wistful look through the car window towards the open spaces of Greenwich Park. She hadn't been out of the house properly for several weeks and it was making her restless and irritable. When Lawrence suggested a trip out she had leapt at the chance, despite the obligation of visiting Eva.

'I don't know if that's such a good idea,' Lawrence said, trying to assess her strength. There were dark shadows beneath Arima's eyes and the loss of weight had given her face a fragile look, the bones a shade too well defined beneath her skin. 'You look a bit pale.'

Arima rolled her eyes.

'It's winter and I've been cooped up. Of course I'm pale. I need fresh air.' She also needed time to gather herself before facing his mother but she could hardly say that to Lawrence. She laid a hand on his arm. 'Please?' she begged. 'I promise to be good.'

Lawrence laughed, unable resist. 'Okay, but wrap up. It's freezing today.' He saw a parking space close to the park entrance and swung in. 'We've got half an hour. Let's go.'

They passed through the arched gates and struck out in the direction of the Observatory, ducking their heads against the wind. The park was bound to be quiet in such weather but there were a few hardy souls dotted here and there; seasoned joggers and a few mothers cajoling frozen children along the paths. They looked like little astronauts, moving awkwardly in their over-padded snowsuits, red-faced with temper or the cold. No doubt the walk would do them good but Lawrence felt sorry for them all the same. Seeing them brought back memories of walking to school in all weathers as a child and spending the first lesson huddled over his desk, certain he'd never be warm again. His reverie was rudely interrupted by Arima prodding him on the arm.

'Will you buy me an ice-cream?' she asked.

'Arima, it's January.'

'How about a lolly?'

'You must be mad.'

'It's not my fault,' Arima pouted. 'It's the hormones.'

'Ah, the hormone excuses. Very convenient.' Lawrence glanced over at Arima, her face wrapped up to the nose in one of her crazy home-knitted creations. If you were generous you might call it a scarf but he strongly suspected she had chopped up one of her stripy blankets and sewn some tassels on the end. She looked like a psychedelic version of a partially mummified Egyptian. 'Is it really the hormones?' he asked, leading her along the same path Sarah had followed with Beatrice in the summer. Now the trees were bare, their branches reaching upwards like clawed hands as though they could grasp the sky and shake down spring. The branches rattled like angry sabres in the breeze.

Lawrence liked the bleak beauty of the park in winter, despite the cold.

'Well . . . no,' admitted Arima. 'I just want an ice-cream.'

'I applaud your honesty.'

'So you'll buy me one?'

He grinned down at her.

'No.'

Without warning, Arima gave him a hard shove so that he toppled off the path onto a muddy patch of grass. Lawrence yelled in surprise and leaped to safety, his shoes coated to the ankle. 'These are brand new!' he spluttered. 'I can't go back to work looking like this!'

'Keep your feet under the desk then,' Arima sniffed. 'Serves you right for being tight.'

Lawrence raised his hands in defeat.

'Alright,' he sighed. 'If you stop trying to beat me up, I'll buy you a wretched ice-cream.'

Arima's eyes glinted with mischief.

'Don't bother,' she replied. 'I've gone off the idea.'

'I don't think I've ever met anybody quite so infuriating as you,' he said, putting an arm around her shoulders to take the sting from his words.

'Thanks,' Arima said smugly.

She leaned into him as they walked on, allowing him to take her weight and shield her from the worst of the wind. It felt good to let herself rely on another person after years of fierce independence.

As they walked, Arima felt something inside her give way. Perhaps knowing that the tiny life she carried was entirely dependent on her made her realize that needing others did not necessarily equal weakness: it could be a good thing. Whatever the catalyst, the part of Arima that had frozen people out in the past through fear of loss or stubborn pride dissolved in Lawrence's nearness like snow in sunshine, unable to survive in his presence. This man wanted to take care of her, as others had before. What was extraordinary was she wanted to let him. It was an alien sensation but not at all unpleasant. She moved closer to him, letting her head drop onto his shoulder as she mulled over the thought again and again.

'Are you ready to go back?' Lawrence asked, mistaking the gesture for fatigue. 'Mum won't mind if we're a bit early.'

'No,' said Arima quickly, pointing to a wooden bench flanked by clusters of budding snowdrops, their teardrop petals swaying in the wind. 'Let's sit. The fresh air is doing me good.' Lawrence guided Arima to the seat and eased himself down beside her.

'Your hands look frozen.'

'They are a bit,' Arima admitted. 'But it's worth it to be out.'

'Here.' Lawrence took her hands and began chafing them between his own.

'My dad brought me here once or twice when I was little,' Arima remarked, inclining her head towards the dome of the Observatory. 'For astronomy lessons.'

'Oh yes, I remember – you're a star watcher.'

'If you want to call it that,' she said offhandedly. 'It was our special thing, Dad and me.' Their only thing, in fact, but she didn't want to share that. 'I keep his telescope in the van.'

'You are endlessly surprising, do you know that?' Arima stared at their hands, her slender fingers dwarfed by Lawrence's. She slid her fingers through his as he rubbed the back of her hand with his thumb. They sat like that for some time, each exploring their own thoughts while guessing at the other's. Eventually, Lawrence broke the silence.

'Doesn't he watch the stars any more?'

'Pardon?'

'Your dad. You say you've got his telescope.'

'Oh.' Arima leaned into Lawrence, dipping her head to conceal her face. 'No. He doesn't use it now.'

Lawrence heard the pain in her voice but didn't pry. Instead, he tilted his head slightly so that it rested on Arima's, offering wordless comfort. She could feel the pulse beating in his neck, the warmth of his breath on her hair. Suddenly, her hand tightened on his.

'Here, quick,' she said, tugging his hand across and pressing it hard against her middle, her fingers splayed over his. 'Feel it?'

Lawrence concentrated. For a moment there was nothing, then just as he was about to withdraw his hand he felt it. No more than a flicker, a tiny ripple against his palm, but it was there.

'Yes,' he said, his throat tight with emotion. 'Yes.'

Love and elation swept over him and Arima pulled back to see his face. He moved closer. Their lips met. They were kissing, carried along on the crest of the wave as the wind gusted round them and the winter flowers nodded their assent. *Yes. They feel it.*

Later, Lawrence couldn't have said how long they stayed like that, wrapped round each other on the bench, heedless of passers-by as they kissed and kissed.

All he remembered was the feeling, the depth of love and pride that had obliterated everything else. Whether it was love for Arima or love for the child, he didn't know. Could they be separated? Guilt and confusion consumed him. He had never kissed anyone but Sarah since they had been married – nor had he ever wanted to. But in the midst of it all, a single point of clarity stood out like a star in the night sky – this encounter with love went beyond anything he'd ever known.

Here, sealed in a kiss on a park bench was the loose thread in the plan, the hidden enemy he had sensed. Now it had struck, and Lawrence was helpless against it.

Arima's heart spoke plainly, her loyalty to Sarah sloughed away like dead skin. This baby bound her to Lawrence for life. Her baby . . . their child . . . all bets were off.

Eva waited all afternoon for her son, sitting by the window to watch for his arrival. Lawrence had never missed a visit. When at last it grew too dark to see, she drew her curtains and left the room, her frail shoulders hunched as though they bore the weight of the world.

Even if Sarah had not received the call from her mother-in-law, she would have known something was wrong when her husband returned home with Arima. The lie that slid off his tongue was too smooth, his eyes over-bright as he filled the silence with inane chatter and questions about her day. He was not himself. And Arima – Arima was glowing, her whole being thrumming with quiet joy as she gave Sarah the news about the baby.

Sarah smiled graciously and said nothing to indicate the cold suspicion consuming her heart, piece by piece. She prepared supper, made cups of tea and watched from the shadows, biding her time. Waiting, always waiting. There would be a time for action, she told herself, gouging her nails into her palms as she lay in bed that night. But not until she had the child.

# Chapter 19

February the fourteenth came quickly; the night before Arima went to the hospital for her twenty-week scan, Lawrence and Sarah argued. It was obvious to Sarah he desperately wanted to go with Arima. Sarah was adamant he would not.

'I don't see why we can't all be there,' Lawrence had protested like an angry child.

'Because . . . there's no need,' Sarah replied. 'Two is plenty.'

'That's not a reason.'

'Tough. It's *my* turn, and you're not going.' Her words were final.

She had drawn the bedcovers up to her chin and turned her back, firmly signalling that the conversation was over. She knew it was petty and almost relented in the morning when she saw how genuinely disappointed Lawrence was.

Then Arima had entered the room and looked at Lawrence. Sarah hardened her heart at the sight of the smile that lit her husband's face. There was nothing 'going on' between them, she repeated over and over, forcing herself to dismiss the idea.

Arima and Lawrence were chalk and cheese, to say nothing of the age difference. And yet, there was something snug developing in their manner towards each other that rankled. The dynamic in the house had shifted. Sarah was the one left out, or so it seemed to her. Plus there'd been that afternoon last month. Why had they lied about where they'd been? And where had they been?

Sarah had asked no questions yet but they were there nonetheless, unwelcome squatters inhabiting the dark corners of her mind. She picked her way delicately through each day, denying suspicions, quelling fears, no longer sure of her ground.

Whenever she and Lawrence were alone, things were as they had always been; he was loving, affectionate, and exasperatingly meticulous. Arima's presence in a room caused an instant change in the atmosphere. Somehow she had put herself centre stage, the spotlight falling full on her face, drawing every scrap of attention from Lawrence. Sarah was left with the uncomfortable sensation of being the understudy in her own life. Her thoughts had become so fractured there was a constant debate playing in her head.

*They're getting too close.*

*You're imagining things, Sarah. She's a friend.*

*Perhaps you should remind her of that.*

*He would never . . . but he IS a man . . .*

On and on it went, impossible to mute. Sarah didn't know what to do but fortify her mental defences, hold tightly to her marriage and soldier on.

The appointment turned out to be the first of the day and was so straightforward the women were home by eleven o'clock, complete with an up-to-date photo of the baby. The frame for it was already waiting on Sarah's dressing table. She hoped they might get one more before the birth so she'd have a trio.

'How about a cup of tea?' suggested Arima, flopping down on the sofa.

'Lovely,' Sarah replied.

She looked expectantly at Arima, who made no move to get up. She had sprawled out full length without even attempting to remove her coat, hat or scarf.

'Sorry,' Arima said, her grin contradicting the apology in her voice. 'I'm exhausted.' She kicked off her shoes and put her feet up on the sofa as if to emphasize her point.

'Already?' Sarah's voice was sharp. 'You've only been up a few hours.'

'Horrible, isn't it?' Arima sighed. 'And no sign of improvement. Honestly, you have no idea. So much for the bursting-with-energy second trimester. I'm so glad you persuaded me to give up work.' Sarah stalked from the room before she said something she might regret. 'Oh, decaff tea, one sugar please,' Arima called after her.

In the kitchen, Sarah peeled off her leather gloves and slapped them down on the counter as though issuing a challenge. *Honestly, you have no idea.* Of course she had no idea! How could she? Arima was deliberately rubbing her nose in it.

Sarah filled the kettle and slammed it down on its base, then took the rest of her temper out on the primrose-yellow teacups, narrowly avoiding breaking the handle off one of them as she crashed it onto the tray. It was insufferable, she thought, allowing herself a silent rant. *She* was insufferable. Pretending she couldn't even make a cup of tea, when Sarah spent every free moment running about after her, making bizarre vegetarian meals, checking her blood sugar hadn't dropped, blending endless fresh fruit smoothies to ensure the right amount of vitamins were taken on board each day and scouring the shops for ginger nuts at all hours of the day and night. All while holding down a full-time job.

Sarah slopped some milk into a jug and picked up the tray, furious her excitement at seeing the baby had now been ruined by *Lady Muck* in the next room. You're being over sensitive, she told herself, trying to be reasonable. You never minded before. Remember you're doing this for the baby and for your future. She glued a smile in place, checked herself at the door to be sure it hadn't slipped, and hustled in with the drinks.

'Here we are,' she said, keeping her tone light and breezy. 'Tea and biscuits, as ordered.'

'You're a star,' Arima mumbled, prising her eyes open and sitting up with difficulty. She was genuinely weary.

Sarah poured with a rock-steady hand and balanced two ginger nuts on the edge of the saucer. 'There are more if you want them,' she said, tapping the lid of the biscuit barrel.

'Great.'

Silence descended, punctuated by the clink of teaspoons on china and Arima's muted crunching. Neither woman knew how to navigate the new, unspoken awkwardness between them.

Sarah leashed her tongue, wanting to pummel Arima with questions but afraid of what she might be told. Arima watched her guardedly, like an opponent in a poker game. Each of them had something the other wanted; each was aware that the other suspected and was seeking to consolidate their position before making their move. Arima needed Lawrence to admit his feelings for her. Sarah was paralyzed until the baby was officially hers. Everything hinged on showing their hand at the right moment. The stakes were high: four lives rode on the outcome of the game. With the baby as her trump card, Arima knew she had the better hand. Who would be the first to blink?

'I've been thinking about male names again,' Sarah blurted out, afraid Arima would read something in her face if the silence went on.

'Oh?' Arima dunked her second ginger nut in her tea and sucked, letting it disintegrate in her mouth. 'What makes you think it's a boy?'

'Just a hunch.'

'That doesn't count for anything.' Arima thought the same but was irritated that Sarah had picked up on the vibe. 'So,' she went on, taking five more ginger nuts from the biscuit barrel to antagonize Sarah into making a plea for moderation. 'What's your list now? Have you gone off Horatio and Maxi-whatnot?'

'Maximilian,' corrected Sarah. 'No, I've discovered a few more that I like.' She took a sip of tea, trying to marshal the names into order of preference in her mind. 'Benedict.'

'That's a bit wet.'

'I don't think so.'

'It's a girl's name in French, did you know that?'

'No.' Sarah immediately struck it off her list. 'Lucas.'

Arima wrinkled her nose.

'Arthur.'

'You already know an Arthur,' Arima objected.

'Well, it's permissible for more than one to exist at a time,' Sarah retorted, stung by Arima's response. Didn't Arima realize she was making polite conversation, nothing more? Her opinion didn't figure. 'Anyway, just those for the time being,' she said, pointedly not asking if there were any names Arima liked.

'Mmm.' Arima was no longer paying attention. In her head, she was going through her own list. Eneko. Jon. Alesander. Luix. Eneko, 'my little one', had a nice ring to it but one had to consider that children do grow up. Perhaps Jon. It was a good Basque name that sounded like its English equivalent. Confident of her prediction, Arima had a single girl's name in reserve. Alaia, for her mother.

Sarah stood up abruptly. 'I must get back to work,' she said stiffly. 'The students are starting to get jittery about their projects for the end of year exhibition.'

'I thought it wasn't until June?'

'It isn't,' Sarah replied, checking her handbag for the house keys. 'But I won't be there so they need my input now.'

'Where will you be?'

Sarah shook the keys free of her bag and looked up. It was an innocent question but she fancied she saw a hint of challenge in Arima's eyes.

'At home, of course,' she said, her voice measured and matter-of-fact. 'With the baby.' And you, she thought as she swept out of the room, will be far away if I have anything to do with it.

The surrogacy information booklet had recommended a holiday for surrogate mothers after the birth. Sarah decided to speak to Lawrence, suggest they pay Arima's fare and accommodation.

That would kill two birds with one stone, making her appear generous while ensuring that Arima was out of the picture. A couple of places sprang to mind, like Outer Mongolia or Siberia. 'Anywhere,' Sarah said through clenched teeth as she slammed the front door with undue force and set off down the road, ducking her head against the wind, 'Anywhere . . . but here.'

Arima left the tea tray on the lounge table and shuffled up to her room for a rest. She needed to be more careful around Sarah. Their friendship was already stretched so thin it was as translucent as cobweb. A sharp tug from either side and it would break apart. If that happened too soon, she risked losing Lawrence. Once the baby was born there would be no contest: the scales would tip irrevocably in Arima's favour. What was there to keep him by Sarah's side but their forgotten youth and the prospect of a slow, dismal slide into joyless old age?

Lying on her front was becoming uncomfortable as her bump expanded, so Arima curled up on her side and laid the scan photo beside her on the pillow. She saw nothing wrong in what she was trying to do, no element of scheming or deceit. In her eyes she wasn't putting a crowbar into the cracks of a marriage and prising them open – she was following her heart. Sarah and Lawrence weren't right for each other, she reasoned, stroking the grainy outline of the baby's face. They must have been unhappy for years. Otherwise Lawrence wouldn't have looked twice at Arima.

Goodness knows she had never looked twice at him in the past. Her old teacher's husband? Not likely. Arima rolled onto her back and frowned up at the ceiling, trying to decipher her feelings. Somewhere along the line Lawrence had shed that old identity and acquired a magnetic quality that drew her irresistibly to him. Suddenly, it didn't matter that he was thirty years older than her, or that he was married to her friend; he embodied all the hidden needs that had gnawed at her for years, craving fulfilment. Wasn't it said that love was the strangest of things, impossible to understand?

In her teenage years, Arima remembered asking her mother why she had married Peter Middleton, knowing him to be proud, difficult and plagued by depression.

'You could have had anyone,' she argued, almost angry that Alaia had willingly subjected herself to such a life. 'Why him?'

Alaia had smiled at her tempestuous daughter and inclined her head graciously, acknowledging the compliment.

'His heart answered mine,' she said simply.

Arima tossed her head irritably.

'His heart answered yours? They're not telephones, Mama. What does that mean?'

Alaia gave a mysterious shrug.

'I can't say. It's different for everyone.'

'Gemma Drayton say she's in love with Adam Crowley and all she does is stare off into space looking dreamy,' Arima said scornfully. 'Either that or she's beefing her eyes out because he smiled at someone else. It's embarrassing.'

'That's not love,' her mother laughed, ruffling her daughter's hair. 'That's a crush. One day we will have this conversation again, with your husband by your side.' Her mother wagged an admonitory finger as her daughter snorted at the idea. 'And you will see that I was right. We don't choose love; it finds us.'

'Well, it's not finding me,' Arima said flatly, with the special brand of utter certainty possessed only by teenagers. 'Who needs the hassle?'

Arima smiled at the memory, appreciating her mother's wisdom now, as she hadn't been able to then.

'His heart answers mine,' she whispered as she thought of him. They were meant to be together. Sarah would get over it, in time. Arima had no wish to hurt her, but these things just . . . happened and there was nothing anyone could do about it. With a happy sigh, she went back to staring at the scan picture.

As she examined the contours of the baby's spine, a sweet way of presenting the photo to Lawrence occurred to her. It would make up for him missing the scan appointment, which was down to Shrew-face, whatever he'd said about having a meeting. Arima pottered downstairs in search of materials, pausing to collect her mobile phone from a pile of her belongings cluttering up the bottom step. Her stomach lurched as she saw the message sign flashing. She pressed the button, hardly daring to look.

*How did it go? Wish I was there with you. L xx*

Two kisses. Arima sat down on the stairs, grinning like a fool. One would be friendly, two was significant. She thought for a minute, then tapped out a message and hit the send button. Mustn't be too flirtatious.

*Fine. Safe to start shopping if you want? Slave needed to carry bags. A xx*

Within seconds, the reply popped up.

*Saturday? Willing slave at the ready. Your wish is my command!*
*L xx And x for bump.*

Arima kissed the scan photo and hugged herself, giddy as a teenager in the throes of a mad infatuation. She could have given Gemma Drayton a run for her money. 'Daddy says hello,' she informed her stomach, delivering a sharp poke to wake the baby. Instantly there was an answering kick. Arima grabbed the phone.

*Bump kicked when I passed the message on!*

Back came the reply.

*Smart child. Obviously knows where the money is xx*

Arima giggled as she hauled herself up and headed for the kitchen, reading and re-reading the messages. Six kisses and one for the baby. She danced around the room. 'Put that in your pipe and smoke it, Shrew-face,' she crowed.

Lawrence finished work as early as he could and managed to miss the rush hour traffic, arriving home at six o'clock. He mounted the steps two at a time, half-noticing that Sarah had planted some snowdrops in the stone pots on sentry duty outside the front door. A smile tugged at his mouth as he remembered the snowdrops in Greenwich Park. He found the house in darkness.

'Hello?' There was no reply.

Lawrence jettisoned his keys and hung up his coat without bothering to switch on the lights. Sarah must be running late. He glanced at his watch, the display illuminated in the gloom.

Lawrence slipped off his shoes and climbed the stairs. 'Arima?' he called softly, knocking on her bedroom door. A sleepy voice mumbled an incoherent reply. Lawrence slid into the room and sat down on the bed. 'Arima?' She was lying on her side with her knees drawn up, her body curved in a protective arch. Her hair formed a curtain across her face, hiding her from sight.

Lawrence extended a hand and rested it lightly on her hip, applying just enough pressure to turn her onto her back. Arima opened her eyes to find Lawrence leaning over her, brushing her hair off her face. Instinctively, she lifted her arms to draw him down for a lingering kiss. He could feel the pulse beating in his neck. His mind spun out of control without a thought for Sarah.

'Hi.'

'Hi yourself.' She could feel him smiling against her mouth. 'Time to wake up.' He helped her sit up, his arm circling her waist for support. 'How are you feeling?'

'Fine,' Arima yawned, snuggling into him and closing her eyes.

'Don't go back to sleep,' he grinned, lifting her head from his shoulder. 'You need to eat something.'

'Not hungry.'

He tilted her chin up so that they were eye to eye, one hand moving to caress her stomach. 'For baby?'

'I really can't face anything.' She didn't want to move. They were so close their lips were almost brushing, their words not airborne but moving directly from mouth to mouth.

'Please,' he begged, tracing the line of her jaw from chin to earlobe with his thumb. 'For me?'

A thrill ran through her, tiny shockwaves of delight from her head to her feet. 'Okay,' she whispered. 'For you, I'll try.'

Lawrence kissed her again, intoxicated by her nearness. When he held Arima it was as if nothing existed beyond his encircling arms. The problem was he had always felt that way about Sarah too, and still did. They were a fantastic team. Was it possible to be in love with both women at the same time? Lawrence's conscience roared but he silenced it with more kisses, pressing closer to Arima. He shouldn't think so much. She was young and beautiful, clever and kind, the mother of his child. And she wanted him. No, he corrected himself, raking his fingers through her hair. She needed him; it was a responsibility. He couldn't ignore that.

They jumped guiltily at the sound of a door slamming downstairs. Sarah was home.

'Hello?' Tiredness made her voice flatline like a dying heart. 'Lawrence, are you there?'

'Yes, I'm here,' he called out. 'Two minutes, darling.'

'Okay. I'll make a start on dinner. See if you can dig Arima out, will you?'

'Will do.' Disgust engulfed him at the sound of her voice, weary, faithful. Thinking of him. What kind of a man was he to betray a good woman like this? It was the only thought his mind would allow. Never had he thought in all his life he could be unfaithful. Yet, he had slipped into this predicament like a hand in a well-worn glove. His heart was torn, twisted like his guts.

'Two more minutes,' Arima murmured, squirming against him. Lawrence pushed her away and stood up.

'No,' he said harshly. 'No, I can't. Oh God, Arima.' He covered his eyes with his hand as tears welled in her eyes. 'I'm sorry, sweetheart. I shouldn't be . . .'

'It's okay,' she interrupted, scrambling off the bed to reach his side. 'I know it's hard for you. I understand.'

Arima knew she mustn't put him under any pressure or force him to choose too soon. It had to come from him. She reached out and smoothed her hand across his face tenderly.

'Arima, I don't know. It's all such a bloody mess. What are we doing?' He hung his head, weariness and desire and shame fighting to conquer each other.

'Take it easy,' she said soothingly, touching his hand to her stomach to remind him of the child. 'We can wait.' Obediently, the child kicked and Lawrence's face cleared.

'Thank you,' he sighed, pressing his lips to her hair.

All's fair in love and war, Arima told herself as they left the room, their fingers interlaced in a lover's knot. She intended to use every weapon to make Lawrence hers for good. Reluctantly, she dropped Lawrence's hand and went ahead of him down the stairs. On the final step she grasped the banister with one hand and swung herself round into the darkened hall, colliding with something solid and heavy. She screamed and fell back, her heart racing.

'Arima!' Lawrence was at her side in seconds. 'What's wrong? Did you slip?'

'No, I . . .' Arima's eyes were fixed on something behind him. Lawrence turned as Sarah advanced, a grim smile stretched across her face.

'Hello, darling. Good day?' She kissed him and moved past to face Arima. 'You should be more careful. We can't have you slipping on the stairs,' she said, every word clipped and precise. 'Here.' She thrust a bundle into Arima's arms and propelled her towards the door. 'I think you should get some fresh air.'

'Sarah, I'm tired,' Arima said, clutching her balled-up coat to her chest.

'So walk slowly. My husband and I have things to discuss. In private.'

Behind them, Lawrence was panicking. Had she heard something? Caught sight of their linked hands at the top of the stairs? He swallowed nervously.

'Sarah, there's no need . . .'

'Shut up.' She yanked the door open and pushed her face right up to Arima's, so close Arima could see the tiny imperfections in her skin. Sarah forced her back across the threshold. 'Don't worry,' she sneered, her smile at odds with the open hostility burning in her eyes. 'I'll give him your little . . . note.' With a jolt of fear, Arima remembered the card she'd made for Lawrence using the scan photo. She must have left it in the kitchen. Sarah saw her eyes widen and knew that she had understood.

'No,' Arima blustered, clutching at the doorframe. 'You've got it all wrong.'

'Really?' Sarah's perfect blonde bob sliced through the air as she whipped her head round to glare at her husband, dumbstruck and paralyzed in the hallway. For a second, she seemed to waver. Arima shifted her weight forwards, inching one foot over the threshold, but the face Sarah turned to Arima held nothing but cold suspicion. 'Dinner in one hour,' she spat and swung the door shut. Arima reeled back and snatched her hand away just in time. She stared at the bold blue-painted wooden panels, frightened tears coursing down her face.

'Keep calm,' she mumbled, leaning her forehead against the cold brass knocker. Sarah couldn't know, not for sure. In a minute the door would open and Lawrence would spring to her rescue. Any minute now. Arima squeezed her eyes shut and counted to a hundred. The door regarded her implacably. No one came.

*You fool.*

Arima tumbled down the steps and ran, her coat billowing out in the wind as she struggled with the fastenings.

It began to rain, bitter and cold.

# Chapter 20

Sarah and Lawrence faced each other in the hallway like gun-fighters. Lawrence kept his eyes on Sarah's hands, fully expecting her to launch herself at him in the next thirty seconds and claw his eyes out with her French-manicured nails. The grandfather clock chimed the half hour, adding to the drama. Both of them jumped. It was enough to break the immediate tension. Lawrence took a step towards Sarah, half-raising his hand in supplication.

'Are you going to tell me what this is all about?' he asked, risking a lopsided smile. 'Before Arima and your baby freeze to death out there?' He saw her face relax a fraction at his careful use of the possessive.

'In the kitchen,' she said brusquely. Lawrence stood aside to let her pass. 'We can talk and chop at the same time.' Lawrence followed her, inwardly questioning the wisdom of conducting this conversation with Sarah while she had a knife in her hand.

He watched her lay out the raw vegetables, silently accepted a chopping board and knife and set to on a pile of carrots. Sarah stationed herself beside him and attacked a swede, hacking viciously into its thick skin. Lawrence's heart quailed. Out of habit, he offered up a prayer for help. It wouldn't be answered — he was as guilty as hell — but the comfort of the ritual provided a modicum of courage. It wasn't too late, he told himself, shooting a sidelong look at his wife, cheeks flushed and jaw set as she worked. It was still possible to make things right. To his shame, he didn't stop to wonder where Arima had gone, or whether she was okay. Out of sight, out of mind. All he could think about was convincing his wife he loved her and wasn't having an affair.

Abruptly, Sarah jabbed her knife in the air, pointing at a spot on the kitchen counter.

'I take it you've seen it?' she said in a casual, conversational tone. Lawrence wasn't fooled. He could see the muscle twitching in her cheek. 'Your Valentine's card.'

There was a tremor of hurt beneath the sarcasm in her voice. Lawrence heard that too and knew there was still hope.

'No,' he replied, adopting the same light tone. When Sarah gestured again with the knife he crossed the room and picked up the homemade card, smoothing out the marks where Sarah had begun to screw it up but changed her mind. Aware that she was watching him like a hawk, Lawrence schooled his features into a neutral expression. Arima had folded a plain rectangle of white card and covered it on both sides with a découpage of hearts, cut to varying sizes from scraps of material, each overlaying the next. The scan photo had been glued onto the bed of hearts so that they protruded around and beneath the edges. It was beautifully done. Inside, Arima had written 'To Daddy, with lots of love from your son.' Caught off guard, Lawrence said the first thing that came into his head.

'It's a boy?'

It was the best thing, perhaps the only thing he could have said to allay Sarah's fears. His immediate focus on the baby gave the impression Arima didn't figure. At this moment in time, that was perfectly true.

'*I* think so,' Sarah answered, still scrutinizing his face. 'Arima didn't. She must have changed her mind.'

'Couldn't you have found out for sure today?' Lawrence asked, moving under one of the angled spotlights to get a clearer look at the photo.

'The baby was in the wrong position.' Sarah put down her knife and took a tentative step towards him. 'Lawrence, why has she made you this card? What's going on? These last few weeks, there's been an atmosphere in the house and I don't like it.' She pointed at the card in Lawrence's hand. 'Now this. Tell me why.' Her face was stern but her voice betrayed her. Forcing the issue like this was unwise, but the sight of that card . . . it was too much. She had to know. Sarah felt bands of fear closing around her chest. What if she was right?

Lawrence kept his eyes on the photo. *Think, man. Think.* What could he tell Sarah that she would believe? She wasn't a fool. It had to be something plausible, a lie with a grain of truth. He couldn't lose her. Taking a deep breath, he turned to face her, careful to meet her eye.

'Darling, I think –' he began. 'I think Arima has got a bit of a bee in her bonnet about me lately.'

'Like a crush?'

'Exactly.' He seized the word and made it his own. 'A crush.'

Sarah watched him warily, unwilling to let the matter drop. 'Why?'

Lawrence closed the gap between them in three long strides, taking her hands in his.

'I suppose, in a funny sort of way, it's understandable,' he offered. 'It's only natural for a pregnant woman to gravitate towards a man for support and . . . and protection. Instinctive, even.'

Sarah nodded slowly, not yet in agreement.

'But you're old enough to be her father.'

'Maybe that's part of it,' Lawrence said, silently absorbing the blow to his ego. 'She never mentions her father, does she?' He expanded the idea a little further. 'Maybe she needs that kind of security in her life at the moment, and she's mistaken my concern for her – our concern, really – for something more.'

'That makes sense, I guess,' Sarah said thoughtfully. 'You've certainly been a lot more sensitive to her needs since Christmas. I thought . . .'

'What? That I was having an affair with her?' He forced a laugh. 'Oh, Sarah.'

'Don't laugh at me.' Sarah twisted free and turned her back on him, weak with relief.

'I'm not.' Lawrence put his arms round her waist and kissed the top of her head, loving her fiercely, even as a small part of him loathed himself for laying everything on Arima. 'I'm laughing at the idea of it. Sarah, I married *you*.' He gave her a gentle squeeze. 'I love *you*.'

Sarah leaned into his embrace, trying to release all the pent-up suspicion of the last weeks.

'Arima doesn't know you very well,' she commented. 'Making you a Valentine's card. We've never bought into that.'

'Never needed to,' Lawrence agreed. He squeezed her again and was about to release her when Sarah turned in his arms, suspicion bubbling to the surface again.

'Where did you go with Arima last month?'

'Eh?'

'You were supposed to visit Eva,' she said, narrowed eyes fixed on his. 'But she waited all afternoon and you never showed up. She called me.'

'Oh, *that*.' Lawrence hoped he looked sheepish rather than guilty. His heart thundered in his chest, lies and truth ricocheting around in his brain. Had she laid a trap for him? Lulled him into a false sense of security so she could catch him out when he thought he was safe? He wondered if they had been seen by someone in the park. Should he just come clean and admit it?

'Why did you lie to me?'

There was no accusation in Sarah's voice this time, only confusion. Looking into her eyes, Lawrence sensed that while she might not believe him, she wanted to. The human capacity for rationalization was unparalleled. If he could come up with something even halfway convincing, she would swallow it because the alternative was too horrible to face.

'I thought it would cause a row,' he confessed. 'It was my fault. When it came to it, Arima was anxious about seeing Mum and got herself all worked up. You were right about Mum being funny with her at Christmas, by the way,' he added. 'I didn't want to force Arima into going and make things worse.'

'So where were you all that time?' Sarah stared up into his face, searching for the slightest hint of a lie.

*Keep it simple*, Lawrence urged himself. *Don't over-egg the pudding.*

'In the end we just went for a drive,' he improvised. 'Arima wanted some fresh air but she wasn't really up to a walk. She agreed to visit Mum another day when she was feeling stronger. I meant to call St Jude's.'

'But . . . why didn't you just tell me?' She asked, knowing the story didn't quite ring true.

'I should have done,' Lawrence apologized, gathering her into his arms again and starting to rub her back with the flat of his hand in small, circular motions. Any more direct eye contact and he would crack. 'But you were concerned about Mum and Arima not getting on and I thought you'd worry if you knew the visit had been postponed.' He kissed her hair and let the lies flow out of him. 'You spend all your time worrying about Arima as it is. I didn't want to add to it. Arima said I was being a fussy but I persuaded her it was better this way.'

'You are a fussy,' Sarah said, her body relaxing against him. Lawrence knew he'd succeeded. Inside, it hurt. It was as if some force was pushing him on as one lie led to another. His love for Sarah was true and a path well trod. His love for Arima was fresh, new and exciting.

'I completely see where you were coming from,' he said, holding her tightly. 'It must have looked really bad.'

'It did.'

'I love you so much, Sarah,' he murmured. 'Don't ever doubt it.' Sarah heard the truth in his words and allowed herself to believe. Inside, Lawrence's conscience was tearing him to shreds. His excuses were feeble but still he tried to justify himself. The words leapt around his brain as he argued with himself.

*I'm not lying. I do love her.*

But you've been with another woman.

*I haven't slept with her.*

You're in love with her. That's far worse.

*I'm not! I'm . . . I'm . . .*

You're in it up to your neck. In love with two women.

Sarah tucked her head beneath Lawrence's chin, nestling closer to him.

'I'm sorry, I should never have doubted you,' she whispered.

The words slid between his ribs like an assassin's knife. There and then, Lawrence vowed to put Arima aside. He was a happily married man and it was madness to jeopardize what he had with Sarah. Utter madness. It would be easy, sensible, the right thing to do. He would tell Arima and that would be it.


Arima had tramped the streets for perhaps half an hour, walking fast and hard with the collar of her coat pulled up high to shield her face from the stinging rain. She had no idea where she was going, or if she would be going back. When she was completely lost and the rain had permeated every layer of clothing and skin, she staggered into a door-way and huddled there, fear mingling with hope in her mind like the rainwater with her tears.

The rain showed no sign of letting up, the camber of the road creating pools of water at the kerb edge. Arima watched the passing cars plough through them, spurting the water up and over the pavement like tiny waves breaking over a miniature sea wall. She clutched her sodden coat round her body as another bout of shivering overtook her. Low blood sugar and shock were making her dizzy and disorientated. Arima shielded her eyes from the glare of oncoming head-lamps and tried to focus. When a thought surfaced through the muddle she snatched at it and clung on. Robin. Call Robin. She couldn't be more than a few miles from home. If he drove about a bit he would find her, somehow. She fumbled in her pockets, only to realize that both her mobile and her keys were at home. Arima sank to the ground and curled up in a ball, vulnerable and alone.

Time passed as she crouched there. People passed but nobody was going to stop on a dark, wet February night, much less approach a figure hunched in a doorway, face hidden by long, rain-matted hair.

Besides, it was Valentine's Day and who wanted to spoil a romantic evening with a trip to the local homeless shelter? Arima would have done the same in their place. Still the rain fell. Gradually, Arima began to sink into unconsciousness. She ought to be getting back, she thought fuzzily, wondering why she no longer felt cold.

It must have been more than an hour. Dinner would be on the table, Sarah had said. Why hadn't Lawrence come to find her? At that moment, the baby woke inside her and began to kick. Nothing else could have roused Arima. Slowly, she got to her knees, then to her feet, using the wall for support. She cried out as her cold fingers scraped against the brickwork.

'Excuse me,' came the unexpected voice.

Arima turned, clasping her arms across her stomach at the sound of the man's voice. She had neither seen nor heard his approach. Dressed in black, he was barely visible in the dark, beyond reach of the glowing spheres of light cast by the streetlamps. A shock of red hair stood out above a pale face unattractively spattered with freckles.

'Are you alright?' he asked, taking a step towards her but checking himself instantly when Arima shrank away from him. 'It's okay,' he said, raising one hand palm up while the other unwound the scarf from around his neck to display the white clerical collar. 'Do you need help?'

Arima pushed her sopping hair out of her eyes, unable to stop herself shaking with cold and relief.

'In-inside,' she stuttered, struggling to articulate through numb lips. The baby kicked its encouragement and she tried again. 'Need to warm up.'

The priest stretched out his hand. 'Are you unwell?' he asked, tactfully trying to ascertain the best place to escort the girl.

She shook her head and let her coat fall open, saw the shock in the man's eyes. 'Come,' he said, taking his coat off and draping it across Arima's shoulders. 'You shouldn't be out in this. My church is just round the corner.'

He took her arm and helped her along, maintaining a comforting flow of banal chatter. The girl staggered, all her concentration devoted to putting one foot in front of the other. She seemed barely aware of his presence, yet when they reached the church he had to gently prise her hands from his arm so that he could unlock the double-fronted oak doors.

'I'm sorry,' he apologized, helping her over the threshold. 'I would take you to my house but one has to be careful these days. The look of it, you know.' Arima nodded automatically, neither knowing nor caring what he meant. All she cared about was being somewhere dry and warm. 'The heating's still on,' the priest continued, scurrying ahead to switch on the lights. 'The evening service didn't finish until nine. Here.' He led her through the porch and into the body of the church, steering her towards a pew. 'If you take your coat off, I'll put it on the radiator for you,' he offered. Arima obediently peeled it off and re-wrapped herself in the priest's coat.

'Nine o'clock?' Arima asked. 'What time is it now?'

'Going on for ten,' he replied, coming back to sit beside her. 'Look, is there someone I can call for you? Family, boyfriend perhaps?' Arima stared at him, her eyes bleak. 'I don't – don't know,' she said through chattering teeth, 'if I want to go back.'

'I see.' The priest digested this. The girl didn't look ill-treated, if such a thing could be judged on first appearance, just very cold. It was difficult to show an appropriate level of concern in pastoral cases without coming across as prying. 'Well, I'm Robert. Father Robert Embles,' he said, pressing a hand to his chest.

'Arima.'

'That's an unusual name. What does it mean?'

'Soul.' He looked very young for a priest, she thought, still shuddering with the cold.

'That's beautiful,' he said. 'Oh, you're frozen. I wish I could offer you a hot drink.' He nodded at the simple wooden altar, dressed with a plain white cloth, the Alpha and Omega symbols carved into the front. 'All I've got is communion wine, I'm afraid.' He beamed as Arima gave a half-smile. 'Look, if there are – problems – at home, I know of an excellent women's refuge.'

Arima shook her head. 'No, no. Please don't worry.'

'Arima, when I see a pregnant girl alone on the street at night and clearly in distress, I *do* worry,' he said earnestly. 'You don't have to tell me anything at all about your situation but please accept my help.' He gave a wry smile. 'It's part of the job description, I suppose, but I genuinely want to.'

'It's . . . complicated.'

'That's okay.'

The simplicity of his kindness opened something up inside Arima. She burst into tears again. Father Robert produced a pristine white handkerchief and sat patiently beside her without saying a word. He didn't stare at her or try to comfort her in any physical way, but silently accompanied her through her grief.

When there were no tears left in her, Arima hiccoughed into the handkerchief, blew her nose and looked up at a statue of the Madonna and child set into a niche of the wall. The child was propped on his mother's arm in a forward-facing pose, chubby arms outstretched to the world as his mother looked on, her serene figure swathed in a dress of traditional white and blue. 'It all started when I came home from travelling last year,' she began, addressing the statue though her words were for the man sitting beside her. Father Robert listened with a sense of growing astonishment.

It was true he was relatively new to the priesthood but as Arima unfolded the tale he began to doubt he would ever hear its like again in all the years of ministry ahead of him. Arima spoke frankly about her love for the baby and for Lawrence, holding nothing back. When she had finished, she kept her eyes on the statue, awaiting the condemnation she was sure would come.

'I think,' said Father Robert with quiet perception, 'that you are a brave and generous woman, Arima. You made a spontaneous offer from the heart and in good faith, without fully understanding the implications. The bond between a mother and child is not easily broken, nor is it designed to be.' He paused, choosing his next words with great care. 'Neither are the bonds of marriage vows.' There was no accusation in his voice or bearing but Arima flinched as though burned by the light touch of his hand on her arm. 'I am not judging you,' he said gently.

'I don't know what to do,' she whispered. 'I love him.'

'I will willingly take you wherever you want to go,' the priest replied, 'but I think that in the first instance and for the sake of your integrity, home may be the best place. Your friends will be concerned for your safety and perhaps, in due course, some honest conversations need to take place.' He glanced at Arima's stomach. 'Sooner rather than later, I should say.'

Arima nodded. 'Okay,' she said.

It was nearing midnight when the car pulled up outside the Abrahams' house. 'The lights are still on,' observed Father Robert, applying the handbrake and peering up at the window. He looked at Arima and saw the combined strain of apprehension and exhaustion overlaying her delicate features. 'Would you like me to come in with you?'

'No, Father. There's no need.' She shuffled along the seat and opened the door, reluctance weighing her movements down. No sooner had she set foot on the pavement than the front door flew open and Sarah came charging down the steps, her arms flung wide.

'Arima, thank God!' she cried. 'Where have you *been*? Look at the state of you! Lawrence has been out searching for two hours, we were on the point of calling the police. I'd never have forgiven myself if anything had happened to you and the baby.' Her anger had vanished, meaningless compared with her relief at Arima's safe return.

The priest watched from the car as Arima was hustled up the steps, robbed of the chance to thank him or say goodbye, though he expected neither. Father Robert flicked the indicator and prepared to pull away. At the last minute, he saw a man appear in the doorway and throw his arms around both women. Did the husband love Arima, he wondered, or were his feelings for her simply an extension of his love for the unborn child? Who could judge where one ended and the other began?

'A riddle fit for King Solomon himself,' Father Robert muttered as he drove away, knowing that Arima would be much in his heart and mind in the coming months. 'God bless them all.'

# Chapter 21

'I can't believe,' Arima said in a pained voice, 'that you're making me go round the Tate Modern in a pushchair.'

'Wheelchair,' corrected Robin, putting a restraining hand on her shoulder as she attempted to climb out for the fourth time in as many minutes. 'I'm not the one with symphysis pubis dysfunction.'

'I find it painful to walk – but I still can . . .' Arima argued.

'Honestly, Arima,' Jemma tutted as they drew alongside with Beatrice. 'Will you please sit still and stop making such a fuss. Beatrice is behaving better than you.'

Arima exchanged a look of shared suffering with the little girl, who shook her rattle and gave a rallying cry as she attempted a Houdini manoeuvre on her harness.

'Beatrice has no choice,' Arima pointed out. 'She's strapped in.'

'That could be arranged,' muttered Robin darkly to Jemma, sizing up the length of her pashmina with a speculative eye. 'Just say the word.'

'We've made it to Level 3 without them escaping,' Jemma responded, delving into her bag for a breadstick. 'That's already a personal best for me.'

'You make it sound like a reality game show challenge.'

'Welcome to the world of parenting.'

'Don't I get a breadstick?' Arima whined. 'Beatrice has one.'

'Oh, good grief.' Robin held out his hand for Jemma to palm him the snack. 'Here.' He thrust it under Arima's nose. 'Now . . . be quiet . . . there's a good girl.'

'I can't believe you just said that,' Jemma mouthed as Arima took a savage bite out of the breadstick and folded her arms moodily.

'I know,' grinned Robin. 'I think I'm getting the hang of it. Don't do that, darling,' he said to Arima as she deliberately sprayed crumbs onto the floor. 'Beatrice will copy you.'

'Shut up,' snarled Arima between crunches. Jemma almost choked with the effort of swallowing her laughter.

'This is the best trip out I've had in ages,' she said, wiping her eyes.

'Always delighted to entertain,' Arima said caustically.

Robin wheeled her into Room 5, part of the Poetry and Dream collection. 'Don't be like that,' he said soothingly. 'Look, here's your fix of twentieth-century modernism. This'll cheer you up.'

'I'm not keen on Francis Bacon,' Arima objected, determined to sustain her bad mood for as long as possible.

'But you love Picasso.' Robin knelt down beside her and took her hand. 'Come on,' he said, rapping the arm of the wheelchair with his knuckles. 'Don't let this spoil your day. I know it's a pain but I'm only following orders.'

When he had arrived to collect Arima, Sarah had treated him to a ten-minute lecture on symphysis pubis dysfunction, a condition that had developed suddenly in Arima a fortnight before.

Her graphic description of the pelvic bones grinding together when walking had been gruesome enough for Robin to call the Tate Modern immediately to reserve a wheelchair, and then text Jemma for a lift instead of using public transport. Just as well, since Arima refused to use the crutches she'd been given.

'I can walk,' she grumbled bitterly, obviously in pain. 'Just feels like I am about to fall apart.'

'Of course you can,' he agreed, squeezing her hand. 'But why struggle when you've got me to do the hard work for you?'

'Over there,' Jemma called. 'I love that one.' Robin trundled Arima across the room and parked her in front of an oil painting entitled, 'Nude Woman In A Red Armchair.' Picasso . . . 1932. Arima stared at it, her brain automatically tracking the exaggerated curves of the subject, the voluptuous body-lines echoed and enhanced by the scrolling arms of the chair.

She did love Picasso but at that moment, Arima saw her own sulky mood reflected in the woman's half-shaded face, the downward turn of her mouth and pensive gaze exactly matching Arima's own. It was true she was in some discomfort but the real source of her ill temper was Sarah's decision to go shopping for baby things with Lawrence while Arima was out.

'Put a brave face on,' Lawrence had whispered urgently while Sarah was out of the room.

'But we were going to go all together,' Arima complained.

'I know,' he said, kissing her furtively on the lips and glancing over his shoulder for Sarah's return. 'But it would look odd, sweetheart. Surely you can see that?'

Arima did see, but that didn't mean she had to like it. Since the fall-out of Valentine's Day Lawrence had been like a cat on hot bricks, going out of his way never to be on his own in the house with her. For a couple of weeks he had kept his distance but had been unable to resist the pull for long. Soon enough they were snatching moments here and there while Sarah was in a different part of the house. It was important, Lawrence argued, to keep things on an even keel for the time being.

There was no need to hurt Sarah. Arima bit her tongue and concentrated on reeling Lawrence in, twining herself ever more tightly about his heart and trusting in her trump card – the baby. Lawrence could barely keep his hands off her stomach and got down on his knees to talk to the baby at every opportunity. Sarah talked at the bump as well, an intrusion Arima endured for Lawrence's sake. It kept up the pretence. Father Robert's subtle warnings had fallen on deaf ears.

Above her head, Jemma and Robin exchanged covert looks. For whatever reason, Arima just wasn't in the right frame of mind for a gallery. Neither knew what the problem was but it was abundantly clear that silent contemplation of modern art was not the solution.

'Who's ready for some lunch?' Jemma asked brightly. 'I feel a disgustingly large slice of cake coming on.'

'Not the lemon and poppy seed drizzle cake, by any chance?' Robin enquired.

'The very same. Fancy going halves?'

'Get lost. I want my own piece.' Robin bent down and scooped Beatrice's rattle off the floor. 'And I'm not sharing with you either, Beetroot.'

'I'll thank you not to refer to my daughter as a vegetable.'

'Some people are so touchy.'

It was very hard to stay angry when your friends were being so jolly, Arima thought as they made their way up to Level 7. After a brief attempt to be cross about that as well, she gave in and began to smile. She loved the monochrome simplicity of the restaurant and *Cold Mouth Prayer*, the panoramic painting displayed along one wall, was a personal favourite.

'I think it's creepy,' Jemma said, turning Beatrice away from the rich, flower-dotted landscape. 'It's the smoke-breathing crows.'

'That's the best part,' Arima protested through a mouthful of pear and cinnamon crumble.

'Deliciously sinister,' Robin added with a raised eyebrow.

'Precisely.'

'Tell you who else would love it,' he went on. 'Your mum, Arima. Have you brought her to see it?'

'I – er . . .' Arima was thrown by the sudden swerve in the conversation. 'No.'

'Do you mind if I invite her for lunch?' Robin asked, chasing cake crumbs around his plate to eke out one last mouthful. 'I've been meaning to ask for your parents' address for ages. We should never have lost touch.'

'Well, life moves on. They did some more house-hopping after we graduated,' Arima mumbled uncomfortably. 'Never stay put for long. You know how it is.'

'Quicksand.'

'Yep.' Arima cast an urgent look at Jemma, which she correctly read as a cry for help.

'Er – another cup of tea, anyone?' Jemma said hastily, brandishing the pot at Robin.

'Me, please.' He held out his cup without taking his eyes off Arima. 'So can I have their number?' He pressed. 'Or an address? Where are they living these days?'

'I'd love another cup,' Arima trilled, pushing her cup towards Jemma. 'It's not decaff but I'll live dangerously.' Jemma filled the cup to the brim, alarmed by her friend's brittle smile. 'Any plans for baby number two yet, Jem?' Arima's hand shook as she raised the cup to her lips.

'Mima.' There was an edge to Robin's voice now, a shadow of suspicion darkening his face.

'What?' In a blind panic, Arima missed her mouth and spilled lukewarm tea down the front of her dress. She dabbed frantically at her chest with a fistful of paper napkins, avoiding Robin's eye.

'What is it that you don't want me to know about?' he asked. 'Have they got divorced or something? Moved back to the Basque country?'

'They . . . I . . .'

Robin's hand shot out and gripped Arima's wrist, forcing her to be still. She dropped the napkins with a cry and tried to shake him off but Robin refused to budge.

'Robin, stop. You're hurting her,' Jemma hissed, aware that they were attracting attention from other diners. Beatrice started to cry. Robin held fast, his jaw set.

'The truth, Arima,' he demanded.

Tears leaked from the corners of her eyes. 'There . . . was an accident,' she said hoarsely, her eyes fixed on the table. 'A fire.'

'When?'

'Three years ago.' Her arm thudded onto the table as Robin threw it away from him and stood up.

'You're a piece of work, Arima Middleton,' he breathed, his voice barely audible. 'You weren't ever going to tell me, were you.' It wasn't a question.

'Didn't – didn't tell anyone,' Arima gulped, terrified by the anger in him.

Robin shook his head. 'I'm not anyone,' he said bitterly. 'But you've never seen it that way, have you.' He scrabbled in his pocket and threw some notes down onto the table. 'If I can trouble you for the location of their graves,' he spat, 'I'd like to go and pay my respects sometime.' He turned on his heel and strode away. Jemma sat white-faced and shaking, Beatrice clasped to her chest.

'He'll . . . he'll come round,' Arima stammered, looking to her friend for reassurance. 'It's just the shock, do you think?' Jemma pressed her lips together and looked away. 'Jemma? I didn't know where he was, I was out of touch with everyone at the time, I . . .' her excuses tailed off. 'He will forgive me, won't he?' she whispered.

Jemma shook her head, knowing enough of their shared past to grasp the selfishness of Arima's deception. Alaia had cared for Robin like her own son, and he, in turn, had never forgotten the debt he owed her from those childhood years.

Arima laid her head on the tea-stained cloth and wept.


Robin was also weeping, but his tears gave vent to rage more than grief. He walked blindly round the Tate Modern, unaware he was virtually mowing people down, striding out without a clue where he was going. He knew this place like the back of his hand but couldn't seem to find the exit. Eventually, he emerged onto the South Bank, blinking as the blustery spring wind blew grit into his eyes. The weather suited Robin's mood and he let the wind push him along the path, offering no resistance. His brain, however, was resisting for all it was worth, refusing to assimilate the shocking news.

Alaia and Peter Middleton were dead.

They couldn't be.

Robin had never thanked Alaia as she deserved, with the benefit of hindsight to illuminate the depth of her care. When had he last seen them? Four, five years ago on graduation day from Goldsmiths? Yes, that was it. A picture of them came vividly to mind, Peter standing by, starched and formal in a linen summer suit, Alaia proud and radiant, laughing at her talented daughter, giving her blessing as Arima shrugged off her achievements and declined all offers of work; accepting that Arima was Arima and there was nothing to be done about it. Robin dashed fresh tears from his eyes, remembering how she had tugged him down to her level, holding his head in her tiny, fine-boned hands. 'Be strong,' she commanded him. 'Make your own happiness.' And he, with a full heart and eyes for nothing but Arima, had not understood, until Arima slipped out of his bed and drove away in a purple camper van the very next day with his heart tied to the bumper. Oh, she was wise, Alaia. She had seen it coming for years and, not loving her daughter any the less, done what she could to protect him.

Now she was dead and it was too late for thanks. Life had got in the way and Robin had allowed them to drift out of his life, never imagining, not even for a second, that one day soon they would be gone for good. So it wasn't all Arima's fault, really. He could have tried harder to keep in touch. Should have tried harder.

'Stop it,' Robin berated himself, thumping his fist against his thigh as he walked. 'You're always doing this. Making excuses for her. Taking the blame on yourself. You've got to stop.' He slumped onto a bench by the Thames and put his head in his hands. 'The whole thing has got to stop. It ends here.'

'Crumbs. That sounds a bit serious.'

Robin peeled his hands from his face and saw a pair of unfashionable lace-up trainers toe to toe with his worn-out loafers. His gaze travelled up past faded jeans and a floral smock to a lilac pac-a-mac, a chubby face and smiling green eyes. He almost burst into tears all over again. 'I haven't even got any emergency cake,' Hannah said, plonking herself down beside him. 'Sorry.'

'Thank God it's you.' Robin wrapped his arms around her and buried his face in her neck. 'How long have you got?'

'Er, all afternoon,' she said, patting his back experimentally as though needing to check this was actually happening. 'It's my day off.'

'Great.' Robin said nothing more for several minutes, during which time Hannah realized several things. Firstly, being crushed in Robin Jennings' arms was something that had hitherto only happened in dreams and that in the flesh it was utterly thrilling. Secondly, this was extremely out of character for him based on their friendship to date and therefore something must be terribly wrong. And thirdly, while being crushed in someone's arms looked incredibly romantic it was, in fact, painful, and rather difficult to breathe, especially with a large purse in your smock pocket digging into your ribs. The screen sirens of the Hollywood golden era must have been a lot tougher than they looked; all that gasping and swooning over leading men was not brilliant acting after all, but a genuine need for oxygen. Interesting.

Hannah bore it for as long as she could, unsure of the protocol in this situation. In films, the crushing hugs usually led up to a bout of passionate kissing, which on the one hand could be well worth hanging on for. On the other hand, if she left it much longer her lungs would pack up before Robin got round to it. Tough call. In the end, Robin solved the dilemma by releasing her of his own accord. He sat back, keeping one arm across her shoulders, and heaved a great sigh. 'Thanks,' he said. 'I really needed that.'

'No problem,' Hannah groaned, discreetly rubbing the sore spot on her ribs to see if it was broken or just bruised. 'Any time, be my guest.'

Robin laughed and kissed her on the cheek. 'You're so funny, Hannah. You always cheer me up.'

'What, even without cake?' she said sceptically.

'Cake is an added bonus,' he conceded, inclining his head, 'but the cheering up is all you.'

'Are you okay?' Hannah ventured timidly.

'Not really,' he said with a tired smile.

'Do you . . . want to tell me about it? You don't have to,' she finished in a rush of embarrassment at the idea that Robin might think her nosey or intrusive.

Robin got to his feet and held out his hand. 'Yes,' he said simply. 'I think I need to get it off my chest.' He pulled her up and tucked her arm through his, keeping hold of her hand.

They strolled along the South Bank, heading nowhere in particular. There was no hurry. Jemma had her car and would see Arima safely home. Even in his anger Robin couldn't quite dismiss the ingrained habit of looking out for her, but as he walked beside Hannah he was struck by how different she was to Arima. They were polar opposites. Where Arima talked, Hannah listened so she could understand what made other people tick. Arima was whimsical, flighty and capricious. Hannah was dependable, funny and kind. Arima was unconsciously selfish, whereas Hannah never gave a thought for her own needs. Arima had a wild, untamed beauty, a description that would never apply to Hannah. And yet, as Robin looked down and met the attentive gaze of those green eyes, he shocked himself by finding in them something far more attractive than Arima's good looks. Hannah matched him quality for quality.

That afternoon, with Hannah as his witness, Robin offloaded several years' worth of baggage and dumped it in the waters of the Thames. For as long as he could remember, he had been trying to mould himself into someone Arima would love, someone she couldn't live without. Now he saw that it wasn't meant to be that way. There would be no moulding with Hannah Templeton. They already fitted. It felt like coming home.

# Chapter 22

Lawrence stood in front of the bedroom mirror, wrestling with the knot in his tie. They were late for Beatrice's birthday party and for once he couldn't lay the blame at Sarah's door. He was still recovering from his own birthday celebrations two days ago and had slept in.

'Listen to yourself,' he snorted, tipping his head to examine the thinning patch of hair at his crown. 'One dinner party and a meal out. Two late nights, that's all. No, three,' he amended.

Sarah had taken to sitting up late with Arima when she was in pain with her joints but she was exhausted herself at the moment and had asked Lawrence to take a turn a few nights ago. No complaints on his part, obviously. Arima was seeking a lot of reassurance from him lately so it worked out well all round but fatigue was catching up with him now.

With a jolt of anxiety he realized there were shortly going to be a lot of late nights and early mornings in his life. How would he cope? At fifty-eight, it sounded appalling to say he was beginning to need his sleep but it appeared to be true. Lawrence tucked his shirt into his trousers, turned sideways and sucked in his stomach. Middle-aged spread was definitely setting in. He reached for his jacket and buttoned it up quickly, masking the evidence.

'Are you ready, darling?' Sarah stuck her head into the room, looking every bit as tired as he felt. She too had gained a bit of weight and the soft jersey dress hung badly, clinging in all the wrong places, the navy colour making her look washed-out.

'Just about,' Lawrence grimaced, crossing the room to kiss her on the forehead. Close up, Sarah looked dreadful. Her eyes were heavy and her hair and skin looked dull and lack-lustre, as though something was leaching all the goodness out of her. 'Are you okay?' he asked, his voice tinged with worry. It upset him to see her this way. 'I don't feel right,' she admitted, brushing her hair off her forehead. 'I've made an appointment at the doctors.'

'Do you think it's a virus or something?'

Sarah gave him a glum smile.

'No. I think it's the menopause. The clock has ticked and it is five minutes to midnight.' She stepped away from him, shaking her head to forestall his reply. 'Bound to happen sooner or later,' she said matter-of-factly, though she felt the weight of it like a stone about her neck. 'It's been coming on for a while.' Menopause was so final, an indelible full stop on a life phase that for her had never achieved its potential. Her failure was absolute. With visible effort she shook the sadness off. 'It doesn't matter now,' she smiled, determined to look ahead. 'The baby will be here soon.' She turned away and left the room, weariness burdening every step. 'I'll sort the car out,' she called as she plodded down the stairs.

'Okay. I'll bring Arima down,' he called back. 'Don't for-get her crutches.'

'Already done.' Of course it was, Lawrence thought rue-fully. Ill or not, Sarah kept on top of everything. That was her way.

'Are you ready, darling?' Arima entered the room, moving gingerly to minimize the pain in her hips and pelvis. She was wearing a long white dress embroidered with cornflowers and poppies on the bodice and hem, the material flowing out over her bump. A soft blue cardigan covered her arms and buttoned under her bust, emphasizing her full, rich curves.

'Just about,' Lawrence repeated, crossing the room to kiss her on the forehead. Close up, she was radiant, her eyes shin-ing, hair and skin finally reflecting the textbook pregnancy glow. At long last the sickness had eased and despite the added complications caused by the widening gap in her pelvis, Arima was blooming. She snaked her arms round his waist and tipped her face up for another kiss. Lawrence felt the years fall away from him.

'Are you coming to the ante-natal class next week?' she asked.

He kissed her on the tip of her nose. 'Of course.'

'Sarah too?'

'Yes.'

'Must she?'

'Darling, you know she must. It's only fair.'

'I don't want her at the birth.'

'Don't worry about that now,' Lawrence said vaguely, burying his face in her hair. He had become tremendously adept at sidestepping awkward questions when pressed, par-ticularly the distant shouts of his thrashing conscience, which

had been lying gagged and bound in the depths of his sub-
conscious for quite some time.

It was madness to think once the baby was born, clarity
would return and everything would fall magically into place
but mad or not, Lawrence was clinging to this belief. On the
few occasions when he had lifted the lid on the dark, tangled
mess of his emotions, they had leapt at him, bombarding him
with uncomfortable truths. He knew he loved both Sarah
and Arima and yet his deceit would bring pain to them all.
His thoughts whirled out of control.

*You can't leave your wife . . . do you even want to?*

*Arima thinks you're going to marry her. What will you lose?*

*Do you honestly think she's going to hand the child over and just
disappear?*

*This isn't love. It can't be.*

*How do you intend to resolve this mess?*

*Stop now before it's too late.*

The sentences from his mind took on that inner voice of
rebuke he feared so much. Until he had met Arima he had
never looked at another woman. He had made a covenant
with his eyes and his faith, beleaguered and fleeting as it was,
held him back from even thinking of anyone else. Many of
his friends had taken a mistress, had an affair or used escorts.
Lawrence had not. He had felt it was his duty, even at times
when married love was not easily to be found, to be loyal
and faithful. Sarah was his friend and yet he found betrayal
so simple.

He thought it far, far better not to think at all.
Compartmentalization was the key to ongoing denial, which
was rapidly reaching epic proportions. The trouble was,

Lawrence reflected, helping Arima slowly down the stairs, there were now so many compartments in his life he was in danger of being permanently boxed in. He held her hand, knowing he wanted to be with her, lying with her in green fields under a summer sun. Yet he did not want to leave Sarah. God seemed far away and completely silent.

Philip and Jemma had pulled out all the stops for Beatrice's first birthday party, though Philip drew the line at hiring a magician to entertain the children.

'They're only a year old,' he pointed out. 'They think it's magic if someone ducks behind the sofa and pops back up again. I'm not paying for it.'

'But do you think we have enough organized activities?' Jemma fretted, anxiously running her pen down her to-do list. Philip held out his hand and read the items aloud. 'Chocolate egg hunt . . . colouring in Easter bunny hats . . . pass the parcel . . . pin the tail on the rabbit . . . *paper basket weaving*? You're kidding, right?'

'I want it to be nice for the children,' Jemma said defensively.

'Jemma, they're still babies,' he replied. 'Half of them can't even walk yet. If we gave them all wooden spoons and pans to bang they'd have a great time. We don't need to go to all this trouble.' At the sight of his wife's crestfallen face, he had wisely given in and gone along with it. Not so many months ago Jemma wouldn't have felt able to face organizing a party at all. Philip kept quiet and counted his blessings.

By the time the Abrahams arrived with Arima, the party was in full swing. The conservatory had been transformed into the party room, with picnic rugs and twenty individually labelled organic lunchboxes spread out for the children and a separate buffet for the parents set up along one wall. The wicker sofas were pushed back to allow maximum crawling space and Jemma had installed the craft table in the garden beneath a portable gazebo. Brightly coloured cardboard rabbits were dotted around the lawn and among the flower borders, marking the treasure spots for the egg hunt. The conservatory floor was heaving with little bodies, some rolling, others crawling.

Led by Beatrice in her red taffeta party frock, a few of the more advanced guests made tottering death-or-glory runs from one point of safety to another, emitting high-pitched shrieks of delight. The noise level was probably illegal.

'Speedy little critters, aren't they?' said Robin to Philip, stepping aside as a crawling child darted through his legs.

'Unbelievable,' agreed Philip, a plate of fresh crudités balanced in each hand. 'It's a health and safety nightmare.' He nodded at the open patio doors, where Hannah was cheerfully rebuffing attempted escapees and guarding the door hinges from exploratory fingers. 'I see Jemma's set your friend to work already. She seems a nice, capable sort.'

'She is,' Robin answered, smiling as Hannah gave him a thumbs up, his presence boosting the confidence she'd previously lacked at social events. Dressed in jeans, a Mr Men T-shirt and a baggy blue hoodie appliquéd with hearts, she struck a jarring note among the groomed Kensington mothers. Robin couldn't have cared less.

Philip regarded him with curiosity. 'Not your usual type, is she?' he queried, the inference to Arima oblique but unmistakeable.

'No,' said Robin, not taking his eyes off Hannah for a second. 'She's much better.'

'Good for you.' Philip clapped him on the shoulder. 'It's about time. Oh, was that the doorbell?' He looked around for a safe place to deposit the loaded plates but there was nowhere within arm's reach. 'Could you hold these for a second?'

'Don't worry, I'll get the door.' Robin picked his way through the maze of children and into the hall.

Sarah was helping Arima up the front steps, watching her grimace as the movement sent pain arcing across her hips and thighs.

'Is it bad today?' she asked, supporting Arima at the waist and elbow.

'No,' growled Arima. 'I'm pulling faces for the hell of it.'

'Pregnancy really hasn't agreed with you, has it,' Sarah said apologetically as they paused for a rest.

'It will be worth it,' Arima said unthinkingly. The old suspicions rose to the surface like air bubbles in Sarah's mind. What did Arima mean by that exactly? Sarah redoubled her grip on Arima, fighting the resurgence of her old paranoia. She wasn't herself lately. Lawrence carted the crutches up behind them and leaned on the bell. They were a whole hour late.

'Prepare for the telling-off,' he warned, anticipating Jemma's displeasure.

It was Robin who swung the door open and bowed, twirling one hand in a courtly flourish.

'Greetings, friends. Welcome to the madhouse,' he said, standing up and beaming at them. There was a tiny pause.

'I'm so sorry!' Arima wailed and burst into noisy sobs.

Lawrence and Sarah closed protectively around her, Sarah supporting her sagging weight while Lawrence patted her arm and searched his pockets for a handkerchief. Neither of them had the faintest idea what to do.

'I was only joking about the telling-off.'

'Is it the pain?'

'Perhaps we should go straight home.'

'Go on in,' Robin said, calmly stepping outside. 'Leave her to me.' He and Hannah had discussed this meeting at length. He knew what he had to do. Baffled, Lawrence and Sarah obeyed. As the door closed, Lawrence saw Robin pull Arima into his arms. Jealousy bit deep.

'I'll, er, wait here,' he said to Sarah, making as if to sit down on the stairs. 'Best to be on hand in case she needs us.'

'She'll be perfectly fine with Robin,' Sarah snapped, holding her hand out to him impatiently. 'Come along, Lawrence. I'm wiped out. The sooner we show our faces, the sooner we can leave.'

'Sorry, darling.' Lawrence took her hand and led her down the hall, steeling himself not to look back.

Try as he might, Robin couldn't get Arima to let go of him. She sobbed into his chest, remorse spreading in a dark patch across his grey sweater.

'Arima, look at me.'

She shook her head and sobbed even harder.

'Mima.' It was no good. Not knowing what else to do, Robin scooped her up, deposited her on the front step and sat down beside her, gently prising her arms from about his neck.

'Listen to me,' he said, turning her tear-streaked face up to his. 'I haven't forgiven you for what you did, not by a long shot. And you've got a hell of a lot of explaining to do. But,' he went on as Arima's bottom lip trembled, 'you don't get rid of me that easily. I still love you, Mima.'

Arima managed a wobbly smile. 'You do?'

'Yes.' Robin gave her a gentle nudge with his shoulder. 'Everybody needs a best friend,' he said. 'We go back a long way and besides, you're such a nuisance no one else would put up with you.'

'I suppose you're right.' Arima wiped her eyes on the sleeve of her cardigan. 'I'll tell you about Mum and Dad,' she said quietly. 'The . . . the house fire. If you want.'

'Yes please,' Robin answered. 'But not today. We have time.' He wrapped his arms round Arima and held her close, valuing Hannah's wise head and generous heart. For better or worse, she had counselled, Arima was an important part of his story and always would be, whether she was in London or halfway round the world. If he cut her off, he would be hurting himself too. There were issues to be resolved on both sides and long conversations to be had. Once that was done, Arima could finally occupy her proper place in Robin's life, as a friend. Behind them the door opened a crack and there was a polite cough.

'Any chance you could come in?' Philip begged. 'The conservatory is wrecked and my flower beds are beyond repair. We need to cut the cake and get these hoodlums out of here before they start on the rest of the house.'

'So how did it go?' Hannah asked, meeting Robin later on over the washing up. The parents had eventually regained control of their offspring and departed, leaving a trail of destruction in their wake. Hannah and Robin were in the vanguard of the clean-up team.

'Pretty well,' Robin grinned, wiping a blob of soap bubbles from Hannah's cheek. 'We're going to meet up for a proper chat. You should be a professional counsellor.'

'No,' she said mournfully, her eyes bright with humour. 'No one would take me seriously in my Santa hat and I couldn't possibly work without it.'

'On second thoughts,' Robin snorted, heading back to the conservatory for more dishes. 'Maybe you need a professional counsellor. I'll pay.' Hannah's laughter followed him.

Armed with an enormous broom, Philip was on his twenty-fourth lap of the conservatory, shunting an ever-growing pile of mud, grass, crumbs, baby wipes and wrapping paper into the middle of the floor. 'Where are the others?' enquired Robin, hoping to get the chance to introduce Arima to Hannah.

'I think they're just leaving,' Jemma said, her rear end protruding from beneath one of the wicker sofas. She reversed out and emerged pink-faced and triumphant, cupping a handful of chewed-up raw carrots. 'Lawrence went to get coats. Sarah's not feeling well. She's been upstairs for most of the party.' She tossed the putrid orange mush onto the rubbish pile and wiped her hands on her jeans. 'You'll catch them if you hurry but go quietly. Beatrice is crashed out in the lounge.'

Robin stepped into the long hallway at the same moment as Sarah appeared at the top of the stairs. Neither was aware of the other's presence but they halted in perfect unison, their attention trained on the couple by the door. With their backs to the stairs, Arima and Lawrence were arguing in hushed voices.

'Put this on,' he ordered, moving behind her to pull the cardigan roughly over her shoulders.

'What's wrong?'

'Nothing. I need to go and wake Sarah, that's all.'

She looked up at him, her fingers busy with the buttons. 'Tell me.'

Lawrence shrugged into his own jacket, fussing over the collar. 'You were outside a long time with Robin,' he said tersely.

'So?'

'So I didn't like the way he looked at you.'

'You're jealous.' She laughed delightedly.

'He's been in love with you for years,' Lawrence grumbled. 'You shouldn't lead him on.'

'I wasn't.'

Poised above in the shadows of the stairway, Sarah gasped as Arima's hand lifted to her husband's cheek and he turned his head to kiss her palm, just as he did with Sarah.

The propriety of the gesture was unmistakeable. Rooted to the spot, Robin heard the slight intake of breath and looked up. Sarah gazed into his eyes, reading in them the truth she had so valiantly tried to deny. Strangely, there was no pain, only a numbing sense of defeat as the plans she had laid imploded and her life came crashing down about her. A single thought materialized.

*You did this. You, Sarah.*

She wondered if she could salvage anything from the wreckage. Closing her eyes as Robin's honest face projected the answer she started to cry.

Arima intended to take Sarah's entire life, piece by piece, starting with her husband. The child would be next, Sarah had no doubt. Had this been Arima's plan from the start, to lure Lawrence away with the promise of something Sarah could not give? Sarah clutched the banister for support. She knew she had to fight but next to Arima she felt old, sick and tired.

As Lawrence stepped away from Arima, Robin and Sarah moved with one accord, signalling their approach with fake coughs and exaggerated footfalls.

'Hey, there you are,' said Lawrence, beaming up at his wife.

'Is it time to go?' yawned Sarah, joining them at the foot of the stairs. 'I've missed the whole party. What a washout.' She kissed her husband and bestowed a loving smile on Arima. 'Let's go home.'

At that moment, Robin admired her courage more than he could say.

'Not without saying goodbye,' he protested, prompting a flurry of handshakes and kisses, then a second round as Jemma and Philip appeared to wave them off.

Robin swept Sarah into a hug and received a bleak smile in return. She intended to tough it out, to win Lawrence back if she could, but the odds were heavily stacked against her in this contest.

Love was Sarah's only weapon, and she knew it was not enough.

# Chapter 23

Sarah was clutching at straws. She knew it but did it anyway because that's what people do when their lives fall apart. They try to turn back time, thwart natural laws, magically make things happen simply by wanting them to. She had read about it in a magazine once: it had to do with the stages of grief. Apparently there were quite a few and the first was denial. Next up were anger and bargaining, but for now there were no windows in Sarah's emotional schedule – she had more than enough denial to be going on with. For several weeks she threw herself into being the most perfect wife imaginable, pushing herself to be brighter, sexier, more organized, more intelligent, a better cook, a more attentive listener. A Fun Person. She left photo albums lying around, dredged up happy memories from the past and found ways of shoe-horning them into conversation.

'Could you pass the salt, please?'

'Remember when we had that lovely holiday in Cornwall, darling, and went surfing every day? The sea was so salty there, wasn't it?'

'I'm so tired I can barely stand up.'

'Like the time we came home from New Zealand and flew off to that gorgeous wedding in Canada the next week?

And I was so tired I walked into a glass door and knocked myself out cold?'

'This fish pie is superb.'

'I used to cook this when we were first married, do you remember?'

By normal standards this would have been exhausting, but in Sarah's weakened state it was almost impossible to sustain. Somehow, she kept going, plastering more and more make-up onto her face to camouflage the dark smudges beneath her eyes and the unhealthy pallor of her skin. Positivity was the key, Sarah told herself a hundred times a day. Don't attack Arima or Lawrence will be forced to take sides. Concentrate on reminding him of all the reasons why he fell in love with you. It was a startling effort on her part, not least because she felt as though somebody had flicked the shut-down switch on her body.

At home Sarah was being all things to all people; work was a different matter. She sat dumbly through meetings, hands clamped to the chair to keep herself upright, mumbled incoherently at her students and sleepwalked from the studio space to her office and back again, often for no reason at all. It did not go unnoticed.

Among the bitchier enclaves, the words 'breakdown' and 'mid-life crisis' were bandied about. Kinder colleagues, such as Marjorie, said nothing but arrived frequently at Sarah's desk bearing industrial-strength coffee and packets of bis-cuits. Each time, Sarah thanked them with a glazed smile and didn't touch a thing. She was barely eating at all, contenting herself with picking over the bones of the last year and try-ing to pinpoint how things had gone so wrong.

At night she thrashed in her sleep, tormented by images of Arima reclining like an Egyptian queen on Sarah's beloved Chesterfield sofa, stroking her enormous stomach while Lawrence looked on adoringly and Sarah ran herself ragged waiting on the pair of them. Smug eyes were what gave Arima away. She looked permanently smug, her eyes following Sarah as if to say, 'I've figured out your game. Go ahead and try – your best isn't even going to come close.'

The menopause was the final insult. Sarah had stalled on going to the doctors for a couple of weeks, cancelling three appointments until Lawrence had got wind of it and forced her to go for the tests. That was another facet of the denial – Sarah knew the change was upon her but if she delayed going back for the results, put off hearing the doctor say the words, maybe for a while it wouldn't be true.

Lawrence didn't get it. Sarah limped on, ignoring his every attempt to reason with her until he finally lost all patience and made the follow-up appointment for her. At least it showed he still cared.

'Now you won't forget your appointment,' he said, waking her with a cup of tea on a sunny mid-May morning. 'Will you.' It wasn't a question.

Sarah tried to roll over but Lawrence put the heel of his hand on her shoulder, pinning her to the mattress. 'Ten-thirty,' he said.

'It's not convenient today,' Sarah complained. 'I have to take Arima for her appointment with the midwife and I'm not trekking to the surgery twice in one day. I can't afford the time off work. Anyway, it's bad time management.'

'No, it isn't,' Lawrence contradicted her. 'The receptionist managed to synchronize your appointments. It's ten-thirty for both of you. In and out, job done.' Sarah batted his hand irritably. Everything hurt. 'Let me sit up.'

'Sorry.' Lawrence sat back on the bed and passed her the cup of tea. 'You will go, Sarah, won't you?' he begged. 'It's better to know for sure.'

'I already know,' Sarah grumbled. 'The menopause isn't something to be cured. You just live with it.'

'Not like this you don't,' Lawrence said emphatically. 'You're not well, darling. There are . . .' he waved a hand vaguely. 'I don't know, supplements you can take, aren't there?' Sarah grunted. There were, but she wasn't going to concede the point.

'Promise me you won't cancel again,' he insisted, getting up to fetch a suit jacket from the wardrobe.

'Don't *fuss*, Lawrence.' The perfect wife act faltered as her temper slipped.

'I'm not leaving until you've promised.' Lawrence stood at the foot of the bed with his arms folded. Sarah glared at him. Lawrence rolled his eyes despairingly. 'Please.'

'Okay. Now please stop nagging and go to work.'

Lawrence stooped over her to steal a victory kiss on his way out but Sarah turned her face away, ungracious in defeat. Her bad mood lasted through a shower, blow-dry, long and painstaking make-up application and choosing clothes. It was bolstered by helping Arima downstairs and continued during breakfast. Hunched at the counter, Sarah crunched her cereal viciously, rather enjoying the fit of temper after weeks of enforced good humour. She paused, spoon dangling half-way to her mouth as a thought struck her. Perhaps she'd moved on to stage two of grief – anger. At least she was progressing.

'Sarah?' Arima's voice floated through from the lounge. 'I'm done with the tray, thanks. A peppermint tea would be great, when you're ready.'

'Just a second.' Sarah shoved the spoon into her mouth and bit down hard to smother her rage. Propped up on cushions in the lounge, Arima traced languid circles on her stomach with one hand and shifted to a more comfortable position.

'Not long now, baby,' she whispered. A smile crept over her face at the sound of crockery clashing in the sink. Sarah was teetering on the edge now. The time was ripe. Confident of her growing hold on Lawrence, Arima was working hard now, building up to the confrontation she had striven to avoid, certain he would choose her over Sarah. In the end it was easy, pitifully easy.

Thanks to the symphysis pubis disorder, Arima genuinely needed assistance; she had no choice but to rest while Sarah ran herself into the ground, playing Superwife.

Poor, sick Sarah. When Lawrence sat beside her in the evenings, Arima was aware of his eyes on his wife, heard genuine tenderness in his voice. He loved her still, Arima could see that, but the truth was Sarah no longer posed a threat. The slightest wince of pain from Arima, a feather-light touch of her fingers on his neck as he bent his head to kiss her stomach and Lawrence was hers again. She teased him with snatched kisses and breathless promises. They would have more children, as many as he wanted. 'Like the stars,' she whispered. 'Star-watchers, like me.'

Only two people in Arima's life could have intervened, throwing themselves between the Abrahams and Arima to halt the impending collision. Together, Alaia and Robin might have prevailed. But Alaia was dead and Robin, who should have tried, stood helplessly by, sensing that his childhood friend had travelled too far along this shadow-path, past reason, beyond recall. Alone, his pleas would have been no more than faint cries in the wilderness, lost on the gathering wind. No voice on earth had the power to reach Arima now.

At ten-fifteen they arrived at the surgery, Arima limping over the threshold with her crutches. Even using them over a short distance made her hot and crotchety, the handgrips digging into her palms and the slightly stooped angle generating a slow burn across her shoulders. Arima lowered herself onto a seat with difficulty while Sarah went to register their arrival on the touch-screen system. The lady next to her offered a sympathetic smile.

'Wrecked your pelvis?' Arima nodded. 'That happened to me with my second,' sighed the lady. 'Hurt like hell.' She saw Sarah approaching and shuffled along to make room, moving her handbag onto her lap. 'Having your mum to help makes all the difference, doesn't it?' she said encouragingly. 'I couldn't have coped without mine.' Sarah gave her a stare that would have felled a giant and she shrank back, clutching her handbag to her chest. Arima didn't bother to hide her smile. The lady began to stammer an apology but was interrupted by the crackle of the intercom.

'Sarah Abrahams to Room Four, please. Sarah Abrahams, Room Four.'

'Arima Middleton to Treatment Room One.'

Sarah rose without a word and strode to the door, leaving Arima to fend for herself. Arima hauled herself up and gave the lady a cheeky wink as she hobbled off. 'Don't worry about it,' she grinned. 'Mum's a bit touchy today.'

Sarah was so incensed by the incident she walked straight into the consultation room without bothering to knock, sat down before being invited and dropped her handbag heavily onto the floor.

'Let's get it over with,' she said belligerently. 'I haven't got all day.'

'Mrs Abrahams?' queried Dr Colman, unfazed by Sarah's rude and abrupt manner.

'Yes.'

He flicked her notes up onto the computer screen.

'Ah. You're here for your test results, is that correct?'

'Yes,' Sarah answered, closing her teeth over the more impatient reply that came to mind. The doctor read the information carefully, appearing to cross-check the details several times. Sarah's foot began to tap against the chair leg. 'Look,' she burst out, 'I'm menopausal but I don't want to discuss it, if it's all the same to you. Just write me a prescription for some tablets and let me go.'

Dr Colman sat back in his chair and regarded Sarah solemnly, his astute gaze noting the salient points of her demeanour, from her open agitation to her slumped shoulders and haggard face. The aura about her was one of mingled exhaustion and defeat. This wasn't going to be straightforward.

'I can't give you a prescription without first discussing your condition,' he began, feeling his way into the conversation.

'I'm not prepared to discuss it.' Sarah folded her arms and stared the doctor out, trying to browbeat him into submission.

'Mrs Abrahams, I'm afraid you must.'

'Must?' she snapped. 'Why must I?' A sliver of fear cut into her. 'Have you found . . . something else, as well?' Surely not. She was healthy, there was no history of cancer in the family, no hereditary diseases.

'No, no, there's no cause for alarm,' replied the doctor, at pains to reassure. 'Your test results show no abnormalities whatsoever.' He paused, waiting for Sarah to meet his eye. 'You're pregnant.'

His words fell into the silence and sank without trace, like a stone tossed into a pond. Slowly, the ripples began to spread.

'I'm – I'm what?'

'You're pregnant,' he repeated.

Sarah laughed. She couldn't help it.

'That's impossible.'

'Not at all,' the doctor assured her, checking the computer screen once more to be sure of the facts. 'It's – unusual – to fall pregnant at forty-six but not unheard of. You'd be surprised.'

Sarah put a hand to her head, incapable of processing the information. 'But . . . but I can't be,' she stuttered. 'Years and years we've been trying. We've spent thousands. They said there was no hope.'

'Sometimes, nature takes its course when the time is right,' said Dr Colman, judging it safe to smile. Sarah's head was shaking of its own accord as her brain went into shock.

'Are you absolutely sure about this?'

'There's no doubt,' the doctor confirmed. 'HCG, the pregnancy hormone, doubles its levels in the body every forty-eight hours in the early stages of a pregnancy. It's very clear.' He glanced back at the screen. 'The levels start to dip after twelve weeks and your HCG level is very high. I'd put you at about ten weeks.'

'Ten weeks?' Sarah grappled with the figures, her mind saturated with joy. 'So . . . so when am I due?'

'Sometime in November. A winter baby,' smiled the doctor, touched by the emotion on Sarah's face. She looked like someone who had been handed a last-minute reprieve on a death sentence.

'November.' Sarah stood up unsteadily, reaching blindly for her bag. 'I have to go,' she mumbled. 'My husband . . .' The room lurched in and out of focus.

'Of course.' The doctor hurried round the desk to show her to the door. 'Call the surgery to make your booking-in appointment with the midwife.' He followed her out into the corridor, concerned by her dazed manner. 'Mrs Abrahams?'

'Yes?'

'Go and have a cup of tea. You look quite faint. And congratulations.'

'Thank you,' Sarah beamed. 'Thank you!' She stumbled out of the surgery and sank to the ground with her back against the wall, heedless of her expensive skirt scuffing in the dirt. Her mobile was buried deep in her handbag and Sarah's urgent scrabbling failed to unearth it. 'Come on, come on.' She tipped the bag upside down, sending a shower of cosmetics and personal effects rolling over the tarmac. With shaking fingers, she punched the speed dial for Lawrence and waited. Voicemail.

'Office,' she muttered, fumbling over the keys. Lawrence's plastic secretary answered in her best Marilyn Monroe voice. 'Yes, hello,' Sarah snapped. The ridiculous woman sounded as though she was having an asthma attack. 'Lawrence Abrahams please. It's Sarah.' There was a pause. 'His wife.' More breathy bleating came down the line. 'I don't care if he's in a meeting, fetch him out. It's urgent.' She waited, heart pounding. 'Yes? No, it's not alright for him to call me back. I told you it was urgent.' Sarah hung up and hurled the phone to the ground, grinding her teeth in frustration. The one time she needed him, life and death, and he was closing a deal. She pressed her hands to her stomach, unable to contain her feelings. The need to tell someone was paramount. Then it would be real. Retrieving her phone, she wiped her coat sleeve over the smeared, cracked screen and dialled a third number.

'Hello?'

'Eva, it's Sarah.'

'Hello, my darling. Is something wrong? You sound anxious.'

Sarah held back for a few seconds, letting the butterflies surge in her stomach. 'I'm pregnant,' she said, revelling in the feel of the word on her lips. 'Pregnant. Ten weeks.' There was a muffled thump as Eva fell back on her bed.

'Eva? Eva?'

'Praise God,' Eva breathed, laughing through her tears. 'What did I tell you, Sarah? Haven't I always said it?'

'You did,' Sarah replied, beaming into the phone. 'But Eva, listen. Lawrence doesn't know yet. You're the first.'

'It's a privilege to share it with you, darling girl. If only you had believed . . .' There was a pause before Eva spoke again, anxiety sharpening her voice. 'And Arima?'

Sarah sucked her breath in with a hiss, wary of speaking ill of Lawrence to his devoted mother. 'Things have become . . . difficult,' she said, deliberately circumspect. 'Arima is confused about her feelings. In all sorts of ways. Lawrence . . .'

'. . . is a man and therefore a fool,' Eva finished, relieving Sarah of the responsibility. 'When it comes to beautiful women, they all are. I saw it at Christmas, but it wasn't my place to speak.' Sarah shut her eyes, the relief at finding an ally indescribable. 'It's you he loves, Sarah,' Eva said with utter certainty. 'Desire burns itself out. Love goes the distance. And of course, now . . .'

'Exactly,' said Sarah, following her mother-in-law's thought. 'Now what?' Suddenly she was holding all the cards and had forgotten how to play.

Eva lowered her voice but there was no mistaking the force of her message. 'Now,' she said slowly, 'you do what any mother would. Protect your family.' Hearing her own instincts articulated, Sarah closed her mind to the surging joy within her and thought fast, assessing options and risks with cold, calculating logic. 'You know what to do,' urged Eva.

At that moment Arima appeared at the door, her crutches slipping as she tried to manhandle both them and her bag down the steps. 'I need a hand here,' she called.

'She's here.' Sarah snapped the phone shut and stood up, making no move to help the struggling girl.

'Sarah? I can't manage,' Arima called. Sarah walked slowly over to the bottom of the steps and stood there, arms folded, watching as Arima tottered down, step by painful step, almost falling as she reached the bottom. 'I need a rest,' she panted, looking up at Sarah through her tangled hair. 'Take me home.'

'I'm afraid that won't be possible,' Sarah said sweetly.

'What?' Arima stared at her, puzzled, then rephrased her statement. 'When we get home, I'll have a rest.'

'Not possible,' Sarah repeated. 'I need to rest too and I can't do that with you there.'

Arima swayed on her feet, beads of sweat forming on her upper lip.

'Listen, Sarah . . .'

'No, you listen.' Sarah ordered. 'You listen to me, you little slut.' Arima's head rocked back as though she'd been slapped. She tried to move back, put some distance between them but she was trapped against the steps with nowhere to go. Sarah came on, firing words like bullets, relishing the impact as every insult thudded into Arima's chest. 'Do you really think my husband wants you?' she scoffed. 'You're nothing to him. A temporary amusement.'

'What . . . the . . .'

'Shut up!' she hissed as Arima tried to speak. 'You think you're going to steal my husband and take the child?' She snapped her fingers right in Arima's face. 'Keep the brat,' she scoffed. 'Take it and be welcome to it, but Lawrence is staying with me.' She locked her hands across her stomach, her lips curving in a triumphant smile as she saw fear kindle in Arima's eyes.

'You're . . .'

'That's right,' said Sarah softly. 'I'm pregnant. After all these years. It's a miracle, don't you think?'

Arima was speechless, her breath coming in laboured gasps. Her crutches clattered to the ground as she collapsed onto the step, hands gripping her stomach.

'Oh dear,' Sarah cooed, bending over her in a show of concern. 'I hope you haven't gone into labour. I've heard shock can do that.'

'Help . . . me,' Arima moaned, turning a pain-wracked face up to her old friend.

Sarah smiled cruelly. This was her moment.

'Don't worry,' she murmured, stroking Arima's hair. 'Everything will be fine.' She waited for the flash of relief in Arima's eyes before stepping away. 'You're in the right place,' she said, pointing up at the surgery door. 'I have to go home and rest now, Arima. Doctor's orders.' She scooped up her belongings, stuffed them into her bag and set off with a cheery wave. 'I'll have your belongings packed up in the camper, don't worry about a thing,' she called cheerily. 'Bye now!'

Arima doubled over as the pain struck again, knifing across her stomach and into her back. Through her tears, she watched Sarah reach the car, pause and turn back. 'Thank God,' she whimpered.

Sarah trotted back, her heels clipping smartly over the pavement. She stopped a few feet away from Arima, a look of mock outrage on her face. 'Come now, Arima,' she chided. 'Aren't you going to congratulate me before I go?'

# Chapter 24

Robin was enjoying a lazy lunch with Hannah at the Borough market when the call came. 'Sorry?' he said, putting a hand to his ear to block out the hustle from the surrounding stalls. 'Where did you say she was?' Hannah put down her minted lamb burger as Robin's face changed, reaching out to lay a reassuring hand on his.

'What's wrong?' asked Hannah.

'It's Arima,' said Robin, hooking his jacket from the back of his chair. 'She's in hospital.'

Hannah swigged the dregs of her cappuccino and jumped up. 'Let's go.'

'You don't have to come, Han.'

'Don't be silly. I want to.' She took his hand and made for the exit. 'Where is she?'

'St Thomas's. I'll explain on the way.' Anxiety blunting their manners, they pushed through the shoppers, picking up speed as the crowd thinned out in the street.

'It'll be just as quick walking,' Hannah puffed, trying to keep pace with Robin as they jogged towards the tube station. 'The tube's rammed today.'

'True.' Robin swerved aside, pulling her along with him.

'Is the baby okay?' Hannah panted, holding her side as a stitch began to develop.

'Yes, but Arima isn't. They can't calm her down.'

'If she's in labour, I'm not surprised.'

'Where are Lawrence and Sarah?'

Robin shook his head grimly. 'God knows.'

Twenty minutes later, they barrelled through the doors of the maternity unit, red-faced and panting from the run. 'Arima Middleton,' wheezed Robin, leaning on the reception desk where a midwife was catching up on paperwork, humming to herself as she sipped a well-earned mug of tea. She had only been on duty since twelve but by two o'clock it was already shaping up to be a busy shift.

The midwife snapped to attention at the mention of Arima's name. 'The surrogate baby? This way,' she said briskly. 'It's good you made it in time.'

'In time?' Robin stammered as she led them smartly down a corridor towards the private wing. 'In time for what?' The midwife stopped by one of the doors, Robin and Hannah almost skidding into the back of her. She knocked before opening the door a few inches, not quite revealing what was inside. 'The intended parents are here,' she announced.

'The – the what? No, I . . .' Robin turned to Hannah for help but before either of them could explain, they were thrust inside.

'Straight in, please,' the midwife said. 'The obstetrician will be here any minute to bring you up to speed. We need to be moving things along.'

As the door closed on their escape route, another midwife bustled forwards. She was a short, kindly looking Afro-Caribbean woman, her hair woven into dozens of intricate plaits that swung about her face. 'Mercy,' she said by way of introduction.

'Pardon?' said Robin, blinking in confusion.

'My name,' she chuckled, leading them to the high hospital bed, its head jacked up to keep the patient upright. 'She's been waiting for you. We gave her some pain relief so she's quite placid at the moment. She was very wound up when they brought her in.'

'Who brought her in?' Robin demanded.

Mercy shot him a curious look. 'The ambulance,' she replied.

Arima was slumped on the bed, some kind of monitor belted to her stomach. Beside her, a machine clicked, emitting occasional anxious beeps. Her eyes were closed and she was sucking on a long tube tipped with a plastic mouthpiece, her head lolling to one side. A second contraption was taped to her upper arm to monitor her blood pressure.

Who on earth, Robin wondered, moving the wheeled stand aside as Hannah took the other side of the bed, had thought turquoise walls would make for a relaxing birth environment? 'Arima?' he said, stroking her hair off her face. She opened her eyes and smiled woozily.

'I knew you'd come,' she slurred. 'Where's Lawrence?'

'He's on his way,' Robin lied, hoping to God that it was true.

Hannah took Arima's hand. 'How are you doing?' she asked.

'Oh, you've brought a little friend,' Arima said, beaming up at Robin. 'That's nice.' She took another long drag from the tube and turned to address Hannah. 'I'm not doing very well at all,' she said seriously. 'I only scored three points in the test. Rubbish. I'm much better at spelling tests.'

Mercy intercepted the glance that passed between Robin and Hannah.

'She's had a pethidine injection and gas and air,' she explained. 'It makes people a bit punch-drunk.'

'Ah,' said Robin, already way out of his comfort zone and accelerating towards hysteria. 'And the, er, three out of ten?'

'She's three centimetres dilated.'

'And we need to get to . . . ?'

'Ten.'

Arima looked up at Hannah. 'I'm not going to make it,' she said frankly.

'You're doing brilliantly,' Hannah said, squeezing Arima's hand. 'It's going to be fine.'

'I like her,' Arima told Robin. 'But why are her eyes all big and cattish?'

'Er . . .'

'I read a lot,' Hannah said swiftly. 'In the dark, you know?'

'Ohhh.' Arima nodded sagely. 'Bad idea, that. Aaaarrrrgh!' She stuck the tube back into her mouth and sucked for all she was worth as another contraction hit her.

'I'm just going to, um, make a call,' Robin said, starting to edge towards the door. Lawrence and Sarah really ought to be here. More to the point, he really, really needed not to be here. Arima's hand closed on his wrist, her fingernails digging into the soft tissue.

'You can't go,' she whimpered.

'It's okay,' said Hannah, stroking Arima's hair and enduring the vice-like grip of her hand with apparent ease. 'He's not going anywhere. Breathe into it, just breathe into it. You're doing great. It'll ease off in a minute.' Beside her, Mercy gave an approving nod. Robin stared at his girlfriend in amazement.

'It's not rocket science, Robin,' Hannah said, ordering him back to his place with a jerk of her head.

'Don't leave me,' Arima begged as the pain carried her off.

'We won't,' said Hannah firmly, her tone leaving Robin no room for negotiation.

The door opened and the obstetrician swept in, his team scuttling deferentially behind him.

'Ah, here's Mr Ledley,' said Mercy, gratefully relinquishing the medical notes to one of the underlings, a thin-faced man with spiky blonde hair. The obstetrician took the notes, scanned them without comment and approached Robin.

'I am Mr Ledley,' he said, grasping Robin's hand. 'You're Mr Abrahams?'

'That's right,' said Hannah loudly. 'And I'm Sarah, his wife.' Robin gaped at her. What the hell was she playing at? Mr Ledley switched his attention to Hannah, who was clearly the more lucid of the couple.

'And you have your surrogate's permission to attend the delivery, is that correct?'

'Absolutely,' said Hannah, assuming her best honest-as-the-day-was-long face and ignoring the looks of alarm Robin was shooting at her. 'Arima has asked us to stay.' At least that part was true. Mr Ledley nodded and introduced himself to Arima, who favoured him with a beatific smile before drifting off into her own world again. After a swift examination, Mr Ledley made his decision.

'I strongly recommend a Caesarean section,' he informed them. 'She's had injections to slow the contractions but they haven't worked. Her pelvic bones have separated too much to allow a comfortable delivery and the baby has been showing signs of distress. At thirty-two weeks it's not ideal but we can cope with it. This baby won't wait.'

Arima opened her eyes and saw Robin standing at the foot of the bed, pale-faced as the dark-haired man in a white shirt and red tie talked rapidly at him. She took another pull on the gas and air, snatches of the conversation floating through the haze to reach her. 'Caesarean section . . . signs of distress . . .' She was aware of a form in front of her, Hannah putting a pen in her hand and encouraging her to sign her name.

'Where's Lawrence?' she mumbled.

'Shush, it's okay,' soothed Hannah, releasing Arima's hand as she was wheeled from the room.

Mercy beckoned to Robin and Hannah. 'This way.'

Robin waited until they were alone in the changing area, scrambling out of their clothes into outfits resembling blue pyjamas and rubbery moon boots. Then he let rip.

'What are you *doing*?' he hissed, looking over his shoulder in case they were overheard. 'We're not allowed in there! What if Lawrence turns up?'

'Look,' said Hannah, tucking her hair into what looked like a blue shower-cap. 'There's no time. Lawrence won't make it.'

'We could get in serious trouble for this!'

'I'm not leaving her on her own in there,' Hannah said calmly. 'Pretty soon the wacky-gas is going to wear off and then she'll be terrified. Giving birth is a frightening experience.'

'You're telling me,' Robin gulped.

'Besides,' Hannah continued, sitting down to pull her moon boots on. 'A labouring woman can have anyone she wants in the delivery room. Arima asked us to stay.'

'But we're impersonating other people,' Robin protested.

'Needs must.' Hannah thrust one of the plastic hats at him and stood up. 'Now put that on and shut up. And when we get into theatre, don't look over the screen.'

'Why not?'

'Just don't. Trust me on this.'

While Robin screwed his courage to the sticking point, the real Lawrence was a few miles away, sitting in a restaurant opposite Philip and looking down the barrel of a confession. Like Robin, he was also taking his courage in both hands, though for entirely different reasons. Philip was a solid man and a good friend. It was time to come clean and seek advice.

'So,' said Philip, hacking into a large steak. 'What did you want to discuss? Is this business or pleasure?'

'Er . . . neither, actually,' said Lawrence, wondering how one was supposed to open a conversation like this. Philip glanced up, his curiosity whetted by the odd remark. Lawrence was normally a straightforward, decisive man. This tentative manner was not something he'd encountered with his friend before.

'Something wrong?' he asked.

'Yes and no, I suppose,' Lawrence hedged. 'It depends how you look at it.'

'Is it the baby?' This was like pulling teeth.

'No, no. The baby's fine.'

Philip put down his cutlery and stared at his friend. 'Spit it out, Lawrence,' he said bluntly. 'What's bothering you?'

Lawrence took a sip of claret, a slight tremor in his hand as he replaced the glass on the table. Best to come right out with it, he decided. 'It's not the baby,' he said. 'It's the women.'

Philip was none the wiser. 'What, they're not getting on?'

Lawrence fiddled with his napkin, unable to meet the other man's gaze.

'Not desperately well, no. But I'm getting on with them . . . *both* . . . of them. Rather . . . well.'

This was excruciating. They sat in silence as Philip fed the inferences into his brain and translated them into plain English. He baulked at the answer that presented itself. That couldn't be right. If Lawrence meant what Philip thought he meant, then . . . no. It couldn't be right. Unfortunately, the only way to find out for sure was to ask. He cleared his throat delicately.

'Are you saying,' he said, keeping his voice low, 'you're having an affair? With Arima?' Lawrence nodded, his eyes fixed on a random point in the middle distance. 'But you're also saying that you still love Sarah?' Another nod. Philip took a long, slow drink from his own wine glass, dabbed at his mouth with his napkin and set it down on the table. 'You prat,' he said quietly. 'You total, utter prat.'

Lawrence hung his head. 'I know, but I love them both . . .'

'Your life wasn't already complicated enough without throwing this into the mix?' Philip shook his head in disbelief.

'Right. Let's approach this thing logically,' he said, engaging the business side of his brain. 'Putting aside the rights and wrongs of it, let's take it from the top. Does Sarah know?'

'She suspected at one time,' Lawrence admitted, 'but I convinced her nothing was going on.'

'Right,' said Philip, suppressing his disgust. 'And Arima? What's her take on the situation?'

'She wants to keep the baby,' Lawrence said.

'And go skipping off through the bluebells to play happy families with you?'

'Yes.' Lawrence squirmed as Philip's incisive questioning exposed him, dragging each uncomfortable truth out into the light, where they writhed like vipers on the tablecloth. 'I didn't mean for this to happen, any of it. The thing is, it just ... did.'

Philip couldn't let the comment pass. 'Things don't just happen, Lawrence,' he spluttered. 'You had a choice, man. Own it.'

'But that's just it, Philip,' Lawrence groaned, his head in his hands. 'I haven't made a choice! I don't know what to do for the best.'

*Try a long walk off a short pier*, thought Philip, keeping his face blank. At this point in time he'd be happy to provide the necessary push. Lawrence was a friend, and anyone could make a mistake but this was much more than a minor slip-up. 'You need to sort this out, Lawrence,' he said forcefully. 'And fast. We're talking about people's lives here. A child's life, for God's sake. You can't muck about.'

'What's your advice?' Lawrence's face filled with hope at the thought someone might take the decision off his shoulders.

Philip shook his head. 'It has to come from you, Lawrence,' he said. 'You know that. Think. What is it that you want?'

'I . . . I want it all,' Lawrence whispered, shame stripping him of all dignity.

'Damn it, man, you can't *have* it all!' Philip struck the table hard with his fist, causing the plates to rattle. The elderly lady at the next table shrieked in fright and dropped her drink. Shards of glass and red wine splattered on the floor, the thick, viscous liquid like droplets of blood. 'I'm so sorry,' Philip apologized, signalling for a waiter to replace her drink. 'Please excuse me.'

'I'd like to move,' the lady quavered, grabbing the waiter's arm for protection as he reached the table.

'We can't tolerate outbursts like that, sir,' the waiter warned, helping the woman up. 'Any more and I'll request you leave.' He accepted Philip's profuse apologies with a toss of his gel-slicked hair and escorted the shaken lady away. Philip snatched up his cutlery and attacked his rapidly-cooling meal, waiting for his temper to subside. Lawrence followed suit, noting with some anxiety that his friend was stabbing his chips with an alarming degree of aggression. By the time the plates were cleared, Philip felt sufficiently in command of himself to resume the conversation.

'Lawrence,' he said wearily. 'You can't run a sodding harem in Kensington. Apart from the obvious flaws in that plan, Sarah would tear you limb from limb. You need to exit Lawrence-Land and get back into the real world before it's too late.' He reached for his wallet as the waiter approached with the bill. Lawrence bowed his head, accepting the rebuke. 'Every man I talk to these days thinks he can have his cake and eat it. We are getting old . . . we have to accept that. We can't live our lives how we want – there are consequences . . .'

'I know . . . and there are also promises.'

While Philip settled up, Lawrence checked his phone for messages, having set it to silent when he left the office for his 'meeting'. To his surprise, there were several missed calls from earlier, first from Sarah, then Arima. There were also two voicemail messages. Lawrence pressed the recall button and lifted the phone to his ear. Philip was right. He needed to take the bull by the horns and sort things out once and for all, do the decent thing. But what was the decent thing? The first message began to play back.

'Lawrence, it's Robin.' He sounded completely hysterical. 'Arima's had the baby.' Lawrence nearly fell of his chair. How could that be? There were still another eight weeks to go. 'It's . . . it's . . .' Lawrence held his breath. Was it the son he'd longed for? '. . . amazing.' Robin stuttered as he breathed hard. 'She's been asking for you. Get here as soon as you can.' There was a pause, then, 'I think it's the least you can do.'

'My God,' Lawrence whispered. 'Oh my God.'

'Lawrence?' Philip was frowning at him as he buttoned his jacket, preparing to head off. 'Everything okay? You looked miles away.'

'Arima's had the baby,' Lawrence said in a quiet choked voice. 'Hang on, there's another message.' It was Sarah, fed up of waiting for him to get in touch, tired of calling his office to harangue Deborah. Lawrence's jaw went slack as he listened to her, the colour draining from his face. Philip moved swiftly round the table.

'Lawrence?' he repeated, placing a hand on his friend's shoulder. 'Is the baby alright?'

Lawrence let the phone fall into his lap, his mouth working. No words would come. He breathed hard, gasping each breath as if it were his last.

Philip increased his grip, beginning to panic.

'What is it?' he demanded. 'Are they okay? Tell me they're okay.' Lawrence made no reply. Philip grabbed both shoulders and shook him roughly. 'Lawrence . . . what is it?'

With enormous effort, Lawrence turned his face towards Philip.

'It's Sarah,' he said, his voice hoarse with shock.

'Yes?' Philip prompted when Lawrence said nothing more. 'Is she okay?'

'Yes,' said Lawrence, his lips clumsily forming the words. 'Yes. She's pregnant.'

'She . . . she . . .' It was Philip's turn to be stunned. He felt behind him for a chair and sat down abruptly. Neither man spoke for some time, forgotten limbs hanging by their sides like puppets with their strings cut.

Lawrence spoke. 'If only she had believed . . . none of this would have happened . . .'

# Chapter 25

Three days passed. Three, tear-filled, pain-riddled days in which the separation of day and night ceased to exist, blending into a fractured, stop-start rhythm of waking and sleeping, the transitions triggered by the insatiable wail of a newborn child. Arima sat in her private room high up in the North Wing, exhausted and in pain, staring blankly at the television and rocking her baby to and fro, to and fro, waiting, waiting. Surely Lawrence would come soon.

There had been a moment of terror after the Caesarean when the midwives had handed the baby to Robin and encouraged him to remove it from Arima's sight, following the policy guidelines for surrogacy. It was better for surrogates not to handle the babies, she said. Bonding caused problems. Robin had stepped past her and gently placed the baby in Arima's arms. 'It's a boy,' he said in an awestruck voice. 'Your little boy.'

'Mr Abrahams,' said the midwife, seizing his arm urgently, 'We don't advise that –'

'No.' Robin cut her off, politely but firmly. 'No. Let her hold him. She's his mother.'

'We can wait,' agreed Hannah, swift to back Robin up. 'There's plenty of time.'

The midwife had glanced from Arima, her arms encircling the baby in a fierce, tender embrace, to Robin and Hannah. All three were in tears.

Arima eventually laid the baby in his little glass cot.

'On your heads be it,' the midwife muttered under her breath as they set off in convoy with the cot, Robin trudging behind with Hannah.

Robin and Hannah had kept vigil by the bedside for the rest of that day, waiting for Lawrence and Sarah to arrive and take their place. The baby was small and would need monitoring for several days but after a thorough examination the doctors pronounced him healthy. Robin was jittery with nerves, fretting about how they were going to get round the thorny issue of mistaken identity.

Hannah, watching Arima with the baby, was worrying about the real issue at stake here. Huddled in the corridor for a team talk, she voiced her concerns. 'I don't think she wants to give this baby up, Robin,' she said, biting her lip. 'They can't make her, can they? Just look at them.' She gestured through the half-curtained window at Arima, tired and doped up on morphine but staring resolutely at the cot, refusing to close her eyes in case her son needed her. 'It wouldn't be right.'

Robin put his arms round her and rested his chin on her head. 'No,' he agreed. 'I feared this all along. She wouldn't listen.' He rubbed a hand tiredly over his unshaven jaw. 'But it's worse than that, Hannah.'

'What?' She looked up at him, pulling back to see his face. 'How could it be worse?' Her face paled as Robin told her what he'd seen at Beatrice's party.

'And . . . and Sarah saw it too?' she gasped. 'You're absolutely sure about that?' Robin nodded. 'So why isn't Lawrence here?' Hannah wondered.

Robin shrugged, no longer able to distinguish between truth and lies in the whole twisted-up situation. 'He hasn't answered my calls.'

'This is way beyond complicated,' Hannah said. 'I just don't understand what's going on.'

'I'm not sure anybody does,' Robin replied, worry etched deep into his forehead. 'Including them.'

He was wrong. Alone and struggling to adjust to the hammer-blow of motherhood, Arima knew. Cocooned in comfort at home and watching Lawrence's every move, Sarah knew. And Lawrence . . . Lawrence slid through the cracks in his conscience and tried to escape his guilt.

Sarah had been jubilant when Lawrence arrived home, doubly so when she heard Arima had given birth that same day. Lawrence had made his choice. A single day later with news of her pregnancy and she might have lost him, she thought, marvelling at the timing. Against all the odds, she had won. Little was said; little needed to be said. Arima's things were missing from the house, the constant pile of clutter on the bottom step vanished as if it had never been there, the keys to the camper van set pointedly by the door. All that remained was the collection of baby things in the box room, intended for one child but destined for another. Sarah's actions conveyed a clear message. *Her or Me*, they screamed. Or rather, *Them or Us*. It was plain Sarah wanted Arima out of their lives with immediate effect. Verbally, they skirted round the subject, shadow-boxing with the truth.

'I think she wants to keep the baby,' Lawrence said hesitantly over a hastily assembled celebration dinner.

'With hindsight, I think she always did,' Sarah replied calmly, equally keen to cover over her husband's transgression. Confronting him again, raking over the pain of the last months would mean acknowledging she had not been enough for him. Pride forbade it. Least said, soonest mended, was the safer way through the danger zone. 'So it works out well for everyone,' Sarah concluded, looking for a sign of regret, a flicker of doubt in her husband's face. 'In the end. Doesn't it, darling?'

'Absolutely,' he replied, reluctantly taking her in his arms.

The word affair was never spoken aloud. Internally, each of them turned down the volume to mute the whisper of betrayal in their souls. Sarah wasn't letting him off the hook, though – she knew her husband. What Lawrence couldn't turn down was the call of blood to blood. In a way that no one else could, Sarah understood being separated from his child was punishment enough, now and forever.

The day came for Arima to be discharged from hospital. The baby was developing well and there had been no complications.

'You're free to go,' smiled the consultant, scrawling his signature on the discharge forms. Arima packed her bags mechanically, folding the tiny vests and Babygros that Hannah had bought, wincing as the small movements of reaching and bending pulled at the fresh scar stretching across her lower abdomen.

'Careful there,' warned the midwife, entering the room to offer assistance. 'You do have someone to help for the next few weeks, don't you?' she continued, heaving Arima's bag onto the bed to avoid her lifting it. 'You mustn't overdo it.'

'Yes,' Arima lied, her voice flat and emotionless. She had no idea where she was going to go, didn't have so much as a carrycot to put the baby in. She was so tired she could barely think at all.

'The Registrar is in today,' the midwife said casually. 'If you're not going through with the surrogacy, you could register the birth.' She raised her hands as Arima's head whipped up. 'I'm not judging you,' she said quickly. 'I'm trying to help. He is your baby,' she said softly.

Arima's head drooped. 'Not today,' she mumbled. 'Another day.'

Lawrence ought to be there to register the birth, she thought numbly. It should be done together. Why hadn't Lawrence come? The baby stirred in his cot and Arima went to settle him.

'Is someone coming to fetch you?' asked the midwife, sensing Arima's reluctance to leave.

'Here we are,' boomed Philip, striding into the room, armed with a baby car seat and blanket.

'All ready?' asked Jemma, hurrying over to the cot. 'Ooh, can I hold him, Arima?'

'I'll leave you to it,' said the midwife tactfully as Arima's eyes filled with grateful tears.

'Where's Beatrice?' she sniffled.

'With friends.'

'But . . . how did you know I was leaving today?'

'I called Robin,' Jemma said, cooing over the baby's shock of dark curls and sleepy eyes.

'Bawled him out, you mean,' snorted Philip, fussing over the bags. 'You're a popular girl, Arima. Everyone wants to have you to stay.' He hugged her awkwardly, embarrassed by her gratitude.

'We've got far more room,' Jemma sniffed. 'Not to mention baby equipment coming out of our ears. The spare room's all set up.'

'Thank you,' whispered Arima, crying helplessly into Philip's shirt.

'So you'll come?' Jemma smiled, stroking the baby's cheek with her little finger. They had agreed, she and Philip, not to take sides. As Philip had said to Lawrence, whatever the rights and wrongs of it, there was a child involved. Even if it was partly of her own making, Arima was the one left high and dry.

'Yes,' sobbed Arima. 'I'm sorry, I can't stop crying. I'm worse than the baby.'

'Don't worry,' said Philip, grinning at his wife. 'Hormones are something we're well acquainted with. Practically on first-name terms in our house.'

'Don't listen to him,' Jemma instructed with a withering glance at her husband.

'May I?' Philip asked, approaching the cot. When Arima nodded, he lifted the baby out, cupping his head gently in the palm of one hand, and strapped him expertly into the car seat. 'Come on, little man,' he said, hoisting the seat into the air. 'I'll be glad of some back-up at home. Surrounded and outnumbered by women, that's what I am.' With the bags in one hand and the baby in the other, he set off, still chuntering under his breath.

Jemma produced a clean handkerchief and gently wiped Arima's eyes. 'Come on,' she said. 'You're in a proper pickle, aren't you.' She tipped Arima's face up. 'What were you thinking?' she asked gently, no hint of blame in her voice. 'They've been together for years, Arima. Almost as long as you've been alive.'

'I . . . I don't know,' Arima said as yet more tears poured down her cheeks. 'I love him, Jemma.' She wiped her eyes again and blew her nose. 'I really do. And he loves me. He does.' She faltered, needing to justify Lawrence's continued absence, his failure to come and meet his son. 'He just needs time to – to sort things out,' she finished, clinging to the tiny chink of hope left in her heart. Jemma said nothing. With her friend in such a precarious emotional state, it was hardly the time for home truths.

The days crawled by at a painfully slow pace, gradually blossoming into weeks. Arima dragged herself along, hour by hour, the baby an exhausting pleasure. Still she waited, unable to reconcile herself to the fact that Lawrence wasn't coming, not now, not ever. Robin fetched the camper van and installed it outside the Hevers' house, where it cut a vibrant dash against the muted colours of the other vehicles on the street. Hannah popped in for regular visits, bringing a never-ending supply of homemade cakes.

Philip called Lawrence several times, trying to persuade him to come and see the child, just once, and make his peace with Arima. Lawrence's refusal was spineless and cowardly, his excuses pathetic. It was too risky, he said. Sarah would find out. He had to protect his marriage. A clean break would be better. Watching Arima labour to mend her wounded heart at night, only to break it anew each day, Jemma thought she'd like to break his neck. Arima needed closure in order to move on.

With gentle, persistent promptings, Jemma and Philip succeeded in persuading Arima to take small steps forwards, registering the birth, planning the christening.

'Just a small service,' Jemma cajoled, a comforting arm around her friend as Arima sat feeding the baby late one afternoon, the sun stretching long, lazy shadows across the conservatory floor. 'Something to celebrate.'

Arima shook her head.

'Christenings are a family celebration,' she said. 'I don't have a family.' A tear dripped onto the baby's downy head. 'It's just me and him. Look at him, Jemma,' she said, gazing down at her son. 'He's so beautiful, so perfect.'

'He's a treasure,' agreed Jemma, leaving her second thought unsaid. The mop of hair matched Arima's but overall the child bore a striking resemblance to his father, Lawrence's strong features evident in the slopes and planes of the tiny face. Her heart ached at the anguish in Arima's eyes.

'How can Lawrence not want him?' she asked, the question echoing in her heart. *How can he not want me?* Her eyes pleaded for an answer that Jemma could not give.

'Let's concentrate on getting you back to full strength for now,' she said, shifting to a safer topic of conversation. 'You've got your six-week check coming up soon. The christening and so on can wait.' She stroked Arima's hair. 'Enjoy this time,' she advised. 'You won't believe me, but they honestly don't stay babies for long.'

'Perhaps not,' Arima acknowledged. 'But I won't forget.' She bent her head to kiss the baby's fingers one by one, her senses absorbing every detail; the smell of his hair, the impossibly soft, flawless skin, the determined grip of his hand around her finger, the solemn dark-eyed stare. 'I'll never forget.'

That night, Arima woke suddenly from a restless sleep, the answer seizing her unexpectedly by the throat. So simple, yet so obvious.

If Lawrence could only see his son, hold him in his arms just for a moment, he would surely change his mind. How could he not fall completely, terrifyingly, in love with his child, as she had? It wasn't too late to make a fresh start. Quickly, she laid her plans.

Beatrice had a packed social programme on Tuesdays, kicking off with story time at the library at nine-thirty, followed by Tadpoles, her weekly swimming class, at eleven. Jemma arrived home, wet-haired and shivering, at half past twelve, to find Hannah on the doorstep, her arms full of cake tins. 'Day off,' she called cheerfully as Jemma bumped the buggy up the steps, Beatrice protesting loudly at every jolt. 'It's our quietest time of year.'

'Arima not answering?' Jemma puffed, jabbing her key into the lock.

'I didn't want to ring for too long,' Hannah said, helping her lift the buggy over the threshold. 'In case she was asleep.'

'No, I think she had a good night with the baby,' Jemma replied, turning to close the door. 'He slept thr- . . .' her sentence derailed as she stared out into the street.

'Oh, no,' she breathed. 'No, no, no.'

'What is it?' Hannah asked, standing on tiptoe to look over Jemma's shoulder.

'That.' Jemma pointed to a large gap between two parked cars. A camper-van-sized gap.

'But . . . but . . . she's not supposed to be driving yet!' Hannah said stupidly.

'More to the point, she's in no fit state,' Jemma said. 'She's not herself.' Both women pulled out their mobile phones. 'Let me,' said Hannah. 'Robin can close the shop, it's easier for him.'

'Okay.' Jemma lowered her phone, acknowledging to herself that if anyone could climb into Arima's mind and work out where she'd gone, it was Robin.

Arima careered to a halt outside Lawrence's office, swinging the camper van across the remaining two staff parking spaces. Lifting the baby from the car seat, she eased herself to the ground, the pains in her stomach defeating the painkillers she'd taken before she left. 'Come on, darling,' she said, gritting her teeth as she limped through the double doors of the building. 'Let's find Daddy.'

Lawrence was in the middle of a conference call when Deborah put her head round the door, gesturing wildly at him. He frowned and waved her away but she kept on, beckoning urgently and mouthing words he couldn't catch.

'I'm terribly sorry,' he said to his clients, 'there seems to be a problem in the office. Can I call you back in a few minutes?' He threw the phone down and strode out of his office. 'Deborah,' he barked, 'that is *not* . . .' Arima flung herself at him, thrusting her crying child into his arms. 'Arima!' Lawrence backed away, pulling her into his office, away from the curious eyes of his staff. She was wild-eyed and dishevelled, trembling with the effort of the journey. 'Sit – sit down,' he said, unsure how much longer she could physically remain upright. He had no idea how to handle the situation.

'I had to come, Lawrence,' Arima gulped, collapsing into his chair. 'I had to. So you could meet him.'

Lawrence looked down at the tiny bundle in his arms, his heart melting as he saw his own likeness imprinted on the little face. 'He's . . . wonderful,' he said, hardly able to speak past the lump in his throat.

'I named him for you,' Arima said softly. 'Lawrence.'

Lawrence began to cry. He kissed the child on the forehead and handed him back to Arima, tears streaming down his face. 'You shouldn't be here,' he said thickly. 'You have to go.'

'I know,' said Arima eagerly, clutching his arm as she took the child back. 'I know. That's why I came.' She stared up at him, her eyes fever-bright. 'Come with me, Lawrence. I've got the van, my passport, the baby's birth certificate. Everything, it's all there. Come away with us.'

Lawrence backed away. Arima was rambling, making no sense.

'What? Arima, no,' he protested.

'Just get your things,' she begged. 'It's not too late. We could go to Spain, France, Italy, anywhere we wanted.' She limped towards him, trying to put the baby back into his arms. 'I know you love me, Lawrence. I . . . I *know* you do. You said so.'

Lawrence's back was literally against the wall, his hands raised as if in surrender – or to prevent her from giving him the child.

'I – darling, I do, but . . . it's complicated. Sarah, the baby . . . I can't leave her.' He put his hands on Arima's shoulders. 'Surely you can see that? She needs me.'

'I need you!' Arima begged. 'We need you.' She was shaking now, every hope and dream disintegrating before her eyes. 'Lawrence, please. I'm begging you.'

'No,' Lawrence said, weeping over her brokenness. 'Arima, no. I'm sorry, so sorry, but no. I can't do this.'

They stared at one another, the tears sluicing away the last relics of hope from Arima's face, Lawrence was dumb before her grief. Then, holding the child close to her chest, Arima stumbled to the door, the pain in her body as nothing compared with the pain in her heart. It was time to leave, she realized. Past time. 'It's just you and me, little one,' she sobbed.

Robin sprinted around the corner of the block as the camper van began to chug away, Arima weeping and coaxing the engine back to life.

'Arima!' he yelled. 'Arima, wait!' He drew level with the window, every muscle straining as he sought to stop her, to hold her back. 'Wait!' Arima turned her face towards him and for a fraction of a second, the future hung in the balance. Robin's breath was like fire in his lungs. This time she wasn't going to run away.

Arima's lips moved in the ghost of a smile, as though reading his thoughts. Then she accelerated hard and pulled away, driving out of his life again as abruptly as she had come. Shedding the skin of one life and striking out in search of another, the wanderlust coursing through her veins. It was who she was.

Robin stood in the road and watched her go, wondering if there was anything he could have done to make her stay. 'Arima,' he whispered, knowing this time she was gone for good. 'It didn't have to be this way.'

As the purple van disappeared from view, Robin turned his back and slowly walked away.